What Others Ar

"There's a new name in
back the mysteries of Ba'al s
reign in her debut novel, Rain. Brillian..,
prophet Elijah's story with the widow of Zarep.....   r
son, McNeely explores a tale not widely told but brought .. _.e
with impeccable research and fascinating fiction. Biblical
novice and scholar alike will be enthralled."

~**Mesu Andrews**, Christy Award winning and bestselling
author

"A splendid debut from Dana McNeely. This engaging,
fascinating tale takes us back to a time of idol worship and
sacrifices. Rain entertains as well as challenges the reader to
ponder life's deeper questions long after the last page. A
must read for all seeking to understand the past as well as
the present."

~**Rachel Hauck,** New York Times Bestselling Author

"Welcome to ancient Israel like you've never imagined it!
McNeely has done the research, pulling aside the veil of time
with astonishing insight and depth. You'll never forget the
days of Elijah after reading RAIN."

~**Linore Rose Burkard**, award-winning historical fiction
author

"Dana McNeely has crafted a story of faith, love, and courage
so thrilling it literally kept me up late reading it! Realizing
Melquart is no god, young Aban travels throughout Israel
trying to find the prophet who promised a drought.
Encountering danger at nearly every turn, he fights to save his
mother and baby brother from the clutches of Israel's Queen
Jezebel. In the end, he finds much more than he was ever
searching for."

~**Carole Towriss,** Author of Sold into Freedom

"Based on biblical history, Rain is set in a pagan society, which gives it both a fantasy feel and a searingly relevant message for our world today. I knew the story of Elijah, but I'd never experienced the depth of it until reading McNeely's refreshing take. Poignant and powerful."

~**Angela Ruth Strong,** Author of The Resort to Love series

"A beautifully written, well-researched, and memorable debut novel. Elijah, King Ahab, and an expansive cast of other characters are rendered vividly in this carefully written biblical fiction. Dana McNeely is an author to watch."

~**Brennan S. McPherson,** author of the bestselling Fall of Man series

Sue ~ thank you so much
for your loyal support
of my writing.
Dana McNeely

Whirlwind

"In whirlwind and storm
is His way, and clouds
are the dust beneath His
feet. The Lord is good, a
stronghold in the day of
trouble, and He knows
those who take refuge in
Him." Nahum 1: 7 NLT

Whirlwind

Whispers on the Wind series
Rain—Book One
Whirlwind—Book Two

Whirlwind
By
Dana McNeely

MBI

Whirlwind
Published by Mountain Brook Ink
White Salmon, WA U.S.A.

The website addresses shown in this book are not intended in any way to be or imply an endorsement on the part of Mountain Brook Ink, nor do we vouch for their content.

This story is a work of fiction. All characters and events are the product of the author's imagination. Any resemblance to any person, living or dead, is coincidental.

© 2022 Dana McNeely
ISBN 9781-953957-23-8

The Team: Miralee Ferrell, Nikki Wright, Cindy Jackson
Cover Design: Indie Cover Design, Lynnette Bonner Designer

Mountain Brook Ink is an inspirational publisher offering fiction you can believe in.
Printed in the United States of America

To Mom ~
Thanks for all the weekend trips to the library
and for letting me hide in the trees to read
instead of cleaning my closet.

To Betty and Laura ~
Who read Whirlwind chapter by chapter as I wrote,
pointed out typos and missing pieces of story, and
sometimes gently suggested,
"Can you write just a little more here?"

Acknowledgments

Early on in my imagination, I saw Miriam, the little girl who trapped birds in Rain, now grown and striding through the hills with an eagle she trained to hunt. The ACFW loop is fabulous for offering up experts, and I was given the name of Valery Smith, Director of Mississippi Wildlife Rehabilitation, Inc., whose work specializes in rescuing raptors.

After I explained a bit about Whirlwind's characters, setting, and biblical storyline, Valery shared invaluable advice about golden eagles, a species that is found in Israel and best fit my story. I had so many questions. What if this or that happens? What does the bird look like at this age? What does it eat? When does it fly? Not only did she answer questions on the phone for more than an hour, she kindly sent links of pictures, websites, and YouTube videos. Thanks to Valery, I learned a lot more about golden eagles than I started with, but surely fell short of all she knows. Any mistakes are my own.

The work Mississippi Wildlife Rehabilitation does is admirable and interesting. I encourage you to visit their website at:

www.mswildliferehab.org.

I received much support in writing Whirlwind. The dynamic duo of Betty and Laura faithfully read and reread the draft. My friend, Vicki Floyd, gave it a last-minute read before my submission deadline and provided a helpful list of actionable items. Many prayer partners provided much-needed support along the way.

Miralee Ferrell, my publisher and editor at Mountain Brook Ink, helped shape the manuscript in ways I could not have achieved alone. Lynnette Bonner created the beautiful cover that was perfect for this story.

I thank God for each of these people, my friends and partners in Whirlwind. For your glory, Lord.

Chapter One

Now Ben-Hadad king of Aram mustered his entire army.
Accompanied by thirty-two kings with their horses and
chariots, he went up and besieged Samaria and attacked it.
~ 1 Kings 20:1

Samaria, capital city of the Northern Kingdom of Israel, around
857 BC
Dov

STANDING ATOP THE CITY WALL, DOV nocked an arrow in his bowstring, grasping several more between his fingers for successive shots. He signaled the men he supervised to rain arrows on the Arameans at his mark. Behind his archers, spearmen pounded their weapon shafts on the wall's stone cap, a percussive battle song. Slingmen pressed behind them, eager to shoot rocks down on the enemy like hailstones.

The enemy king, Ben-Hadad, shouted harsh insults from below the city wall. Dov translated to Hebrew for King Ahab. "Your situation is hopeless. We comprise the armies of thirty-two kings, well supplied with food and drink we've seized from your cities. We can camp in comfort for months—years—eating the harvests of your farms while you starve."

So many. Dov tried to estimate the enemy's number. Fifty thousand? A hundred? They had besieged Samaria for three months, devoured crops for miles around, and their ranks kept growing. In the city food supplies were low, and cistern levels fell at a worrisome rate. The city could weather a few more months' privation, but soon ... Dov caught King Ahab's gaze and saw the same realization in his grim expression. "Shall I silence him, my lord?"

Giving a swift shake of his head, the king motioned Dov to draw near. He lowered his bow and dropped the arrows back into his quiver.

"Bid them send a negotiator." The king's expression was grim as he headed for the palace.

Dov struck his fist against his breastplate, strode to the wall's edge, and shouted the instruction in Aramaic, adding a demand for the rest of the army to stay back from the gate.

Dov watched as several well-dressed men conferred with Ben-Hadad. He selected three. If typical, one would be spokesman and the others witnesses to his honesty. Dov ran down the wall's stone steps to the city entrance, instructing the gatekeepers to open only the small gate, the *Eye of the Needle*. Aaron, head gatekeeper, muttered under his breath. "Twenty years on the gates, and he tells me how to—"

Dov suppressed a grin but threw his weight into shutting the *Eye* quickly after the Arameans entered. The tallest, clad in a long-sleeved green tunic, strode forward confidently, stopped in front of Dov, and held out his arms to be checked for weapons. Dov did so, nodded his satisfaction, and motioned for Aaron to check the other two.

When Aaron gave him the nod, Dov spoke in Hebrew. "Come with me." He repeated the command in Aramaic, but the tall messenger had already stepped out. Dov led them to the palace. They waited in an outer room until Obadiah, the king's steward, requested they enter the throne room.

Unlike other times Dov had seen Ahab on his throne, the king wore his military armor, rather than robes of Phoenician purple. While standing at attention, Dov observed the three messengers. The spokesmen, as Dov had concluded, took in the throne room through strange gray eyes. Its opulent hangings and ivory carvings intimidated most guests, but the man's calculating gaze lingered on them as if taking inventory.

Queen Jezebel stood beside the king, looking much the same as when Dov had first laid eyes on the flame-haired, foreign princess. Her slanted eyes were lined with green malachite, and unlike King Ahab, she had donned royal purple. She was still a striking woman, though her three children were nearly grown.

The king stared at the spokesman, waiting. Dov knew the king would not speak first.

This didn't appear to trouble the Aramean, who dipped his head then spoke Aramaic. At his second demand, Dov glanced at the queen. Only her eyes flickered.

When the man finished, Dov translated. "This is what Ben-Hadad says. Your silver and gold are mine, and the best of your wives and children are mine."

King Ahab averted his gaze from the queen and muttered. "Tell him, 'Just as you say, my lord. I and all I have are yours.'"

At the king's immediate capitulation, Dov was glad of his military training, which ensured no emotion crossed his face. Likewise, the queen appeared unmoved, except for a tightening of her lips.

The king motioned to Dov to escort them out. It appeared the *negotiations* were concluded.

He accompanied the men to the gate. Would the Arameans withdraw with such easily won terms? He thought not. Once a tyrant's demands were met, he usually exacted more. Dov thought about the queen's stoic expression as the king gave her to the enemy without argument. She wasn't the kind of woman who'd open her veins with a jeweled dagger rather than face humiliation ... or worse. But would she slice open the king's veins, for giving her up? Yes. Should she find an opportunity.

"What'd he say, up at the palace?" asked Aaron. The old soldier had been badly wounded in battle and was no longer fit to make sweeping treks to protect the Jezreel valley, but despite a bad leg, his ever-present axe made him a good man to keep close in hand-to-hand battle.

In the city square, a crowd of farmers and shepherds milled about, grasping makeshift weapons—sharpened plowshares, cudgels, the occasional ass jaw. Many of these lived outside the city but took refuge within its walls upon spotting the dust of approaching armies. Townsfolk took them in when they could, especially women and children. Others slept in the streets. Fortunately, mild weather favored them. Unfortunately, it also favored the Arameans.

Dov raised his voice to toss a scrap of hope. "They discussed terms for troop withdrawal."

"Withdraw!" Aaron spat in the dirt. "Why would they?"

Dov shook his head. "I have no details." None he would tell them, at least. He imagined the people's reaction should he reveal the enemy's demands and the king's response. This crowd, who rarely took more than one wife, would be all for Ahab getting rid of his Phoenician queen. Although some still followed the Ba'als, the Yahwists hated her and for good reason. The king did his best to restrain Jezebel's bloodthirsty tendencies, but during the long drought she had secretly hired assassins to target the school of the prophets, headed by the reclusive prophet Elijah. Jezebel would never forgive him for proving her priests impotent in the contest on Mount Carmel. Many wondered if cutthroats still stalked the prophets.

"Samaria could use that Elijah fellow again." Aaron leaned back against the gate to take pressure off his bad leg. "Rain down fire on 'em all, I say."

Jezreel, Northern Kingdom, the same day
Miriam

Gazing across the Jezreel valley from atop the city wall, Miriam clutched Jaedon's small hand. For several weeks, they'd watched a pair of eagles carry tree branches and trailing reeds to their nest, repairing damages from winter storms. Then the eagles appeared singly for a long while, and she explained to the boy if eggs had been laid, the pair would take turns sitting on them. Bird watching provided relief from the isolation insisted upon by Jaedon's father ... Miriam's betrothed.

It was still hard to think of her cousin Gershon in that way.

"There!" She pointed at a far-off stand of cypress which provided a convenient marker for the cliff ledge just beyond. "See, she's heading for the nest."

"Yes!" Quickly, Jaedon stepped forward. Catching the neck of his tunic, she pulled him back, away from the edge. She stared down at the drop to the terraced vineyards below, the height of at least three men. This boy. He needed to run free in the valley outside the walls, or at least help his father in the vineyard. Since he could do neither until Gershon deemed it safe, she must always be alert, if he were to reach manhood.

Settling both hands on the boy's shoulders, she watched a magnificent golden eagle hover above the nest with what looked like a hyrax clutched in its talons.

"Is the mother feeding the chicks?"

"Mmm. Perhaps they've hatched by now."

"I want to see them." He scuffed his foot, sending pebbles skittering over the wall into his grandfather's land, the nearest of several terraced vineyards embracing the hill of Jezreel. She heard the pout in his voice and hoped he wouldn't start crying again. Poor motherless boy.

He lived in a different world than Miriam had. She and her brothers had roamed the fields surrounding their home in Samaria, with only Seth's sling for protection. But that was then.

Keeping her eyes trained on the eagle, Miriam bent to speak in his ear. "Listen, little one. You must learn to stand motionless and silent to observe wildlife. If you don't, how can I ever take you hunting? Remember now, this is important." She gave his shoulder a squeeze. "Besides, what do I tell your *savta* if you fall from the city wall?"

Jaedon tucked his chin and giggled. "Tell her, 'He went *splat* in *Saba's* vineyard.'"

A chuckle escaped her. The seven-year-old felt more like a little brother to her eighteen summers than the son he would become upon her marriage, although it was hard to imagine herself, at last, a wife and mother.

She'd not been surprised to watch her friends in Samaria, so pretty, petite, and compliant, become betrothed and married before her. Though she'd been small as a young girl, around her twelfth year she shot up past her eldest brother and stood eye-to-eye with most men in Samaria. Her shoulders grew muscled from carrying crates she built, filled with birds snared in Abba's vineyard or the valley.

Despite her success selling birds in Samaria's marketplace, no one offered her father a *mohar*, a bride price for his ungainly daughter. Her mother despaired. When *Dohd* Naboth wrote that his son's wife expected a child, Miriam's parents volunteered her assistance with the couple's active young son as Rasha neared her time of confinement, hoping Miriam's stay in Jezreel might throw her into the path of an eligible farmer or tradesman. After all, the king had built a winter palace in Jezreel, and the city had prospered.

At first, Miriam hesitated to go. Active boys, she could handle, but as the youngest child in her family, she'd never attended a birth. She agreed, however, when she understood a midwife would supervise the birthing.

Her brothers had helped her uncle harvest his vineyard a few times, but because she was a girl, Miriam was not allowed to go. The boys returned with stories of bountiful crops and lush grasslands in the Jezreel valley. With her brothers' stories in mind, Miriam looked forward to exploring the grasslands around Jezreel with her cousin's young son, though she dreaded the thought of meeting the marriageable young men of the city.

But Miriam found no more admirers in Jezreel than she had in Samaria. To be fair, minding Jaedon had filled her time in the final weeks of Rasha's pregnancy. Then, tragedy struck. No one could have expected the death of Gershon's wife and baby son during childbirth. Nor that Miriam would be trapped in Jezreel when the Arameans attacked Samaria.

At least she wasn't marrying a stranger.

"Can we do it tomorrow?"

Jaedon's question drew Miriam back from her musing. His eyes widened beseechingly.

"Do what?"

"Find the eagles."

Her gaze crossed the valley to the cliffs. A breeze carried the earthy scents of new grass and the cluster of sheep that grazed beyond the city walls. A black lamb darted from the herd, leaping and frolicking, but the shepherd's whistle sent a speckled dog in pursuit. The lamb turned to rejoin the flock, dragging its heels like a truculent child. What she wouldn't give to trade places with that shepherd.

Cupping Jaedon's shoulder, she turned him toward the steps leading down to the street. "We'll see," she said. "But for now, let's play a game."

"What game?"

She reached for his hand before answering. "A game my brothers taught me. Desert cat."

He jumped to the next step and shouted his approval.

Good thing she'd taken hold of him.

"I'll teach you how to hide in plain sight."

They played in the alleys of Jezreel, moving stealthily and freezing in place like their game's namesake, until the sun hid behind the rooftops, one of which was the last place she found him.

"Perfect. I almost didn't think to look above," Miriam said. "Silent and still, that's how the cat hides from its enemies."

"Or catches its prey!" He bounded down the steps.

She laid her finger across her lips.

He mouthed, "*Sorry.*"

She grinned. "You need a little more practice."

"You'll never find my next spot."

"Your boast must wait. Your *savta* needs our help with supper."

They wound their way through the alleys, as Jaedon discussed the potentials of various hiding spots, evidently not feeling the need to keep his own counsel from a pursuer. The yeasty aroma of bread wafted through windows of neighboring houses as they approached her Uncle Naboth's three-story structure, its plaster-washed facade the color of sunshine.

The wooden door stood propped open. Miriam ducked through the length of woven cloth fluttering from the header, which allowed cooking smoke to escape while preserving privacy. Jaedon's grandmother knelt beside the hearth, stirring what smelled like her simple, yet delicious, lentil stew. She glanced over her shoulder and dipped a spoonful from the pot. "Give this a taste, my dear."

Jaedon hurried to grasp the spoon. "Not sure." He smacked his lips. "Might need more cumin. Better give me another taste."

Rolling her eyes, Yaffa refilled the spoon.

"The best you've ever made, *Savta.*"

Miriam felt her face flush. They were late. Supper was ready—without her aid. "Doda Yaffa, how can I help?"

"Bring me the wooden bowls, dear. Jaedon, get your father. He left something at your house." She studied Miriam for a moment. "Don't worry. There's plenty you can help with.

Arrange the cushions around the mat. No guests tonight, only Gershon and Jaedon. No need to use the upper room."

Jaedon's grandfather walked from a back room, drying his face on a cloth. "Waste no time, Grandson," he called after Jaedon. "I am hungry as a wolf."

"Sit yourself, husband," Yaffa said, handing him a small bowl of roasted grain. "Let this slake your appetite. How did it go at the gate today?" Yaffa turned to Miriam, her voice deepening with pleasure. "Your uncle has become a prominent man in the city, child. He sits in consultation at the city gate when important matters must be settled by someone of sense."

Naboth sighed, hunching his shoulders. "Disagreements between neighbors are ... disagreeable. Neither fellow was satisfied by my decision." He shook his head. "A bad business."

"I'm sure your decision was right, my love. Sit, sit." She bustled about settling him on the thickest cushion.

Jaedon flung back the door cloth and ran to plop down beside Naboth. The boy whispered in his grandfather's ear, throwing Miriam a knowing look she could not interpret. Gershon entered behind him, carefully rolled the hanging cloth, then shut and latched the plank door.

The man she would marry carried a small parchment, loosely rolled and tied with a strip of cloth. He placed it carefully beside his cushion as he sat on the other side of his father. Looking up, he caught her gaze and nodded. "Shalom, Miriam."

She smiled, though he had not. He seemed a quiet man, unlike his gregarious son. His grief was too near. She bit her lip, searching for a topic, something she never had to do at home. "How did you find the vineyard today? Are the vines beginning to bud?" She carried bowls of lentils to the men, waiting for an answer. The first swellings of spring growth were a topic guaranteed to spur discussion among her father and brothers.

"No, not yet." He reached for his bowl. She waited a moment, thinking he would expand on his brief reply. Her own mother and father could chat endlessly on the slightest greening of the wood. Finally, she turned away, disappointed.

So that was to be it?

Outside, fragments of cheerful discussion and laughter floated into the room. Miriam felt her gaze drawn to the window. They needed lighthearted conversation in this room. Guests. If Gershon's wife had not died, there would be guests. Everyone would have wanted to see the new babe. Then there would be conversation. Of course, the women would eat downstairs while the men reclined in the upper room, but there would be plenty of discourse if women were present. They told stories, true and not, about husbands, children, in-laws, and forays into the marketplace where good bargaining skills could be admired. Sometimes they would speak of the king and queen—especially the queen— always in hushed tones, as if Jezebel might station spies outside their window.

What odd thoughts. If Gershon's wife had not died, Miriam wouldn't care if she had conversation with him or not. She felt her mouth tighten and immediately turned her gaze to Jaedon. Again, he whispered in his grandfather's ear, then giggled and looked her way. Naboth's responding smile intensified his resemblance to her father. Miriam felt tension fall away, like a cloak tossed aside.

As was his habit, Naboth waited for Yaffa and Miriam to sit, then he prayed. "Give thanks to the Lord, for He is good. His love endures forever. May He keep safe each person under this roof and also Kadesh, my son whose duty has taken him far from us." Her uncle recited more of the psalm, ending "He gives food to every creature."

Miriam breathed her own prayer for Gershon's absent brother, adding a request for her brothers Caleb and Seth. All able-bodied men within her hometown city of Samaria, would have been conscripted into Ahab's army.

Jaedon piped up, "Give thanks to the God of Heaven! His love endures forever!" Gershon gave his son a stern look when they all opened their eyes, but Naboth laughed aloud, spooned up a mouthful of stew, and the moment passed.

Miriam tore off a piece of bread, folding it to scoop up the stew. It was fragrant and delicious. Her mother made a similar stew, but this tasted of a spice she didn't recognize. "Yaffa, what is—"

"I'm going to the cliffs tomorrow to see the eagle chicks," Jaedon interrupted. "Miriam promised to take me."

Yaffa, who had turned to listen to Miriam, raised her eyebrows. "What's this?"

"Oh, well, we've been—"

"Why would you promise such a thing?" Gershon turned to Miriam scowling. "You know my feelings on this matter. It's too dangerous for either of you to venture outside the walls."

She felt her forehead crease at his sharp tone. Yes, she did know his feelings, though she disagreed. When the Arameans had marched through the Jezreel pass on their way to attack the capitol of Samaria, everyone in the city spotted the cloud of dust, long before the chariots and soldiers had passed by. There'd been ample notice to take shelter behind the walls, and the city's hilltop perch guaranteed there would be similar warning of the army's return. Still, her cousin—her betrothed—had reason to be protective of Jaedon. He'd barely had time to mourn the deaths of his wife and infant son in the weeks since their deaths.

"Gershon, we've only watched the eagles—from the wall—and he's understandably excited about the nest, but I told him, *we'll see*. Of course, I planned to consult you first."

He looked down at his hands, drawing her eyes there as well. They were clenched around the scroll he'd carried in.

"Of course. We'll talk of that later. Right now, I ..." He glanced again at the scroll.

"Son," Naboth began, "perhaps now isn't the time—"

"When might be the time, Abba? My wife is dead, my baby son"—he cut himself off, shaking his head slowly. "We are at war. If the Arameans return, Abba, if there is a battle ... Jaedon is unprotected. Matters must be resolved."

"Son, surely I—"

"This is the *Ketubah*, Miriam." Gershon held it out. "The marriage agreement," he said, as if she didn't know the meaning of the word. He shoved it closer.

Belatedly she realized she was meant to take the scroll. She fiddled with the string holding it closed. "Shall I read it?"

"Not yet. I want to say ... I'm sorry I am not what you ...

you must have had many …" Gershon glanced at his mother as if asking for help, but Yaffa remained silent.

Miriam cleared her throat. Did he think she'd been overwhelmed with offers? Certainly not. He must understand, with two older brothers, she had no expectation of a share in the family's vineyard in Samaria. Despite the fact that she had worked in the vineyard, along with her entire family, the men of Samaria had decided Miriam could bring little of worth to a marriage. She was no beauty. Gershon spoke kindly, that was all. "I understand," she said. "The situation is difficult."

"There has been no reply to the message I sent to your father. We've heard rumors the siege continues. It's likely a runner can't get through. If Samaria is overrun …"

She nodded, speechless, when he did not continue. Samaria overrun? *No word from her father?* Icy fingers grasped her throat.

"Surely, your family is safe, dear," Yaffa said. "The walls of Samaria are higher even than Jezreel's. It's only that, with the besieging army, it must be impossible for a messenger to get through."

Naboth spoke up. "You are like a daughter to us, Miriam. Gershon is my eldest son. I know your father will be satisfied with the arrangement."

Miriam fidgeted. Of course, her father would be satisfied with any arrangement his brother proffered. It wasn't fairness she worried about, it was—

"You'll be well provided for," Gershon said. "You and my son. If I die before Jaedon reaches manhood, as his guardian, you will control half the vineyard and receive a portion of the income."

"But your father and brother—"

"I will control the other half," Naboth said. "As for Kadesh, his desire was never to farm, but to market the products of the vineyard—a benefit to us all. You will be my co-beneficiary as well as Jaedon's guardian. If the Lord is willing, we will work together until my grandson can take responsibility."

Gershon looked intently at her. "It is a good arrangement. As good as I can make it. The king"—he glanced at Jaedon uncertainly, then seemed to make up his mind to speak plainly. "The last runner to get through was accompanied by a general of the king's army. He came to recruit and train soldiers from Jezreel. If Samaria falls to the Arameans, they will pass by Jezreel on their return victory march."

"You're concerned about the crop?" The grapes had been mere nubs when the Arameans marched by on their way to Samaria. Now they were too green for wine, but large enough to tempt hungry soldiers.

"What—the crop—no. It's my son. My son needs a mother. A protector."

She felt an empty place in her heart she hadn't expected at the cold practicality of this discussion of marriage. She knew Gershon did not love her, how could he? He still loved his wife.

Her grandmother had spoken often of love, of her Nathaniel, that tall soldier who had stolen her heart when it was almost too late. "It will not be that way for you, my beautiful girl. You will have your choice of the young men." Miriam scoffed softly under her breath. She could not expect a love match. *Savta* was blind, after all.

"Gershon, will you walk with me?" She headed for the door, not waiting for his answer. If he did not mind discussing such matters before his impressionable young son, she did. She did not hear his footsteps, but when she unlatched the door, he was at her side to wrest it open.

Night had fallen. Lights from oil lamps and hearths flickered from a few windows. Overhead, a sliver of moon held court over a spill of stars.

"How soon will we wed?" she asked.

"Before the fullness of the moon."

So, there would be no celebratory feast with friends, no wedding procession through the streets of Jezreel. Not for her, readings from *The Song of Songs*. *'Who is this that cometh from the wilderness, like pillars of smoke?'*

Why would she want that? Her family could not attend. She waited the space of three deep breaths.

"No. That is too soon."

"But you haven't opened the—"

"I am assured my father's brother will have been more than fair." She glanced quickly at the ketubah. "It's not that."

"But Jaedon—"

"There is no question. I love Jaedon. The betrothal is settled if I agree to its terms, yes? From that time, he will be my son." She reached for Gershon's hand, feeling him withdraw under her touch. *Was she that repulsive to him?*

"But you ... you have not had time to mourn." She looked pointedly at their hands, hers open, reaching, his closed in a fist, a portrait of their relationship. "Young couples may wait a year before the *chuppah*. I want to wait the full period of mourning for your beloved wife. For Rasha."

His hand uncurled when she spoke his wife's name, and then he slowly lifted it to stroke his beard. His forehead had smoothed, with relief, she was sure. "You will agree to the terms?"

She slid the cord from the rolled parchment and read aloud. "... guardian to my son, Jaedon." She rolled it loosely and repositioned the cord. "Write '*mother* and guardian'. Then, I agree."

"You are satisfied with the financial agreements?"

"What do I care for houses and land? Ah, but a son!"

For the first time, Gershon smiled, and he reached for her hand.

Chapter Two

The messengers came again and said, "This is what Ben-Hadad says: 'I sent to demand your silver and gold, your wives and your children. But about this time tomorrow I am going to send my officials to search your palace and the houses of your officials. They will seize everything you value and carry it away.
~ 1 Kings 20:5-6

Samaria, a day later
Dov

HEAVY CLOUDS DARKENED THE SKY ABOVE Samaria, begrudging the dawn. Dov strode along the parapet, encouraging his archers with a word or clap on the shoulder while he studied the enemy troops below. More tents squatted in the valley today. Shrouded forms converged like ants from an anthill. He let his gaze flick momentarily to the farmland at the far end of the valley. After more than twenty years, little remained of the burned-out house, only a pile of stone where the firepit had stood. Even the dark smudge of ash had become one with the earth.

Straightening, Dov wrenched his attention back to the city gate and its ancient bronze fittings. He considered today's exchange. It was one thing to allow in a few messengers, yet another to throw open the gates for transport wagons to carry the silver, gold, and royal wives and children King Ahab had promised Ben-Hadad. If the main gate was opened for wagons, the enemy hoard camped around the city could storm through.

Disaster. For the city and for his king.

Striding up to the gate's right hinge, Dov leaned over. A shield bearer leapt forward to protect his head and torso as he searched the exterior area in front of the gate. No sign of digging or firestarters.

Nodding his thanks to the shield bearer, Dov resumed

his review of the archers, breathing in the noxious smoke from firepots and hot oil at the ready. In the square below, his superior officer, Ocran, stationed the rest of their archers at ground level to protect the gate from the inside, in the event of a breech.

Provincial officers leading either horsemen or foot soldiers, lined their troops facing the gate, prepared for defense or attack. Valley dwellers who had sought shelter inside the city's walls grouped behind them, armed with staffs, cudgels, and plowshares. Yesterday after King Ahab capitulated to the Aramean king's demands, everyone felt on edge. Everyone had a stake in today's events.

King Ben-Hadad's opulent tent had been moved up from the valley to one of the hill's terraced vineyards. Dov calculated it was out-of-range of his best archer and a fiery arrow, but to be sure, he caught the archer's gaze, jutting his chin toward the wind-whipped banners. The archer grinned at the implied question, dipped the cloth-wrapped head of an arrow in oil, and motioned toward the firepot with an upraised palm. *Just give the word.*

Suddenly Dov caught movement below. He fisted his hand. *Hold.*

A cadre of Arameans milled around Ben-Hadad's tent. When a servant held open the tent flap, several ducked inside. After a long while they filed out and headed for the city gate. Six armored soldiers and the same three messengers Ben-Hadad sent yesterday. But why the soldiers? To transport the silver and gold their king demanded? Perhaps. Yet, to transport silver and gold, let alone the wives and children, armored soldiers would not be his first choice. Protection then? But why would they need protection? Despite their demands, the messengers had entered and left the city without escort, and unharmed. Frowning, Dov hurried down the steps to meet them.

A mace pounded the gate, iron on iron. The regiment of foot soldiers guarded one side of the entrance. Dov planted himself beside the other side, waiting for Aaron to move into position. The gatekeeper limped more slowly than usual, shoved back the wooden window covering, and hollered through the bars. "Drop your weapons right there. I have my eye on that mace for myself. You, too, big fellow, or we'll add that pretty bronze dagger to our arsenal."

The old soldier made them wait until he confirmed they dropped all visible weapons. Dov's mouth twitched.

Inside, they submitted to a second search, displeasure evident on their faces. Finally, the weaponless soldiers formed a protective circle around their messengers. As Dov led the group toward the palace, he motioned for a troop of foot soldiers to fall in behind. It was one thing to allow Ben-Hadad's envoys into the throne room, quite another to allow trained enemy soldiers to outnumber Israelite guards in close quarters.

King Ahab sat on the elevated throne platform, his face absent of all expression. His steward, Obadiah, waited at the base of the steps nearest the king.

After the last Aramean crossed the threshold, the group halted half a room away from the king. They stood motionless. Would they not bow to the king? Then, with supreme slowness, they did bow. A veiled affront.

Dov watched for a signal from the king, but none came. The spokesman stepped forward, the other messengers angled their heads toward the spokesman—one to deliver the message, the others to ensure Ben-Hadad's words were accurately delivered. The gray-eyed messenger read from a scroll.

"This is what Ben-Hadad says," Dov translated. "Yesterday I demanded your silver and gold, your wives and children. But tomorrow, I am going to send my officials to search your palace and the houses of your officials. They will seize everything you value and carry it away."

King Ahab's face suffused with red. He stood, marched down the stairs, and motioned for Dov to follow. Not waiting for orders, Obadiah fell in behind the king. Ahab stopped in the alcove between the throne room and the royal quarters. Gurgling water from a tiled fountain obscured their discussion.

"Send those fellows to the smaller banquet room," Ahab told his steward. "Serve them my best wine. Then summon the city elders and any military generals who can be spared from the city's defense." The king paced the length of the niche, wheeling just as the steward reached the hall. "Obadiah."

"Yes, my lord?"

"I changed my mind. Give them the worst wine."

The steward inclined his head and hurried away.

Having crossed paths with the steward several times during the years of the drought, Dov knew him to be capable, resourceful, and loyal—up to a point. A point upon which Dov agreed. As a follower of Yahweh, Obadiah would do nothing against the Lord's commands.

Dov's brow creased. Something had shifted in the king's decision-making. From the time Dov advanced from temple guard to provincial leader, Ahab consulted only with his generals. Now he was calling in the city elders? Civilians? Ahab was known as a brilliant military tactician. Even yesterday's capitulation, in the face of the long siege, had met with the approval of the king's general. *What were a few wives and children to the King of Israel?*

Although Dov's military service stretched less than two years, he had been Ahab's palace guard for several years. He could not understand the king meeting with elders over anything except city planning or a judgment involving powerful citizens. Never a battle decision.

"Those scoundrels are otherwise occupied by now." Ahab headed back to the throne room.

Dov followed, and when beckoned closer, positioned himself next to Obadiah at the foot of the throne.

After a while, the elders filed into the room. Their long-sleeved tunics and embroidered cloaks identified men of words rather than deeds. Dov recognized a craftsman who headed the metalworker's guild and one of the priests of the Yahweh temple. Why was Caleb's father, Lemuel, not among this company? Most considered the vintner a discerning man.

Ahab greeted them cordially and began speaking. "Allow me to hear your opinions on a matter. Yesterday, when the messenger brought Ben-Hadad's demand for the best of my wives and children, my silver and gold, I did not refuse him. With the great strength of their numbers, I thought it best to end the siege and let Samaria's people return to their lives and daily pursuits. But today his demand is, 'About this time tomorrow, I am going to send my men to search your palace and the houses of your officials. They will seize everything you value and carry it away.'

Sharp cries of concern erupted from the elders.

The king continued, "You see how the fellow causes trouble? If we allow them in the city, your families, your riches will be at risk, as well as mine. What say you?"

Aha. So this was the king's strategy. By confiding the enemy's plan to seize their wealth, he gained support for a refusal that could lead to the war's escalation.

After briefly putting their heads together, they shoved one gray-haired representative forward.

"Welcome, Nagid." King Ahab beckoned the elder to approach the throne. "I see you have conferred. What is your advice?"

"You are right, my king. Do not agree to Ben-Hadad's new demands."

The king tapped the armrest of his throne. "So be it." He nodded to Dov. "Send for the emissaries."

Hurrying to the lesser banquet hall, Dov found them enjoying the king's wine. Even the soldiers had partaken, although they were on duty. Evidently, they found no fault with the king's worst wine.

Which gave him an idea.

"King Ahab has asked to see you once more. Please follow me." Messengers and soldiers traded looks, pushed their goblets back, and followed Dov. Only the sound of their leather sandals clicking on the polished floor interrupted the silence.

The elders gathered near the throne steps, forcing the Arameans to take the lower position. King Ahab remained seated as he addressed them. "Tell Ben-Hadad, 'Your servant will do all you demanded yesterday, but this new demand I will not meet.'"

The spokesman frowned at Dov after his translation. "Do I understand correctly? Your king refuses Ben-Hadad's new demand?"

"Correct. King Ahab will meet the first demand, as agreed. He will not open the city to unlimited search and seizure."

The three messengers deliberated amongst themselves. Meanwhile, Dov pulled aside two Aramean soldiers. "The rest of that wine should not go to waste. Perhaps it will put your king in a better mood—if it makes its way to his tent. Come."

The larger soldier grinned and followed Dov back to the banquet room.

"Is it a trick?" The second soldier hurried to catch up. "Could it be poisoned?"

"How do you feel? You drank enough."

Dov lifted one of the storage vessels. "True. This is nearly empty. If you're assured the wine is safe, please allow me to send enough for you and your king. And remind Ben-Hadad—our king will pay the tribute he already promised." He motioned to Obadiah. "Send for full casks, one for each man. No—two apiece."

Obadiah summoned several servants to fulfill Dov's request.

When they left, each messenger carried a cask, and the soldiers hefted one on each shoulder. When they reached the gate, Aaron creaked open the Eye of the Needle. When the last wine-laden Aramean passed through, the old soldier raised his eyebrows.

Dov bounded up the steps to the top of the wall and watched the visiting party make their way back to Ben-Hadad's tent. What would be his reaction? Would there be another message today? The sun had topped the mountains, but plenty of morning remained.

Below, he watched the negotiator enter the tent, the other messengers close behind. One staggered under his barrel, and a countryman hurried forward to steady him.

Dov had watched the army arrive, marching in a column that curved like a serpent along the road from Jezreel. But more worrisome than the crowd of tents, were the dirt ramps that had sprung up against the wall like anthills and the battering ram with obscene iron poles on a wheeled cart.

Dov spotted Ocran climbing the stairs. When his commander reached the top, he strode along the lines of archers, stopping a few times to talk. Ocran had a way with the men. Though a veteran fighter who had fought for Omri before Ahab, he had singled out Dov to mentor when he transitioned to the military.

"Your report?" Ocran asked.

"Yes, sir." Dov detailed the events at the palace, including summoning the elders. When he heard the king's decision, Ocran's face settled in hard lines. "The king did right, but we'll have a fight on our hands tomorrow. Watch for fires under the gates, overnight. Their war engines are placed to bring forward at the right opportunity, so they'll seek to weaken the gates and storm the city at dawn. When our forces were strong, an enemy would be satisfied with tribute. Battle is costly for both sides, in lives and goods. But the drought took its toll on Israel, and Ben-Hadad knows it. They have the advantage."

There was a flurry of activity from a tent adjacent to Ben-Hadad's. Two huge men emerged, carrying kettledrums capped with black skins. The *Anakim* pounded on the flat tops with knobbed sticks. The weighty sound reverberated to the top of the wall. Dov grimaced, recognizing the drumsticks as human thigh bones.

In the marketplace below, a few horses snorted nervously, rolling their eyes. "Steady your animals," a cavalry officer shouted.

Two normal-sized Arameans came to stand beside the giants. They lifted long brass horns to their lips.

"*Anafils!*" Ocran shouted to the horsemen in the square. "Cover your ears," he blurted to Dov. The horns shrieked like wounded mountain lions. Horses plunged and added high-pitched whinnies to the cacophony.

Dov spotted King Ahab in the crowd, banked by the king's Guard. Townsfolk and soldiers bowed low as he made his way through the square. Meanwhile, drums kept beating a dirge, punctuated by earsplitting peals from war horns.

Finally, Ben-Hadad emerged from his tent, resplendent in bronze scaled armor from shoulder to calf. His skirt armor split in front, underlaid by a white tunic. Most impressive was a copper helmet topped with long *houbara* feathers.

The players on either side of Ben-Hadad's tent raised the *anafils* once more.

But Ben-Hadad held up his hand, palm flattened. The

drums ceased and the brass horns remained silent.

King Ahab and his cohort strode through the archers. Dov stepped aside so the king, wearing his own scale armor, could confer with Ocran. But he stayed close. Ahab might need Dov to translate a message to the enemy king.

Ben-Hadad, seeming to recognize the Israelite king, shouted, "I could scarcely believe the response my messengers brought. Can you not be reasonable?"

Dov quickly translated, and Ahab shouted his answer in Hebrew. "As I told your messengers, I will do all you demanded the first time, but I will not let you have free access to the city."

This message was meant for the Israelites to understand. A show of strength—nay, defiance—they could rally behind.

Without waiting for translation, Ben-Hadad replied, "May the gods deal with me severely, if enough dust remains in Samaria to give each of my men a handful." His vehement reply propelled spittle from his mouth.

When Dov translated, Ahab's jaw clenched. He leaned over the balustrade. "One who puts on his armor in the morning should not boast like one who takes it off at day's end!" He turned to Dov. "Translate that. Shout it, so all the Arameans understand."

Dov complied. Then he noticed the big soldier who had accompanied the messengers into the city. He sought and gained entry to the king's tent. A few more soldiers approached Ben-Hadad's tent carrying familiar casks—Israelite wine.

"What are you looking at?" asked King Ahab.

"Oh, king, forgive me. But this morning I noticed the enemy soldiers drank even your worst wine with gusto. I sent more with them as a gift to their leader."

"Poisoned, I presume?"

"No sir. That would serve only to slay the cupbearer. I thought the wine of Israel might make Ben-Hadad look kindly on your response."

"Hmm. What say you, Ocran?"

"Our wine is potent, but not that potent." He indicated a group of enemy soldiers packing dirt into baskets. "Each night they have built packed-earth ramps against several locations of the wall. We've attacked when we caught them at it. When they've attempted to scale the walls, we poured hot oil upon them or shot fiery arrows. They paid the price. But their numbers are such that tomorrow, they may prevail."

The king nodded grimly.

"We will fight like lions, my king."

"Yes, Commander. I know you will." Ahab trudged down the steps and headed to the palace.

"He will talk to his harem tonight," Ocran said.

"Talk?" Dov said.

"*Instruct* them. Don't you have a woman?"

"No."

"Best you don't," Ocran mused. He eyed Dov, opened his mouth to speak, then evidently thinking better, snapped it shut.

But Dov had heard it before. Some version of 'Why are you alone, a strapping young man like you?' There had been a woman he'd thought on once, a priestess. Dov's Hebrew father, although he'd not been devout, had taught his son enough of the Law to make him hesitate about desiring a priestess. But then she fled from Jezebel with her son, Aban, and all choice in the matter was removed. After Dov joined Ahab's army, war made it foolish to form attachments of any kind. Besides, now he had old Maalik to care for. What woman would join a household with a career soldier and a eunuch?

"You live alone, then?"

His commander had never asked about his personal life before. He was making up for it.

"I live with the temple guard, Maalik."

"I know him. He once served Jezebel."

Dov nodded. Ocran looked over the valley, bumping his fist against the balustrade.

"Listen to me. If my wife hears the gates fall, she knows to kill the babe, then herself. They might leave an old eunuch be. Or they might ... practice on him new methods of torture."

Scowling, Dov gazed behind, down the narrow street leading away from the wall, little more than an alley. Maalik's one-room house stood at the end. When Dov entered it the first time, winter had set in. An orphan, he ran the streets with a group of ragged boys, snatching kernels of grain or rotting fruit where they could, sleeping in alleys in a shivering heap. He'd snagged a huge raisin cake, and a bigger boy demanded Dov give it to him. The best scores were meant to be shared by all, but the bigger boys often robbed the smaller before the food made it to the community pile. Vowing the little ones would not go hungry another night, Dov put up his fists, but the boy took it anyway, after beating Dov unconscious.

Maalik carried him home, tended his wounds, and fed him the first warm meal he'd eaten since his father's death. The eunuch and the orphan formed an unlikely family, almost father and son, a bond that had strengthened through the years as Maalik taught Dov everything about working for the royal family.

Maalik had accompanied Jezebel on her journey from Tyre as a treaty bride. Later, the queen had put him in charge of guarding the priestesses. Respectful of Dov's Israelite heritage, Maalik steered him away from the temples of Melqart and Astarte. Instead, he trained Dov to serve as a palace runner, then a guard, and later in the king's army. It was there he rose through the ranks and became a junior officer.

Dov served King Ahab wholeheartedly. But to Maalik, he owed his life.

Ocran braced his hands on the balustrade and leaned over the wall. He perused the landscape below. "Be at ease, lad. They cannot work on the ramps until dark. Be morning before they batter through the gate. You'll have time."

Time for what? Dov could never put the sword to Maalik, not even to save him from torture.

Dov's mind twisted through the labyrinth of possible solutions. He thought again of Mara, the priestess, and young Aban, who he'd watched grow up. When the mother fled from Jezebel, they took sanctuary in a secret cave in Caleb's family vineyard. Now the enemy swarmed that entire area. Had they found the crevasse that opened to the cave? No matter. Dov would need to bring Maalik through the enemy troops to reach it.

Nothing could be done but wait until morning and face the enemy, sword in hand. He was glad he had no wife. He could not protect even one old man, let alone a woman and children. After Mara had left, he'd never been tempted again. How could he raise a family? His life was the king's. He was not a part-time soldier, like a farmer or vintner, who enlisted for a single season, then laid aside weapons to go home for harvest.

Not all were like that. There were some farmers, early settlers like Caleb's family, who were bound to the city. Their terraced vineyards were built outside the walls during the founding of Samaria and most also kept a house inside the city. Like the other citizens, they were safe—like a lion is safe in a pit—until men come with spears to kill the animal, trapped in its enclosure. So they stood by the king and his men when enemies threatened the town.

Ocran tapped Dov with the butt of his spear. "Take yourself off for a few hours. Eat a meal with Maalik. Check the palace for messages. Then return, so I may go ... make sure my wife understands."

When Dov walked through the door, Maalik looked up from his workbench. "What are you doing home, boy?" he asked, surprise etching his features. He grasped a club made of fire-hardened acacia limb. He had just finished nailing the last iron spike into its round knob. "As you're here, walk with me to Lemuel's house. He and Caleb are to fight atop the wall. I'm to protect the women."

"They take a later shift. Why are you going so early?"

Maalik winked, causing Dov to wonder if the man who brought him up would be any good at protecting anyone. Dov threw his hand up in an attack position and feinted toward him.

"Careful, there, lad!" Maalik swung the club to meet Dov's attack, stopping just in time to save him a broken forearm.

"You react better than I thought, old man. Answer my question."

"That Hadassah is quite a cook. Quite a woman, as a matter of fact. She promised me chickpea stew with barley bread—hinted she might yet have honey from her granddaughter's hive."

Dov nodded, stirred by the old eunuch and the glint in his eyes. He had protected Jezebel without question most of his life, now he proposed to guard some of the Yahwists the queen hated. The same Yahwists Dov had befriended.

Maalik tied his cloak rakishly over one shoulder and picked up the lethal-looking club.

"Need we bring anything else?" Dov asked.

"Not when I'm eating at the home of the best cook and finest vintner in the city." Maalik grinned, but in the next moment dropped his swagger. "What do you think of our chances?"

"Not good. My commander said, if the city gate falls, his wife is instructed to kill their child and then herself."

Maalik nodded grimly.

Dov pointed to the club. "Is that why—"

"You mean, the women—no! There is a difference between those who follow the Ba'als and those who follow Yahweh. They believe life is precious—given by their Creator. This club will protect them. But if it comes to it, they will face death without fear."

"I met Caleb's grandmother and sister before the drought. They are brave."

"You met them before the drought?"

Dov smiled. "When I was part of the Temple Guard, I searched houses to find the acolyte who helped Elijah evade the king's soldiers. It was Aban, of course. The grandmother had disguised him as a girl and spread flour paste on his face. I recognized him at once, but the other guard threatened to 'question the girl in private.' Hadassah put herself between them, shouting 'Come no closer—the girl is unclean!' It was only then the guard noticed the crusty white patches and concluded they were leprosy. I tell you, I could hardly keep from laughing when he leapt backward and left me to finish the investigation."

"You said Caleb's sister was there at the time?"

"Yes. The grandmother had placed Caleb and his little

sister in the opposite corner, but before the guard noticed her, Aban drew attention to himself shouting 'Don't hurt my grandmother!'" Dov laughed, remembering, and Maalik joined in.

When they reached the house, Dov stepped in to greet Caleb's family. After he'd spoken with the parents, Lemuel and Dorcas, the grandmother offered Dov flatbread, warm and fragrant with honey. Gratefully, he sank his teeth into the bread. "Maalik said you had honey from your granddaughter's hive." He looked around the room, not seeing the young girl he remembered from that time. "Miriam's not here?" This was not the time to be visiting a friend. Not when it could be the last night with your family.

"I sent her to Jezreel, just before the Arameans attacked Samaria," Lemuel said. "My brother's daughter-in-law was expecting a child."

"Oh. And then she could not return."

"We're grateful, of course. She's safe, at least for now."

Dov nodded, his lips tightening. If the Arameans took Samaria, they'd attack Jezreel next. There was no need to say it.

As Dov hurried back to the wall, he noticed a lanky stranger making for the steps. Glancing to the top, he saw a flash of scaled armor—the king or the king's guard. The man climbed the steps toward them. Why? Dov broke into a run.

While the city was under siege, only soldiers, officers, and the king and his retinue were allowed atop the wall. A guard had been placed to keep others at bay, yet this man strode by unchallenged. He wore the undyed tunic and head covering of a shepherd, his sandals roughly made and worn. Dov shoved his way past soldiers and archers, keeping his eye on the man.

What business would a shepherd have on the wall during a siege? This was no time to bring up a dispute over sheep or grazing rights. *An Aramean spy? Assassin?*

The guard had let the stranger pass. Was treachery afoot? Dov charged up the remaining steps to draw level with the stranger. Though many newcomers had taken refuge inside the walls, Dov made rounds among them each evening. If the fellow was one of that lot, Dov would recognize him. Still, there was no reason for one of them to approach the king.

Dov caught up before the man reached the king's guards. But when he turned, his cloak was pulled low on his brow and wrapped across the lower part of his face.

Dov grabbed his arm. "Halt, stranger. What is your business here?"

"I bring a message for King Ahab."

Dov looked him up and down. No accent, so not Aramean. He even sounded like a common shepherd, but why the disguise? "Message from who?"

"Yahweh."

A prophet? Dov hesitated. He'd witnessed the mighty contest on Mount Carmel between Ba'al Melqart and Yahweh's prophet. Seen fire shoot from the sky at Elijah's command. Yet, since Jezebel put a price on their heads, no prophet of Yahweh had set foot in the city. Under those conditions, disguise might make sense, but Dov was responsible for the king's safety.

"What is your name?"

"My name is unimportant. I am merely the servant of Yahweh."

Dov thumped the man's chest with his forefinger. Less than a blow, more than a tap. "No one speaks to the king without identification."

"You are known, Dov, as a man of character. A worthy servant of an unworthy ruler. Yet, the Lord has sent me to speak with the king, not you. Search me for weapons, if you wish. I need none."

Dov stared into unwavering eyes. He could swear they'd never met. He thrust his hand beneath the prophet's sash, the one place a weapon could be hidden. The man endured it without protest. There was no weapon, not even a dagger, like most shepherds carried.

Who was he?

Elijah had been known by his long, grizzled hair, leather belt, and sheepskin mantle. This man's garments were old woolen cloth, worn smooth in spots. Was he Elijah? His assurance reminded Dov of Elijah facing down the priests of Ba'al Melqart, but with his face covered, Dov couldn't be sure. Hadn't Elijah been a larger man? He had never hidden his face, but even Elijah had fled when Jezebel threatened to kill him and all the other prophets of Yahweh. Fear of the queen was enough reason for any prophet to cover his face.

Momentarily, Dov considered ripping the cloth from the man's face. But surely this was a man of God, whether he was Elijah or not. Memory of fire called down from heaven on Mount Carmel restrained Dov. Yahweh might object to His prophet being treated roughly. Dov took a deep breath.

"I will ask if the king will see you."

The man stood quietly, hands clasped loosely together. Dov left him gazing curiously at Aramean soldiers wheeling the battering ram closer to the gate.

King Ahab scowled at Dov. "You aren't sure it's Elijah?"

"He would not give his name—said he was merely a servant."

"Sounds like Elijah. That troubler of Israel!"

Dov shifted uneasily. "I remembered Elijah as a larger man. The drought, food shortage, his advancing age—all might have changed him. I believe he is a prophet, but Elijah? I don't know."

"Let us hear him." King Ahab cast his gaze over those atop the wall. His shoulders sagged. After a year, the siege weighed heavy upon him. Or was it dread of another interview with a prophet? The last had brought drought and famine to his kingdom.

Dov walked slowly as he returned with the mysterious stranger—was he bringing friend or foe into the presence of the king?

The prophet spoke loudly enough to be heard by nearby archers and soldiers. "This is what the Lord says: 'Do you see this vast army? I will give it into your hand today, and then you will know that I am the Lord.'"

Dov felt his forehead crease. How could it be? Outside the wall, Aramean war machines stood in position to attack. Seven or eight chariots raced around the foot of the hill, drivers whooping derisively as if to flaunt the strength of their army.

Bringing his gaze back from the spectacle below, Ahab appeared doubtful. "But who will do this?"

The prophet stood straight as a pillar, turning his face up as if searching the heavens for the answer. "This is what the Lord says, 'The young officers of the provincial commanders will do it.'"

Dov's gut twisted. The young officers—him!

Ahab also seemed conflicted. "And who will start the battle?"

The prophet answered, "You will." Then he turned and walked down the steps, where he quickly disappeared into the crowded marketplace of townsfolk, farmers, and refugees.

Ahab stared after him for a while, then walked slowly to the balustrade. "Give me the battle? All these?" The king shook his head. "Do you think it was Elijah?" he asked those gathered close—the king's guard, Ocran and another commander, and several archers who had moved closer to hear the exchange between the prophet and king.

Dov looked down, hoping someone else would answer. The king had met Elijah several times. Why hadn't he asked the prophet his name? Surely, he would answer the king of Samaria.

But would he?

King Ahab motioned Ocran to approach. "Send word for the provincial commanders to summon their young officers. I want to meet with them."

"Here, on the wall?"

"No, on the palace steps."

Ocran saluted and strode away to brief the commanders.

Dov peered over the wall. In the enemy camp, officials in fine clothing headed toward Ben-Hadad's tent, laughing and gesticulating toward the city. Quickly he tabulated their number—eight, fifteen, twenty-five, thirty-two—these were the kings of the ally armies. Likely, they planned a victory tomorrow and counted their riches today. Understandable. All the Israelite men of fighting age totaled less than ten thousand, a paltry number compared to the enemy that blanketed the hillside and valley.

Yet, Dov felt his mind unfold the rest of the prophet's message. *I will give this vast army into your hand today, and then you shall know that I am the Lord.*

Hadn't Elijah said something like that, when he cursed the land with drought? *You will know there is a God in Israel, and that I am His servant.*

After witnessing Elijah's miracles on Mount Carmel, Dov was willing to follow his orders.

And if it wasn't Elijah? If it was his servant Elisha, the one who had supplanted Aban? Or one of the others in the school of the prophets, those who sheltered in Caleb's cave when Jezebel hunted them. He no longer remembered their names. But did it matter who the prophet was, as long as he spoke for Yahweh?

The king had agreed with the instructions and put orders in motion. Besides, Dov's commander, Ocran, had painted a picture of complete devastation if the Arameans stormed the gates in the morning. What other options did they have? Obey the prophet's instructions—or die.

Vague instructions, though. *I will give this vast army into your hand—today.* That was not vague. He had said *today*, hadn't he?

Dov looked down on a nearly finished earthen ramp. A battering ram stood ready at its base, a fearsome wheeled contraption made of wood reinforced with iron. An iron pole menaced the gate like a striking viper. From a military standpoint, *today* was the only chance for Samaria. Tomorrow, the ramp would be complete, the war machine mobile, and the enemy would pour into the city.

Today. The younger officers. Those were the only instructions.

"Why are you still here?" Ocran's sharp tone matched his scowl. "Junior officers to lead—bah! You're capable, Dov, but the others—well, I count on you to see the attack through."

Chapter Three

*Meanwhile a prophet came to Ahab king of Israel and
announced, "This is what the Lord says: 'Do you see this
vast army? I will give it into your hand today, and then you
will know that I am the Lord.'"*
~ *1 Kings 20:13*

Samaria, later that morning
Dov

WHILE WAITING AMONG THOSE GATHERED NEAR the palace steps,
Dov counted the assembled junior officers. Including himself,
two-hundred thirty-two—a paltry number. Most were skilled
fighters, but they had little leadership experience. Behind
them, however, several thousand Israelites of fighting age
wielded an odd assortment of weapons—clubs, plowshares,
and slingshots. Farmers, shepherds—not military men.
Would they stand firm in battle?

King Ahab strode out of the palace, halting on the
topmost step. As he surveyed the crowd, the late morning
sun revealed lines of stress and concern.

"We've had a message from Yahweh." The king scowled
as if ingesting something distasteful. "His prophet says
Yahweh is with us—with you, in fact. You junior officers will
lead the charge."

A ripple of murmurs passed through the crowd—not
from the officers, young or seasoned. The military training of
either group would restrain expressing emotion at the king's
order, no matter their opinion. The murmurs of questioning,
wonder, and disapproval came from the civilians of fighting
age.

"Silence!" The king turned a scowl on the volunteers. "I
give the orders. You obey without hesitation or face
execution."

No one made a sound. Ahab needed discipline in the
ranks, and he knew how to get it. Then the lines in his face
softened, as if he realized the need to encourage the men.

"The prophet said the Lord will fight on Israel's side. He will give us the battle—through your hands. Here is the plan."

Ben-Hadad hoisted a silver goblet, sloshing wine over its polished rim. A pity to waste even a drop, but there'd be more after tomorrow's battle. He would send a special envoy to raid Ahab's reserves. "To victory," he intoned.

"Victory!" Word had spread quickly about the quality of Israel's wine. The allied kings had crowded into Ben-Hadad's tent. The close quarters intensified bodily odors perfumed oils could not mask.

"Open the tent flaps," Ben-Hadad instructed his servant. "We need a breeze. Let there be music." The king chuckled and staggered slightly. Waving his hand at the servant had unbalanced him. Keeping both arms pinned to his side, he called to another. "It's nearly midday, is it not? Bring food—and more wine."

With the flaps tied back, a breeze threaded through the tent. The hill had been a pleasant setting on which to stage a siege, elevated above the heat of the plain and conveniently terraced with vineyards and gardens for his fellow kings to pitch their tents upon. Its position also made it more difficult to attack the elevated city, but the siege had done its work. Victory was imminent.

Ben-Hadad leaned back on a cushion, smiling at the gentle tune a musician played on a lute, interrupted when one of his scouts blocked the entrance.

"Men are advancing from Samaria."

"Generals?"

The scout shook his head. "Younger men. Some dressed as civilians."

Ben-Hadad steadied himself against the tent's center pole. "Ah. They're ready to make terms. If they have come out for peace, take them alive. If they have come out for war, take them ... alive."

The scout hesitated. "Alive, Sir? Either way?"

Ben-Hadad said sharply, "Have I not said it?" He shoved past the scout, squinting against the noon-day sun. Yes, there was a regiment of young men marching down from the city gate. They would reach the terrace where his tent was pitched quite soon. Certainly they intended to parley.

The scout quickly ordered Ben-Hadad's soldiers to approach the group and take them for questioning.

Ben-Hadad watched as one of his soldiers fell, then another. Had they lost their footing? *Drunken oafs!*

The young Israelites rushed his men, striking with daggers and spears. Each killed his Aramean opponent. Behind the first line, archers surged down the hill, setting arrows to flight. Then he understood. The Israelites had not come seeking terms of surrender.

He had foolishly—drunkenly—underestimated his enemy.

Someone grasped his arm. "Sire, your horse." His groom, Faraz, held the fleetest horse in the string, already bridled. He tried to toss a saddle on its back, but it shied away. An arrow flew past Ben-Hadad's head.

"There's no time," shouted the groom, pointing at an even larger regiment close behind the archers. "They come." He bent, making a step of his back.

Ben-Hadad swore as he climbed atop the horse, clutching with his knees as it sped from the soldiers flooding from the gate, this group led by Ahab. Ben-Hadad turned his mount down the hill, clinging as it jumped down terraces. As his horse galloped past the deserted battering ram, he glanced behind. Some of his fellow kings also fled, some on foot, others on horseback if their grooms were as prepared as Faraz. Israelites waded through his men, hewing them down like barley. Arrows found their marks. Where were his shield bearers? These Israelites—many of them civilians—were decimating his mighty army! How had power shifted so fast?

A flaming arrow hit a tent in his path. Fire licked hungrily across its surface. The horse reared violently, throwing him against its neck. Instinct drove him to rake his fingers into the horse's mane. Curse the wine, he was a better horseman than this, saddle or not. He mourned the absence of his painted chariot until he saw a dead king slumped on the floor of his own, arrows protruding from his back. Despite the steep downgrade, Ben-Hadad grimly urged the horse faster, weaving to dodge arrows. Ahead, two of his soldiers ran toward him, shouting something unintelligible. Ben-Hadad veered away, but when they lunged for the horse's reins, he dispatched each with a slash of his sword.

When he reached the plain, he risked another backward glance. So many tents burned, the hill appeared aflame. Some kings who had thought to hide from the battle, ran out screaming, long robes on fire. *Soft, stupid lap dogs!*

He watched as a few charioteers attempted to charge up the hill, likely the soldiers earlier racing around the city for sport. There had been no time for others to harness horses to vehicles. He grimaced as Israelites overwhelmed them, clubbed the drivers to death, and confiscated horses and chariots.

He took one last look. A regiment of foot soldiers had stayed on the hill to fight, rather than follow their retreating kings. Valiant men. But to no avail. Arrows rained down and Israelites wielding clubs and spears surged from the city. Ben-Hadad searched the melee for Faraz but couldn't locate him. He recognized some of his ally kings, who had also acquired horses, riding hard out of the battle. He did not slow for them to catch up, but every time he looked back, they followed.

Ben-Hadad set his sights for the mountain pass that would take him to Jezreel. On the army's march to Samaria, he remembered craggy cliffs. There must be caves. He looked back again and saw the Israelite army closing in, shouting as they cut down the Aramean foot soldiers. Where were his chariots? One moment he'd had his foot on Ahab's neck, the next everything turned. Thanking the gods for quick-thinking, probably-dead Faraz, Ben-Hadad kicked his horse into a gallop.

His mind filled with the images of kings running from their tents like human torches. He had judged them foolish, but he was no better. So assured of his army's superior strength, he drank with his officers, rather than lead his soldiers.

He reassessed the wisdom of hiding in caves so close to Samaria. He'd misjudged the Israelites once and lost the battle. One more mistake could cost his life.

He considered his options. He'd lost most of his army.

His helmet lay on a table in his tent. He had no provisions. But his short sword hung from his belt and a dagger was strapped to his ankle. Two hours of daylight remained. He would press on toward Jezreel instead. The rough terrain around Mount Gilboa would offer refuge. There was a spring.

He looked back at the remaining kings, pulled his sword, and raised it over his head. They saluted him from their cloud of dust.

Chapter Four

*Afterward, the prophet came to the king of Israel and said,
"Strengthen your position and see what must be done,
because next spring the king of Aram will attack you again."*
~ 1 Kings 20:22

Samaria, later that day
Dov

A SWEAT-FLECKED BAY CHARGED TOWARD Dov, dragging its reins. Dov spread his arms, moving slowly and crooning, "Whoa, whoa." When the horse shied away, he seized the trailing rein, ran a few strides alongside, then leaped for its back. He'd seen an Israelite arrow catch its rider in the chest, and the Aramean had toppled off backwards. Sweeping his gaze down the hill, he spotted several other riderless horses. "Any man who can sit a horse, follow my lead!"

He set off in pursuit of enemy soldiers, raising his bow over his head. Roaring their approval, his archers fell in and fanned out across the hill.

A young officer in Ahab's cavalry led riders from the city. "You, and you!" he shouted. "Capture loose horses. Find riders among the foot soldiers and the townsfolk." Soon, newly mounted on Aramean steeds, a larger Israelite cavalry galloped after the enemy.

King Ahab thundered by, grasping the reins of a brilliantly-painted, iron-wheeled chariot. After him came about twenty more captured chariots driven by a conglomeration of farmers and men from the city. Dov laughed aloud when he saw Aaron the gatekeeper, wild-eyed and clinging white-knuckled to the front of one chariot.

Dov raced after the Arameans, employing his sword for the most part. After he grew accustomed to the warhorse, who thundered steady as a mountain torrent after the enemy, Dov tucked the reins under his leg and shot arrows, cutting a swath through the faltering Arameans.

He crossed the battlefield searching for Ben-Hadad. He

found bodies, some of the allied kings, but not the powerful leader he sought. It seemed many of the leaders had obtained mounts and escaped, deserting their own armies. Even the king of Aram. Unfathomable. No wonder confusion reigned among the enemy forces, despite the advantage of their numbers. A crushing loss of face for Aram.

Dov pulled up next to King Ahab's chariot. "Ben-Hadad is among the missing and about a third of the allied kings. Shall we press after them?"

"How did he escape? I'm driving his chariot."

"He fled on horseback. Word is, he had no saddle."

"Nor do you." The king smiled grimly. "Let's continue on. At a faster pace."

"Yes, my lord." Dov swung back and rallied his men. "Onward! Forge a path for your king."

They made good time across level ground, not slowing until they neared a mountain pass. At the first rocky ridge, scouts rode before the foot soldiers hunting for signs that the enemy had splintered off into landslips, wadis, or caves.

A full moon lit the plain, but when they rode past hills and outcroppings, visibility and rough terrain hampered the pursuit. Finally, King Ahab called a halt. Dov rode back to his side.

"Enough. The leaders have escaped. Yet, the victory is ours ..." The king cleared his throat. "That is, the victory is the Lord's. You have dispatched your duty well, men of Samaria."

The king's message was relayed across the army until the last man had heard. "My lord," said Dov. "With your permission, my fellow officers and I will continue in the hope of yet capturing Ben-Hadad. Surely, we will pick up a trail."

"I leave it to your judgement." Ahab turned his chariot, then paused. "May the Lord be with you." Then he and the battle-weary civilians headed toward home. Dov saw Caleb, his brother Seth, and their father among them. The three hesitated, then turned to follow after Dov and the mounted rag-tag cavalry. He galloped back to them. "Go back to Samaria with the others. We must move fast, without fear that you might be ambushed from the rear. See to your family—and mine. Maalik is guarding your women."

"If you are sure," Caleb said. "I can use the sleep. Tomorrow, or the next day, the king will send me to Jezreel, to bring news of our victory."

Dov waved off his friend and swung round to rejoin the hunting party. Layered hills offered many hiding places. The moon had crossed the sky when they lost hope of finding a trail in the rocky ground, and he gave the order to return to Samaria.

When they finally approached the city, torches moved randomly across the hill. Men dragged away debris, tended to the wounded, and carted off the dead. Others piled up food, clothing, weapons, sometimes even silver and gold. The spoils of war included not only what they found in tents and on bodies, but the large, grand tents that had not been set afire. In their haste to retreat, the Arameans had abandoned many chariots, their drivers either killed or fleeing on horseback. Some now doubled as carts, filled with clothing, other goods, and weapons. The two war machines had also been left behind. Soldiers and townsmen hitched mules to their traces and dragged them toward the city.

Moonlight revealed the city wall undamaged, the gate intact. Ben-Hadad's curse—*May the gods deal with me severely if enough dust remains in Samaria to give each of my men a handful*—had fallen on his own head.

Dov urged his horse to a trot, anxious to see how those inside had fared. The battle had quickly turned against the Arameans, so it was doubtful any forced their way into the city. Still, he had to see for himself—set his eyes on Maalik and the others. After he reported to the king, Dov would head for Caleb's house.

Aaron stood by the open gate, looking decidedly more comfortable than when Dov saw him clinging to the speeding chariot. Torch-bearing soldiers flanked him on either side. Each man wore gleaming new weapons, secure in tooled leather scabbards of Aramean fabrication. Dov's horse sidestepped through the gates, tugging at the reins. How did the animal have such energy, after the night they'd been through?

"Officer!" Aaron barked, and all three saluted. "Did you chase them all the way back to Aram?"

Dov smiled at the exaggeration. "Some escaped on horseback. We kept on toward Jezreel a while, but never sighted them."

"Will they attack Jezreel?"

Dov's horse snorted and shoved its muzzle against Aaron's chest. Laughing, the gatekeeper stumbled back.

"I need to report to the king," Dov said, "and this fellow wants his barley. But, I do not believe there are enough left to trouble another walled city."

Aaron gave the horse a light slap as Dov rode past. "May the Lord make His face to shine upon you."

Dov kept the horse to a walk as they crossed the wide square, normally a market during times of peace, but for these many months a refuge for farmers from the valley who took shelter during the siege. Dov squinted at the temporary residents bustling about, rolling up sleeping mats and piling them against the wall to create a large open space, as if they meant to stay awake throughout the night's remaining hours.

Women prepared meat for roasting in the community ovens at the edge of the market square. Musicians pitched their instruments with one another, stirring up a cacophonous muddle rather than a melody. Neighbors carried oil lamps from their homes and placed them strategically around the center fountain, at the top of the gates, and along the parapets of nearby homes where they glowed festively.

As Dov reached the fringe of the activity, he was stopped by a cluster of the townsfolk. "You were there, among the first out of the city." Hands reached up to grasp his, making the horse dance sideways. "Such bravery—you saved us. Yahweh was with you."

Weariness weighed on Dov like scaled armor. He hadn't sought to lead men into battle, nor take the place of his commanding officer. He had done his duty, but he was no hero. Considering how he'd come to lead the battle, at the behest of the prophet, something in their praise felt dangerous. Almost blasphemous.

"You are right in the last," he said. "Yahweh was with Israel, as the prophet promised. All of you followed. The victory is the Lord's."

The people moved back, opening a path for him to ride through. "It's true," someone said. "Yesterday the king was ready to pay tribute and surrender. The victory belongs to the Lord."

"Not sure Ahab will agree," muttered a shepherd, and there was a round of quiet laughter. Dov moved on, pretending not to hear.

He rode to the palace, where more oil lamps lit the entrance steps. A servant hurried out to take the horse, promising to give it a good feed and stable it with the king's own animals. He was glad of the assurance. The stallion had served him well, tireless and steady. A comfortable ride, too, considering he had no saddle.

"Have all the captured horses been stabled here?"

"Yes. It's a tight fit, but we've managed for now—until the king decides what's to be done." The servant eyed Dov with concern. "Sir, are you reporting to the king? Your tunic is bloodied."

Dov nodded, thinking of his second tunic, hanging on a peg at Maalik's house. "I'm to report upon my return. It will have to do."

"Sir, we've a number of fine garments taken from the enemy camp." He tipped his head toward a lean-to attached to the stable. "Let me find something suitable. Meanwhile—the water in this trough is fresh."

Stepping into the dimly lit stable, Dov pulled off the offending tunic, plunged the cleanest half into the trough, and scrubbed his face, arms, and torso until his skin prickled from the cold. The servant hurried back with a clean tunic and a vest of scaled armor that appeared never to have seen battle. He handed Dov a dripping waterskin. "I keep it cool weighted down in the trough," he said.

Dov drank deeply. When he crossed the palace threshold, he saw King Ahab surrounded by most of the city elders. Servants roamed the room offering wine and honeyed almonds. Everyone was dressed for a celebration and the air reeked of perfume. An advisor raised his goblet to Ahab. "I offer congratulations, my king. You threw the Arameans into complete disarray."

Dov glimpsed the queen standing apart, half hidden by a column. She eyed the king as he received accolades from prominent citizens but made no move to join them. What a contrast to her previous boldness, she who once positioned herself as co-ruler of Israel, a strong queen who held the heart of her king. But the king had offered her as a war prize, only one among many. Now she stood at a distance. An impartial observer might have thought her humbled by the incident. But Dov had not forgotten the aftermath of Mount Carmel.

"Officer Dov." The king smiled and beckoned him approach. Dov saluted and strode forward.

"You have not brought me Ben-Hadad."

"No, my lord. We searched several miles farther, to no avail. After the passes, nothing, though we were careful to explore every turnoff."

Dov heard something out-of-place under the hum of conversation, quiet, like the click of a deathwatch beetle. How foolish. He was exhausted, his battle-weary mind imagining the movement of insects within the palace walls.

King Ahab frowned at a point just beyond Dov's right shoulder. Before he turned, he caught a whiff of sheep wool. *The prophet.*

As before, the prophet had draped his cloak across the lower part of his face. Black eyes held Dov's gaze. Across the room, Queen Jezebel took several quick steps, then halted, as if intercepted by an invisible hand.

"This is what the Lord says." The prophet's voice stilled all others. "You will not find Ben-Hadad or his fellow kings. Not until next spring, when he will again attack. Strengthen your defenses. Rebuild your army. Prepare."

By the time Dov left the palace, the celebration in the square was pulsing like a runner's heart. The musical instruments played joyous dance music. Maidens and matrons circled the fountain holding hands when they weren't clapping or beating tambourines. They wore their best raiment but even these showed the grime of the long siege, when water was meant only for drinking, not washing. Women stamped their feet and bells on their anklets chimed.

Men circled the women like a wall of protection, their deep voices chanting with the drums. As Dov skirted the perimeter, he was pulled, protesting, into their company.

Yet why should he hang back? Shouldn't he celebrate with his countrymen? On the heels of his question, images came—arrows flying, sword thrusts, lifeless eyes staring into Sheol.

Should he celebrate death? No. He would not wish death on another, but the enemy had chosen their path, and he followed his duty—to protect his people.

The merriment brought an antidote to the poison of the siege and the horrors of battle.

Dov gave himself to the dance, only extricating himself when he caught sight of a familiar face on the sideline, dark hair uncharacteristically slicked with oil.

"Is the whole city holding up my guest?" Caleb asked.

"My apologies—"

Wordlessly, Caleb grabbed Dov's arm and reached back toward the dancers. Several arms extended his way. In an instant, the festivities swallowed them.

"I could find myself a wife this way." Caleb raised his voice over the music. "All these beautiful maidens!" A petite young woman gave Caleb a sideways glance, then danced away. But in a moment, she swung by again, and this time she loosed herself from the line of women and swirled in front of Caleb, arching an eyebrow.

He stopped in his tracks, tossing a grin at Dov, who had also plowed to a halt. Suddenly the entire line of women broke and moved apart, surrounding Dov and Caleb like a cluster of butterflies, flitting under one another and twirling, their skirts fluttering like wings.

A tall woman paused before Dov, juddering a tambourine, at the same time feathering strokes upon it, bringing forth a soft, insistent thrumming countered by the clinking of silvery discs. Dark eyes, framed by not-unpleasant lines at their corners, held his as she began to dance slowly around him. Tension clouded the air in a way he had not felt even on the battlefield.

He gave a half bow and stepped back, smiling

apologetically. Turning to Caleb, he said, "Let's go now. I must see to Maalik." He ignored the wink Caleb shot him. Then he strode off toward the house, not looking back to see if his supposed friend followed.

"Come sit by the fire." Caleb's mother Dorcas took his hand and guided Dov to sit by her husband Lemuel. A pot simmered on the coals, filling the room with a savory aroma.

Dov's gaze latched on the face he sought above all others. Maalik sat beside Hadassah, Caleb's blind grandmother. He spoke quietly into her ear, and she smiled with surprising accuracy in Dov's direction.

"Shalom, Dov. You have not met my wife, Avigail." Seth, Caleb's older brother, rested his hand on her shoulder. His young wife ducked her head and smiled shyly. Dov was no expert when it came to women, but Seth's pretty spouse had a look about her, especially in the way she rested her hand protectively on her belly, that set Dov wondering if there would be a child in the spring.

"Shalom, Seth. Avigail."

"You must tell us of the day's events," Maalik said.

"All in good time." Dorcas swirled her wooden spoon in the stew pot and stood. "Dov must certainly be hungry, and the food is ready. Talk while we eat."

Lemuel stood, raised his hands, and looked toward heaven. "Let us thank the Lord for this day's great blessings.

Have mercy on me, O God, have mercy on me,
for in you my soul takes refuge.
I will take refuge in the shadow of your wings
until the disaster has passed.
I cry out to God Most High,
to God, who fulfills his purpose for me.
He sends from heaven and saves me,
rebuking those who hotly pursue me;
God sends his love and his faithfulness.

They spread a net for my feet,
I was bowed down in distress.

They dug a pit in my path,
but they have fallen into it themselves.

I will praise you, O Lord, among the nations;
I will sing of you among the peoples.
For great is your love, reaching to the heavens;
your faithfulness reaches to the skies.
Be exalted, O God, above the heavens;
let your glory be over all the earth."

The room was silent a moment, but then, in a sweet clear voice, the grandmother sang the first phrase of the prayer. One by one, Dorcas, Lemuel, Caleb, and even Maalik joined in to lift the words in song. Dov had not spent much time in the temple, but even he knew the tune of *Do Not Destroy* and his spirit soared as he sang phrases he remembered.

Dorcas filled bowls with a stew of lentils, root vegetables, and bits of meat. She handed them to Caleb.

"You can see why I had to come pull you from the arms of your dance partner. I thought I'd die of hunger awaiting your return." Caleb addressed his complaint to Dov, while distributing bowls.

Dorcas swatted his hand when he came for more. "You did not suffer, my son." She handed him a basket filled with round loaves of bread.

"Eat, eat," Lemuel urged. "My wife will think you do not like her cooking."

Dov broke his loaf, dipping into the stew. "Delicious! Mmm, I taste lamb." He ignored a pang of guilt. Food had been scarce during the siege, but tomorrow, each family would gain food, clothing, and weapons, courtesy of the Arameans.

Dorcas smiled. "We dressed a lamb when we knew the Lord had given Israel the victory."

As they chatted over the supper, Dov began to relax in the humble atmosphere. "We did not find Ben-Hadad," he answered when asked. "But you will find this interesting—I had scarcely given my report when the prophet showed up— or *appeared*. He was not there when I arrived, and I heard no footsteps behind me. He was simply there."

"Did he have another message from the Lord?" Lemuel asked.

"He said, 'Strengthen your position and see what must be done, because next spring the king of Aram will attack you again.'"

Lemuel stroked his beard, taking this in. "The interaction between the prophet and the king. Did you find it strange?"

"All of it," Dov responded. "Starting with the disguise."

"That is not strange," said Hadassah. "Remember how Queen Jezebel sought to kill the prophet Elijah."

Dov nodded, then said, "Yes." He would never get used to the way Hadassah's blind eyes turned toward the sound of his voice. "At first I thought Elijah might be the prophet. Not now. Tonight, the man's head covering was not pulled completely over his hair. Elijah's hair was white."

"And this prophet's?" Caleb's grandmother asked.

"Black as a raven's wing. And I tell you, he would do well to continue his disguise, now that the queen is not Ben-Hadad's war prize. I saw the look she fixed on the prophet when he said the Arameans would be back in the spring."

After Dorcas and Avigail cleared away the remains of the meal, the women guided Hadassah to a back room and did not return. Lemuel stood and retrieved a wine skin from a corner. He reached to fill Dov's cup, but he covered it with his hand. "I will seek my bed soon. And I must rise early."

"A moment, then." Lemuel said, "I find it strange that Yahweh is giving Ahab another chance."

"You mean—"

"Ahab never admitted the Lord was the one who ended the drought, let alone thanked Him. Then the prophet tells the king the Lord would give Him this battle, despite that the enemy greatly outnumbered us—and Yahweh would do this so Ahab would know He alone is Lord in Israel. Did the king show any sign that he attributed this victory to the Lord?"

Dov thought on it. "King Ahab was careful to follow each of the prophet's instructions," he said. "He sent the young officers out first to start the fighting, as instructed. Then he rode out behind them, leading the rest of the men in the city—farmers, shepherds, and vintners. Not an officer among them, just as the prophet said. Yet the king led them fiercely, and they answered his call."

"Yes, I was among them," said Lemuel. "Perhaps this time King Ahab understands. Perhaps the kingdom will change—things will be different."

"Next year we will be prepared." Seth spoke for the first time. "Dov, the farmers and shepherds need more training with weapons. I, for one, am no soldier."

"You acquitted yourself admirably," Dov replied. "But next year *will* be different. The king will conscript men from other cities. We will have more men, more training, and we already have many more weapons."

"I'm anxious to bring the good news to Jezreel—and see my sister," Caleb said. "I hope the king sends me tomorrow."

"It's likely he will, especially since he is anxious to begin building his new army," Dov said. "I will accompany you. We lost Ben-Hadad somewhere on the way to Jezreel. It's possible he holed up in a cave or culvert."

"Your company is welcome. But can you keep up with the king's fastest runner?"

Dov laughed. "The gazelle of Samaria? Not on foot. We go on horseback."

Caleb raised his eyebrows. "Indeed?"

"Many fine horses were captured and the stable is crowded. I will ask the king for a horse for you."

As Dov and Maalik walked home, the watchman called the third watch. *"Sleep in safety, oh Israel, the Lord has given you victory over your enemies."*

Dov draped his arm over Maalik's shoulder. "How different this proclamation from those we heard in past months. 'Unknown army approaching from the north. Activity in the enemy camp. Attempt to build ramps. Enemy preparing to storm the south gate.'"

"No one slept more than a few hours at a time. Especially you." Maalik craned his neck to look at Dov. "Last time I looked, you stood this high." He set his palm on his heart. "When did you get so tall, my son?"

It felt good to laugh.

Chapter Five

You will not fear the terror of night, nor the arrow that flies by day, nor the pestilence that stalks in the darkness, nor the plague that destroys at midday. A thousand may fall at your side, ten thousand at your right hand, but it will not come near you.
~ Psalm 91:5-7

Jezreel, morning of the battle
Miriam

"I WANT TO SET TRAPS. PLEASE, Gershon, let me go with you to the vineyard. Think of it—roast partridge for supper, leftovers to flavor lentils ..." Miriam saw his refusal forming. "There's no need for me to go to the valley," she rushed to explain. "I've seen birds in the vineyard hunting insects. Haven't you grown tired of plain lentils? It will not take long and then I can help you—"

"Say no more. It is not safe." He turned from her, but then paused at the door. "Give me the traps. I'll set them for you."

Not safe? The vineyard was only steps from the city gate. Gershon was worse than an old woman. Huffing a sigh of irritation, Miriam described where she'd seen the birds feeding and gave him bait she prepared. He left, carrying two basket traps she wove since arriving.

The house was quiet with Yaffa ministering to a sick neighbor, Jaedon visiting his friend Samuel, and the men working in the vineyard. Kneeling, Miriam ground flour with such vigor she had plenty for supper in half the time. She kept on until she had enough for tomorrow, then sat back on her heels, vibrating with pent up energy. She measured out lentils to soak. Why not mix dough and let it rise? That would make a change from flatbread. That done, she dusted flour from her hands, swept the floor, and tidied the room. She looked around for something else to fill her time. She should have gone with Yaffa.

Miriam donned her head covering and wandered outside. The blue dome of sky stretched overhead, expansive and peaceful. She searched for the eagles. Seeing nothing but sky, she climbed the stairs to the roof then stepped atop the wall. When she looked over the parapet, Naboth and Gershon were bent over, tying up drooping vines. Gershon had already placed the traps—not where she had told him. She didn't hail the men, telling herself she didn't want to frighten any unseen birds considering the bait, but in truth, irritation still left her tetchy.

Again, she searched the sky. There they were! Both eagles, one above the other, crossing and re-crossing paths in a synchronized dance. As if the two were of one mind, they veered to change directions, heading south toward Samaria. As her eyes followed the pair, something beyond them caught her eye.

At first, it was just a wisp in the sky, trivial, like a dandelion puff. Then it billowed, and her mouth fell open, soundlessly at first, but then she shouted. "Smoke! Smoke over Samaria."

Gershon looked up from the vineyard and she gestured toward clouds that rose higher, smudging the sky over the mountains. He and Naboth stared as if paralyzed, then turned and ran across the rim of the hill to the city gate.

Once inside the city, Naboth helped the gatekeeper shut the gates while Gershon rushed up the steps to her side. "Get down from here," he ordered. "We don't know what has happened—or who is coming."

Frowning, she stormed down the steps. Who was he to order her about? Her family was in Samaria! "Do you see a runner?" She yelled to Gershon from the foot of the steps. "Do you see Arameans?"

She feared the Arameans had lost patience with the siege and finally put fire, catapult, and battering ram to use. Samaria had fallen to the enemy. What else could it mean? There would be no fire if a treaty had been struck. She twisted a fold of her tunic.

"I see no one." Gershon shouted down to her. He fingered the sling he'd untied from his waist, searched the valley between the mountains once more, and hurried down.

"Caleb will come as soon as he is able. Try not to worry."

Impossible, while the southern sky continued to darken with smoke.

Yaffa returned home, but Gershon went with Miriam to bring Jaedon from Samuel's house.

"Why do I have to come home early, Abba? I'm not afraid of the Arameans."

"Do as I say, son. We three men must protect the women—and our home."

It was nice not to deal with the boy's pouting alone.

That night, Gershon did not stay in his own house. Instead he lay down in front of the barred door beside Naboth, while Jaedon "guarded" Miriam and Yaffa in the room the grandparents usually shared. Sometime during the night, Miriam awakened to hear the men whispering in the front room, the earthy slide of wooden door scraping dirt, and footsteps outside climbing the stairs. She rose silently and crept after them.

Hoofbeats thundered on the road. It sounded like twenty riders or more coming from the direction of Samaria. Dust rising over the wall filled Miriam's nostrils. Heart pounding, she tip-toed up the steps.

Gershon and Naboth crouched behind the parapet, their heads barely above its rim as they scrutinized the landscape below. The hoofbeats diminished as the riders passed the city, not circling it, but fading into the distance.

Miriam tip-toed back down the steps, trailing her fingers along the side of the house for balance. At the bottom of the steps, Yaffa waited. She reached for Miriam's hand and silently pulled her into the house.

At daylight, Miriam and Yaffa prepared bread together.

Miriam leveled the coals and carefully positioned the grate. It had been all she could do this morning not to bang the grate against the rock wall so that Gershon would wake and she could ask what they saw and heard. He and her uncle had stayed atop the wall for hours after the last hoofbeat had faded away, and she finally fell asleep. The men's snores woke her sometime during the night. She had lain awake until dawn.

"How nice you ground the flour already," Yaffa murmured, when the dough was transformed to palm-sized rounds. She tilted her chin toward the threshold, where Naboth and Gershon still slept. "Gives us time to chat. Privately."

Did *Doda* Yaffa want to talk about the disturbance in the night? To caution Miriam against danger? Instruct her in a wife's duty of obedience?

"Yes, Doda?"

Yaffa whispered, glancing over at the men. "Sometimes—although it is always important to respect one's husband—we must speak to them of their shortcomings. Of course, it is a mother's duty to raise her son in the ways of the Lord, and I hope I have done so, but—"

"Aunt!" Miriam whispered hoarsely. "No one could accuse you of not—"

"Let me finish, child. It is only that each woman must school her husband, gently, of course, in the ways she wants to be treated. It is like teaching a bull that the ring in his nose can turn him."

Miriam chuckled. "I am not sure—"

"Perhaps a better example is ... I once knew a woman who kept a house dog."

"Truly!"

"It was a pretty creature, speckled and small, no bigger than a newborn child. She treated it thus. She actually taught the little thing to relieve itself only in the field. A husband is like that."

Miriam smiled, positioning a circle of dough on the grate. "Surely Gershon does not—"

"No, no, of course not. But he must be taught what you need. While I see your affection for Jaedon and believe you will come to care for my son, you are not a woman like Rasha, content to live a quiet life tending only to your house and children. I believe that each day you need to feel the earth beneath your feet and the sun on your head. Gershon has known one woman. You must introduce him to another. You must tell him who you are, Miriam. I am afraid he cannot see you for himself."

"I see you, Miriam," piped a small voice. Jaedon rubbed his eyes, shoved up from his mat, and looked around. "Since I am first awake, may I have the first loaf?"

Yaffa rolled her eyes. "Put away your mat, Jaedon."

Naboth made some indiscernible sound, then muttered hoarsely, "Is it daybreak?"

"Only just, husband," Yaffa said. "You had a hard night, I think." She brought a jar of water and a cloth. "Here. Wash, clear your mind, and then we will eat. Miriam has made bread."

Miriam slanted a gaze at her aunt. There was an orderliness to her speech. Kind understanding, offering time for reflection, promising food. Her own mother had often postponed important conversations until after *Abba* had eaten his meal. 'A full stomach helps a man make good decisions,' *Imma* had advised.

While the men stored their sleeping mats, Miriam wrapped the warm bread in a clean cloth, prepared olive oil with garlic for dipping, and poured cups of cool buttermilk.

Miriam cast veiled glances at Gershon as she worked. He folded back the shutters over the street-facing window, standing there a while, as if sorting the morning sounds for danger. She dropped her gaze. Why had she spoken sharply to him yesterday? He only meant to keep them safe.

"The meal is ready." Yaffa plumped the last cushion. "Come sit."

Naboth said the prayer of thanks for bread. While they ate, Jaedon chattered about a dream. Miriam paid little attention until he said, "And then a wild herd of horses raced by. Abba, I would love a horse of my own."

"I am afraid only kings own horses, my son," Gershon said. "Or very wealthy men. Your father is neither."

"A donkey, then? Of my very own?"

Gershon gaped at him, nonplussed. "Where do you get such ideas?" He glanced at Miriam and she threw up her hands in denial. Did he think every troublesome idea the child had must come from her? Jaedon had heard the horses in his sleep and his dream had woven its own story.

She drew a deep breath. "Owning an animal requires great responsibility, don't you agree Gershon?"

"Yesss." He drew out the word as if wary to let go of it.

"Perhaps Jaedon could practice on the family goat before we discuss owning other animals. He could feed the goat, keep it clean and safe, and milk it. I can teach him to make buttermilk for our meals, even cheese." Miriam had taken on care of the docile animal which was at this moment tethered in the shade of the courtyard. It was her favorite of the tasks she'd undertaken, but Jaedon would learn responsibility while caring for the goat.

"Truly?" asked Jaedon. "Then I could sell cheese in the marketplace and buy a donkey."

"Hmm," said Miriam. "Let us see how the feeding, caring, and cheese-making goes before further discussion. We will also need to make a trip to the vineyard, to gather large, pliable grape leaves in which to wrap the cheese."

"A very good plan," Yaffa said quickly. Gershon looked as if a camel herd had just rushed through the house. Naboth gazed at his wife and smiled.

"Husband," her aunt continued, "this talk of goats, donkeys, and horses has reminded me that I was awakened by hoofbeats in the night, sometime after the third watch, I should think. You and Gershon had left your mats, so I assumed you investigated the matter. What did you learn?"

Miriam stifled a smile. Yaffa had picked up on Miriam's intent to gain permission to visit the vineyard and then smoothly inserted the question to which they both wanted an answer.

Naboth stroked his beard. His gaze rested a moment on his grandson, and Miriam saw him take time to order his words.

"Nothing to be overly concerned over," Naboth said. "Twenty or thirty riders, heading north on the main road at a fast pace."

The main road north went to Aram. "Could you see who they were?" Miriam asked.

"It was hard to make out much in the dark," Naboth answered. "A few had long sleeves, and they were riding horses, so—as Gershon just explained—they may have been wealthy. Or the horses stolen. We did notice only a few rode saddled animals."

Wealthy riders, heading toward Aram—lacking saddles. A bubble of hope shoved words out of her mouth. "Fleeing Arameans? Could it mean an Israelite victory?"

"Maybe they are horse thieves," Jaedon said. "I would steal an Aramean horse if I got the chance."

This time, Miriam could not stifle her grin. "Now where did you get such an idea?" she asked, slanting a glance at her betrothed. "From your father?"

Chapter Six

How beautiful on the mountains are the
feet of those who bring good news, who
proclaim peace, who bring good tidings, who
proclaim salvation, who say to Zion,
"Your God reigns!"
~ Isaiah 52:7

The road to Jezreel
Dov

"WRAP YOUR HAND IN THE HORSE'S mane," Dov bellowed. Caleb was far ahead, way too far. "Hold the reins steady. Straighten up. No, you're sliding to the side. Slow down! Slow downnnn!"

Caleb's horse, a pleasant gray mare, seemed to be listening to Dov's desperate shouts. She slowed her ground-eating trot to a jog, but Caleb, the saddle, and the gifts he had tied behind inexorably slipped sideways. He landed on the road with a grunt and a puff of dust. Planting her hooves to avoid stepping on him, the mare turned her long neck to gaze at her former rider with curious brown eyes.

Dov stopped his bay beside the pair. "Are you hurt?"

Caleb stood, straightened the split tunic and loose trousers he had appropriated from the Aramean booty. He looked dubiously at the sagging saddle girth. "You think this strap is too loose?"

"Didn't I say so before? And it's called a girth. We'll make adjustments."

Caleb nodded.

After checking the pack tied behind his own saddle, Dov slid from his horse, looped the reins in his hand, and stepped next to Caleb. "Take hold and pull it snug. Make sure it is tight enough. Like this." Dov shoved three fingers under the girth. "You should be able to wiggle them."

Caleb complied and shot him a glance, seeking approval.

Dov grinned. "Good. One more thing." He took hold of

the girth strap, shoved his knee into the mare's belly, and yanked. The mare snorted and shifted her weight.

"Horses hold air when you tighten the strap and let it out when you are in the saddle."

"Wretched animals." Caleb rubbed his backside.

Dov gave a final yank. "Now the saddle should stay where it belongs."

Moving stiffly, Caleb led the mare beside a boulder, stepping on it to remount. Once settled, he gathered the reins in one hand, grasped the mane with the other, and nudged the gray with his heel.

Dov rode his horse alongside Caleb's. "Keep to a walk until you have the feel of the horse."

"At this rate, I think we'd be faster on foot."

"All in good time," Dov said. Did his friend's voice hold a note of unease? "Are you worried about your sister?"

Caleb shrugged. "She is the youngest. My aunt and uncle will keep her safe, but I am sure she misses home. My parents sent her to Jezreel to meet …"

Dov waited, but Caleb did not finish the thought. "I remember her. A sassy little thing—one hand on her hip, proud of her birds and the crates she made."

Caleb grinned. "That's Miriam. All but the little part."

"She would be fourteen now, fifteen?"

"Seventeen." Caleb slanted Dov a look he could not interpret.

Dov let out a long whistle. "Hard to fathom."

Caleb rolled his eyes. "You sound like our father. Although his greatest concern is that she hasn't, she won't—"

Dov studied Caleb. His lips were pressed tightly. Twice he'd started to say something and stopped. "What is Lemuel concerned about? Miriam won't what?"

Caleb shrugged. "Our cousin's wife was expecting a new baby. Miriam never attended a birth."

Lemuel sent his daughter as a midwife, though she had never attended a birth? Dov felt his face grow hot. Never mind, he didn't want to hear more. Childbirth was a topic best avoided. "Shall we try trotting again?"

Caleb groaned.

"Just keep it slow. Gather up the reins a bit."

Dov kept his bay at the mare's shoulder, both to steady her and to keep a close eye on Caleb. He seemed to have found his balance. After trotting a while, Dov encouraged his friend to try a slow canter.

Once he grew comfortable with the pace, Caleb risked talking again. "This is the road I sometimes take when carrying messages to Jezreel or farther north. There is a shorter route I've run, over and between some of the lower hills, but I wouldn't like to take the horses that way. I'm sure they could jump the fissures, but I am not ready for that lesson."

"Nor I." Dov shaded his eyes, peering farther down the road. "We searched here last night after the battle but turned back only a few miles further on. If you were the Arameans, where would you hide?"

"Depends how large their group. There are many places for one or two men on foot to hide, but fewer places to hide men and horses. Do you have an idea how many escaped?"

Dov shrugged. "Could be as few as twenty, could be several hundred, but they are all on horseback. I suppose foot soldiers could have escaped, but I doubt so." He relived the battle scene, the Israelites on horseback cutting down soldiers as they fled. So many dead. *But not Ben-Hadad.*

"Strange, wasn't it?" Caleb said. "They far outnumbered us. Were better equipped. Yet you just walked out to meet them—and killed your opponents." His voice jounced as they hit a rough patch in the road and the mare slowed again to a trot.

"Ben-Hadad's men assumed we'd come to surrender. Their swords hung in their scabbards, while I gripped a dagger behind my back. When the first man reached out as if to take hold of me, bind me perhaps, I plunged my weapon into him, then I killed two more soldiers before anyone realized I was not surrendering. My companions did likewise. It threw everyone into confusion." Dov studied his friend's face. "This was your first battle?"

"Yes."

"You learn to expect the unexpected. Close yourself to the horror. Remember what you are protecting. But this time, even I was unprepared."

Caleb eyed Dov. "Remember those chariots that had been racing around the city?"

"Yes, I saw," Dov said. "Two kings jumped in with a charioteer, threw him out, and picked up another king. Despite duplicity toward their own countrymen, they did not escape the justice our archers dispensed."

"Other kings escaped on horseback. Not many of their cavalry escaped, because they stayed to fight—at first. They should have beaten us." Caleb mused. "We were far outnumbered."

"When they realized their leaders had fled, the soldiers lost heart. The entire army turned, like wind driving a sandstorm." They both grew quiet.

"It is just. They should have stayed home," Dov finally continued. "Instead, they came to our hill, our home."

Caleb started to list sideways again.

Dov reined his horse in. A breeze cooled his face, carrying the scent of cedar from the surrounding hills. "Let's walk a while. The horses need to catch their breath."

"Do you realize"—Caleb adjusted himself in the saddle—"we could be on foot now, walking not just to Jezreel, but all the way to Aram, for a life of slave labor."

"Instead, we ride like kings."

"I wish all messages could be carried on horseback."

Dov thought about it. "We captured a lot of horses. The stable is crowded. I suppose some might be distributed as a share of the plunder."

"To you, maybe. A valued soldier. Not to someone like me."

Dov patted his horse's neck. He'd hesitated to saddle this particular horse after the hard use it had endured. Like him, the animal slept only a few hours. Yet it had whinnied a greeting when he entered the stable looking for mounts. He reasoned all the captured horses had been in yesterday's battle. This one he knew, and it knew him.

"An appealing thought. I like this fellow, but even if the king were to offer the horse, Maalik's house is small and has no courtyard."

"Well, Miriam will be excited. She loves animals—gives

them names. Might she ride one while we are there?"

"If there is a safe area."

"*Safe.*" Caleb scoffed. "If a walled city isn't safe, what is?"

"You ask a soldier this question? Your own father spoke of safety when he prayed, thanking Yahweh for our victory. Remember 'I will take refuge in the shadow of your wings until the disaster has passed.'"

Dov indicated the gentle hills flanking the road. "I can speak of disaster, duty, and name a hundred ways to die. Yet today we ride a smooth path, sun on our shoulders, bringing news of peace. It is a good day."

"Yes, we carry Samaria's celebration to Jezreel." Caleb grinned. "Speaking of which—the widow you danced with was very pretty. I learned she owns a vineyard in the valley."

"You learned that overnight?"

"You forget, there are three women in our household, even though Miriam is away. Women talk at the well, and not only about the water level. Imma, Savta, and my sister-in-law all know the widow. Do you want her name?"

"I do not." Dov chuckled. "She is a handsome woman, but a soldier has no need for a vineyard or a wife."

"If you're not interested, perhaps I should pursue *Tiran*," Caleb drawled out the woman's name and winked.

Dov shot him a look.

Caleb continued in an exaggeratedly innocent tone. "Even though our family owns a vineyard, I am the second son. Two vineyards would support a growing family clan so much better. My brother may have many children, and my sister, well ... my sister is unmarried."

With that, Caleb urged his horse into a canter, the wrapped bundle bumping his horse's rump.

Dov scratched his head, grinning. His mount tugged at the reins, jogging sideways until Dov allowed him to follow. Caleb was like all young men, constantly dwelling on women. He meant well, pairing Dov first with a widow near his age, next with a maiden—Caleb's own sister. The boy didn't realize how little Dov had to offer.

His life was uncertain. Each spring, he would be on the front lines of battle, from which he might not return. His pay was unpredictable, based on the treasury of a drought-ravaged, war-torn land.

His future in the army was undecided. King Ahab had made no promises, had given no promotions to the young officers who led in this battle.

He didn't own land, not even a home. Maalik owned the home in which they lived, and Dov could not imagine bringing a wife into Maalik's home, although he had assured Dov a daughter-in-law would be welcome.

But all these were pretexts, covering the wound in his soul. If there had been a time for a wife and family, it had passed for Dov. He had longed for a woman once. There would not be another.

Chapter Seven

It is good to wait quietly for the salvation of the LORD.
~ Lamentations 3:26

The vineyard at Jezreel
Miriam

THREE FAT GRAY PARTRIDGES HUDDLED IN the back of Miriam's snare. Their striped wings were so pretty, their eyes so black and round with fright, she yearned to set them free. *Almost.*

"Jaedon, come watch."

Slipping her arm deep into the snare, she grasped the birds one by one, their nervous chuck-chuckar rising to a piercing screech as she transferred them to the smaller crate she'd brought for this purpose. She glanced at Jaedon for his reaction, keeping her voice matter-of-fact. "We'll reset the traps and carry the birds to the house. If we leave them here making this ruckus, they'll scare off other birds and lure a fox." More important, Gershon might change his mind about allowing her outside the gates, and she hoped to snare two or three more birds.

"Do we have to kill them?"

Miriam thought on her answer. When she'd finished shifting the last bird, she stood, clapping the grit from her hands.

"One, at least, if we want roast partridge for supper. We can keep the others in a crate until we need them. You can feed them grain and all the cutter worms you can find."

Gershon pulled weeds only a few steps away. He turned toward her, taking in Jaedon's interest in her instruction. His lips worked, as if he would speak, but then he dropped his gaze, turning back to his task without remark. Several rows beyond, Naboth tied vines to a horizontal support between posts.

She set her hands on her hips. "I'm not ready to go back yet, though, are you? I hope to see the eagles." It would be good for him to see the wild creatures—he always brightened when they appeared.

"I don't want to go either." Jaedon shoved his hands onto his hips, his eyes as round as the partridges. He kept throwing uncertain glances their way.

"We will help your father while we watch. Waiting is the most important part of sighting the eagles. But let us shorten our wait by filling time with important work. Do you know why we pull the weeds from the vines?"

Jaedon shook his head.

"They steal water. They sip through their roots, leaving the grapes thirsty. That is why it's important to get the entire plant, not just the top."

"Abba showed me already." He closed his hand around the base of a weed and pulled. "But I don't like—"

She grinned and yanked three weeds in quick succession. "Since you are already an expert, let us see who is fastest. But any you pull without a root do not count."

Shadows moved overhead. Miriam touched his shoulder. "Look, Jaedon."

The eagles winged their way purposefully toward the mountain, feathers on their heads glinting gold like crowns. Some large prey hung from the talons of the larger eagle, the female.

Jaedon ran to his father and clutched his sleeve. "The eagles, Abba." Gershon stood, his hand atop the boy's head. "They have a nest nearby. Probably in the cliffs, Miriam says."

Gershon shaded his eyes, following the eagles' flight. "They carry food. We'll spot their young ones soon."

Miriam stood watching their backs, father and son. The tightness that sometimes clung to her like a wet tunic, eased somewhat. She exhaled. He was forgetting Rasha. No, not forgetting. But it would be all right.

The morning passed in a bright haze of hard work, sunshine, and giggles. When the dew burned away and the drying earth clung tight to weed roots, Miriam straightened, braced a hand against her back, and stretched. "I will take the birds back and help Yaffa with our meal."

"Jaedon, carry the cage for Miriam," Gershon said. "Saba and I won't be long."

Naboth stood at the far end of the vineyard, a length of loose vine in his hand. "Tell Yaffa I'd like some of her sweet bread, if she has dates."

With a wave, Miriam walked toward the vineyard gate. Jaedon came behind, carrying the crates and puffing self-importantly. Miriam swung back the little gate, leaving it open for Jaedon. The men would latch it when they came to eat.

The city gate arched ahead, a bit of a walk across the upper slope. Her gaze drifted to the road that hugged the foot of the hill. In the distance, she saw riders. Her throat tightened and she ordered, "Jaedon, go ahead very quickly into the gate." He started to question her, and she shoved him, hard. "Go!"

He stumbled, almost dropping the birds. Then, shooting her a glare, he stomped toward the gate, the heavy crate bumping against his knees.

"I said quickly!" She grabbed his hand, took hold of the crate, and shouted over her shoulder. "Gershon, Uncle— riders!" She heard the horses, coming fast now, hoofs pounding the hard dirt.

She shot another look at the road. They had gained ground, two riders on warhorses, one huge and dark colored and one gray, smaller but closing in on the city fast, ahead of the larger horse. Its rider brandished a sword over his head.

Miriam turned, leaping over stones, dropping the crate to the ground and hauling Jaedon after her. She looked back once more, and the foremost rider again brandished the sword and shouted.

"Miriam!"

She stopped, whirled, and sucked in air. Not a sword, an arm. *Her brother's arm.*

"Caleb!" She spun and shouted at Gershon, hearing the relief in her voice. "It is Caleb. My brother."

Dov reined in the bay, giving Caleb a chance to greet his sister and more importantly, allowing her to collect herself.

He stifled a grin as she embraced her brother. A moment ago, she had yanked him off his mare and shook him until he cried out, "Have mercy, Miriam. It is not my fault you didn't know me. I called your name."

"Not until you nearly trod on our heels." She pushed him away, holding him at arm's length. "You are wearing Aramean garments—riding a horse! Oh!" She threw her arms around him again.

Dov nudged his horse next to the gray, slid to the ground, and hung back.

"You remember Dov, don't you?" Caleb asked. His Aramean tunic had shifted askew from Miriam's exuberant greeting. In fact, he looked very agreeably rumpled. It must be a pleasant thing, to have a younger sister.

"Of course." In quick succession she glared at her brother and smiled at Dov.

He would never have recognized Miriam on his own, not this long-legged young woman leaping like a gazelle up the mountain, with the strength to drag a half-grown boy behind her. Only her smile, self-assured and merry, belonged to the girl he remembered. Now she stood a half-head taller than Caleb and leveled a brown-eyed gaze into his without lifting her chin.

"Shalom, Dov."

He twisted the reins. "Shalom, Miriam." He hoped she meant it, after the scare she'd received. Of course, Caleb's Aramean garments would be cause for alarm—why had they not considered that? They should have trotted on the approach to the city, never galloped. Dov shifted his attention to the men running from a nearby vineyard. He patted his horse's neck, purposefully moving his hand out of reach of his sword.

"My uncle and one of my cousins," Caleb said quietly, then raised his voice to address the younger, who arrived first. "I bring you good news, Gershon—and a guest."

"I am twice blessed." Gershon slowed and then bowed slightly, touching heart, mouth, and forehead when he straightened.

Dov bowed in return. This would be the cousin whose wife was expecting, who Miriam had come to help. He resembled his father about the eyes.

Naboth came close behind. "Dov, welcome. How much time has passed since we met in Samaria? And you are still a soldier?"

"May peace be on your house," Dov said. "Yes, though no longer a guard. I've joined the archers."

"Dov is too modest to say he leads Samaria's archers. And more—Uncle, we bring news of peace," Caleb said. "The Lord gave Israel a great victory over the Arameans, Hittites, and their allies."

Miriam breathed something between a gasp and a sigh.

Gershon clasped his hands. "Thanks be to Yahweh."

"Then the siege has ended?" Naboth asked. "Samaria has opened again? What of the spies? Have any returned? You know my youngest, Kadesh—"

"I'm sorry, Uncle, none of the spies have returned," Caleb answered. "We've heard nothing for months, but this is not surprising. No one could get through the blockade, not messengers, not spies. But Kadesh is resourceful. His Aramean is flawless."

Naboth nodded, appearing to shrink at the news. "Truly, he can pass among them like a fellow countryman. He has traded our wine to Damascene merchants for years. Without being taxed!"

"One day soon, he will walk through your door," Caleb said.

"May it be as you have said. But what of the battle? How many Arameans escaped your swords and arrows?" Gershon asked. "We heard riders in the night."

"King Ben-Hadad made off on horseback, with some of the ally kings," Dov said. "We lost their trail before Jezreel. Perhaps those were your riders."

"When was this?"

"Only last night. They must have gone to ground a while, then fled before dawn."

Gershon raised his eyebrows in surprise. "You were in pursuit last night, reported back to the king, and now you are here?"

Caleb laughed. "On horseback, as you see. King Ahab wanted the news to reach Jezreel immediately, but he took pity on his messenger—or maybe he feared my weariness would slow my delivery."

Dov laughed at his friend. "Arameans are still at large in the land. King Ahab asked me to accompany Caleb to ensure his safety and offered the use of horses taken in battle. Happily, my weapons were not needed."

Miriam's eyes lit on the sword, then the bow and quiver on his shoulder. She had grown quiet with the arrival of Naboth and Gershon. The boy, whose hand she still clutched, felt no such inhibition. "Will you show me how to shoot arrows, Dov? I want to fight the Arameans."

Dov bowed to the lad, mentally reviewing the contents of the saddle pack. Was there one small enough? "At my very first opportunity."

"Your son, Gershon?" Caleb asked. "I think he had seen only three years when I last set eyes on him."

"Yes, this is Jaedon." Gershon set a hand on the boy's shoulders. "Run up to the house, son, and tell your *savta* guests are coming." He gave him a gentle push, and the boy did as he was told.

"A fine boy," Caleb said. "And the new little one? Boy or girl?"

A shadow fell over Gershon's countenance, and Naboth's smile wavered. Miriam looked at them both with what seemed concern.

"A son," Gershon replied, his tone brusque. "He did not live."

"My cousin! I am truly sorry."

Gershon glanced at the ground, then at Miriam who had not left with the boy. Her face went pale. "A sad day for us all," he said. "Come, you both are thirsty and hungry. Let us see to the horses—then to you."

They walked through the city gate, leading the horses. Gershon introduced them to the watchman and gave him a brief account of the victory. Miriam stood beside Caleb's mare, running her fingers through its long mane and speaking soothingly, although the animal appeared untroubled.

Caleb turned to his cousin. "Where does the city manager stay?"

"His home is adjacent to the palace."

"In the king's absence, I must give the news to him first, then in some other public place."

"The manager and the stables are both near the palace," Gershon said. "There is a town square fronting the palace where you could speak to nearby residents and business owners. But the market here by the gate is where most public announcements are made." He gestured at the rows of houses and nearby merchant booths. "A large audience is guaranteed. And gatekeepers, of course, spread news far and wide."

Caleb nodded. "All right. After I speak to the city manager, I may as well make a public announcement at the town square. Then, I'll come back to the city gate. Can you give me directions?"

"Better than that, I will take you." Gershon turned to Miriam. "First, I will walk you home."

Dov glanced down the narrow alley bordering the wall. During their ride, Caleb had described where Miriam was staying during her visit. He'd mentioned his uncle's home was built against the wall, only four houses from the gate. Dov spotted an open door that might be the very house. The cousin certainly showed kind concern for Caleb's sister.

"No need. It's only a few steps." Miriam picked up the bird crate and hurried down the narrow street. Gershon stayed where he was but watched as she slowed her steps, then entered the door half-way down the row. Then he turned back to Caleb.

"Cousin, may I have a private word with you? Perhaps you and I could walk together—take the horses to the stable. Just the two of us."

Caleb looked surprised. He nodded slowly, glancing at Dov.

"Certainly," Dov said. "I saw where Miriam—your sister—"

"I will see to our guest, Gershon," Naboth said, his manner lighthearted. "Best not delay, or there may not be enough supper left to fill your bellies."

Gershon nodded. He and Caleb walked toward the inner city, leading the horses. The cousin seemed a little nervous leading the bay, who arched its neck and made a great show of keeping a distance away, almost as if to assure the man he would not be stepped upon.

"Beautiful animals," said Naboth. "Well, let us hurry home. Either Miriam or my own Yaffa will have something tasty waiting when we walk in the door. I assure you, two women cooking at one hearth makes for a very happy man." He patted his belly.

Dov smiled. "As a bachelor who lives with another, any day I enjoy a woman's cooking is a good day." He followed Naboth to the house, thinking on Gershon's words. *Just the two of us.* After Miriam left, Dov had thought all four men would walk together to the home of the city manager, and he reckoned Naboth thought likewise. Gershon's request had been unplanned. Of course it was. No one had known the war had ended and they were coming. It piqued Dov's curiosity.

Dov glanced over his shoulder. The gatekeeper was speaking to a guard. Both men looked his way with broad grins. Gershon had been right. The good news would spread quickly, even before it was formally declared.

Chapter Eight

When justice is done, it brings joy to
the righteous but terror to evildoers.
~ Proverbs 21:15

Jezreel
Miriam

MIRIAM WALKED SLOWLY THE LAST FEW steps to the house. The
bird crate was not heavy, but she wished a moment alone.
The battle news bubbled in her mind like porridge over hot
coals. Now that Israel had won the war, all would return to
normal. But no, it wouldn't, at least not for her. She would
marry soon, gaining a husband and a son. A son she had
already grown to love and a husband she hoped soon to
understand.

She walked into the tidy house, where she knew the
emmer was ground and the lentils soaking—the outcome of
her troubled spirit yesterday. Yaffa would be proud to provide
hospitality to the surprise arrivals, with her home in such
good order. Not that her aunt would feel flustered by a
surprise visit from Caleb, who had helped them harvest
several years, nor even Dov, who she had encountered once
before in Jezreel, after the contest on Mount Carmel.

Miriam set the crate of birds near the door and sighed.

Yaffa hurried over to inspect its occupants. "Oh, they
are fat and beautiful!" She clasped her hands together. "Shall
we have one in the stew?"

"Yes." Miriam cast a thoughtful glance at Jaedon.
Perhaps she should show him how to dress fowl, but she saw
he feigned deep interest in a parchment she'd used to teach
him to write his name. Pondering her own aversion to killing
anything, even their supper, she decided to leave that lesson
for another day. "I'll prepare it."

"Jaedon said Dov and Caleb are coming soon," Yaffa
said.

Miriam filled a large cooking pot with water. "Not quite
yet. Caleb needed to take the king's message to the city

manager. After that they needed to stable the horses." As she set the pot to boil, she pictured the beautiful animals, one red-gold like the sun, the other dappled like a rainy day.

Jaedon jumped up, starting for the door. "I want to go with them. Maybe they'll let me ride a horse."

Miriam grabbed his arm. "Not so fast. Your father sent you to help your grandmother."

"I did help. I arranged the cushions."

She looked at the unevenly placed cushions and nodded slowly. As a girl, she had always been in a hurry to finish the tasks her mother gave her so she could run outside with her brothers. "Very nice. If you are helpful the rest of the day, I will ask my brother to let you ride his horse tomorrow. Perhaps your friend Samuel can ride also, if you want to invite him."

Miriam lifted the crate, intending to move the birds to the courtyard. Across the room, Jaedon hugged his grandmother around the middle. "What else can I do for you, Savta?" Miriam hid a smile. The boy was good at manipulating circumstances to his own will, but Yaffa was no fool.

"Bring the foot basin, a pitcher of water, and a towel— you know how to set it up for guests who have traveled far." He ran off to comply, whistling loudly.

Quickly, Miriam carried the birds to the courtyard, selected a partridge, and killed it before Jaedon could return. When she heard familiar male voices outside, she covered it with a cloth and set it aside on a wooden plank.

"A guest, Yaffa!" Naboth called from the door. "I have brought Dov."

Dov stood beside her uncle, shouldering the large packs she'd seen strapped on the horses.

"Come in, come in. It is good to see you. Set those packs in the corner." Yaffa bustled about plumping cushions, settling Dov and Naboth near the window, and placing cups of watered wine in their hands. Scooting behind them, she peered out the window, searching up and down the street. "I thought you all went together."

"Caleb and Gershon can handle two well-mannered horses themselves." Naboth gestured for her to sit beside them. "Now, Dov, don't make Yaffa wait for the news. Tell her at least a little."

Miriam stood in the doorway, watching the activity in the front room but listening for sounds the others had arrived. Before she headed for the house, Gershon had indicated they all were going together. What had changed? It seemed strange. Wasn't Dov responsible for the horses? Yet here he was and Gershon—Gershon must have wanted to talk to Caleb alone, but what could he—*Of course.* Caleb was the only available member of her family. Gershon was going to ask her brother's permission for their betrothal. She felt a pinch of annoyance. Caleb was not her father and Miriam had already agreed to the betrothal. Gershon should have left it to her to tell her brother.

Hearing the burble of boiling water, she rushed to the hearth. Snatching up rags to protect her hands, she carried the pot to the courtyard, plunged the bird under the steaming water, and began plucking feathers.

"We do bring good news," Miriam heard through the open window, "and you will want to hear Caleb give the full account in the marketplace, but ..." Dov continued a recitation about Ben-Hadad's demands and Israel's surprising victory that seemed summarized, as if he had told the story many times and shortened it each telling.

After she finished cleaning the bird and carried it inside, he was still talking but in such broad terms she longed to press for details. Perhaps questions should wait until Gershon and Caleb returned so answers need be given only once. But when Dov mentioned the prophet, she looked up from cleaning the pot.

"A prophet? Was it Elijah?" Miriam had only seen him that one time on Mount Carmel, boldly shouting his prayer to the heavens. Then fire shot down from the sky, licked up the bullock and the soaking wood beneath, as if it were drenched in oil instead of water. Ever since, she had hoped to see the prophet again one day.

"He covered his face," Dov said. "Only his eyes showed. You can imagine how much talk this stirred up."

"The queen hates Elijah." Her aunt sniffed dismissively. "I suppose hiding his identity is understandable."

"True," Dov agreed. "Yet she has acted with restraint toward the Yahwist prophets since the end of the drought. After the contest between the Melqart priests and Elijah, the attitudes in Samaria changed. Enough people turned from Melqart to Yahweh that even the king began worshipping in the Yahweh temple, although he worships the Ba'als as well."

"Paying lip service," Naboth said.

Miriam shifted her gaze to observe Dov while she refilled and settled the pot among the coals. He avoided her eyes. Of course, a soldier in Ahab's army could not be openly critical of his king or the queen. Perhaps Naboth and Yaffa should be more circumspect around Dov, even though they had trusted him in the past. He was no longer a temple guard. He was a soldier, moving up in the army's ranks. How close might he be to King Ahab's inner circle? He had ridden to Jezreel on a horse taken as plunder, even borrowed one for Caleb.

Jaedon, who had perched on a cushion beside her, leaned forward and opened his mouth, ready to interject his own thoughts on the conversation. She laid a hand on his shoulder and squeezed gently. The boy needed to learn when to be silent among his elders.

"My aunt may have the right of it. The prophet may be prudent to remain unknown, at least for now," she offered. "Especially if he is Elijah."

"Actually, I don't think he was Elijah. I saw strands of black hair under his head covering," Dov said. "Although, I noticed his hair only the second time a prophet appeared. There *could* have been two different prophets. It is rumored many young men are being mentored by Elijah at secret locations in the desert. They call themselves *Sons of the Prophets*."

Naboth stroked his beard. "Hmm. Elisha, perhaps. He was anointed to be Elijah's successor."

"Could be, but I don't think so. I heard he was bald. We may never know. It could have been any of the followers— even an impostor. Wearing a disguise would have made more sense if we *lost* the battle. We know this was a true prophet because what he foretold came about exactly as he said."

Miriam leaned forward. "I take your meaning. If the

prophecy came from his own mind, he did well to hide his identity. False prophets could be stoned."

Dov nodded thoughtfully. "And true prophets persecuted. Fifty prophets sheltered in your own father's cave during Jezebel's hunts. Did you get to know them?"

"Not really, although I sometimes helped carry food and stayed to listen to stories. I remember Binyamin, Micaiah, and Javan." Abruptly Miriam stood and fetched a pitcher of water. She should not have volunteered names. Yet Dov's remark—*true prophets persecuted*—seemed to put him in the same camp as her.

"They mourned fellow prophets killed during the persecutions," she said more slowly. She refilled Dov's empty cup and almost poured water on her uncle's hand when he covered his. "I might recognize a few if I saw them, but years have passed," she said. "I don't remember their names and they will have changed."

Dov chuckled. "That is true. You were a little bit of a girl when I saw you last."

Miriam's smile felt tight. She remembered being impressed by the king's guard Dov had been at that time. So tall, brave, and handsome. A grown man, a little intimidating, perhaps, but then, she'd been *a little bit of a girl*. He meant she'd been a petite and pretty child. Now he thought her a giant. But what did this soldier's opinion matter to a betrothed woman?

"While the mysterious prophet is quite remarkable, I'm sure there is much more to hear," she said, striving for a courteous tone. "I long to know precisely how Yahweh gave Israel the battle."

"You will be interested to know your father and brothers fought." Catching sight of her expression, he quickly added, "They suffered no harm, Yahweh was good."

Then Dov shifted into story-telling mode—the Arameans getting drunk in their tents at midday, how Dov and his fellow provincial officers quickly overcame their captains, the surprising retreat by Ben-Hadad and the other enemy kings. She saw Yahweh's hand in the astonishing tale and, she had to admit, Dov had been an instrument of the Lord.

Jaedon fixed rapt attention on Dov's exciting tale.

Miriam slipped to the other side of the room.

Sometimes, describing galloping horses and racing chariots, his voice grew loud and his arms whipped about to demonstrate the action. Other times, as he described searching in the dark for hidden enemies, his voice grew sinister and his shoulders hunched toward his ears. Possibly for Jaedon's sake, perhaps also for her and Yaffa, he omitted mention of death or gore, but even so she felt gripped by terror. She chopped the fowl as she listened, dropping pieces into the simmering water. Her father and brothers had fought in this battle—they could have been killed. The whole city could have been overrun, her mother and grandmother slain—or worse.

From outside the door she heard Gershon's voice, then Caleb's. In short order, the two men stepped through the threshold.

"Caleb!" Yaffa ran to hug her nephew, who heartily kissed her on both cheeks.

"I gave the news to the city manager and spoke outside the palace," he said. "Now I must spread the news in the market square. Will you all come?"

"I will!" Jaedon scrambled to the door.

Naboth and Dov got to their feet. Caleb looked at Miriam expectantly.

She shook her head. "I've heard much from Dov and expect to hear more from you during supper, brother. I will see to the stew. Doda, go. I can manage."

"No, dear, I will help." Yaffa slipped her arm around Miriam. "The meal will be ready soon, Caleb. Don't be long-winded. Save some stories for us."

After the men left, Miriam added lentils to the simmering fowl and seasoned the stew with the last of their cumin and dried wild garlic. Now that the war was over, she could once again forage in the valley and replenish her garlic and herbs. She eyed the level of the stew. Would that be enough to feed two more hungry men? She measured out more lentils and added them to the pot.

Yaffa mixed dough for flatbread. Her eyes twinkled as she looked up from her kneading. "I think Gershon must have asked Caleb for permission to marry you. That's why he sent Naboth and Dov back to the house while they went together to see the city manager."

Miriam ducked her chin. "I had the same thought."

"We will see. If so, Gershon will announce it during supper."

"Do you really think so? When there is a battle to discuss? All those horses and chariots."

"Yes, daughter, I think your betrothal will take precedent." Yaffa smiled. Miriam felt her face warm. How did this woman so often soothe her tangled heart? She seemed to understand Miriam's thoughts. Averting her face, she sent up a prayer that Gershon might be equally understanding once they were wed.

And now that day might be sooner than she had thought. With the siege ended, and Arameans chased back to their homeland, trade would again flow freely between Jezreel and Samaria. The king and queen might resume their visits, at least during Jezreel's milder winter. Their presence would make Jezreel a safer place, with troops stationed throughout the city and security protocols to protect the royal family. Miriam slowly stirred the stew, trying to ignore the niggling worry that the king's troops had not stopped Samaria from being besieged for nearly half a year.

The savory aroma of partridge, garlic, and cumin must have lured the men home, because they returned sooner than Miriam expected. Yaffa started the meal by passing warm flatbread and herbed olive oil for dipping. Miriam served bowls of hearty stew from the bubbling pot on the hearth.

After Naboth prayed the blessings for bread and grains, Dov said, "Caleb, when you were speaking in the square, I was reminded of something you will not have heard. The king asked me to make this known so preparations can begin. He and Queen Jezebel will visit Jezreel later this summer, rather than wait for winter. Reconstruction is needed in the capital, and they want to avoid the disorder. They reason Jezreel did not suffer war damage, so their stay will be peaceful while Samaria is put to rights."

"That is so," said Naboth. "We were never under siege. When the Arameans rode through on their way to Samaria, they were too early for our crops. Thankfully, they didn't destroy our unripe grain."

"They probably expected to eat our harvest on their triumphal march home," Gershon said. "Now we expect a rich yield. Although we kept our women and children inside the city walls, the men worked all the local vineyards and farms, banding together in groups and rotating among them. With careful management, our crops will sustain both Jezreel and Samaria through the winter."

Dov said, "The king will be glad to hear that. Not only did the Arameans devour Samaria's harvest like a swarm of locusts, they cleared the countryside of game. He looks forward to hunting while he visits Jezreel."

Caleb smiled. "He probably is anxious to try his fine new horses. The king and queen should have a pleasant stay." Her brother paused, glancing pointedly at Gershon, as if offering him an opportunity to speak. Miriam's heart seized. *Was this the moment?*

Gershon stood, cleared his throat, and tugged at the neck of his tunic. When he looked at Miriam, she held his gaze, transfixed by the intensity she saw there.

"This has been a difficult time for us," he said quietly, as if he spoke only to her. "We were isolated. Although only a day's journey to Samaria, we couldn't travel or send messages because of the siege. Even though Jezreel wasn't surrounded by armies, we faced threat from enemy spies and Aramean reinforcements making for Samaria."

Miriam gripped the folds of cloth over her knees. Her eyes stung with surprising empathy for the decisions he had made—all to keep them safe.

Caleb offered a grunt of agreement. The sound seemed to capture Gershon's attention, for he turned around to face her brother.

"I told you about my loss—the death of my wife, Rasha, and the babe. I feared—at any moment—I would be called to serve—to leave my son without protection."

A slight movement drew Miriam's gaze to Dov, who had sat silent and unmoving beside Caleb until this moment. At the mention of Rasha's death, his brows furrowed in what looked like confusion. Miriam sought the moment Caleb asked Gershon about the baby, and Gershon said ... my son did not live. He did not mention his wife's death.

"I'm a farmer and have never fought in a war. My father is old—"

Naboth made a grunt of protest.

Gershon paused a moment and Miriam almost sighed with relief. But in the next instant, she knew he would continue and suddenly she was desperate with the desire to silence him. He was going to talk of their betrothal and pour out her personal life in the presence of a near stranger. She pushed aside her untouched stew.

"Father, you are a staunch man. But you know my son needed a parent in my absence, a strong woman to guide and protect him should the worst happen, and here was my cousin, an admirable woman and I ..."

Why had he not waited, sent Dov with the horses and discussed this with her alone? Must she be humiliated? *Please, please, do not let him imply my parents sent me to Jezreel hoping a new pool of prospective husbands would present at least one man who would have me.*

"I offered Miriam all that I have, which is insignificant indeed. But she has agreed, and so I have asked her brother for his permission and blessing."

Caleb got to his feet, giving his response a measure of formality. "Cousin, as we discussed, I have known and worked beside you for many years. With all my heart you have my blessing. But I am not Miriam's father. If Samaria were still under siege, if I had secretly stolen through enemy lines, my father would approve of my speaking for him. But now we have peace, and he must be the one who gives permission. You understand this."

Miriam's eyes flicked between them. Gershon gave Caleb a puzzled look. Hadn't Caleb made his position clear when they talked privately? He spoke slowly. "Then I will go to Samaria and speak to him."

Naboth nodded in assent.

It was over. Miriam took a deep breath. Despite Gershon's apparent unease, her father's agreement was a formality. She thought he would agree to any Yahweh-worshipping Hebrew in Jezreel. That was why they had sent her, after all.

Jaedon plopped down beside her, nearly upsetting her abandoned bowl. "You are going to be my mother," he stated, grinning. "It's not a secret now." Then, looking down, "Are you going to eat that?"

Pressing her lips into what she hoped was a smile, she nudged her bowl toward him, letting her gaze drift. Naboth and Yaffa seemed pleased with Caleb's remarks, also confident that her father would agree to the match. She caught Dov staring at her with a strange expression.

She held the soldier's eyes for a moment trying to interpret his thoughts, then slid her attention to her brother, who tilted his head and gave her a bemused smile. Her betrothal surprised him and Dov, nothing more than that. Neither could have guessed what had transpired between the cousins while the country was embroiled in war. Her brother had been told privately and had time to take it in, but Dov's first indication was Gershon's speech in this room.

Yaffa stood and began gathering the bowls. "We must celebrate. Husband, bring a skin from your special vintage."

"I have saved one for just such an occasion!" Dod Naboth shoved to his feet.

Miriam felt the throb of an incipient headache. She stood to clear away the remains. When she reached for Dov's bowl, he murmured, "My congratulations."

She nodded. "I thank you." She carried the bowl to the wash pan. He seemed uncomfortable—was it being forced to listen to the betrothal negotiations, discussions usually private between father and suitor? Or was he simply uncomfortable with her? It occurred to her it might not be only with her, but women in general.

But how could that be? He could feel no discomfort with her, who he remembered as the child she'd been. And it was absurd to imagine that this strong, handsome soldier would not be admired by most women.

"Soon we'll have date bread," Yaffa said, her voice a trill of pride. "I hid dried dates where no one would find them."

"Where was that, aunt?" Miriam thought she knew. She had spotted a bulky parcel behind rags Yaffa used for cleaning and said nothing of it.

"I am not telling. I may need such a hiding place again."

Straightaway, Jaedon leaped to his grandmother's side and began to pester her for the secret. Adroitly, Yaffa assigned him a task. After trudging outside to sweep the street in front of their door, Jaedon could be heard muttering, *Another time, let her keep her hiding place.*

Miriam grinned. He was learning.

Yaffa patted out small round cakes studded with dates, cheerfully humming one of the tunes of ascension. Soon the men joined in singing the words.

When Jaedon finished his sweeping, he came to sit quietly beside his grandfather. Naboth gave him a shoulder nudge, handed him some honeyed water, and whispered something in his ear. The boy broke into a rueful smile.

Miriam felt her own smile take shape. Jaedon would test her resolve and humor until he reached manhood—and possibly beyond. But oh, how her father would welcome the boy into his family, relish sharing a grandchild with his only living brother. And someday, she mused, she and Gershon might have a child of their own.

Yaffa wandered over to the hearth. Before long, the scent of dates and almonds filled the room. "I have this in hand, daughter. Go visit with your brother."

"I have more happy news," Caleb said, when she sat beside him.

"Oh yes?"

"Seth and Avigail expect a child this winter."

Miriam felt her eyebrows pinch together. "And you only tell me this now? Not when you first saw me at the vineyard? Or as we walked to the gate? Or even when you—"

"Miriam, please! It is hard for a man to speak of these things."

Dov laughed first, then Naboth, then the whole room joined in.

"Is there anything else, Caleb? How is Savta?"

"She is well, bossy still, and states unequivocally, Avigail's child is a boy. I will tell her of your betrothal immediately upon returning, upon pain of death. You can rest assured there is nothing else of any import, my sister."

A nephew this winter. Her first nephew. What if ... now

the land was at peace, she and Gershon chose a date for the wedding? There was nothing to stop them, nothing more than her own reticence. But now, Seth's news. If Miriam were to get pregnant soon, the two cousins would grow up friends, seeing each other on festivals and holidays. Yes. Why not set a date? A time when her whole family could attend. After harvest. Perhaps as early as late summer? No, no, that was too soon ... wasn't it? Miriam hugged herself, as if to hold the sudden burst of giddiness inside.

"The bread is ready. If I must say, it smells better than any I have made in the past." Yaffa popped a small cake into Naboth's open mouth.

"Oh! Hot." He chewed judiciously. "But delicious."

Miriam filled a tray and served bread to everyone. When she bit into her own cake, dates and almonds filled her senses with sweet, crunchy pleasure. She leaned back on her cushion with a sigh.

Gershon cleared his throat. "In the marketplace, Caleb spoke of the prophet's warning. The Arameans will attack again next spring. Israel must begin preparations now. This means building an army."

Yaffa's hand stole to her mouth.

"Caleb?" Miriam asked.

"That's right," her brother said. "Dov must recruit soldiers, starting here in Jezreel. He and other officers will seek volunteers throughout all Israel."

Dov spoke in a quiet voice. "The civilians in Samaria fought bravely and well, but they were inexperienced, and we were greatly outnumbered. Yahweh protected us, but we need to be obedient and build the army as He said. We need recruits from every city in Israel. Then we will train them to drive chariots, ride horses, and become proficient in the use of all weapons."

Gershon took a deep breath, and Miriam held hers, as though she stood in an empty riverbed while the pebbles under her feet shook with coming floodwaters.

"I will join."

"But—you can't," Miriam said. "The marriage year."

Yaffa folded her hands. "That's right, son. The law says a newly married man must not be drafted into the army. He must be free to spend one year at home, bringing happiness to the wife he has married."

Naboth spoke slowly. "Normally, that is true. But the law may not apply in this case. Their betrothal agreement was made in a time of war, when permission could not be granted. But now there is peace, and Caleb did not give his permission—"

"Hold a moment. It is not that I—"

"I understand your reasons," Gershon said, "but Abba is right. You told us, quite properly, that you could not give permission, that as her father, Lemuel must be the one. He has not yet given his permission."

Miriam felt the room tilt. What was he saying? That they were not betrothed? Gershon had made her an offer, given her a *ketubah*. She had agreed. Hadn't he told her he wanted to know Jaedon would be taken care of, in case something happened to him, in case he were conscripted? Before supper he told how as a farmer he'd never fought, his concern for his only son should he be conscripted. And now he argued to join the army, when he should thank the Lord for sparing him that duty.

A cool wind blustered through the open window. Miriam rubbed her hands up and down her arms.

He wanted to go. It was only a marriage of convenience he wanted. A mother for his son. She thought of Rasha, the wife of his youth, the beloved one. If war had broken out their marriage year, he would have stayed. Miriam, he would leave. Her breaths beat quick, sharp, stabbing her heart. She would never be enough for any man.

Dov had gotten up and walked away from the discussion. Miriam felt her face warm, the worst of her fears having come true as an outsider witnessed this personal, devastating moment. The soldier walked to the corner where he'd dropped the packs, knelt to untie the largest, and stood holding aloft two unstrung bows. Caleb leapt to his feet and hurried over to help untie the second pack.

Dov handed Jaedon the smaller bow. While the boy crooned over his new possession, the soldier crossed the room to put the larger one in her hand. The polished wood felt smooth to her hand and there seemed to be some design painted on its surface. She moved closer to the hearth. Firelight danced over a simple and meaningful etching. "Birds in flight!" Her breathing slowed.

Dov smiled in obvious pleasure. "I thought it would suit you. The arrows for that bow are fletched with eagle feathers, I think. More weapons are coming by cart tomorrow, but Caleb and I picked the choicest bows and arrows for your family."

"This is yours, cousin." Caleb extended a darkly stained bow to Gershon. "And you, uncle."

Naboth reached for a bow longer than Miriam's, shorter than his son's. "I'll need a lesson—haven't owned a bow since I outgrew the one I owned as a boy. Thank you, Dov."

Caleb huffed. "Ho, uncle—I earned a share in the spoils!"

"Indeed, he did. And you shall all have lessons—that is, all who want one—when we meet with recruits in the valley. Soldiers are coming to guard the weapons shipment, and they have agreed to stay and help with training."

Miriam gripped her bow. She would practice until she became an expert with this weapon. It seemed she would need to.

Chapter Nine

Meanwhile, the officials of the king of Aram advised him,
"Their gods are gods of the hills. That is why they were too
strong for us. But if we fight them on the plains, surely we
will be stronger than they."
~1 Kings 20:23 NIV

Jezreel
Miriam

THE NEXT MORNING, CALEB OFFERED TO accompany Miriam to
the city well and carry her water jug.

"Perhaps we should each carry one." She chuckled.
"Then when you drop yours, we will still have water."

Caleb slumped his shoulders in mock dejection, put the
jar on his head, then staggered so that it teetered
precariously, and she gasped.

"Two! What are you thinking?" he asked. "Imma taught
me the proper way to carry a jug before you were born. Trust
me, sister." He demonstrated, chin up, swishing his hands
at his sides, with a ridiculous sway to his walk that somehow
did not send the pot sliding to the ground.

Miriam heard a giggle behind them. She turned to see a
maiden emerge from a side path, her hand hiding her mouth.
"Chloe! Shalom. How is your mother?"

Removing her hand, Chloe smiled prettily. "Imma had a
bout with fever, which quite frightened us. But she has
improved and can take broth now."

"I'm glad to hear it. This is my brother, Caleb. He often
carries messages from Samaria."

"Oh, a runner?"

"Usually, but this time I rode horseback."

"Ah, with the soldier? I heard he came with another. My
father works in the stables."

The three chatted a while, leaning against the rim of the
well. They discussed the rout of the Arameans as well as local
gossip, while Caleb gallantly filled both vessels.

A sudden shower brought quick, close drops. Chloe and Miriam laughed and huddled under their head coverings against intermittent gusts, then the storm ended as quickly as it began. A rain-washed breeze caressed them with the clean scent of grass.

"I must get back to Imma," Chloe peeked at Caleb through lowered lashes. "Come visit when you can, Miriam."

They said their goodbyes where the path branched to Chloe's house.

Miriam took Caleb's arm, eyeing the jar on his head. "It's a shame she had to leave so quickly, brother. Chloe is a worthy young woman. I believe she sent tender glances your way."

"Truly?" He looked after her as she disappeared around a corner, then turned back, clearing his throat. "But you are the woman I need to speak with, sister."

Miriam thought she knew what was coming. It was if he donned his cloak of *elder brother*.

"When Father sent you to Jezreel, I believe he expected you would have opportunities to meet hard-working young men of sense. To find a man you could respect and ... and love. But Gershon! He is our cousin, and a good man, but I fear he is far too staid for you. I know you are not a silly woman, but you have so much heart and he is so ... practical. And his talk of joining the army—it seems thoughtless of him. Do you truly want this betrothal?"

"Much of what you have said is true, my brother. Gershon is practical—and yes, even staid. But as you said, Father hoped I would meet a hard-working young man of sense. I respect Gershon. He is a good man and will treat me well." Her hands needing employment, she twisted a fold of her tunic. "And if I do not love him—yet—I do love his son, with all my heart. I have no desire to live an aging spinster, a burden on our family, shunted from one home to another when one of your wives is in a family way." She chuckled quietly. "Because I am no midwife."

"Oh! Did you—were you—?" Caleb's jaw dropped, a horrified expression on his face. He made a grab for his teetering jar, sloshed its contents, and hugged it to his sopping wet chest.

"What? Oh, no! I was not there at all. Caring for Jaedon filled my days."

They both stared at his half-empty jug and turned again to the well.

A long, yearning *scree* sounded overhead. One of the eagles circled, magnificent brown wings spread wide to drift on the wind. When it tipped lazily to glide north, it displayed its crown of iridescent gold. Her brother snaked an arm around her shoulders, and she interlaced her fingers with his. Despite her up-in-the-air betrothal, Miriam felt her life unfurling like a leaf, this rain-washed morning.

The eagle soared high above the trees of the northern forest seeking sustenance for her ravenous chicks. Increasingly, her two white nestlings fought savagely over strips of marmot or dove until she interfered, lest one heave the other from the nest. The eagle must find bigger game.

She ranged north and west, far from the city and its busy throughway leading like a river from north to south. Three times her hunt had been disrupted by bands of horsemen thundering past, raising dust, sending game into hiding for days.

As the eagle flew, hills and trees gave way to open plain, large spreads of gold, green, and red, flecked with ptarmigan feeding among the foliage. The eagle ignored the birds, for they had already spotted her shadow and planned their escape routes, but more than that, she sought a larger kill for her hungry youngsters. A young sheep or goat.

The cultivated plain merged into grassy meadow bounded by distant hills. She dipped low over a small flock of black goats grazing the side of a mountain, but no sooner had she honed in on a fat kid who had wandered from its mother, she heard a shout and a stone whizzed like an angry bee and clipped the tip of her wing. With a furious *scree* she veered from the man's flock and changed her course toward the more rugged terrain of the distant cliffs.

She listened for the voice of the Creator who fed her, His whisper always on the wind when she sought direction. Following His leading, her wings beat a path toward the mountains. Rocks and hills passed beneath her, the warm sunshine a balm to the insult of the stone. Suddenly, there it was on the side of a cliff, as if waiting for her, another black kid, the white streak on its back a target. The eagle folded her wings and dived. The goat gave a frightened bleat when her talons raked its back, finding purchase.

The eagle struggled under the weight as her wings pulled her upwards, soaring higher, higher, until bones and tendons cried, *no more,* and she let go of her prey, watching it fall, its legs stiff as if seeking to halt its fast, airborne slide. Then it hit the sharp rocks and tumbled down the mountain.

The goat's fall ended on a cliff outcropping. The eagle perched on a nearby ledge, tilting her head to take measure of the carcass while she rested from her exertion. As she fluffed her feathers and panted through her open beak, she heard a voice. It was not the Creator, but another. She hopped sideways, spreading her wings, preparing for flight if she must again dodge a stone. But the voice came from a distance away, seemingly from within the mountain.

Her eyes swiveled to take in the cliff landscape. Not far from her perch was another outcropping. A trail led up from the foothills to a cave slightly below where she sat, an abandoned lion's lair from the rank, dusty scent. The voices came from within that cave.

"The Israelite's gods are gods of the hills. That is why they were too strong for us. But if we fight them on the plains, surely we will be stronger than they.

We must do this—remove all the kings from their commands and replace them with military officers. We need generals not politicians. You must also raise an army like the one you lost—horse for horse and chariot for chariot—so we can fight Israel on the plains. Then surely we will be stronger than they."

The eagle could not fathom their odd language, the clipped barks almost doglike, the angry huffs like an ox in heat. Even among their own kind, it seemed much was spoken but little understood. But she did comprehend they spoke of the Creator and ascribed to Him a boundary beyond which He could not pass. The Creator, of course, heard this as well, and His laughter floated all around her.

Bathed in that healing laughter the eagle grasped her kill, flapped her wings with renewed strength, and flew home to her nest and her chicks.

Ben-Hadad strolled from the cave. Strong wind hit him full in the face. Turning away from its force, he spotted a huge bird rising in the sky. What an odd sight! He shouted for his men.

"Look, a golden eagle carries a goat. It is an omen, is it not? Aram will triumph over Israel." The king jammed his fist into the air. "We will prevail."

The Arameans watched the eagle slowly flap its long wings, carrying the half-grown kid, as if borne aloft by the breeze.

When they could no longer make it out, they cast their gaze down over the landscape where the eagle had disappeared. "That is the city of Aphek," said Ben-Hadad. "Look at the size of the surrounding plain. We can stage at least a hundred chariots there."

Chapter Ten

Praise be to the Lord my Rock,
who trains my hands for war, my fingers for battle.
~ Psalm 144:1

Jezreel, A day later
Miriam

The day dawned bright with promise, and sedge warblers chittered merrily along the path. Miriam carried one empty water jug on her head and a second in her arms. She would willingly have made an extra trip to the well to draw enough water for the guests. Anything to ease Yaffa's load.

But Yaffa had said, "It is not seemly for a maiden to go unaccompanied." So her mother-in-law walked alongside, the smallest vessel on her head. Miriam insisted on that.

Did Yaffa appear paler than usual? Were the shadows darker under her eyes? Entertaining guests brought additional work, though Miriam tried to take on the heaviest tasks. Noting the beads of sweat on the older woman's upper lip, Miriam slowed her steps. "I'm glad the men allowed Jaedon to go with them to the valley."

Yaffa chuckled softly. "If they had not, my grandson would have pestered us to death, seeking to escape such mundane work as this."

When the weapons cart had arrived earlier than expected, Gershon, Naboth, and Caleb eagerly went with Dov to prepare an area in the valley for distribution and training. Miriam bit her lip. "He carried his bow. He expects to train with the men."

Yaffa replied slowly. "He is so young."

Miriam shifted the pot in her arms. "But he has seen seven years, and it is good for him to be with his father, learn the ways of men. Gershon will make sure he is careful. Your son is a good man."

Yaffa dipped her head in agreement, immediately reaching to steady her jug. "Of my two boys, he has always been the most thoughtful, wanting to do the right thing. Kadesh, on the other hand, is quick to act. A bit like Jaedon."

Miriam wondered about the absent brother, the impulsive son, the spy. Yaffa and Naboth fretted, his name often on their tongues. Why had he not returned by now? How deeply was he entrenched with the Arameans, who valued him as a supplier of fine wine? Now that they had been defeated, would distrust arise with this supposed ally? Miriam glanced again at Yaffa, whose mouth compressed into a thin line. Was she thinking of her missing son? *Yahweh, protect this man who is part of my family. If he lives, bring him home to his mother.*

As they rounded a turn in the path, Miriam heard a woman speaking excitedly, followed by a burst of high-pitched laughter.

"Most of the men of Jezreel and several soldiers from Samaria will be there."

Miriam did not recognize the young woman who spoke, her hand resting on one hip. A tall, slender woman, though not as tall as Miriam, she wore a striped head covering, its tails tossed jauntily behind her shoulders.

"That is Davita, the baker's unmarried daughter," whispered Yaffa. "Can you believe she approached Naboth in the marketplace *herself?* Not her father, mind you, and only one day after our poor Rasha died in childbirth." Yaffa huffed a throaty rumble, like a disgruntled hen.

Miriam studied the baker's daughter, whose flashing gaze fixed on hers. A girl who knew what she wanted and went after it. That she had wanted Gershon, troubled Miriam not at all—he was a man worth having.

She didn't see anyone she knew in the group. A woman, who bent over the rim of the well, straightened and waved. "Oh, there is Chloe. We've spoken several times at the well."

"A sweet child. I've known her mother since childhood."

When they reached the well, Yaffa introduced Miriam to several of her friends and, with an almost undetectable quirk of eyebrow, to Davita. Davita introduced a woman wearing a dark tunic and heavy veil, her widowed aunt, Puah.

Davita's comment about the men of the city made more sense when one of Yaffa's friends remarked, "That big soldier told Aaron, the gatekeeper, to send men to help with the training session. My husband went in hopes of getting an iron-tipped spear. Not that he knows how to wield one."

"Why would he?" Yaffa responded. "Most of our men are farmers, merchants, or shepherds. Few are men of war."

"Spears, bows, and swords have always been scarce," said another matron. "In our town, even those who have seen battle, carried only slings or clubs. Still, the trained warriors were glad of their support."

"Scarcity will no longer be a problem. Did you see that cart, stacked high with Aramean weapons? Aaron said any man who asks, will receive a weapon and be trained to use it. Our men will be well able to protect us," Yaffa said.

"Not only the men," Miriam said. "I own a bow. I will go to the valley and be taught."

Davita looked at her with interest.

"But you are a woman," said the girl's aunt with a sniff. "That is not fitting."

Miriam regarded the older woman. What a dour expression. Was she the baker's sister? Had Davita's father brought her to Jezreel for feminine influence? Striving to keep a respectful tone, she answered, "Perhaps you are right, Puah. But sometimes women must protect themselves, especially when men go to war. Remember our history. Jael killed the wicked commander of the Canaanite army with a tent peg and saved Israel."

"Well! She used a household tool she had at hand," said the aunt. "And she only did what she had to do."

Miriam chose not to argue. If she explained that a bow was a tool of the trade for many fowlers, though one she'd never before had the means to own, would that convince the woman? No, the aunt would probably chide the heroic Jael herself for unwomanly actions. Davita's aunt could keep her opinions, but she could say nothing that would keep Miriam from attending the training.

"Do you think I could learn?" Chloe asked softly.

"I do. After we take the water home, we will go there together," Miriam said. She tossed Davita a look. "And anyone else who wants to come."

"Caleb! Come help me with this." Dov motioned for Caleb to take the other side of an immense fallen tree. They struggled to drag it near the pile of bows and arrow-filled quivers. Dov stood back and measured its thick trunk with his eyes. It would do nicely.

"Bring those sheaves over here," he shouted to the valley farmers who helped set up their fallow fields. Dov would train archers on this end. Leaving sufficient space for safety, a soldier would teach spear throwing beside Dov, and another would demonstrate the basics of sword fighting and hand-to-hand combat in the farthest field.

"What about shields?" Caleb pointed at the haphazard bronze stack still in the cart. "Do we unload these?"

"Not today. We will teach the offensive skills first and send weapons home with those who show promise." He glanced toward the city. A group of men were tramping down the hill, Naboth, Gershon, and the lad among them. Perhaps fifty. Was that all? He'd hoped for more. He could issue an order in the name of the king, but he wanted only motivated recruits.

"Will you look at that!" Caleb jutted his chin toward the gate.

Dov saw her first. *Miriam.* Striding down the hill, her headscarf rippling back from her face, she wore the determined expression he'd seen often since he arrived. He smiled. A crowd of women followed, nearly as many as the men—Yaffa among them! He laughed aloud.

"Don't let Miriam catch you laughing at her." Caleb said.

"Oh no, my friend. It is your aunt who surprised me."

Caleb turned. "My aunt—and look there—that soft-spoken young woman Miriam introduced at the well. She isn't"—he turned back to Dov. "You realize they are not just coming to watch us spar? Miriam will have convinced them they can fight as well as men."

"And they can, but—"

"I tell you, their fathers would not want them put in harm's way. Nor would I." Caleb crossed his arms over his chest and scowled. Belatedly he added, "Gershon won't stand for it, either."

Dov extended his hands palm up. "I agree, Caleb. But we need not inflame the women. I may not have a wife—nor a mother for that matter—but I think I understand that a home can become uncomfortable if a woman is discounted. Here is what I propose." He quickly explained and sent Caleb to invite Miriam and her followers to approach.

He beckoned to the soldiers who agreed to teach and the new recruits they would train. "Welcome, men," he called. "You are embarking on a noble purpose to protect your country. The Arameans have besieged Samaria and stalked your roads and fields. But Yahweh has spoken through His prophet. If we obey the Lord, He will fight for us, as He has already done."

"What do you mean? What did the prophet say?" shouted someone in the back of the group of men, which had steadily grown while Dov, Caleb, and other soldiers were arranging the training area.

"He gave us this word from the Lord. 'Prepare, strengthen your army, because the king of Aram will attack again next spring.' That is why we are here. To build your skills and enlarge our fighting force. But there is something even more important. Something you may think is unrelated."

The women had reached the valley floor but hung back behind the circle of men. Dov raised his voice and spoke directly to them. "This concerns you women as well. Can you hear?"

A few raised a hand or shouted high-pitched affirmations. Men in the crowd swiveled their heads toward the women, frowns on some faces when they turned back.

Dov spotted Gershon among them and saw the moment he spotted Miriam at the front of the women. But Dov could not read his expression. Deep murmurs began winding through the crowd until Dov motioned for silence.

"On the last day of the siege, Yahweh spoke through his prophet with these words, 'Do you see all these enemy forces? Today I will hand them over to you. Then you will know that I am the Lord.'

"I tell you, His last sentence is of vital importance. We

have not acted as if we *know* Yahweh is the Lord, the One. Our nation has worshipped the Ba'als, yet no Canaanite god came to our aid when an enemy overtook us. We were helpless under the siege, with no option but surrender, until the Lord gave us the battle. He is the true God. We must honor Him. We cannot go back to our old ways."

"But we *are* worshipping at the Yahweh temple," someone called from the crowd.

"*And* also worshipping the Ba'als in the high places," another accused.

Heads studied the ground, sandals scuffed uneasily.

Dov raised a fisted hand. "We must do right. Worship only the Lord. Follow His laws. Treat one other with kindness. Help your neighbor, protect orphans and widows—"

"Does that include forcing those widows to fight like men?" The man pointed an accusing finger at Miriam and her followers. "Why are these women here?"

Dov began, "The women should—"

Three or four women began to shout arguments at the same time. When they realized they were talking over each other, they stopped, confused about who should go first. Miriam had not spoken, but her face was set in those familiar indomitable lines.

"Listen to me. If any disagree, we can speak later, but make no mistake. In a fighting force, obedience is imperative." Dov's gaze traveled across both groups of volunteers, purposefully making eye contact with those he deemed leaders and not moving on until he sensed compliance.

"Who among you would wish your wife, daughter, or mother to be without defense when you are away at war?"

At first there were no answers, then one young man called out, "If my wife were fighting beside me, I would be so concerned for her safety, I would be useless in the battle." The man stared hard at the group of women. There were a few shouts of agreement. One of the women gave another a playful shove—the wife of the young speaker? Her face blushed like an autumn pomegranate.

"But what if your women were safe behind the city

walls? Or on the roofs of your own homes? I propose we teach these women to use bows. There are many ways to use the weapon. You have seen archers standing, on horseback, or riding in chariots with bows in vertical position. But there are other ways."

Dov paused, glancing toward Miriam. Would she be upset if he asked for her help? He studied her face. Wary. *Uncertain.*

"Miriam. Will you assist me ... and bring two or three others?" Without waiting to see whether she complied or who she picked, he walked to the pile of bows and selected four small weapons.

Miriam strode forward, carrying the bow he gave her last night. Dov smiled at seeing Yaffa among the four women. No wonder Gershon's expression appeared neutral—his own mother supported Miriam. He handed Yaffa the smallest bow.

Miriam quickly introduced Chloe and Davita. Chloe was young, doe-eyed. This was the girl whose appearance had set Caleb stuttering. And she ... was trembling. He handed her a bow, and she blushed.

Davita met his eyes with something akin to Miriam's determination, underlaid with ... was it anger? Disappointment? Did all women wear two guises?

A better question—was he dissolving into a philosopher in his advancing years, rather than a soldier?

He handed Davita the last weapon. She took it with a firm hand.

He cleared his throat. "Have any of you shot a bow before?"

Brief shakes of the head from Miriam and Davita, giggles from Yaffa and Chloe.

He gave them the few arm guards he had garnered, demonstrated posture, grasping the bow, and nocking the arrow. One by one, he bade them shoot. Yaffa surprised him by sending her arrow straight and level. "Very good. You just killed an Aramean captain." At her horrified look, he amended, "A terrible man, murderer of thousands and, in so doing, you saved your husband's life."

Chloe's arrow fell to the side only a stride in front. "A

fine attempt," he said. "This time, raise your elbow—just so—and pull the string just a little farther—wait—now, release." Though her arrow still listed right, it flew farther. He praised her.

Davita strode forward taking Chloe's place, followed his instructions admirably, and loosed an arrow with similar accuracy to Yaffa's and more distance. "Excellent," he said, judging that praise was as necessary for this one, despite her confident demeanor.

Finally, it was Miriam's turn. Her first arrow fell short, but she quickly nocked another, took aim, and released a shot that eclipsed Davita's. Why did pride warm his chest? She wasn't *his* sister. He glanced at Naboth and Gershon among the group of men, staring his way, ignoring the boy seeking their attention. From their expressions, Dov wagered neither had been consulted about their women joining the training. He needed to get to the point of this demonstration before he set off a family spat.

Dov walked over behind the wheat sheaf. "We just demonstrated the vertical stance. If an archer stands on the wall, near a tower or turret, he—or she—can nock an arrow behind it, step out briefly, aim, and shoot. Like this." He demonstrated. "But that allows exposure to the enemy's return volleys. Unacceptable risk for the women." He glanced at Naboth. Though his expression did not change, he gave a slow nod.

Dov walked toward the fallen tree, hunkered down, and lay alongside. Ignoring soft giggles, he raised his bow parallel to the log's topside, aimed a little high, and fired. Without changing position, he called, "This log is about the height of your roof parapets. In this position, archers can shoot with very low exposure to return fire, but soldiers surrounding the city are vulnerable to arrows raining down from above."

Dov moved to his knees and motioned to Yaffa. Slowly she knelt and settled into his former position with a little grunt. "On my rooftop, you say? I will bring my sleeping mat and cushions."

Smiling, helped her position the bow and nock an arrow. "A fine idea. A cushion under your shoulder makes it more comfortable and easier to shoot." After she had shot several more times, he sent her to rest in the shade of a nearby tree.

"Men, think about what you have seen. These are your wives and daughters—I believe it is good they learn protection skills, should the walls be breached—but you have the final word."

"I call a bow an attack weapon," someone shouted from the crowd.

"Yes," Dov responded. "But it also is protection—from a safe distance. I would rather a woman stop an attacker before he has his hands around her throat."

Dov waited until he heard murmurs of agreement. In Samaria, he would not have faced any disapproval to his suggestion. The siege had come too close to a breach.

"I will work with any women who wish to learn the bow, teaching the horizontal, defensive position I have demonstrated. Aaron will teach the standing position there by the wheat sheaves. Men, this will also suit for horseback or chariot shooting if that interests you." Dov pointed at other trainers as they raised their example weapons—slings, axes, and spears.

"Finally, if you do not already know how, everyone should learn to use a dagger. They are small, easy to hide in your clothing, and lethal. They may offer your last means of defense."

Wiping sweat from his brow, Dov continued. "Volunteers in the next field will assign sparring partners and demonstrate the use of swords and spears. We have only a few wooden swords, so I ask those skilled in woodworking to make copies. No one is to practice with iron swords today. We will save that for future sessions, but not until your trainer approves. Since spear-throwing does not involve a partner, select a spear that suits you and practice while the swordfighters are sparring.

"Some who are younger may not realize that Aaron, your respected gatekeeper, is one of our most experienced soldiers. While Aaron is not as swift on his feet as he once was, he is adept with the axe, club, scythe, and many other weapons, some of which you may have in your tool shed. He is only one man, but one you need to seek out for instruction. Gather around and watch when he gives a demonstration. If the battle turns, a fighter with good hand-to-hand combat skills survives."

The recruits moved to the different stations. The women who had shot their bows from the standing position, stayed to learn the second method. Dov motioned Davita to approach. After she had gotten into a comfortable position, he knelt just behind her shoulders. "Remember, you will be on a rooftop and the enemy will be on the hill below, so your aim can be straight, slightly up, or down. If the city is under attack, your shot will likely find a target."

She shot three arrows, then raised her head to see where they landed. "I thought that first one went wild—my hand slipped on the string. The other two went where I intended, even though I couldn't see over the log."

"You have a steady hand. Want to shoot a few more?"

She nodded, so he placed a handful of arrows in front of her. She shot until her bow arm began to tremble, then angled herself up. "Thank you for teaching me. Will you be here tomorrow?"

"I'm not sure. Take this bow, one of those quivers, and some arrows with you. If I am called back to Samaria, practice with your friends." Davita looked uneasily at Miriam, who returned a friendly grin. "Stay until we are finished, though. Sit in the shade with Yaffa—watch the others, including the men. Should it come to fighting, I want you women behind a wall, but a good archer is comfortable shooting from any position."

He turned then to Miriam. "Are you ready?" She nodded once and hurried over. While she got into position, following the examples of Yaffa and Davita, he glanced across the field. Caleb was casting glances their way from amongst the spear throwers. Taking pity, Dov motioned him over, jutting his chin toward Chloe, who stood blinking as Miriam's brother walked toward her.

"You noticed, too?" Miriam slanted a grin up at him, raised her bow, and nocked the arrow. "Is this right? It doesn't feel—"

"If you roll back this way." He took hold of her shoulder and angled her slightly toward him. A mistake. He took his hand away.

"Yes, that is better. I can move my arm." Her concentration was fixed on the bow, her lips pressed together as she drew. He shouldn't have touched her in that way. Yet, with any soldier, he would adjust an arm, move a shoulder. It was different, training women. He must take more care.

She released the arrow.

"A fine shot," he said. "Straight and true."

She twisted her head back. "You are a good teacher."

He was. It was only that she confused him somehow. Was it because he had known her as a child? He must remember, she was a child no longer.

"Not as good as the man who taught me." He smiled, remembering. "An ambidextrous Benjamite. That man could shoot from the back of a running horse—left, right, and behind." He dropped a fistful of arrows in front of her.

"Where did a Benjamite get a horse?" She pulled, released, and looked back at him.

He scratched his head. "I don't know. I never asked."

She laughed, a sound like water over smooth stones. "Where did you get the bay horse?"

Dov stood and extended his hand. "The king gave him to me."

"What did you name him?" She allowed him to pull her to her feet.

"Name a horse? Right. Caleb told me you name animals." He chuckled, immediately chiding himself for his dismissive tone.

If Miriam noticed any slight, she ignored it. "You should call him Uriel."

He paused, liking it. Lion-like. Flame of God.

"I will think on it," he said.

She quirked one side of her mouth. When she did, a small dimple appeared. "Will you continue to teach us to shoot lying down or standing?"

"Depends on you. Both take considerable practice. Though I demonstrated two methods, the fact is, you teach yourself. Carry your bow everywhere, shoot often, consider the weapon an extension of your own arm. But I think you and the others—even your aunt—are capable of defending a section of wall. More important, of defending yourselves."

"Can we bring more women to the training tomorrow?"

Slowly, he scuffed the toe of his sandal across the ground, giving himself time to form an answer. "When we saw you coming down that hill—Caleb, at least, saw trouble. You heard the men this morning. Most are uncertain at least, some are unhappy. My job is to train men for battle. I cannot let anything interfere with that. But if the women come tomorrow—and their men agree—they can learn the bow."

"And daggers? In Samaria, every girl of my acquaintance was handy with a sling from childhood. We shot targets, playing, not training for war."

He glimpsed Gershon, who had joined the male archers in the adjacent field, looking their way again. Dov turned his attention back to Miriam—his student. "Daggers, definitely. In fact, take your friends to Aaron's station when we finish. Tell him I asked that he fit you with daggers and show you the basics." Dov brushed dust from the front of his tunic. The older man's gruff humor, his experience with more than warfare, might make him the best teacher for the women.

"You all did well. Before I move on to help others, we will retrieve the arrows so you can take them with you." He shouted to Caleb, instructors, and recruits down the line. "Archers, hold and recover your arrows."

When the shooting paused, they walked with the others to find where their arrows had flown. It was like the history of the young King David and Jonathan meeting in the field, the secret pact between the two of them because of King Saul. The last time the two friends saw each other alive. Why had he thought of such a thing?

Miriam stooped to retrieve one of her eagle-fletched arrows and lightly ran a finger down the feather edge. "This belonged to our enemy. Yet the eagle feathers—the birds etched on the bow—it's as if it were given me by a friend."

Dov smiled. "Was it not a friend, little bird girl?"

Miriam stood in the far field towards evening, chortling with Davita and Chloe as they slashed the air with deadly little daggers. She had learned six ways to kill a man before supper—if that was when the foe attacked. Aaron stood by grinning, arms crossed. "Easy girls, save something for the enemy."

Gershon walked over. "I can accompany you all to the city, if you are finished," he offered politely.

Chloe and Davita thanked him and they walked up the hill together.

"Where is Jaedon?" Miriam asked.

"He tired early, as did Imma. Abba took them home."

"And Caleb?"

"Still training with the archers."

Miriam glanced at Chloe. The girl's eyes were on the path, but a blush fanned her cheeks. Davita, walking the other side of Chloe, arched an eyebrow.

Both women lived south of the gate, so they turned aside after entering the city, vowing to meet on the morrow for training. Gershon was quiet as she wished them a good night.

But he was not silent long. "You did not ask me about this plan of yours."

Miriam stared straight ahead as they continued walking. Should she have asked him? "You had already gone to the fields preparing to train."

"You should have waited—or asked me to show you what I learned."

She looked away from him, off to the distance where the sky met the mountain in a blue smudge of shadow. Though the sun had dropped behind the mountain, dusk gilded what was left of day. An in-between time. "I have not been in the habit of asking permission for every action I take."

"Not even of your father? I cannot imagine that you did not ask him—"

"You are not my father."

"But I am your betrothed."

She turned toward him, looking him full in the face, musing. There would be no going back if she spoke now. "Am I? Am I your betrothed?"

"Of course you are," he said. "I asked, you agreed—"

"And then you changed the agreement. Decided you would volunteer for the military, knowing that means we cannot marry until you come home. If you come home. And in the meantime, I am to wait here, care for your son, with none of the protections you promised me in the *ketubah*. As of today, we are not betrothed, and my father is not here to *ask permission*. So you have nothing to say to me about today's lessons. Which I enjoyed and was very good at."

He stared at her a moment, nonplussed. Finally, he sputtered, "You—you are willful!"

"Yes. It is good you learned before giving me a real promise." Feeling lighter, Miriam lengthened her stride and left him and their angry words behind. All fell away, as if she was back in her familiar landscape, the foothills of Samaria she roamed as a girl, employing the ground-covering pace that her long, ungainly legs were good for.

Chapter Eleven

Then Miriam the prophet, Aaron's sister, took a timbrel
in her hand, and all the women followed her,
with timbrels and dancing. Miriam sang to them:
"Sing to the Lord, for He is highly exalted.
Both horse and driver He has hurled into the sea."
~ Exodus 15:20-21

Jezreel
Miriam

MIRIAM FLIPPED ANOTHER WET HANK OF flax, scrunching her nose at the putrid smell. Gershon worked a few paces away. An uneasy peace existed between them. After avoiding all but necessary conversation after their argument, Gershon had apologized for speaking harshly. He said nothing more about her asking permission, for the training or other activities. They didn't speak of it again, though nearly a month had passed, but neither did they speak of their betrothal. Uncomfortable, stilted courtesy hung over every interaction.

She swiped sweat from her face and glared across the adjacent roofs, detesting the way the grit and smell seemed to penetrate her skin, while the other women turned the rotting stalks as if they were fragrant loaves of bread. Jaedon, only a few steps away, tossed a forkful up in the air. She jumped back to avoid getting covered with the stuff. She stifled the rebuke that threatened to erupt. After all, she wasn't angry with *Jaedon.*

It was wrong to let her frustration with Gershon spill over into this day, even tinge her feelings toward his son. She jammed her wooden fork under another bundle, reminding herself of the reward for this task—new wedding raiment of soft linen. If the day ever came, Miriam hoped the garment wouldn't smell like wet flax. She hung her head at her sulky thoughts, as sour as the rotting stalks.

When she looked up, she saw a great cloud of dust afar off, on the road from Samaria.

"They're coming!" Jaedon shouted. "Must be the king and queen. I see the horses!" He dropped everything and sprang toward the stairs.

Miriam grasped his sleeve. "Hold a moment." She saw the horses, too, at the front at what appeared to be the entire Israelite army, although dust obscured all but the front riders. She opened her mouth to instruct him to stay close and loosened her grip. A mistake. Jaedon darted down the steps from his grandfather's roof like a mountain goat.

"Wait!" Miriam hurried in pursuit, with a quick glance to ensure Gershon followed. Others on the roofs alerted to Jaedon's shout, shoppers at the gate market pointed at the royal entourage, and curious people swarmed from houses. She didn't want to lose her boy in the swelling crowd.

Jaedon had snagged a spot for the three of them on the stairs to the gate tower. She chuckled as he boldly shooed others away, motioning for her and Gershon to stand on either side of him. Some glanced at the boy, wrinkled their noses, and stepped aside without argument. Miriam grinned. Perhaps there was more than one advantage to rotting flax.

They squeezed their way up the stairs to reach him. As others jostled to take viewing positions, Gershon draped his hands over their shoulders, steadying them against pushes and shoves. The warmth of his hand through her tunic only sent a chill through her frame. Why could she not shake the bitterness over his sharp words?

She forced herself to relax, reminding herself what Yaffa had said about his first wife—shy, a keeper-at-home, looking to Gershon for guidance. A different kind of woman than Miriam. She slanted a glance at his face, so near to hers. He looked uncertain.

Like she felt.

She switched her attention to the arrivals. King Ahab rode at the head of the cavalcade, his black war horse framed by the sharp blue sky. A troop of soldiers in red and gold dress uniforms flanked their ruler. Next came the queen's litter, carried on the shoulders of four bearers and escorted by more soldiers. A covey of chariots followed, war vehicles captured during the rout of the Arameans. Silvery conveyances followed horses of a similar hue, red chariots were drawn by blood bays. One gleaming black cart was hitched to horses spotted all over like leopards. Bronze trim flashed around the rims and wheel hubs. Each chariot carried a driver and archer.

A quick sweep of the occupants revealed Dov in the first vehicle. He glanced up just then, stealing Miriam's focus.

"Look!" She leaned forward, her cheek near Jaedon's. "Your cousin Caleb. The fifth row back."

"I see them. They have bows and arrows, like the other soldiers. Oh! There is Dov!" Jaedon pressed his hand against her cheek, turning her face.

She smoothed his curly hair, much like her brother Caleb's. How she loved him. Resolve began to congeal, to press Gershon to set an early wedding date as they had originally planned, and as her family wanted. Delaying so that he could go to war, left Jaedon vulnerable. Her as well. Without the betrothal, she would merely be the boy's aunt. If she went back to her family, they would be separated, not to mention if her father betrothed her to someone else.

What if her father's choice of husband lived in a distant city? Miriam might never see Jaedon again. She swallowed against the painful tightness in her throat. "You have sharp eyes, my boy."

The troops saluted the crowd as they passed beneath the flower-festooned arch. Jaedon tossed blossoms into the king's chariot when he passed, saving a few for the queen's litter, and tossing more into Dov's chariot. Miriam saw the boy search his empty basket as Caleb and Seth approached and she quickly slipped him all her remaining blooms save one. She glanced at Gershon, caught him smiling, and handed him the last flower. He threaded its stem through the weave of his tunic.

The man continued to surprise her. Yesterday he'd trained all day with the men of the village. But early this morning, he had accompanied Miriam and Jaedon when they gathered flowers and vines, although few men joined the women and children in the task. He had even helped them weave garlands for the gate's arch and the palace balustrade.

Flowers weren't Jezreel's only adornments. Every street and alley had been cleared and swept. Colorful banners streamed from roofs, houses displayed fresh whitewash, and doors shone with oil. It was as if the city tried to erase, not only their hardship, but Samaria's oppression as well—to adorn all the ugly memories with beauty.

As the chariots passed, Miriam gripped Jaedon's hand. "Stay close." The crowds pressed as the parade made its way toward the palace. Bottlenecks formed and shifting bodies threatened to separate them. The narrow streets weren't made to accommodate crowds on foot as well as chariots and mounted troops. The most enthusiastic citizens climbed atop the wall or roofs lining the route to the palace. Others dropped back, satisfied with cheering the king and queen, shouting praises to Yahweh and singing.

> Though hostile nations surrounded me,
> I destroyed them all with the authority of the LORD.
> They swarmed around me like bees;
> they blazed against me like a crackling fire.
> But I destroyed them all with the authority of the LORD.
> My enemies did their best to kill me,
> but the LORD rescued me.
> The LORD is my strength and my song;
> he has given me victory.

After the last chariot passed, the people fell in behind, singing and dancing their way to the palace square where a city-wide celebration was building. Called outside by the festivity, Naboth and Yaffa strolled not far ahead, arm in arm. Gershon took Jaedon's free hand and they hurried to catch up. Miriam breathed in the aromas wafting over the city since early morning—roasting pheasants, partridges, goats, and sheep, parched grain, breads fragrant with cinnamon and honey, stews seasoned with garlic, cumin, cardamom, and wild onion. The king had provided many sacrificial bullocks. Tomorrow, after the priests offered thanksgiving sacrifices to the Lord, the people would enjoy the undedicated portions of the rare treat. Miriam's mouth watered at the thought.

She surveyed the line of musicians on rooftops above her, recognizing a neighbor who lived in the blue house down their street, and beside him, the father of Jaedon's best friend, Samuel. She made a mental note to invite the boy to their house again. As she watched, more musicians assembled in corners, tuning harps and lyres to harmonize with flutes and trumpets. Cymbals clashed and drums underscored it all, with no attempt to synchronize. The dissonant confusion was strangely exhilarating.

But suddenly the odor of rotting flax penetrated everything. If only the king had come a day earlier or later. "Gershon, we smell terrible. If there is to be a celebration, I must go home and wash."

Gershon didn't argue, and he hushed Jaedon, who did. They hurried to the two houses, the men going to Gershon's and Miriam and Yaffa to Naboth's. After washing and putting on her best garment, a white tunic Yaffa had woven, tied at the waist with a striped sash, Miriam felt prepared to enjoy the celebrations.

"Darling girl, let me share this nard perfume. Naboth bought it for me after a particularly fine harvest, but there is rarely an occasion. After that flax—well, this is the occasion." Yaffa laughed.

Gershon waited outside, handsome in his best tunic, woven from wool of spotted sheep. "You smell nice," he said, smiling.

Naboth hurried forward holding Jaedon's hand. "Is Yaffa not ready?" he asked. "She did not work on the rooftop today."

Yaffa walked outside. "Nor did you, husband. Sometimes I move a little slower, but I am here."

"I would wait an eternity for you," he said.

She rolled her eyes.

Jaedon laughed. "You always say that, Saba."

Gershon took Miriam's arm and they headed toward the palace. "The king will make his entrance before long," Gershon said. "He delivers a speech when he visits."

"In Samaria, too," Miriam replied. "Will the celebration begin afterward? I cannot wait to sample the delicacies teasing my every breath. And I long to hear the musical instruments in tune—at last!" She paused, wondering if she chattered too much. But it was pleasant to finally feel free of the constraint their disagreement had brought.

"With so many musicians, I'm sure there will be singing and dancing," Gershon said.

"Abba is a fine dancer." Miriam clasped her hands. "If only he were here. Oh, when he performs the dance of the pomegranate tree! He can leap as high as any young man. What about my uncle?"

"Who do you think taught your father to dance? He is the older brother, after all. But this is a victory celebration. The men will have a small part, but the maidens—"

His final words were drowned by ringing tambourines and tinkling bells. Miriam turned to watch Chloe and a string of other women trot past. Chloe had introduced her to others at the well, but many were strangers.

"The maidens will dance? After the end of the great drought, one of the vineyards below Samaria hosted a celebration." Miriam gazed after Chloe and the women. She and her childhood friends had held hands and danced with the young women, but that was years ago. And now, would she be considered a maiden, in this strange in-between place she inhabited?

Even though Gershon had apologized, and a *ketubah* was tucked among her belongings, he had not spoken to her father. She did not know where she stood.

Gershon smiled. "Yes. The maidens will dance through the vineyards. You should dance with them."

"Oh ... no, no, I never learned." Immediately she regretted the lie. She loved to dance. "I am too tall, too ungainly." That much was true, but the previous lie still rebuked her.

"You, ungainly!" he scoffed. "You are like a graceful, long-necked heron."

She stared at him, knowing her mouth had fallen open.

A flush spread upward from his neck, and he quickly leaned over to tie the lace on Jaedon's sandal. "This is always coming undone," he muttered.

"Caw, caw." Jaedon vocalized. "Is that what a heron sounds like?"

"That would be a crow, I think." Was her face as red as Gershon's?

Turning to hide her blush, she saw Naboth lead Yaffa

toward a vendor of dyed wool. He examined fibers dyed a soft shade of blue. That particular color held a place of honor in their family history.

Before they left Jerusalem, *Saba* Nathaniel had given *Savta* Hadassah a blue tunic. Now Naboth, their firstborn, bent to whisper in his wife's ear. When she nodded, smiling, he said, "What say we strike up a trade, Enan—my fine wine for your equally fine wool?"

After a little haggling, Yaffa cradled enough blue fiber to weave a shawl. She called Miriam to come admire it. While she felt its softness, Jaedon drew Gershon away.

Miriam watched father and son wander from vendor to vendor. They stopped to talk with an Edomite burned dark by the sun. Gershon pointed at a stack of pelts, and the two men entered into discussion, while Jaedon scrutinized contents of a frayed basket. He motioned to his father, turning that pleading face upon him. Gershon extended his hand toward the Edomite, palm up. He poured out an answer accompanied by extravagant arm motions. When they returned, Jaedon clutched a wooden donkey and Gershon had slipped something small between the folds of his sash.

"Miriam, my donkey has real woven baskets!" Jaedon gushed. "When we go on a journey, he'll carry sticks for campfires and grass to eat."

"When you journey?" She looked at Gershon for clarity. To her knowledge, other than occasional visits to her family in Samaria, Naboth's clan never left Jezreel.

He shrugged. "You know how Savta talks about celebrating Passover in Jerusalem, one day. To say "one day" around Jaedon, is as good as a promise."

Miriam grinned. When she was Jaedon's age and listened to their grandmother spin tales about the holy city, she longed to go. But relations were uneasy, then, between the northern tribes and Judah.

"Maybe—" Gershon halted, then started again. "Many things are uncertain." He glanced down at Jaedon, who appeared engrossed in his toy donkey. Miriam wasn't fooled. "But Yahweh has promised to be with us in the coming battle, and King Ahab and King Jehoshaphat have formed an alliance. Perhaps ... one day ..." He stretched out the words, glancing meaningfully at the top of Jaedon's head.

"And our grandmother?" Miriam folded her hands tightly, searching for the right words to frame this request. "She has longed to celebrate Passover in Jerusalem. How many more years will she have to satisfy that longing?

Gershon shrugged. "Do you think Savta would allow us to leave her behind?"

"You are not leaving me behind either." Jaedon stated. Miriam smiled. So he had been listening.

His father ruffled his son's hair. "What do you think we are talking about?"

"To see the eagles. Can we go tomorrow?"

Listening, but not quite following.

Gershon raised an eyebrow. "If we go, *one day*, what time would be best?" Miriam studied first father and then son, foreseeing a lifetime of challenges, negotiations, and contests of will.

"Before dawn."

Shofars sounded from atop the wall, their haunting call hushing the clatter of the marketplace. All eyes turned to the palace. Two of the king's guard folded back shuttered doors that faced a walled balcony on the upper level. The guards surveyed the crowd, and apparently satisfied, took positions on each side of the platform.

Once more the shofars blew, and the king and queen strolled out arm-in-arm. The queen smiled demurely, first at the king, then at the crowd. She wore a pale green gown and her matching head covering was held in place by a golden circlet. Thick strands of her famed red hair escaped the veil, with artful intent, Miriam thought. What stirred the queen's thoughts, beneath that crown? How could she forgive her husband for promising her to the enemy as a tribute?

The king dropped her hand and Jezebel stepped back, continuing to gaze at Ahab as he began his speech. He spoke of the long siege and thanked Yahweh for the surprising victory. Interesting how the royal couple seemed to lean apart, even when they touched. Miriam didn't believe that tender gaze. Yet she sensed a strange kinship with Jezebel.

Although she was queen, she was vulnerable as any woman to her husband's whim.

The crowd interrupted the king with cheers, especially at his final announcement. His servants had prepared special food for the citizens, which would soon be carried to banquet tables outside the palace entrance.

The king continued to speak, briefly mentioning the prophet's warning that the Arameans would attack again in the spring. Then he motioned to someone standing inside the chamber, and Dov walked onto the balcony.

"Dov is one of the officers who led our troops to victory. I have put him in charge of coordinating military recruits and training." The king motioned for Dov to stand beside him. Miriam felt a spark of something akin to pride that he was given this honor, and that she had known him from her childhood. Even when she was young, he had seemed brave and heroic in her girlish eyes.

"It is not necessary to have fought before," Dov shouted to the crowd. "We have instructors and have already begun distributing weapons and training recruits. But we need more men to volunteer.

"Remember, Yahweh has promised to go with us. With His help, we will prevail. I heard the prophecy from the mouth of His seer, when he spoke to our king."

Miriam stood on her toes to see better. Enthusiastic murmurs rippled through the crowd as Dov continued speaking. She glanced at Gershon. He also seemed attuned to Dov. His stance exuded confidence and wisdom, he spoke about tactics and strength. This was why men followed him to battle. If she were a man, she, too would be inspired.

Again, she fixed her attention on Gershon, and as she did, she felt a turning. One part of her wanted to wed soon, as she and Gershon had first planned. But knowing he wanted to stand with his countrymen—she would not deter him. Her heart scoffed at her oh-so-noble decision, whispering she could not stop him if she tried.

Dov closed, bowed to the king, and stepped to the rear of the balcony. The shofar sounded once more and then, arm-in-arm, the king and queen walked back inside.

After they sampled all the king's delicacies and the sun dipped lower, the musicians began to play again. Tentative at first, one or two lutes played in synchrony, then harps and double-piped horns wove a thread of harmony. When the drums thumped a rhythm, dancers lined up. Women gathered first, many with tambourines, others linking hands to shoulders in a human chain. First stepping left, then returning right, they swayed to the music and dipped to the drums. As Miriam watched, she found a pattern to their movements, slowing as the music slowed, reversing direction at the next single drum beat, picking up the pace as hand-drums chirred and the music intensified. Miriam clapped her hands, enthralled with the dancers' grace.

Gershon fumbled with the sash around his waist, pulling out a small object. It dangled from his fingers as he extended it to her. "For you," he said. "For the dancing."

The piece chimed as he dropped it into her cupped palm. She fingered a pretty little ankle bracelet. Braided threads of jute and silk dangled brass bells and spotted seashells. She gave it a shake and smiled at the resonant clicks and chimes.

She closed her hand around the gift, her first from a man not her father or brother. The shells felt cool against her skin. "Thank you."

He smiled. "Put it on quickly. The dancing begins soon."

"No, I—"

"The women will head for the vineyards—likely ours will be first. You must lead them away from the tender vines."

He glanced away when he said it. It was true, strangers might carelessly tread upon the young cuttings he nurtured. But the family could just as easily position themselves to direct dancers away from the delicate plants. Surely it was immodest for her to dance.

His brown eyes seemed to bore into hers. Some trick of the light. "You are always working. See—your friends are waiting."

She tore her gaze from his to another crowd of girls, who jostled, pushed, and giggled into their hands as they formed a loosely structured line. Among them, she saw a familiar face. Chloe waved vigorously at Miriam, beckoning her to join the fun.

And part of her wanted to, but ... She looked thoughtfully at the pretty trinket, uneasy about bending in the street to tie it to her ankle. Yet, how much worse to allow Gershon to kneel and assist.

Gershon smiled at her. "Go on."

What had he said, when she called herself ungainly? *A graceful, long-necked heron.* Perhaps she could balance on one leg, the other bent up—fasten the ankle bracelet that way. She fought the urge to laugh at the ridiculous image.

With decisive movements, she wrapped the anklet twice around her wrist, accepting Gershon's help to tie it tight enough that she would not lose it dancing, but loose enough to quiver, click, and chime when she moved. The music called to her. It was time to leave behind her hesitation. It was twilight. Darkness would conceal any blunders. What did it matter that she was tall and ungainly? This would be her last chance to dance with the maidens.

Giving Gershon a quick smile, she ran toward the dancers, shaking her arm to set the bells chiming. Chloe made space for Miriam next to a girl with long black curls.

"Shalom, Miriam. I am Kyra." The pretty girl tilted her head toward Chloe. "She told me your name."

"And that you have a handsome brother." Chloe handed her a tambourine. "Is he here?"

"I saw him ride in with the king's procession, but I haven't seen him since then."

Music interrupted their conversation. The first line of dancers pranced past, and their group scurried to attach themselves at the end. With whoops, tambourines, and singing, the mass of women dipped and swayed their way toward the gate. Colorful head coverings fluttered like butterflies in a meadow of wildflowers.

Ahead, the women pranced faster through the open gate, pulling those at the tail of the line with ever increasing speed. Some of the musicians followed alongside. Turning onto the highest terrace, they all headed for Naboth's vineyard.

Naboth's vineyard! Gershon had said it would be first.

Miriam was meant to guide them away from the tender vines, and here she was at the end of the train. She pulled back, intending to halt the line and twist its tail into lead position. Instead, she nearly got pulled off her feet. Chloe tossed her a frown and shouted over the singing. "Are you all right?"

"I need to get to the front. Our vineyard has a patch of new shoots." A cymbal clashed.

"What?" Chloe turned her ear toward Miriam. It was no use. The instruments, singing, drums, and laughter drowned everything. She extricated herself from Chloe and Kyra, intending to sprint for the front of the train, but suddenly it slowed of itself and stopped. What had happened? Couldn't they find the gate?

Miriam stepped up the mountain's slope to get a better view. Another group of dancers, a line of men, had entered the gate from the opposite direction, temporarily blocking passage for the women. Several carried lit torches that cast ruddy light on faces and shoulders. They had begun to circle the vineyard and were heading toward the far end, their backs to her. But even so, she recognized Gershon leading the line. She breathed a sigh of relief. He could surely direct the revelers where they could do no harm. The men took up a position at the end of the vineyard, forming several rows in front of the delicate vines Gershon wanted protected. They began a slow dance with many dips and leaps, underscored by flames that wavered and sparked. Their lines crossed each other as alternate rows danced left and right, blocking the protected section. Their dance had something of the strut of mating waterfowl, reminding her of Gershon's description— like a graceful heron. Miriam searched the group again, glimpsing him in the back line. He lifted a hand in acknowledgment, and despite the growing darkness, she imagined she saw him smile.

Moon, stars, and torches cast sufficient light to prevent missteps. The chain of women snaked into the vineyard, no longer linking arms, but undulating to the music like lake grass obeying a breeze.

Miriam gave herself to the persuasive beat. While women spun and twirled around her, she lifted her arms, imagining wings. Swaying in place, stretching her fingers into

DANA MCNEELY | 113

feathery tips, her body responded to remembered rhythms, long-legged strides, powerful flight.

Suddenly Chloe clutched her arm, hissing in her ear. "Your brother is here." She brushed her hand across Miriam's cheek, directing her gaze. Indeed, there was Caleb, next to a torch carrier who, in that moment, tossed his flickering torch overhead. She watched it spin end-over-end into the darkening sky, casting sparks of spiraling light, up, up, and then falling, the man snatching it effortlessly from the air by its rope-bound handle—*just like Abba.*

"Has your brother spoken for a maiden back in Samaria?" Chloe asked. "Because I—"

Miriam grabbed Chloe by both arms. "That is my father!" When had he arrived? How had she not seen him?

Chloe's face crinkled in confusion. "But I see your—"

"My father is *beside* Caleb! The man with the torch."

Kyra moved closer, an eyebrow raised. "Your brother is here?"

Chloe pointed. "There. Curly-haired, next to the one with the torch."

Quickly Miriam scanned the rest of the row. "My uncle Naboth is there, too, on the right. Watch him."

"Too old," Kyra said.

Miriam shot her a look.

Kyra laughed, crossing her arms. "Handsome enough, though."

"Stop teasing her," Chloe said. "Miriam is a serious woman."

As Naboth flipped his torch into the air, Miriam pressed her hand to her mouth, holding back laughter that threatened to spill, partly because of the teasing, but more at the surprise of seeing her father in Jezreel and anticipating what would come next between these two brothers.

Who do you think taught your father, Gershon had said.

It had already started. After catching his torch on its downward spiral, Naboth lobbed it over the heads of three men to Abba, a trail of falling embers streaking the dark. Her father caught the torch in his left hand, simultaneously tossing his up in the air. He gave Naboth's torch a spin and tossed it high to follow the other. Soon two torches spun above the vineyard, to the whoops and howls of the dancers, who had halted in place to watch, shout, and clap to the drums. The musicians also stopped with the dancers, to watch her father juggle fire.

Naboth tossed his brother a third, unlit torch. That was nothing to her abba. She had seen him juggle four, even five lit torches together. Miriam squealed with the others, when he lit the new torch while continuing to juggle.

"Whoop!" Miriam shouted and slapped her tambourine, establishing a hand-hip beat her friends quickly followed. Drummers joined their beat as torches lit the sky, flying higher and faster above the vineyard in mesmerizing fiery trails. Caleb and Gershon tossed more lit torches, and soon each brother juggled multiple torches, never missing a catch as they whirled, leapt, caught behind their back, or flung torches up and across to each other. Miriam grinned. All eyes were on these two older men—her father and her uncle.

At the culmination of their torch exhibition, the musicians again played the victory tune sung when the king and queen entered the city. One by one, to slowing music, Naboth and Abba rid themselves of torches. As a torch fell from the sky, they handed it off to a neighbor who passed it down the line of men.

The men sang as they staged a mock battle. The torch staves doubled as spears, clubs, and swords in the confrontation.

They swarmed around me like bees;
they blazed against me like a crackling fire.

Beating their tambourines in admiration, the women responded.

But I destroyed them all with the authority of the LORD.

They continued their call and response, drawing close or away from one another, their ebb and flow guided only by music.

My enemies did their best to kill me,

but the LORD rescued me.
The LORD is my strength and my song;
he has given me victory.

When they sang the final words, the music started again, but now the line of men headed toward the watchtower at the center of the vineyard. They circled around once, then made their way among the vines to leave through the gate. The women followed, but because there were so many more women than men, their lines crossed several times, interlacing like knee-high sandals.

Gershon slowed as he approached Miriam. He lifted his torch so that its flame lit her face. He leaned close. "You dance beautifully."

Then he took her hand, wrapped her fingers around the torch handle, and marched away to rejoin the line of men.

"Who was that?" Kyra asked, her voice sultry as she emphasized the last word.

"We are—cousins." Miriam had almost said they were betrothed. Wouldn't that be proper, so a maiden wouldn't consider him free? But though they were not betrothed, it also seemed dishonest to say they were mere cousins.

"Not him—the tall soldier looking at you."

The drumbeats quickened, drowning any possible answer. Miriam looked in the direction of Kyra's gaze and spotted Dov, but he was talking to a musician outside the vineyard, not looking at her. Nor did his gaze settle on any woman, she noticed as they left for the next vineyard, though Kyra gave an extra shake to her tambourine when she passed him.

Miriam shrugged. "He is a friend of the family. Perhaps he thought my brother was nearby."

She didn't blame the girl. Dov was an admirable man, heroic even, especially in the wake of the recent victory in which he'd had a prominent part. But Miriam sensed he would disappoint the beautiful Kyra. Dov, even more than Gershon, was focused on his duty to the country.

After the dance, Miriam returned to the square, looking for

her father and for Gershon. She spotted them through the crowd, along with Dod Naboth. *Abba!* A smile lit her heart as she pushed her way toward them, longing to throw her arms around him, to hear from his own mouth how Imma and Savta fared.

But Abba was frowning at Gershon. All three were deep in conversation. Instinctively she drew back behind a jutting stairwell, peering around the corner. Though she strained to hear them, the babble of the crowd defeated her. Still she could see words pouring from Gershon's lips, his hands upturned, pleading his case. Her father stood with arms crossed, his mouth downturned. She knew that expression, that stance. She had seen it often enough, as a young girl, when her father found her in the wrong. Unease rippled through her and she backed deeper into the shadows. Although she wondered about the details of their conversation, she didn't want to charge in. She waited until the musicians finished playing the current song. Then she strode around the corner, forging a confidence she did not feel.

Chapter Twelve

There are three things that are too amazing for me,
four that I do not understand: the way of an
eagle in the sky, the way of a snake on a rock,
the way of a ship on the high seas, and
the way of a man with a maiden.
~ Proverbs 30:18-19

Jezreel, early the next day
Miriam

IT HAD BECOME MIRIAM'S HABIT TO rise before dawn and grind grain before Yaffa woke, but the next morning she rolled from her sleeping mat even earlier. She listened at the shuttered window in the small room in which she slept. A rustle of wind, the watchman's call. At least two hours until sunrise.

After last night's celebration, perhaps Gershon and Jaedon would not show up at Naboth's door before dawn, as they had agreed, but if they came, she would be ready. She had been wakeful all night, though she feigned sleep when she heard her father and Naboth arguing in hoarse whispers, especially disturbing because they were impossible to understand.

Best to focus on today's tasks, forget incomprehensible whispers. She knelt at the hearth, stirred the banked coals with a twig, and lit an oil lamp against the dark. Next, she retrieved the sack of emmer wheat from the wooden chest, which was impervious to mice. Shielding the flame with her cupped hand, she headed for the courtyard, smiling at the memory of last night's dancing, singing, even the impromptu boxing match between two youths who had imbibed vast quantities of wine.

Miriam tiptoed as she passed the area where her father had spread his sleeping mat. She listened for the heavy snores that often plagued Abba during flax harvest when the air was full of dust and stench, but he slept soundly, even though the fields were near. Carefully lifting the latch, she slipped through the door.

"Good morning, daughter."

She gasped and jostled the oil lamp, nearly extinguishing the flame. "Father! I thought—but you're awake."

His garments rustled as he moved closer. "I wanted to speak to you alone."

She nodded stiffly, then realized, with only the lamp's dim flame, he would not see her small movement in the early hours of cockcrowing. "Sit while I grind the grain. Take the lamp."

The flame marked her father's descent as he lowered himself against the courtyard wall. Feeling for the grinding stone with her foot, Miriam knelt beside it. Her fingers trembled only a little as she untied the sack of emmer. As she dipped a measure into the stone's depression, she mouthed, *help me, Lord.*

"I spoke to your cousin last night. I'll admit, I do not find his actions toward you to be honorable. He did not speak to me first ..."

Words surged on her tongue like a dammed-up stream, but a breeze filtered through the courtyard entrance, and a quiet voice whispered. *Wait.*

It was not her voice.

She bent over the grinding stone and scraped it across the wheat.

"I almost could understand his reasons for haste—his wife's untimely death, the uncertainty of war, his motherless son—he spoke of the *ketubah*, of his provision for you apart from the boy. He even took me to his home and showed it to me. He states he has treated you honorably. That you have lived here, in my brother's home, and Gershon in his. Is this true, my daughter?"

"It is true." She leaned harder on the millstone.

Abba went silent. He rested the lamp on his bent knee. "The *ketubah* is generous, but the promise of a gift means nothing without a formal betrothal. You have no protection. He did not give the *ketubah* to me, nor to the temple priest. He said he would do so now, providing it was not made public until after the battle next spring. He explained his reason. I admire his devotion to our country, but you are my daughter—my first concern. I cannot agree to such an arrangement."

Miriam looked away from the lamplight, her thoughts at war within her. She agreed with everything Abba said. She had even planned to talk to Gershon today, with the hope of changing his decision. Her father had spoken. A daughter's vow could not stand without her father's approval. Most important, she had heard the whispered command. And yet—

She set the millstone on edge. "You were so anxious I wed. Isn't that why you sent me to Jezreel? To meet a suitable husband?" She cringed at her disrespect, even as further retorts fought for release.

"It is not seemly you live in his father's household—"

"Your brother's household, remember. Where you sent me."

She felt the stern look he must be giving her, though darkness cloaked his face. After a long pause, he said, "I will not argue with you, Miriam. You know I am right. I have told Gershon either he marries you now, or you come with me when I return to Samaria. I will not have him use you in this way, caring for his son, while muddying your reputation."

Once more Miriam bent over the grinding stone, scraping it over the wheat until her calloused hands chafed. She reasoned with herself. Why should Abba's interference fill her with anger? She had not wanted to marry. She planned to live as a spinster in her father's house, and should Yahweh will it, to help care for her nieces, nephews, and possibly their children in her old age. If she now wanted her own family, specifically this family—Jaedon and Gershon—that was her father's fault for sending her here to attract a suitor.

She took a long breath, her strokes slowing, the stone's complaints growing quieter between her words. "Father, most of what you say is good. But caring for Jaedon is not a burden. I love him as though he is my own. Gershon … I care for Gershon, too. I am content to wait while he fulfills what he considers his duty." She stilled the millstone. "I ask you not to interfere."

The lamp flame jerked. "I have spoken to Gershon and given you my decision." His voice rasped as though he forced himself not to say more.

Grimly, she bent again to her task. She meant to make flatbread, enough for her father, aunt, and uncle to break their fast, and enough for her, Gershon, and Jaedon to carry with them. She trailed her fingers through the flour on the stone, scooped it into a wooden bowl, and poured more emmer into the lower stone's depression.

"It is my understanding that you two have planned a jaunt into the countryside with only the boy as your escort." He scoffed. "It is hard to understand my brother's apparent lack of supervision—or why Yaffa has not planned to accompany you. Therefore, I will go with you."

Yahweh, this is how you help me? Miriam scraped the stone faster.

A flock of ducks flew low over the courtyard, their soft quacking like laughter.

Dawn was still an hour away when the two arrived. Gershon carried a torch tilted crookedly and stretched his mouth in a mighty yawn. Jaedon couldn't keep his hands and feet still. Both father and son wore cloaks over the bows and quivers. They planned to look for the eagles, but practice shooting as well.

Miriam plucked her bow from the wall hook, grabbed the pouch of provisions, and stepped into the cool morning air. She pulled the door to close it, but felt resistance.

"Hello, Gershon, Jaedon. Mind if I come along?" Abba stepped through the door. So he hadn't gone back to sleep.

"Come, and welcome," Gershon said slowly, catching her gaze. Jaedon eyed her father curiously.

"Ah! You are hunting. I will need to borrow a bow."

Gershon put a hand on his son's shoulder. "My father will gladly loan his. But we are not hunting today, sir, only target practice. Dov and Caleb have been giving lessons in the valley, but we need practice."

"I carry my bow everywhere," Jaedon said, flipping his cloak aside and reaching for the bow.

Gershon laid his hand on the boy's shoulder, giving him a stern look. "What did we discuss?"

"I ... I am not to ever, ever take an arrow from the quiver without permission from an adult." He grinned when his father gave him an affectionate squeeze.

With the exception of a cock crow, the city was silent as they headed for the gate, and so were they. Gershon led the way. He had alerted the gatekeeper about their early morning outing, so the Eye of the Needle swung open when they approached.

Giving him a little push, Miriam told Jaedon to walk behind his father. She followed closely, picking her way down the city mound. Gershon's torch formed a dome of light that revealed rough patches. She glanced back at her father. "Can you see your footing, Abba?"

Smiling, he nodded. "I have not begun to dodder in your absence, my girl."

When they reached the valley, knee-high grasses and wild herbs brushed their tunics. Jaedon fell back to walk beside her, whispering questions.

Burred seeds attached to the tassels on their garments. Sometimes grasshoppers bounced off their cloaks. Once a wall of feathery, white-flowered plants towered in their path, and when Miriam stepped around them, she dowsed her sandals in a puddle.

"Jaedon, watch out here." She shook her feet, winning his grin as well as her father's.

Before long, the sun peeked through the distant hills, illuminating the colors of the landscape—green, gold, deep purple, yellow, even splashes of red that were wild calanit. Did everything grow here with more vigor than home in Samaria? The forested hills and lush shrubs provided a deep green backdrop for the silvery wheat and tall grasses that grew in the valley. Golden sunflowers turned wide faces toward the dawn. She marked patches of mustard, dill, and mint she'd forage as they returned home.

When they neared the cliffs, Miriam placed a restraining hand on Gershon's shoulder. Nodding, he waited while she took bearings. She spotted an outcropping half-way up the cliff that might be the nest location. Did it line up with the route she saw the parent eagles take, when they carried kills to their young? She looked behind to the city, catching her father's considering gaze. Shifting her focus to the city gate, she traced the line of the wall eastward until she spotted Naboth's vineyard, its upper fence near the top of the hill.

She made a half turn and looked up. There it was. Her eyes traced the jagged outline of sticks and branches, the building tools of these mighty birds.

She pointed her chin at the cliff outcropping. Jaedon and Gershon looked where she indicated and nodded. Jaedon raised his finger against his mouth. Pleasure warmed her. He had finally learned the need for silence from those games of desert cat. But Gershon? Was he just a quiet man? The workings of his mind still mystified her.

She caught her father's gaze. Little mystery about his mind. He doted on her, his only daughter. She captured and sold birds for food and pets. He appreciated her contributions to the family coffers. But did he think her capable of deciding her own future? Apparently not.

She looked around for a place to keep wait for the eagles to make an appearance. A nearby copse of sycamores provided deep shade. She caught Gershon's gaze, tilted her head toward the trees. Soon they settled down among the grasses, Jaedon beside her, Gershon beside him, her father on her other side. The four were nearly hidden by long blades of grass.

As yellow light washed over the cliffs, a series of chirrups and sharp cries broke the silence.

"They are talking," Jaedon whispered. "Is it the chicks or the parents?"

Miriam's father glanced at his nephew, then at her, waiting for her answer.

She scanned the empty sky. "Both, I think."

"What are they saying?" Jaedon squirmed beside her, hidden up to his chin in rippling grass.

"What do you think?"

He squinted in apparent thought. "I am hungry."

Miriam felt her lips curve. "Are you speaking for yourself or the eagles."

"Both, I think." Jaedon smirked as he reached for the

sack of provisions, his raised eyebrows asking permission. When she nodded, he pulled out four small loaves and handed them around.

"Look!" He whispered loudly around a mouthful of bread. Two dark slashes launched from the nest.

The adult eagles circled the valley, heads swiveling as they floated on the breeze with only a lift of wing from time to time as they caught a passing current. At first, they flew abreast, wingtips nearly touching, their heads veiled in gold. Then one, the larger of the two, dipped a wing and slid down a ramp of sky, as neatly as a chariot drawn by swift horses.

Miriam turned her mouth to Jaedon's ear. "The female."

"How do you know this?" he whispered, his gaze fixed on the eagle's flight.

"She is larger. When we first began watching them, I noticed the smaller eagle spent more time hunting, while she"—Miriam pointed her chin toward the sky—"brooded over the nest."

The eagle circled closer to the ground, eyes fixed on a spot where grass rippled as an animal darted through. The raptor folded her wings and dove like a loosed arrow. Her mate shot after her.

Miriam heard a shriek and sounds of struggle. Bleating, plaintive cries, and the whump, whump of wings beating the grass ensued. Jaedon clasped Miriam's hand.

When the female flapped her way upwards, she gripped a young goat in her talons. Its legs hung limply, stunned or dead. When the eagle reached the height of an old pine, she dropped the goat, then circled and joined her mate on the ground. But though the two eagles ripped at the corpse, flinging bits of fur and hide over their heads, they did not stay long. When they flew toward the cliffs, neither bore any part of the carcass in their bloodied talons.

"I don't understand," Gershon said. "They kill a goat and leave it?"

"Maybe they sensed bitterness or taint. Goats will eat anything," Abba said. Looking at Miriam, he added, "That foolish youngster separated from shepherd and flock. Went her own way."

Miriam kept her gaze on the sky. She would wait before

adding her opinion. But she remembered the feathery plants they had bypassed on their trek. Rooted in a boggy puddle, smooth stems, taller than her head. A memory of Savta ...

"Let us keep silent a while longer," she whispered. "I think it is not over yet."

"What is not over?" Her father whispered.

"I'm not sure. Wait. Watch."

Jaedon nestled against her. "That's what she always tells me," he confided to his uncle. Sitting the other side of the boy, Gershon glanced their way, smiled, and draped his arms across his bent knees.

As the sun topped the cliffs, it set a patch of calanit ablaze. It had been such a day, when Miriam had seen no more than four summers. She and her grandmother foraged for greens to augment lentil stew. She clutched a wilted red flower in one hand as she hopped two steps to each one of her grandmother's. From her child's gaze, the grasses seemed as tall as her brothers, and at the edge of the bog, a white-flowered, feathery plant loomed big as a tree.

Her grandmother flung out a cautionary hand, stopping Miriam from plucking a low-hanging flower. "Hemlock, Miriam. Look closely. You must never eat, nor touch it."

"Like the fruit of the tree of good and evil?"

"The knowledge of good and evil, dear. And Elohim did not say do not touch—he said, do not eat. But, my sweet, even touching hemlock can harm you. Eating only a few leaves can kill an animal—and then, the animal must not be eaten. But you already know—"

"We must never eat an animal that has died by unknown ... by unknown ..."

"Unknown cause, dear. Very good. And what did you learn about hemlock?"

"It is very pretty—and would look nice with my flower—but I must not touch it or eat it. But why did you call Him Elohim and not Yahweh, Savta?"

And there had been another little lesson. There had been many, as she grew, for constant questions bubbled out of her. They still bubbled—but she had learned not to let all go free.

Miriam had never seen hemlock again until today. Her

grandmother had told Abba, and he and other farmers, fearing for their flocks, went into the valley with hoes and torches. She wanted to ask Abba if he had seen the plant, if she was right. But she had shushed everyone. Best to follow her own advice and wait.

Over by the cliffs, the eagles circled just beyond the nest. Strange. Why didn't they land? Miriam heard the chicks, chirping hungrily. The parents brought no food. If the goat was tainted, why didn't they continue to hunt?

"They must want to eat," whispered Jaedon. "I ate, but I'm hungry again."

She patted his arm.

The eagles circled close to the nest, then soared away, edged closer, flew off again. The chicks hopped on the side of the nest, flapping their wings, demanding food, demanding attention—

Then as the female flew close to the nest, one of the chicks hopped over the edge and fell. Miriam sucked in her breath. Would the eaglet fall to its death? The mother dove after it flapping her own wings encouragingly as she swooped beneath it. Whether from instinct, or imitation, the young eagle beat its wings, slowing its fall, leveling off. When the female swung away from the nest and the young one followed, Miriam breathed again. Sometimes it wavered, once a breeze seemed to flip it like a leaf in a gale, but it climbed the heavens and doggedly followed its mother as she circled the kill.

Meanwhile, the male swooped over the head of the remaining nestling. This seemed to surprise the young one, who tottered on a leafy edge. When the male swooped by again, the chick gave a sharp cry and lunged to nip its parent's tail feathers. Seeming to misjudge the edge of the nest, it too fell, flapping its wings in confusion, but quickly finding a rhythm. The parents circled the field, as if demonstrating the varieties of flight. Ascending, descending, drifting on currents. The youngsters sometimes followed their parents' lead, but more often tried their own way. After a while, when the youngsters appeared to falter, the parents turned, but not toward the nest—toward the kill.

"Good instincts, my girl," Abba said. "The meat wasn't

tainted, but rather their lure to get the young ones to fly. How did you know?"

"I didn't. Not really. But I've learned it is usually best to wait—see what happens."

Her father nodded slowly.

They watched the eagles feed for a while. Jaedon had many questions, but this once, Miriam did not rush to teach. Gershon was here. Let him answer the boy's questions, give him a father's attention. There would be little enough time for that if she must return to Samaria with her father and Gershon went off to war. How would Jaedon fare, staying alone with Yaffa and Naboth?

They loved their grandson, but they increased in years. She had watched Yaffa smile with relief when Miriam took Jaedon with her to carry water from the well, visit a neighbor, or help in the vineyard.

Gershon motioned to his son to sit beside him. He put his arm around the boy and spoke quietly to him, as they both gazed at the feeding birds.

Miriam watched the pair of them, feeling the warmth of possession fill her. *Her own. Her heart's own.*

Chapter Thirteen

Like an eagle that stirs up its nest and hovers over its young,
that spreads its wings to catch them and carries them aloft.
The Lord alone led him; no foreign god was with him.
Deuteronomy 32:11-12

Jezreel
Miriam

LATE MORNING, THE EAGLES LEFT THE kill and returned to their nest. Jaedon begged to go see the carcass, but Gershon refused. "Two reasons. Can you think why?" He picked up a dead branch the length of his forearm.

Jaedon sucked in his upper lip. "The eagles might return?"

"And if our scent is around the nest, they won't stay and eat. Would you deprive them of their midday meal?"

Jaedon shook his head. "The other reason?"

"A hint. What other animals eat goat?" Gershon held out the branch for inspection. But it was a bone, not a branch. He snapped it.

"Lions." Jaedon picked up the two pieces of bone, studied them, and clicked them together. "Let's find targets and practice instead."

They set up a number of objects atop boulders or on tree branches—clods of dirt, a rabbit skin, a stump.

"We will go in order of age, backward," Gershon said, ignoring Jaedon's moan. Miriam suppressed a smile. When would the boy learn patience?

"Watch Dod Lemuel," Gershon told his son. "Track where his arrows go, because you will gather all our arrows before your turn."

Walking slowly to a small clearing, Abba picked up his borrowed bow, laid an arrow against the string, and aimed. His shot flew high and far beyond the row of animal skulls balanced on the stump. Her father had defended Samaria with the sword under Omri and had not lost his strength.

But he often said he was handier with pruning hooks than a bow.

Gershon showed him the aim and stance Dov taught. Her father's next attempts neared the target, but he shook his head and sighed. "Yahweh knew what He was doing when He made me a farmer."

Gershon missed his first shot but shattered a dirt clod with his second. Quickly, he swung and aimed at the rotting rabbit carcass hanging from a tree limb. He missed, took more careful aim, and shot again. Another miss. When he missed two more, he shrugged, rubbed his shoulder, and beckoned to Miriam. "Your turn."

She aimed at the rabbit skin, imagining an Aramean threatening Jaedon. She hit its side, not piercing the skin, but making it spin.

Grinning, Gershon whistled through his teeth. "Next time, dead center."

It wasn't. Her second flew far beyond the tree to the right. But her third, hit the rabbit close to center. She waved her bow above her head, and the men whooped.

"Defender of the city!" her father shouted, pounding her back.

She shot the rest of her arrows, missing all but the last target, a snake skin that whipped around realistically when she hit it.

After Miriam finished, Jaedon ran toward the farthest spot one of her arrows had landed. Her stomach grumbled. Noting the sun's position, she thought they would eat the midday meal when the boy returned. But when he was out of hearing, Gershon turned to her father. "He'll be a while gathering them up. Can we continue last night's conversation?" He motioned toward the shady copse where their provision sack still lay. Miriam would rather do anything than have that conversation again. Her appetite withered.

Lemuel nodded, his mouth a grim line. Miriam felt an urge to help Jaedon gather arrows. She braced herself. She would be present during decision-making concerning her. Gershon gestured to her father. "Make yourself comfortable against the trunk."

Abba sank into the grass and leaned back, his eyes fixed on Gershon.

"Uncle, please forgive my rudeness and stupidity. When I first spoke to Miriam about marriage, messengers could not penetrate Aram's siege. I could not seek your permission. I wanted to marry immediately, but she convinced me to wait through a time of mourning."

Heaving a sigh, Gershon ran his hand through his hair, making it stand on end. "But I have no excuse for not speaking to you later. When Israel triumphed, I should have returned with Caleb to ask your permission. I deserve your censure. But still I ask, will you give me your daughter?"

Miriam felt her lips part. What of his desire to fight with Israel's army? *Don't speak, don't speak.*

Her father's unrelenting gaze held firm. "Do you have anything else to add?"

"Only this." Gershon reached into his empty quiver and pulled out a small scroll. "Here is a copy of the *ketubah.* I have given another to the priest."

Her father reached for the scroll, removed the leather tie, and flicked his eyes down the inked characters. "Hmm. You will protect and care for my daughter? Stay with her the required year to … comfort her?"

"I will."

"Then all is in order." He nodded toward her, his eyes crinkling at the corners. "But—it is Miriam's decision. Do you agree, daughter?"

A sudden movement in the tall grass made them all turn. Jaedon crawled toward them on elbows and belly, clutching the recovered arrows in each hand. Dirt smudged his face, seedpods clung everywhere, and desiccated mustard blooms streaked his back. "Say yes, Miriam, say yes!"

They talked about wedding plans as they ate. "Abba, do you think Seth and Avigail will come?"

"Why do you ask who will come to Jezreel, daughter? The bridegroom comes to your house, to take you to his."

Miriam chewed a morsel of cheese she had just put in

her mouth. "Yes, that is the tradition. Is there a tradition, however, when a widower with a young son remarries?"

"Why would it be different?"

Jaedon leaned forward, but Gershon gave him a little shove and gestured for silence.

"Abba, you are wise. Of course, I will do as you say. But Jaedon needs me. His mother only recently died."

Her father glanced at Jaedon, whose eyes welled up at the reminder of his loss.

"I am needed here. Gershon and Naboth work hard in the vineyard each day. Yaffa can't care for the boy and manage the household alone. If Imma will come—and you— I am content."

Her father snorted. "I will borrow a cart. Your grandmother will not stand for you to be married without her."

Miriam flung her arms around his neck. "Thank you, Abba." She reached for the provision sack, pulled out a honeycomb wrapped in fig leaves, and offered her father the biggest piece. When she glanced at Jaedon, he only smiled.

"When shall we marry?" Gershon asked. "For my part, I would choose tomorrow, but I know women want ... that is ..."

She ended his discomfort. It was no secret that, as a widower, he was more versed in the ways of women than she of men. It seemed a good thing. "I can be ready in two weeks—or when Abba returns with my mother and grandmother."

"It may take two or three weeks—no more," her father assured.

As they continued eating, the wedding conversation turned, a few times, to foolish banter. Miriam's face grew warm, until she feared she'd rival the crimson field flowers. How many brides were compelled to discuss wedding plans with their father, bridegroom, and stepson? Well, it wasn't as if she was surrounded by female friends. She thought of Chloe, even Davita who she'd only recently met. Those two, though only recent acquaintances, were closer friends than any she'd left in Samaria. They, along with Yaffa, Imma, and Savta, would provide womanly wisdom in the coming days.

Miriam smiled to herself as she gathered up their belongings and prepared to go home. No, not *home*. To Yaffa's house. Gershon's house—that would soon be her new home.

Miriam wiped sweat from her face as they trod the dusty road back to Jezreel. Closing her eyes, she tried to evoke the cool, smoothness of the meadow grass, the deep, green shade of the sycamore grove behind them. She opened her eyes again, letting her eyes wander to the shoulder of a mountain, studded with a thicket of pines. It was easier to imagine the coolness of—

"Look there! A traveler." Jaeden pointed at the pines.

A man emerged from the shadows, making for the road ahead. Simply dressed, he carried a small pack.

Gershon pulled the bow off his shoulder and casually transferred it to his right hand. "Probably a shepherd returning home to his family."

Miriam studied the stranger more closely. He didn't carry a staff.

Lemuel came alongside. "Two of us," he said quietly. His bow was in his hand, but Miriam had seen him shoot.

"Three," she said, reaching for her weapon. Jaedon trotted ahead. "Jaedon!" she called sharply. "Get behind us."

He obeyed, surprising her.

"Is that a sword strapped to his waist?" Gershon squinted against the sun. "Wait—" He turned toward her. "It's my brother. It's Kadesh!" And then he slung the bow over his shoulder and started running.

The celebration in the house of Naboth was far more joyous than the grand victory celebration the city held the night before. Yaffa could not stop touching their younger son, and Miriam spotted Naboth dab his eyes before asking Kadesh about spy missions. Jaedon, of course, asked countless questions. When tears, laughter, and exclamations subsided, Gershon announced their decision to marry as soon as word could be gotten to Samaria. At the thought of seeing her mother and grandmother at her wedding, Miriam dabbed her eyes with the edge of her cloak.

The quiet moment after supper was sweet. Was it only because the lost brother was home? Or because her position was finally settled? Even the homey task of cleaning the bowls and cups from supper filled her with gratitude. *Thank you, Yahweh, for the work you have done today.*

The men wanted to carry the wash water to the vineyard to nurture the young vines. Naboth struggled to his feet. Yaffa's eyes drooped with weariness.

"Jaedon and I will help," Miriam said, "No need for everyone to come." Abba's steps had slowed as they walked the steep path to the city, but he would do as he willed.

Gershon helped her to her feet. Hoisting one of the wash pots, he instructed Jaedon to bring the large ladle and a basket. Kadesh carried the second pot, and Miriam took the pitcher.

Still seated, Lemuel rested his hands on his thighs. "I believe you four are sufficient to the task. I'll visit with my brother, then take to my bed. I plan to return to Samaria at daybreak." He cleared his throat. "Jaedon, you must see that Miriam is safe at all times. She is to be your Imma."

The stars were popping out one by one as they walked to the gate. The gatekeeper grumbled at having to open the door again for them, twice in one day. "Come by in the morning," Gershon told him. "In celebration of my betrothal and for your kindness—let me offer a gift—a skin of new wine."

After they emerged the other side of the wall, Kadesh gave his brother's shoulder a playful shove. "That old extortioner! It is his job to man the gate, and surely others need to empty wash water. Better you should drop a ladder from our roof into the vineyard. In celebration for your betrothal indeed." He scoffed.

Gershon laughed. "Are you peeved, my brother, because I did not honor your return sufficiently? Rest assured, I am glad to have you home again—to offer your opinions. A ladder is a fine idea—when we are not toting full water pots."

While the three watered the young vines, Miriam climbed the ladder of old, pruned grapevine to the top of the watch tower. Slowly she circled the platform, admiring the view. Her gaze swept over the mountains, across the valley, and to the darkened cliffs where she could only imagine the eagles' nest. She looked up at the stars dusting the sky, and the sliver of moon, before turning back to the city, with its dark sweep of wall dotted with torches. The winter palace loomed two stories higher than the wall, one balcony underscored by a row of oil lamps. More torches slashed the darkness either side of the balcony.

A lone figure walked onto the upper tier, his looming presence a dark shadow, the torches limning his crown with cold light. He turned, his gaze traveling slowly over the landscape, surveying all which fell under his domain, until it finally settled on the small vineyard in which she stood.

Chapter Fourteen

You have stolen my heart, my sister, my bride;
you have stolen my heart with one glance of your eyes,
with one jewel of your necklace.
~ Song of Songs 4:9

Jezreel
Miriam

THOUGH MIRIAM HAD EXPECTED SUNSHINE IN the hot, sundrenched month of Av, her wedding day dawned dark and wet. Chloe and Davita swept and polished the already clean house. As she helped Yaffa and Savta bake crisp breads studded with raisins and other refreshments for the guests who would drop by with gifts or come later for the feast, Miriam imagined them soaked and bedraggled, their sloshing sandals tracking mud across her aunt's floor.

Stop that. Rain is a blessing—it waters crops, brings fertility ...

The sky continued to weep. Would it never cease? By midday, Miriam lost all hope of a traditional wedding procession through the watery streets.

She sighed as she considered the wedding chair her father had brought for the procession—a gift he had specially made for her. Its high armrests curved invitingly, and carved eagles flew in tandem across its back. Friends of the groom were meant to carry Miriam aloft through the streets, giggling and clinging to this chair, as the wedding party proceeded to Gershon's house where her marriage would be celebrated— the wedding feast, toasts, and dancing into the night. The priest would pronounce his blessing on their union and the couple would retreat to the private bridal chamber where ... their marriage would be consummated. She supposed Yaffa, standing in for Miriam's mother, would show the stained sheet to the priest. Proof of her virginity.

Miriam's cheeks heated, as they had when Abba had given her the chair. A parade through the streets—so many eyes on her, strangers commenting, laughing at this gawky, too-large, too-old bride. Had she ever wanted such a thing? She must have, for when she saw the morning sky the heavy clouds dampened her spirit.

She leaned against the chair and shut her eyes. *Yahweh, is a farmer in dire need of rain? Could you not send it another day?*

A frivolous prayer. Yahweh sent rain where and when it pleased Him. But was it too much that she wanted the tradition every other bride experienced? Had it rained on Rasha's wedding day?

For shame! What a despicable, petty thought toward a dead woman. Even worse, the jealousy beneath, like maggot-infested rot—that her groom had known another wife. Miriam pressed her lips together, blinking back the threat of sudden tears.

What was wrong with her? Why was she not grateful this day had finally come? For her kind bridegroom? For Jaedon, who she already loved as her own?

If her mother were here, what would she say to Miriam's despair over unexpected rain and silly jealousy? Would she tell Miriam these were normal anxieties, experienced by every bride? Or would she rebuke her?

She missed her mother. And she had hoped that Seth would bring Avigail to share a young wife's advice. But her sister-in-law, heavily pregnant and ill, could not come. And Miriam's mother, concerned for Avigail's first child, also stayed behind.

Miriam walked to the window again. Water poured from the roof and fat drops splashed puddles, creating layers of expanding rings. It seemed a farmer needed rain today.

Her grandmother came to stand beside her, feeling her way with a shepherd's staff. "Don't fret my girl." She twined her fingers in Miriam's. "Remember your childhood during the great drought, when all Israel languished in thirst. How can we not rejoice in rain, whenever it falls?"

"Yes, rain is a blessing." Chloe took Miriam's other arm, pulling her away from the window. "Come, my friend. You must not spot your beautiful blue tunic. And your bridegroom must not find you watching, like an over-eager—

"

"Spinster?" Davita filled in with a chuckle. "Not our lovely Miriam. No, that will be me, should my wedding ever come about."

"Davita, dear, your day will come," Yaffa said. Because of the archery training, the three girls had become inseparable, meeting several times each week to practice. Davita's troublesome aunt protested this freedom, but her father surprised them all by sending her back to her own home, saying her new friends were a better influence than his prickly sister. And Yaffa had warmed to the motherless girl despite her earlier brashness.

Savta, in spite of her blindness, turned unerringly in Davita's direction. "Come here, young woman." Davita complied and then stood wide-eyed as the grandmother's fingers trailed down her hair and across the planes of her face. "Yaffa is right. You are comely enough," she announced, the testimony of her touch accurate and eerie. "If you do what we tell you, you will be married by winter."

"Praise God!" Davita winked at Miriam. "I am of adequate comeliness, and if I marry in winter, my husband must stay home a year to comfort me—and miss the war entirely." She laughed. "Sufficient incentive for a handsome soldier, weary of war."

Chloe simultaneously blushed and giggled.

Miriam smiled, but talk of avoiding the war still stung, with the whole of Israel preparing to take back Aphek. And Gershon's eyes held a faraway look when his brother talked of spy missions among the enemy.

But talk of war was not the only uncomfortable topic. Yaffa and Savta proceeded to give perplexing yet embarrassing advice about the wedding night, while Davita and Chloe smirked, teased, and added their own uninformed and slightly wanton opinions. This was when she most missed Imma and Avigail.

Despite the teasing, as the hour approached when wedding guests were expected, Miriam enjoyed the camaraderie between the younger and older women. It was like mornings at the well, when the city's women lingered to talk as they filled their water jugs, not concerned, during those stolen moments, about men's opinions or household tasks.

The tightness in Miriam's throat eased. These women the Lord had brought into her life! When girlhood friends had turned on her, she had only family for companionship. She had tried not to care that marriage passed her by, but now the day had arrived—albeit covered with clouds—and she was flanked by these friends.

And if she did not have her mother and sister-in-law, she did have *some* family to celebrate with her. Her father and Caleb had brought her grandmother in a cart, along with household linens she and Imma had woven—sheets, towels, and blankets for winter. Their gifts were stacked by the door, all except the blue wedding tunic she wore. Miriam smoothed the cloth over her thighs, pleased anew at its soft, pliable texture. The tunic replicated her grandmother's wedding garment and, Savta boasted, was dyed according to her specific list of flowers and herbs.

Chloe picked up her harp and played a tune without structure, somehow akin to the pattering rainfall. The music colored the afternoon with happiness, made even the words they spoke melodious, almost translucent. Like rain drops.

While Miriam relaxed to the music, Davita coaxed her to sit in the wedding chair. She unbraided Miriam's hair, loosening the waves with gentle fingers. "Your hair is so pretty. You should always wear it loose."

Miriam reached back and patted Davita's hand. "You are kind, my friend."

Yaffa served the women raisin cakes and honeyed water before sitting opposite Miriam. "It is customary for the mother of the groom to also give practical advice to the bride. Daughter, I am so happy you agreed to be Gershon's wife. He is an easy man to please if his supper is there when he returns from the vineyard."

Miriam couldn't help it, her eyebrows shot up, remembering his ire when she took actions without consulting him first—or when he imagined she did.

Yaffa tilted her head and chuckled. "I know, I know, but that is my piece of advice. You already know all my recipes. Hadassah, have you something to offer?"

Savta nodded, folding her hands like a sage. "There are three secrets that guarantee a wife will please her husband." Her grandmother paused, and Davita and Chloe leaned forward. "Unfortunately, Eve took her secrets to the grave."

Davita and Chloe laughed aloud, which would greatly advance them in Savta's estimation. Miriam smiled, having heard that piece of wisdom from her grandmother's lips at several weddings. Another piece was yet coming. One that would be hers alone.

"I have two more pieces of wisdom for you, my girl, from the man purported to be the wisest who ever lived. I'm not entirely convinced of that claim, but King Solomon did have the benefit—or detriment—of a thousand women to learn from."

Miriam grinned. Savta had always been ambivalent about Solomon.

"He said, 'Finishing is better than starting' and 'Patience is better than pride,' words pertinent to marriage but also to nearly everything else in life. Simple words, but with these, the king may have deserved his reputation. Live by those words each day, and you will finish well."

Miriam's grandmother had modeled that proverb throughout her life. She never left a job unfinished. The daughter of a scribe, she patiently taught her grandchildren, even Miriam, to read and write, using a scroll of the Torah her father had copied. When she had begun to lose her eyesight, she had pushed Miriam even harder, though she was young enough to want to run outside after her older brothers, rather than study. Miriam reached for her grandmother's hand and held it.

Savta paused. "On the day of my wedding, my father whispered to me, 'Speak these words to your husband on the day you are wed, and he will be bound to your heart forever.'" And then she leaned forward and whispered in Miriam's ear.

"Not fair!" Davita protested. "Unless you will be my grandmother, too?"

Savta leaned back and folded her hands across her stomach. "The guests are coming."

"Can you indeed hear them, Hadassah?" Yaffa strode over to the window.

Having grown up with her blind grandmother a member of the household, Miriam had no doubt. Savta also had an uncanny ability, her grandchildren learned early, to discern lies from truth.

"I heard voices." Tilting her ear toward the street, Savta added, "And now, footsteps."

Yaffa smoothed her tunic and opened the door, ready to receive the first callers. "Shalom. Thank you so much for coming—and oh, a gift—how generous. Please set it over there," she repeated to each new arrival. "Samuel, Jaedon will be happy to see you, when he comes with his father."

Chloe whispered, "Sit still, Miriam. All you need do is speak to your friends when they pass by to greet you. Davita and I will see to the food and drink."

The house quickly filled with rain-soaked guests, who ate, drank, and rejoiced with harp music and song. The corner of the front room filled with an amazing pile of wedding gifts—pottery, lengths of cloth, wooden utensils, a laying hen in a crate, even a lamb, bleating loudly for its mother. The chicken and the lamb, first paraded in front of Miriam and the other wedding guests, did not go to the corner with the other gifts, but were taken to the courtyard.

Aching from sitting so long, Miriam got up and strolled around the room, thanking individuals for attending the celebration, for their gifts, and their well-wishes. She had never met the elderly neighbor Elishama, who brought an intricately embroidered shawl. She laughed and clapped for young Samuel who performed his short-legged version of a wedding dance, accompanied by a pipe-playing shepherd.

Miriam listened in vain for sounds of Gershon's arrival, and the patter of rain grew less insistent. She glanced at Savta for confirmation, but she was engrossed in a chat with Samuel's mother. Soon patches of sunlight darted through the west-facing window, dappling the room. And then the shofar sounded.

Her bridegroom was coming! Like fingers walking down her spine, she felt the horn's proclamation, his imminent presence, even her changing status. Soon she would step from one world into another.

Chloe darted over to fuss with Miriam's unbound hair,

dab her lips with dregs of red wine, and drape the veil over her head. Miriam fingered a necklace of silver and amber beads, Gershon's wedding present, along with matching earrings that dangled from her ears. Her grandmother began singing a wedding song, quickly joined by Yaffa, more hesitantly by Chloe and Davita, who did not know the words, but still wove their voices into the melody. Soon all the guests were singing, but Miriam's heart thudded with something like fear, though she was not afraid, no, not at all. Still it thudded, as if to make itself known.

"Miriam! *Ishti.*"

She ran to the door.

Gershon stood in the courtyard, her handsome bridegroom. His dark hair and neatly trimmed beard streamed rainwater. He wore the long-sleeved garment, once-spotless white, she had helped Yaffa weave. That it was now streaked with rain, spoiled his appearance not at all. Her father, Dod Naboth, Kadesh, and Caleb stood near Gershon, and more of his friends clustered behind, spilling into the street. Several carried long poles, canopies stretched between them. Did she hear the clip-clop of hooves beyond?

Dod Naboth spread his hands wide and prayed. "Blessed are you, Adonai, Ruler of the Universe, we ask you to gladden the hearts of this man and this woman as you gladdened the first couple in the garden of Eden ..."

Miriam's eyes fluttered as her father-in-law continued. A rain-dampened breeze blew the translucent veil against her face, blurring the scene into a dreamlike mist.

Miriam's father walked slowly forward, then said, "When our ancestor Abraham sought a wife for his son Isaac, God said He would send His angel ahead to help the search. He said the maid must be willing to return with the servant to live with Isaac in God's Promised Land. But her relatives wanted her to stay with them. And so the servant asked her, 'Will you go to this man and be his wife?'"

Once more Miriam fingered her beads. "I answer as Rebecca did. I will go."

Gershon walked close, taking her hands in his. "The teacher wrote, 'The man who finds a wife finds a treasure, and he receives favor from the Lord.' And 'Who can find a

virtuous and capable wife? She is more precious than rubies.'
I have found these in you, my love."

She had not known what words he would speak to her.
A treasure. More precious than rubies. She had heard her
parents recite these words to each other, sometimes
chuckling when they did so. Suddenly, she was aware of
silence, of all eyes fixed on her. She was to speak!

She blinked several times, trying to remember the first
line, then she blurted, "'Two people are better off than one,
my love, for they can help each other succeed. If one falls
down, the other can reach out and help. But pity the one who
falls and has no one to help him up. Likewise, if two lie down
together, they will keep warm. But how can one keep warm
alone?'" Hearing soft chuckles, she halted, feeling heat rise
to her face. Swallowing a cough, she continued. "'Though one
may be overpowered, two can defend themselves. A cord of
three strands is not quickly broken.' May Yahweh be the
center, the everlasting third cord, binding our union."

Soft murmurs filled the pause. Then someone said,
"Better check under the veil."

"Yes, don't be fooled like Jacob was by Leah. Make sure
you have the right bride."

Then Gershon moved his hands to her shoulders, lifted
her veil, and bent his face close. "I have found everything in
you," he whispered. "*Ishti.* My beautiful, capable bride."

And then he kissed her. Warm lips on hers, mustache
tickling her nose, her veil draping over their heads, secluding
them in a misty world. A strange, hitherto unknown
sensation.

Shouts of congratulations filled the room and they were
hugged, jostled, and separated as the well-wishers hustled
Miriam, her protests choked by laughter, to the wedding
chair. Gershon and Kadesh tied poles to its legs, stretched a
canopy across, and grasped the chair. It swayed precariously
as they hoisted it to their shoulders. Jaedon ran over,
shouting he wanted to help carry *Imma Miriam.* Grabbing
hold of a corner leg, he nearly toppled them backwards.

Dov hurried out of the crowd and handed Jaedon a flag
of many colors. "This is for you, little man. Don't forget that
white pony outside waiting for you to ride ahead and clear a

path for the bride."

When had Jaedon learned to ride a pony?

Dov took the boy by the hand and headed outside, grinning over his shoulder before they disappeared.

Arguing about who would help first, Gershon's friends pressed forward. Gershon pointed. "You and you," and two brothers helped steady her chair. After they pranced a practice circle in the house, they squeezed through the front door. Cheers erupted outside, and more musicians, a few she recognized and others she didn't, began playing the processional song with pipes, reeds, and drums, punctuated every so often by a blast of the shofar. She looked for Chloe, thinking she might play her harp, but she and Davita hurried forward with burning oil lamps.

Miriam clung to the chair, gasping as they made their way through the crowd in the courtyard and the well-wishers lining the street. She saw Dov, on Uriel, the bay she had named. Beside him, Jaedon sat on a fat white pony with flowers braided into its mane and tail. A long lead looped from Dov's hand to the pony's bridle.

"Look at me, Miriam!" Jaeden called. He waved his flag. "I'll clear the way for you."

A wagon rattled over the cobblestones, pulling up behind Davita and Chloe. Naboth and Caleb helped Savta and Yaffa climb inside. Savta protested she could walk the short distance, but Naboth said, "Would you deprive me of the great joy of driving this conveyance through the streets?" He gallantly spread his cloak over wet cushions and offered Savta his arm.

Muttering something that sounded like "contraption not conveyance," Savta settled into the vehicle.

They proceeded through the streets, picking up more followers as they went. Would the whole city crowd into Gershon's house for the feast? Some were dancing already, kicking their way through puddles, ignoring the falling rain.

Miriam turned to Gershon, smiling. "Your canopy has kept me dry. I was afraid—"

"Aach!" Gershon yelped as he stumbled, his side of the chair plunged, and the canopy collapsed, dousing Miriam with its contents.

Miriam sputtered, coughed, and reached under her veil to palm water off her face. Seeing the expression on his face, she burst out laughing.

Gershon bowed his head. "I'm sorry, Ishti. You were afraid you would get wet, and now you are soaked."

Ishti. My wife. She could grow used to hearing those words on his tongue.

"No." She smiled through the veil. "I was afraid I would not have the procession, like every other bride. Vanity, I suppose."

"Of course you would want the tradition."

Miriam playfully shook water from her veil, splashing Gershon and her other bearers. And then she gasped. A shimmering rainbow painted the sky.

Chapter Fifteen

When you go to war against your enemies and see
horses and chariots and an army greater than yours,
do not be afraid of them, because the Lord your God,
who brought you up out of Egypt, will be with you.
~ Deuteronomy 20:1

Tishri, eight months later
Dov

DARK CLOUDS LINED THE MOUNTAINS BEYOND Jezreel, promising rain on the morrow. Although there were hours before dusk, Dov dismissed the men and officers that met regularly in the fields below the city. They had practiced hard today. "But even if it rains in the morning, we will meet to practice," he said. "The time grows near for the battle the prophet predicted—and it sometimes rains during war."

Though he heard a few groans, the men smiled and waved as they made for home. They had gained military discipline as well as skill in the past months. They were soldiers.

He chatted with the officers as he prepared to go home, pleased to hear positive reports about their teams. As he picked up his gear, he noticed a man striding out of the forest. "Kadesh!"

Dov ran between the wheat fields along the swath of dirt the farmer had left for Dov's soldiers. "Shalom." He greeted Gershon's brother with a kiss on each cheek. "What did you learn?"

"I spent months scouting routes the Arameans might use to attack, but when I heard rumors of a great army on the march from the north, I secretly tracked their advance. They are heading for the plain near the Israelite city of Aphek. War is imminent. We either face them, or they take Aphek and begin picking off other cities on the plain. This is where we must take our stand."

"I agree. Do you know where they will make camp? What

is the lay of the land?"

Kadesh looked around, picked up a stone, and dropped to his knees in a clay-like patch of earth between the fields.

"This is the sea of Chinnereth." He sketched a rough oval with the stone. "The city is here"—he jabbed his finger in the dirt about a palm's width from the oval—"about three miles east of the sea, and north of"—he dragged his finger across the dirt in a wavy diagonal—"the Yarmuk River. You can marshal your forces right here." An ant strode busily across the area carrying a grain of wheat. Kadesh waited for it to cross safely, then scrabbled the rock back and forth several times, indicating an area between the city of Aphek and the Aramean camp. "Get there before the Arameans, so you can choose your spot protecting the city."

Dov nodded slowly as he studied the map. "I can set up a supply line through here." He scraped a route from Jezreel through the Harod Valley then pivoted north.

Kadesh nodded. "Good. You will camp here—there's a narrow pass and a steep incline to the plain, so supplies must come through your rear guard. Less chance of enemy intercept. Is King Ahab still at the capital?"

"Yes. When your messenger arrived, the king sent me to Jezreel with half the troops. He will follow in a day or two with the chariots and more troops. Tell me—what led you to believe Aram would not attack Samaria again?"

"My father's wine works wonders around a campfire. My Aramean is such I can pass for one of them. At more than one campfire I heard that Yahweh, a god of the mountains, is powerless on the plains."

Kadesh drew another long oval east of the Sea of Chinnereth. "Many mountains around Samaria. So, I assumed the Arameans would stage their battle on a plain. They are headed here." He scooped pebbles and dribbled them over the enemy camp. Then he scooped another handful to indicate a larger camp.

Dov's throat went dry. "How many?"

Kadesh scratched his head, frowning. "Not sure you want to hear."

"Tell me."

"A hundred fifty, maybe two hundred thousand. How

many did you recruit while I reconnoitered?"

Dov whistled softly through his teeth. Kadesh should have spread grains of sand, not pebbles, in the enemy camp. "Not enough. To make it harder, the maidens of Jezreel have captured some of my best soldiers."

Kadesh chuckled. "And now your soldiers are too busy "comforting their wives" to go to war? I heard there were several weddings while I scouted. I saw you at my brother's. I also heard there was one bold maiden who aimed for your heart."

Dov smiled, careful not to glance back at the city and relieved that Kadesh spoke lightly. It simplified a reply.

"I would not say bold. A *beautiful* maiden, also wise. She chose a handsome young merchant with a thriving trade." Kyra had been both bold and beautiful. Not an unattractive combination, but Dov planned to stay clear of all marriageable women.

"I see. You told her you are a career soldier." Kadesh shook his head ruefully. "The Arameans are a war machine, that is certain. Men like you—like us—never marry. So long as our enemies seek to destroy Israel, we are wed to war."

"True. But it was in jest I spoke of the maidens. Only a handful have wed this year, not enough to turn the war. We must have faith in Yahweh."

"Do you doubt?"

Dov paused, chewing on the question. "If I waver, I remind myself of last year when, far outnumbered, we chased our enemy out of Samaria."

Kadesh studied him. "You grew up an orphan on the streets. You were always a fighter."

"But not on the streets for long. Maalik took me in." Dov dribbled a few pebbles in the area Kadesh had suggested for the Israelite camp. Here was Israel's army, small and ill-supplied. There was Aram, glutted with men and chariots. The grim comparison hollowed his insides like those early days, scrabbling for food on the streets.

"Dov, before you ever joined the king's archers, you were an experienced fighter. A career soldier, in anyone's book. And you just said you trust in the Lord."

"And I do. But each time this prophet appears, his face

is covered. How do we know he isn't a follower of Ba'al, seeking revenge for their losses at Mount Carmel?"

"To me, it is not surprising any prophet covers his face when speaking for Yahweh—Jezebel still leads followers of the fertility cults. But I don't understand your uncertainty, especially since you were on the front lines of the battle. You know the prophet spoke the Lord's truth. Do you think this is a different prophet? A false one?"

Dov lifted a shoulder. "Not really. I am nearly sure he is Micaiah."

"I have met him in my travels—one of the schools of prophets in the wilderness where they teach and encourage each other. Micaiah is an honest man, full of Yahweh's spirit." Kadesh smiled. "Perhaps you suffer from pre-battle nerves."

Dov threw back his head and laughed. "Perhaps."

"My friend, you may fear your army is small, but think how Yahweh thinned Gideon's forces, from twenty-two thousand to three hundred. He said, 'You have too many warriors. If I let all of you fight the Midianites, Israel will boast they saved themselves.' Be glad there's no danger you will make such a boast."

Dov groaned. "Thank you for your encouragement."

Kadesh gave him a playful shove, nearly causing Dov to sprawl over the map. "If you haven't as many chariots as the Arameans, you have more than last year. Their chariots, their weapons."

"For such a slight man, you swat like a bear."

"Arm-wrestling at Aramean campfires."

They chuckled, but then the spy's countenance grew serious. "I have more to say you may not find as encouraging. But you need to know everything I learned."

"Tell me."

"The Arameans learned from their loss last summer."

Dov slapped his knee. "Thus their decision to threaten Aphek. Force us to fight them on a plain."

"Yes. The terrain is favorable for their wheeled and mounted troops. But even more, Aphek has ties to the Arameans of Damascus. Damascene traders constantly come and go. Some reside in the city or farm on the plain. Which is not to say there aren't loyal Israelites in Aphek. I have not detected internal strife. But you can't count on the complete loyalty of the citizens."

This was not what Dov wanted to hear. And Kadesh looked poised to continue. Dov sighed. "Is there more campfire talk?"

"The thirty-two kings have been replaced by experienced generals. Ben-Hadad considered the kings weak and more devoted to their feudal lands than to the coalition. He has rebuilt his armed forces to full strength." Kadesh paused, his forehead creased in thought. "What was it Yahweh said before the last battle? 'Do you see all these enemy forces? Today I will hand them all over to you. Then you will know—'"

Dov finished the Lord's promise. "'Then you will know that I am the Lord.' You are saying—no prophet of the Ba'als would give the glory to Yahweh. This prophet, though he hid his face, proclaimed the one true God. And we obeyed. Attacked with less experienced officers. Now we have raised an army as the Lord told us and are prepared to fight as He directs."

Kadesh grinned. "Now you speak with confidence."

Dov bent over the map, paying special attention to the markings where Kadesh had drawn the two armies. Dov would trust in the Lord and count on His prophet. He had told Dov to raise an army and prepare for battle, and he had done so. Now, to the best of his ability, he would devise a battle plan. And here with him was a man familiar with the landscape of the battlefield.

"What is beyond this stretch of plain, farther east?"

"Low hills, with a wadi beyond."

Dov felt excitement building. "You know the terrain better than I. Would it be possible to"—he drew a line branching east from the supply route—"send chariots and foot soldiers up this wadi—"

"And circle behind the Aramean encampment?" Kadesh threw his hands in the air. "A two-pronged attack. Brilliant!"

"Could our men lie in wait there, undetected, until the battle begins?"

"Yes. They would be well hidden. The wadi is deep, and

the hills, though not steep, are covered with brush. There is a break in the hill—only a slight rise, easy for chariots to ascend." Kadesh drew a curved line through the hills, back into the northern side of the battlefield. "When the battle begins, your rear force will hear the shofars and come over the hills. And you will crush the enemy between your two divisions like a vise."

chapter Sixteen

*The man of God came up and told the king of Israel,
"This is what the Lord says: 'Because the Arameans
think the Lord is a god of the hills and not a god of
the valleys, I will deliver this vast army into your
hands, and you will know that I am the Lord.'"*
~ 1 Kings 20:28

A gorge near the approach of Aphek
Dov

FOR FOUR DAYS, DOV'S MEN HAD hunkered down in the gorge.
He didn't have a good feeling about the rain, which had fallen
steadily on the last two nights of the standoff. Men and
horses slipped, feet became encased in mud, and there was
danger of broken bones, or worse. Still, Dov rode his
surefooted bay down the line of soldiers, quietly alerting them
to be ready to attack on his command.

He marshaled his thoughts to the present dilemma. The
Arameans had established themselves on the plateau before
the Israelites arrived, foiling Dov's plan to establish their
camp first. The enemy guarded the only entrance to the
plain, this steep gorge which narrowed at the top to less than
the width of a city gate. The situation was not going according
to plan—at least not according to Dov's plan. He gazed up at
the watery sky. *Yahweh, what is Your plan?*

It was not as if he hadn't prayed for guidance before, but
the heavens had been silent. Still, the silence had been that
of a commander who had already given orders, expecting to
be obeyed. But what to do next? Dov had followed Yahweh's
instructions, but here they were in the muck.

Suddenly Uriel sidestepped, tossed his head, and
whinnied. A hooded figure materialized from the dark. "Take
me to the king. I have a message from the Lord."

A sheet of lightning lit the man's covered face, but Dov
would have recognized the voice of the prophet anyway.

"Micaiah?"

"Now is not the time to reveal my name."

Nor any time, it seemed. Yet, the prophet had appeared only moments after Dov's prayer.

"All right," Dov said. "Ride with me." He slid his foot from the stirrup and reached to assist the prophet. When he was secure behind the saddle, Dov turned his horse's nose downhill.

The king slept in a tent guarded by two soldiers. When roused, he quickly emerged with the instant lucidity of a seasoned soldier. Dov slid to the ground and saluted. The king enjoyed his comforts, but he was not soft.

King Ahab stared at the prophet, still atop the horse. As Dov helped him dismount, the prophet slid his hand across the horse's neck. It turned to nuzzle him. The prophet whispered in Uriel's ear.

"You have a message for me?" the king asked.

"This is what the Lord says: 'Because the Arameans think the Lord is a god of the hills and not of the valleys, I will deliver this vast army into your hands, and you will know that I am the Lord.'"

The king nodded, as if waiting for further instructions. When none came, he turned to Dov. "The path is no less slippery, I presume?"

"More so."

"What say you? Shall we wait for the rain to stop?"

Dov had not grown used to the king asking his opinion. Each time it happened, he found himself gaping like a callow youth. He drew a breath and plunged in. "We should immediately do what the Lord has said. He is with us."

"Follow your original plan?"

"With adjustment for rain. If we send chariots up this slick defile, we risk serious accidents. The horses would attempt to drag them through the mud, but going up such a steep incline, the vehicles would need soldiers to push from behind. If they overturned, or began to slide back down, well—"

"What then?" The king responded curtly.

"Half our forces—soldiers, spearmen, and archers— attack through the narrows as planned." Dov paused and then pointed northeast. "But *all* chariots and the remaining forces maneuver behind the Aramean army, prepared to attack down the Golan slope when they hear the shofar." Dov detailed routes the chariots could take to the flanking position.

Ahab rubbed his hands together as if warming them, though the rain was not cold. Then he laughed. "With my chariot, I have the better side of the battle," he said. "A good plan, Dov. You lead the main force. We will go immediately and stand ready to surprise Ben-Hadad's troops from the rear."

The king sent his two guards to inform the charioteers and divide the remaining forces into two divisions. Dov turned to the prophet, "Shall I have someone take you home or will you wait?"

"I know the outcome," he said. "And I am not far from my fellows."

Dov watched as the prophet set off without another word. Lightning struck a tall tree, starting a fire in its uppermost branches. The prophet walked on, undeterred. The rain intensified, drops hissing as they hit the burning tree.

Thunder crashed and Uriel plunged about in the mud. "Steady, fellow," he soothed, stroking the animal's neck. "We've more than thunder to face tonight, you and me. Don't fail me now."

Horse and man watched the sky as lightning flashed once more, this time a sheet that trembled a long time in the sky like the surface of Chinnereth in a squall. It backlit the prophet as he departed the ridge and melted into the trees.

Chapter Seventeen

*Have you visited the storehouses of the snow or seen the
storehouses of the hail, which I reserve for times of trouble,
for days of war and battle. What is the way to the place
where the lightning is dispersed, or the place where the
east winds are scattered over the earth? Who cuts a
channel for the torrents of rain, and a path for the
thunderstorm, to water a land were no
man lives, a desert with no one in it?*
~ *Job 38:22-26*

*At the Israelite Base Camp, bottom of the gorge near the city
of Aphek*
Dov

"WE ATTACK AT FIRST LIGHT," DOV said.

Water streamed from Dov's helmet and his horse Uriel,
standing beside him, shook a spray of water from its neck.
Dov eyed the black shapes of foot soldiers and horsemen
huddled outside his tent like a scruffy flock of half-drowned
sheep. Sheep, when he needed a pack of wolves. Many
inexperienced fighters, despite a year of training. He had
demanded hard work and practice, but sparring with wooden
swords among friends was nothing like facing the enemy.
With no practical experience, would it be enough?

"You may have noticed the rain."

Quiet laughter was muted still more by the downpour.

"And that all our chariots have left."

No laughter followed this announcement.

"Chariots would not make it up this gorge, with the slick
footing the rain brought. The king took the chariots and will
circle the enemy's flank. We bear the frontal attack. We must
break through the Arameans guarding the neck of the
gorge—and we will."

Dov's horse pawed impatiently, splattering mud in an
arc over his armor. Taking a moment to settle the animal,
Dov sluiced water from its face. He prayed the king was well

on his way to the Golan ridge. The footing must be slippery the whole way.

"It's true, we did not expect the Arameans to entrench themselves at the neck of the gorge. You all know Kadesh the scout. He thought if we left immediately, we could choose our position—rally near the city. But the Arameans beat us here. Yet the plan we discussed stands, with only minor changes."

Dov explained the strategy, still based on dividing the troops and surprising the Arameans with a dual frontal and rear attack. "The main differences being, all the chariots will amass behind the Arameans. The mild Golan slope can be driven, despite rain.

"Men, we have the more difficult task. Mud, and a lot of it. But we are strong, determined, and Yahweh promised to give us the battle. We will rush the pass despite the conditions, taking the enemy by surprise."

Dov looked toward heaven, breathing a quick prayer for wisdom. "I have heard you say, 'We are like a flock of goats against them.' And this is true. But remember last year, when the Lord promised us victory. He said, 'Then you will know that I am the Lord.' We won then and will win now."

"But divided, we will be two even smaller flocks of goats." In the darkness, Dov could not identify the voice that came from the crowd. Nervous laughter rumbled through the company, melding with a roll of thunder.

Fear stalked their number. How could he help them? His bedraggled army needed more than strategy. *Yahweh, help me encourage your people.*

"That is true. Yet you, little flock, must break through their barricade and engage the enemy's attention. When the king's chariots attack from the rear, the Arameans will be shaken. Never forget that Yahweh vowed by His own name to give us the victory. Though your force is small, attack with vigor. Call out the name of Yahweh as you attack. Remind the Arameans of their fatal mistake in belittling our God. He is not, as they say, a god only of the mountains. He is God over all."

Then Dov began to pray aloud, lines he remembered from the battle prayer of King David.

The LORD is my rock, my fortress, and my savior;

my God is my rock, in whom I find protection.
I called on the LORD, who is worthy of praise,
and he saved me from my enemies.

Dov looked toward heaven. Rain poured over his face and into the neck of his bronze armor. Voices joined his, words Maalik had drummed into his six-year-old head.

The Lord thundered from heaven; the voice of the Most High resounded;
He shot arrows and scattered his enemies;
his lightning flashed, and they were confused.
He reached down from heaven and rescued me,
from those who hated me and were too strong for me.

The heavens crackled at the mention of thunder. Dov shivered, although the rain was warm. The air around them felt charged. The soldiers needed to hear these words, and Dov needed to speak them.

The rain's tempo lessened. A cheer broke out. Though he could not see Caleb in the dark mass of soldiers, he recognized his voice leading the chant. "For Yahweh! For the Lord!"

Too loud. Despite the storm, the enemy guarding the neck of the gorge must have heard. Not what Dov wanted. Not yet, when he had planned for a surprise attack. But hadn't he asked, *Yahweh, what is your plan?*

So be it.

"Men, arm yourselves. We will not wait for first light. Trumpeters, sound the shofars as soon as we top the ridge. We attack now!"

Activity churned around him as soldiers seized shields, spears, strapped on swords, and slung bows over their shoulders. Spearmen and shield bearers charged together up the hill, their gait awkward and plunging in the slick mud. The bowmen, Caleb somewhere among them, followed on their heels.

"Archers, kneel! Fire." The bowmen obeyed, sending a storm of arrows over the heads of their fellow soldiers.

Screams from atop the hill declared arrows had hit their marks.

Swordsmen, slingers, and axmen crowded past the

archers, growling their anticipation of meeting the enemy in hand-to-hand combat. Shofars boomed a war cry. "Louder!" Dov shouted. "Let the message reach our king."

"Archers, spearmen, up the hill. It's up to us. Push your way through. Make a path for the others." Dov drew his sword and followed through nearly blinding rain, his bay the lead horse on the hill. He had instructed the other horsemen to follow only if his horse reached the top without mishap. But he trusted Uriel's surefootedness. If any horse could make it, this one could.

As Israel's first soldiers swarmed over the hilltop, the din of battle filled his ears. Clashing swords, agonized shrieks. Arrows whizzed overhead. Gripping his sword, Dov bellowed orders, warnings, and encouragement. Halfway up the narrow path, the bay slipped under him and struggled to regain its footing. Its hindquarters lurched sideways as it lost traction, then it thrashed and strained its neck forward. With a mighty surge, the horse regained its purchase and crested the hill surrounded by Israelite swordsmen.

An enemy aimed his spear at the bay's chest. One of Dov's swordsmen charged the warrior. At the same time, a shield bearer stepped in front of Dov's horse, fending off the threat. Felled by the sword, the enemy spearman dropped into the mud.

Several Arameans surrounded two Israelites who fought back to back. Their swords set up a clanging brawl. The Israelites fought at double speed while the enemy pushed closer. Dov urged his horse into the thick of the skirmish. It trampled one Aramean and Dov's sword dispatched another.

He reached for his bow, glancing behind at the entrance to the plain. More Israelites had gained the top of the hill, but the enemy opposed them resolutely. Dov shouted, "Follow me, men." The Israelites intensified their efforts, under a cloudburst almost as fierce. Drops shot up from puddles. Soldiers in both armies staggered like drunks through mud that tore at their sandals.

Where was Caleb? Dov glanced over his shoulder and spotted him at the forefront of the archers, who moved shoulder to shoulder. He was well situated with his fellows, at least for the moment.

The fighting intensified. Dov pushed the bay further into the battle, watching for Israelites in trouble. When in close combat, he used his sword. But he grabbed his bow when he spotted unequal skirmishes across the field.

Dov shot three Arameans in quick succession, his arrows felling them like trees. He reined his horse around, taking in the lay of the battle. His army was outnumbered, but they fought boldly, as though they held the upper hand. Dov spotted a stout Israelite wielding an axe, laying the enemy flat in an ever-widening circle. He reminded Dov of— no, it couldn't be—he had repeatedly denied Aaron's demands to join the attack force, telling the old man he was needed to guard Jezreel's wall. That stubborn, insubordinate, order-flouting—just then the axe man took five running steps toward a sword-wielding Aramean. No limp! Not Aaron, then—but the build, the swing—

The stout axe man engaged with the taller swordsman. Though his opponent's reach was longer, the broad-shouldered soldier was undeterred. He ducked the first slash, swinging his axe up to clash with the return slice. The sword flew from the Aramean's hand, and in a blur of movement, the axe buried deep in his chest. The Israelite yanked it loose and wheeled to face his next opponent.

Dov urged his horse forward, mowing down Aramean warriors who blocked his path. Despite the significant force guarding the neck of the gorge, his soldiers had fought their way through. Dov estimated they had overcome more than half the blockade, pushed back the rest. Though the remaining Arameans fought savagely, the Israelites met their attack blow for blow.

The axe wielder was again surrounded by the enemy. Swords drawn, they prudently kept their distance as he taunted them to come on. One lunged forward, shrieked, then fell cradling his forearm—minus a hand. Aaron's lookalike threw back his head and howled triumphantly. Dov half laughed, half growled as he drew his bow. There was his wolf!

He urged the bay toward them, his progress obstructed by an ever-increasing storm of opponents. Dodging the encounters, he fixed his attention on the Israelite. His manner of wielding his axe was too like Dov's old friend Aaron to be coincidence. A student? Brother? Whoever he was, Dov must help if he could.

The rain nearly blinding him, Dov sent arrows into two more attackers. A shield bearer thrust up a handful of arrows he'd retrieved from the battlefield. Dov grabbed them and swept his gaze across the plain. The axe man yanked his weapon from another opponent's body. A jagged lightning bolt lit the landscape. Dov made out tents on the horizon—the main Aramean camp, where Kadesh had said they would be. They had split their forces too—the troops guarding the pass, and these on the plain. Indistinct figures emerged, flooding toward the battle. Far to the left, Dov spotted the line of a wall. A lightning flash revealed the city of Aphek.

Another strike illuminated movement, shadowy horses milling about. *Flash.* Soldiers mounted. *Boom. Flash.* Shofars resounded behind him. Shouting for his troops to follow, he wheeled the bay and hurtled toward Aaron's kin—and the charging Aramean cavalry.

The clash of army and cavalry was terrible. Awful, in Dov's ears, the shrieking whinnies of injured horses. But the lives of his men were far more precious. His army was outnumbered and mostly afoot. More enemy horsemen galloped towards them. And near the tents, soldiers harnessed horses to Aramean chariots. Several began wheeling toward the battle.

I called on the Lord—He reached down from heaven— rescued me from my powerful enemies—

Yahweh, help us!

Though he couldn't find Caleb, he noticed Israelite archers and shield bearers teaming up, as they had practiced, pushing into the conflict to pick off the enemy as they could. A flame kindled in Dov's chest, fiery pride in his men, these inexperienced fighters. Before his eyes, they were becoming warriors.

Then a shofar sounded from the north. Dov gasped in relief when the attacking Aramean chariots wavered and turned aside as if to retreat. When another lightning flash backlit chariots streaming down the Golan slopes, the reason became apparent. Ahab's flank attack! The chariots captured in last year's victory, many of them still painted in national Aramean designs, were at the forefront.

The Arameans that had retreated from the pass to the plain looked to their cavalry for aid. But the enemy horsemen had also halted in apparent indecision. Did they think the chariots were their own reinforcements? They churned about, finally circling to face in both directions. Ahab's chariot force advanced on the plain, more foot troops and horsemen running behind.

Lightning flashed again. The Arameans panicked when they realized Israelites, not their countrymen, were driving the chariots, and they were boxed in from two sides. When the two armies clashed, the din vied with thunder and rain. Iron clanged against iron, chariots screeched as they came together, horses squealed. As the torrent increased, the battle turned. Arameans fell like wheat to a scythe, and Israelites flailed the retreating army. A shofar blew.

Israelites shouted, "The Lord, He is God of the plains." Then the enemy broke ranks and swarmed toward the city, ants fleeing a torched hill. "The Lord, He is God of the mountains. The Lord, He is God of all."

The retreating chariots and horses, being fastest, reached the city first. Why did the gate stand open—a traitor's bribe? Too many chariots vied for the opening, crashing against each other, tangling like toys. The wheel of one chariot went deep into the muck and with a reverberating crack, the axel broke.

But it was the storm of soldiers that tipped the battle. They scrambled over the horses and chariots that now blocked the gate, surged even over their fellow soldiers, as they scaled the walls. For a moment Dov stood transfixed, watching the sheer number of mud-coated bodies, sometimes five and six deep, slipping, digging their heel into another's neck, as they fought to crowd through the gate or reach the top of Aphek's wall and the supposed safety within.

Slowly, the wall rippled like a water snake swimming upstream. Dov wheeled Uriel away from the danger he felt rather than understood. The bay whinnied shrilly, desperate to convey its instinctive fear. The Israelite army followed Dov's lead and scrambled back from the wall. The Arameans who clung to its wavering surface grew frenzied in their efforts to reach the other side. Crawling bodies turned the wall into a living thing.

A lightning bolt struck the fortification, sparking a chain along the soldiers who had reached the top. Screams and the stench of burnt flesh clawed the air. The wall sagged as bricks and mortar collapsed. Torrential rain rushed to fill the gap, the wall's foundation crumbled, giving way to the massive weight of an army and the pressure of a divine finger.

Each progression—waver—bow—slump—framed sluggishly in Dov's mind, though they could have taken only moments. The wall groaned like a dying beast as it toppled and crushed screaming thousands in its wake.

Immense sheets of lightning pulsed the sky. Silence fell across the Israelites as the heavens flashed a message of victory. Dov flinched as thunder crashed louder than a thousand cymbals.

Then you will know that I AM the Lord.

Trembling, Dov tightened the reins as the bay threatened to bolt. Was this a waking dream, resulting from the dreadful battle? Or had he heard the voice of God in the thunder?

No matter. The prophet had said Yahweh would completely destroy the Aramean army. Would give them into Israel's hands. Dov had a job to complete.

He stood in the stirrups and shouted. "Follow me, men. It's time to finish this fight."

As soon as he loosed the reins, the bay charged ahead, jumping some bodies, weaving through. Dov entered the city.

"Form search parties," he yelled. "Do not trouble the townsfolk, but let none of the enemy escape."

The sky, shrouded all day with rainclouds, began to clear for a sunset that ignited the retreating clouds with orange and gold fire.

After they cleared the city, Dov rode back to the battlefield. Israelites helped their wounded and closed the eyes of the dead. As he searched for Caleb, and the axe man who reminded him so strongly of Aaron, Dov's heart contracted. Many lay dead beneath the walls of Aphek. How long would it be before all bodies were recovered?

When Dov spotted the king's chariot parked high on a slope, he patted Uriel. "Got any strength left in you, old fellow?" The horse did not fail him and galloped toward the royal chariot though he would gladly have allowed the faithful animal a slower pace.

Dov saluted the king, slowly bringing his clenched fist to his heart. Blood stained his hand. The Lord had given them the battle as He said. But men had lost their lives today, perhaps his best friend. Would the victory bring peace to Israel?

"You've done well, Dov. Take your share of plunder from the field."

"May it please the king, you have already treated me generously." He indicated the horse and his armor. He fastened his gaze on his men. "But the army has served you well. Many leaving farms and family to fight for Israel and for you, their king."

The king nodded. "Divide the spoils however you see fit." He looked around. "If there is a royal chariot or gold ..."

"We did not find King Ben-Hadad."

Ahab made a face that reflected the same sourness Dov felt. A year ago, a drunken Ben-Hadad fled the battle on horseback, leaving his men on foot and helpless to retreat as best they could. Had he deserted his troops again?

Then he saw three archers, Caleb in their center, striding across the battlefield. He breathed a prayer of thanks. Caleb lived. The archers herded a group of men dressed only in loincloths made of sackcloth. Ropes around their heads indicated surrender.

"Bring them close," the king said. He jutted his chin toward Dov's sword.

Dov straightened. He was responsible to execute prisoners. He steadied himself for the awful task.

Recognizing their fate, the prisoners muttered amongst themselves. One spoke up in broken Hebrew. "Oh king, great and powerful, your servant Ben-Hadad sent us—"

The man looked nervously between the archers, Dov,

and the king. "Your servant Ben-Hadad sent us to say, 'I pray, let me live.'"

A slow smile broke across the king's face. Dov tightened his grip on the sword. The king would let none of them live. Not after last year's long siege and the threat to ravage not only the city, but Ahab's wives and children. And then this year's battle, the lives lost—

"My brother. Does he live?" The king stood straight and regal in his chariot.

The prisoners stared at him, seeming confused. Perhaps only the speaker understood Hebrew. Then he seemed to latch on the king's appellation for Ben-Hadad. "Yes, yes, your brother. Your brother, Ben-Hadad."

"Is he still alive? He is my brother. Where is he?"

Dov forced himself not to gape at the king. Certainly, he would not pardon Ben-Hadad. The king only wanted to find his enemy's location. Dov disliked the ruse, but it was not for him to judge the king.

The Arameans again looked puzzled. They muttered quietly and the spokesman said, "Near where we were found. In an inner room."

"Go and get him," Ahab ordered his shield bearer.

But before the shield bearer could depart, they saw Ben-Hadad stumble toward them, dressed in garments of surrender like his soldiers. Aaron's kinsman swaggered behind, swinging his axe. Every once in a while, he shoved the king with the blunt edge of the axe. "Look who I found, hiding in a closet." He grinned, showing a bloodied gap in his front teeth.

"What is your name, soldier?" Dov asked.

"Zuar. Zuar ben Aaron." Dov felt his lips quirk in a smile. *Little* did not fit this hulking soldier. But he almost guessed right. This was Aaron's son, though the gatekeeper had never spoken of him.

"Bring the prisoner closer," King Ahab ordered. After Zuar shoved the prisoner close, the king studied Ben-Hadad's attire—sackcloth and a noose looped around his neck.

"Come up in my chariot," the king said.

Dov stifled the urge to debate the decision. It was not

his place. And after all, Ben-Hadad had nowhere to stash a weapon. Still, Dov slid from the saddle, dropping his reins to ground-tie the horse.

Ben-Hadad shuffled forward, Zuar dropping back when Dov took the potentate's arm. He stumbled in apparent weakness, and Dov helped him into the chariot, against all his soldier's instincts.

The two stood dangerously close in the chariot. In deference to the king's order, Dov remained silent, but as he loosed his hold on Ben-Hadad's arm, he grasped the rope that trailed from the noose.

The enemy leader stared at King Ahab, dropping his eyes to the sword strapped at his side. "I will return the cities my father took from your father," Ben-Hadad offered. "You may set up your own market areas in Damascus, as my father did in Samaria."

Dov scoffed silently while the kings took each other's measure. The offer was insane. The Israelites were only beginning to bury their dead. Thousands had died on both sides. The city wall had crumbled under the sheer weight of fleeing Arameans. Surely Ahab would not treat with an enemy he had soundly defeated, as he might with an equal. Not after the insult to King Ahab, his wives, and children last year. Not after attacks two years in succession. When Ben-Hadad's offer was the return of Israelite cities previously taken in combat? In a moment, the king would draw his sword and—

"On the basis of such a treaty, I will set you free."

While Dov stood aghast, the two rulers struck hands in agreement.

Chapter Eighteen

*And when the lord your God has delivered them over to you
and you have defeated them, then you must destroy them
totally. Make no treaty with them, and show them no mercy.*
~ Deuteronomy 7:2 NIV

The camp of the prophets,
*several miles from the battlefield, on the road to Ramoth-
Gilead*
Elijah

ELIJAH STOOD BEHIND AN ANCIENT PINE, apart from the others.
The fire burned brightly. Not only the fire around which the
prophets sat warming themselves, but the fire of the Lord's
presence. Elijah slid the cloak off his head. Warmth spread
through him, despite his distance from the campfire. He
sensed the divine flame hovering.

I am here.

Elijah bowed his head a moment, waiting for the Lord to
continue. When He did not, Elijah swept his gaze across the
firelit faces. He generally sat among them, but tonight's task
was to witness, not teach. Each son of the prophets owned a
spark of understanding. Elijah had taught them to listen—
and obey. None needed him to interpret Yahweh's voice.

From behind half-closed eyes, Elijah watched Micaiah
strum his lyre as he stared into the campfire, the ghostly
music merging with the dance of the flames. Elijah sank
deeper into reflection. The other young prophets admired
Micaiah. His devotion to God encouraged them. Among the
school of the prophets, Elijah considered him second only to
Elisha.

Worthy successors, Elisha and Micaiah. And all those
here and in other hidden places throughout Israel who
sought the Lord. *I will reserve for me seven thousand who
have not kissed Ba'al.* Yahweh was good. He had given
purpose to Elijah's life once again. The schools of prophets
had already begun training others, not only prophets, but
followers of the Lord.

Mercifully, Elijah had not been called again to public confrontation. He hoped never to see the faces of Ahab nor Jezebel again. He longed to remain in the wilderness teaching and encouraging the prophets, among whom the Spirit of God moved. They were all as one. Kind, caring, deferential to him and to one another. Humble, despite their gifts. Not jealous of one another, greatest or least. Except for—

Imrah strode into the circle, sword swinging, his crunching footsteps careless of the contemplative mood around the fire. Elijah gazed down at his folded hands, not wanting to look into the face of the young prophet who often wore an insolent expression. Imrah moved about noisily, repositioning the log he had chosen to sit upon. He clicked the heel of his sandal against the old wood several times. *Tap, tap, tap.*

Micaiah's strumming slowed, indicating the music drew to a close. He set the lyre on a flat stone.

Elijah closed his eyes. He had failed Imrah. Had not tamed his pride. *Yahweh, forgive him.*

But a hot wind brushed through the camp, its moan like a wail of mourning.

Micaiah stood, slowly, as if he also heard the keening. His face shone in the firelight.

Recognizing the infilling, Elijah unclasped his hands, making ready to stand beside his fellow prophet. But the Lord lay an invisible hand on his shoulder. *The lad will say nothing, save what I put on his lips. The prophets know this.*

Micaiah slowly turned to Imrah and pointed at his sword. He seemed to cringe a little before he said, "God has ordered—strike me. I must be wounded."

"With my just-cleaned sword?" Imrah scoffed. "No. I'll not play with you at battle."

"By the word of the Lord." Micaiah waited.

Elijah pulled his cloak around him, suddenly cold. It was often hard to understand the word of God. But Imrah must understand Micaiah's claim of divine authority. No prophet of Yahweh would dare falsely attribute their own will to God.

Imrah abruptly turned away. Elijah had to force himself not to run after the lad, beg him to yield. The young prophet had shown signs of jealousy when Micaiah had been given the task of prophesying to the king, as if talking to that evil man was a sign of honor. Why didn't Imrah understand the honor was in being Yahweh's servant?

Micaiah sighed. "Because you have not obeyed the Lord, when you leave me, a lion will attack and kill you."

Elijah tensed, willing Imrah to yield. *Do not leave the circle of firelight. You must obey, even when you do not understand.*

His mind flashed to all the times he had not understood. When told to stand before Ahab and tell him there would be no rain for three years. When told to go hide beside a small brook and be fed by ravens. When told to leave the brook and go to Zarephath, Jezebel's homeland, and be fed by a widow. When told to leave the widow and her son and find the king who wanted him dead.

Imrah snarled. "You are not the only one who hears the voice of the Lord." He lit a torch in the fire and walked toward the tents holding the flame high. Had he not listened to a word of Elijah's teaching? Did he think a torch would stay the word of God?

Imrah crunched twigs and dried leaves under foot as he walked into the darkness. Then came a deep growl.

The lion must have crouched beyond the firelight. Elijah heard a scuffle, and the torch hit the ground. Imrah cried out as the lion took him down, but the struggle was over quickly. Had he time to draw his sword?

The others leapt to their feet.

"Stay!" Elijah ordered, stepping into view. "Imrah is gone. But the lion is not." The truth of his statement was proven when they heard bones crunch and the sound of a body being dragged away.

Micaiah turned to the others. "Who else has a weapon?"

Phineas stood, but he trembled. He was the youngest of the prophets, slight of build, and of a compassionate spirit. His beard had not yet sprouted. He fumbled a small dagger from his sash.

"By the word of the Lord, strike me."

The boy shook violently. "Strike you where?"

"Here." Micaiah drew a line across the top of his

forehead. "Also here and here." He drew another line beneath the first and a third down the length of his left cheek. "Make it jagged—as though received in battle."

Phineas held his breath as he complied. The first cut was tentative and shallow. Micaiah pressed down on the boy's hand for the second, and blood gushed from the wound. He locked eyes with the boy the third time. It did not bleed as much but being in a fleshier spot, it spread wide.

"You have done well," Micaiah said. Then he girded up his tunic and ran where the Lord had sent him. Elijah was certain of that fact, even though Yahweh had not revealed more to him than to the younger prophets.

Phineas' knees buckled and he sat on the recently vacated log. His fellows murmured sympathetic encouragement.

Elijah, feeling very old, felt for his staff and moved to sit among them, close to the fire. Tonight, he would again tell the stories of long and fervent prayers. Of trusting the Lord and listening for His voice. And that Yahweh demanded swift and complete obedience from His followers. Especially His prophets.

The king's steward shook Dov awake. "The king has asked his driver to make ready the chariot."

Stifling a moan, Dov stood and looked around the makeshift camp, not far from the battlefield. His soldiers lay where they had thrown themselves after the battle. Some had circled banked campfires, but many simply wrapped themselves in cloaks and slept where they fell.

"All right," Dov said. "Wake the others who go with us."

He walked over to where Uriel was tied with other horses to a rope between two trees. Untying the bay, he led him away from the others and scooped several handfuls of grain onto a flat rock. Dov saddled the horse while it ate, grinding grain between its teeth with gusto. "Eat quickly, Uriel. We don't want to start another battle."

Dov cringed when the noise elicited whickers of protest from the line of horses. He quickly tied his belongings behind the saddle, save for his weapons. He had hand-picked mature soldiers, well-schooled in war and measured in their conversation, to ride with him and the king. If they hid passionate opinions in their deepest hearts, they knew to keep that door shut. Not like Caleb.

After Caleb learned Ahab pardoned Ben-Hadad, he had cursed their king at length. Thankfully, Dov saw his rage building and pulled his friend behind a stand of trees a safe distance from listening ears. There Caleb let loose a blistering denunciation of the king's action. "Why did we fight this battle if Ahab was going to trade our blood for a few cities?" And there had been more ranting. Pointless. One did not argue with a king.

Dov had tried to express both concern and the voice of reason. "I fear you are right, my friend. Israel will pay. But your words are reckless. You cannot speak so impulsively. You are a king's soldier. You owe King Ahab your loyalty, or *you* will pay with your life. Think of your parents, your brother and sister. Think of Chloe."

Caleb had blanched then, and nodded, thinking of the innocent young girl to whom he had lost his heart.

In time, he would learn to temper his tongue. Until then, it was best he not be in proximity to the king. So Caleb would stay with the rest of the army to continue the job they hadn't been able to finish yesterday—burying the dead, Israelite and Aramean. Dov disliked leaving his soldiers to the grim undertaking, especially Caleb, who he had put in charge of organizing the work force and dividing the plunder. His friend's jovial, teasing manner would suffer from this duty. But hard responsibilities belonged to all men. At least Caleb would go home to his family.

He heard footsteps approach. Caleb hailed him quietly. "Ho there. Leaving so early?"

"Uri woke you?"

"Nah. Jealous horses woke me when an iron sledge drove through a field of rocks."

"Sorry to have disturbed your sleep," Dov said.

"The king's man passed me. He summoned you?"

"They make ready the king's chariot."

Caleb swore under his breath, but Dov heard.

"That is just why you are not coming with me. I value

your head too much, even if you do not."

Dov climbed onto the bay, adjusted the sword in its scabbard, and repositioned the bow over his shoulder. He looked down at Caleb, wishing his expression was not hidden by the dark. "Remember what I said." He stared off toward the battlefield, seeking one more reason to convince his friend to be circumspect. "I'm sorry to leave you to this ugly chore. But with your share of battle spoils, perhaps you will court your gentle young woman"

Caleb grunted. Dov bent and slapped him on the shoulder. Then he nudged his horse into a brisk trot, heading for the king's tent.

The sun was rising when they reached the hill. Scattered clouds streaked the yellow light. A servant held the reins of the harnessed horses as Ahab walked toward his chariot. More servants had broken down the king's camel skin tent and packed it in two other chariots.

After his driver and archer boarded, King Ahab climbed into the chariot. He nodded as Dov rode up. "Looks to be a fine day for my victory procession."

The king took the reins from the driver, wheeled the chariot around, and whipped his horses into a gallop toward Samaria.

At that pace they would reach home well before sunset. Dov nudged Uri into a lope, the stallion's ground-covering strides easily catching the king's high-stepping beauties. Yet the royal horses were not all flare. Steady and resolute, they held their own in the crush of battle. Just as the king was not all pomp and glory, despite his love for pageantry. He was a seasoned soldier. A shrewd negotiator.

Dov frowned. But what about Ahab allowing Ben-Hadad his pick of the royal wives and children? Some had thought it a wise move, to rid himself of Jezebel who, though beautiful, had a fearsome temper. Some thought it foolish— his foreign bride brought a treaty with Phoenicia and a trading route to the sea. Handing his daughter over to the king of Aram was an insult to the king of Tyre and would transfer Israel's goodwill to the Arameans. Yet, in the end Ahab did not give his wife as tribute, but instead routed the Arameans with a surprise attack.

But that was because of the Lord's help, not Ahab's military expertise.

Dov relaxed into the bay's rocking gait. Maybe it was both. The prophet had spoken, and Israel won the battle. As the Lord had said.

Ahab and his father before him were admired as strong military leaders. The king must have had a reason for pardoning his enemy. He had visibly brightened when Ben-Hadad mentioned the cities his father had taken from Omri and the Damascus market. Those geographic and economic advantages proved strong bait, and Ahab bit the hook.

But had he pardoned Ben-Hadad because he didn't trust Yahweh to be Israel's protector? To be the strong wall between their two countries? Caleb was right. The king thought nothing of the price his people had paid. He put their lives at risk again. Ben-Hadad had attacked them twice. Freed, he would build up his army, and he would attack Israel again. If not next year, then soon.

The king slowed his sweating horses. "I am over anxious to be home," he said. "But my horses shouldn't suffer." He stopped and let the animals catch their breath before they walked on. The contingent of soldiers had surrounded the king when they first left the battle camp, but those ahead had rounded a bend and had not noticed the king stop.

A bedraggled man shuffled from a line of trees and stood watching at the side of the road. He appeared to have been in the battle, with a bandage over part of his face. Yet how did he get here ahead of them? Dov and the king had left at first light. One man alone. He looked harmless enough. Still, there could be others, hidden behind the trees.

Dov glanced behind, making gestures to alert the soldiers behind them. He rode forward, put himself between the king and the man.

King Ahab appeared to regard the man with only mild curiosity. As they drew closer, Dov saw he was wounded. With dawning recognition, he observed his stance and the odor of sweat and sheep surrounding the man who had ridden with him on Uriel last night. Micaiah.

"My king! I am your servant." Micaiah called out as they passed.

Did the king recognize him? Should Dov explain? But as he opened his mouth to speak, he choked in a fit of coughing, as if a handful of dust were thrown in his face.

Ahab stopped the chariot and looked back at the prophet, impatience clipping his words. "Yes, my good man?"

"I was with you, in the thick of the battle. Someone came to me with a captive and said, 'Guard this man. If you let him get away, it will mean your life, or you must pay a talent of silver.'" While I was busy here and there, the man disappeared. But I am a humble shepherd. I will never see a talent of silver."

"Busy here and there! Well, you know your sentence," the king said. "Your life for his. You have pronounced it yourself. Why bother me with the matter?"

Micaiah pulled the bandage from his eyes. Dov saw from the king's expression he now recognized him as one of the prophets, though perhaps did not know his name.

"This is what the Lord says: You have set free a man I had determined should die. Therefore, it is your life for his life, your people for his people."

A shadow fell on the landscape. Dark clouds had moved across the sun, turning the rest of the sky a bilious shade.

Micaiah turned and walked back into the trees, seemingly unconcerned about the king's reaction. Glancing at the king's purpled face, Dov held his breath. Would Ahab send an arrow into the prophet's back? Order Dov to pursue and slay him?

It did not seem Ahab intended to beg Yahweh's forgiveness.

Instead, the king once again lashed his horses into a gallop. They quickly caught up with the other riders and rode hard all the way to Samaria, up to the door of the palace. The king threw down the reins and strode up the steps. His driver quickly picked up the reins and drove the horses to the stables. Dov followed and saw to it that Uri as well as the king's animals received water and a good feed.

Your life for his life. Your people for his people.

The king's fury cast a pall over Israel's victory. What would come of this?

Chapter Nineteen

*'Cursed is anyone who withholds justice from the foreigner,
the fatherless, or the widow.' Then all the people shall say,
'Amen.' 'Cursed is anyone who kills their neighbor secretly.'
Then all the people shall say, 'Amen.' 'Cursed is
anyone who accepts a bribe to kill an innocent
person.' Then all the people shall say, 'Amen.'*
~ Deuteronomy 27: 19,24-25

Jezreel, shortly after the battle at Aphek, month of Sivan
Dov

DOV PACED THE DIRT FLOOR IN the small house he shared with
Maalik. "What do you think I should do?"

"I think you should sit down and eat this fine meal
Hadassah sent us," Maalik said, dishing up lentils flavored
with what smelled like venison. "You have grown thin,
battling Israel's enemies, only to have them turned loose to
fight another day. Besides, you are digging a trench in my
floor. What the king has done is his doing."

"But if I talk to him—"

"You!" Maalik snorted. "He grew furious when a prophet
of God pronounced judgment. *Your life for his life. Your people
for his people.* What more can you say—and live?"

Dov took the bowl and sat. "What about the people? Why
should they suffer for the king's mistakes?"

"Is it not always so, my son? On that, I have a word of
wisdom from Hadassah."

Dov smiled in spite of his agitation. "Each time I go
away, I come back wondering if you will have set up
housekeeping with Caleb's grandmother." He should not
have said such a thing. He did not want to hurt Maalik with
a careless remark. Yet they found such happiness in each
other's company.

"Do not jest. I would, for the sake of her company and
cooking. But I would be a poor bargain for Hadassah."

"What is her word of wisdom?"

"It is a king's job—not only Ahab, but every king of Israel—to be the word of the Lord to the people. Instead, our king turned his back on his responsibility and taught Israel to worship the Ba'als."

Dov stirred his stew. "Once she said Yahweh sent the drought to capture Ahab's attention."

"Captured everyone's attention when Elijah called down the rain. For a time." Maalik scooped several spoonfuls into his mouth. "Mmm." He rolled his eyes upwards. "What is that spice?"

"Did you ask her?"

"Said it was a family secret."

"Sounds like a marriage proposal to me." He had done it again. Good thing he was leaving town.

Maalik rolled his eyes.

Dov lifted the bowl and poured stew down his throat. "I must go. I lead the king's guard to Jezreel."

"Not his normal time to visit Jezreel."

"No. He wants something pleasant to rest his mind on. The valley is beautiful. So green and lush." Dov paused, scraping his wooden spoon around the bowl. "Did Hadassah say anything about the victories? I've wondered why ... as you said, rain after three years' drought caught Israel's attention ... for a time. Yet some Israelites continue to worship Ba'al Melqart and Asherah in the high places. So why did Yahweh favor Israel with victories? Why the prophecies?"

"She did say something." Maalik shook his head, perplexed. "She said Yahweh is merciful."

Miriam

Miriam breathed in the sweet smell of a vineyard in summer as she followed the others through the gate. Her father-in-law's vineyard smelled nearly the same as Abba's with small differences. Abba's vineyard was farther down the hill from the city, and its rock outcropping and hidden cave lent their own earthy odors. But both vineyards exhaled a green, almost peppery smell of mature leaves baking in the sun mingled with the honeyed smell of fruit bursting with juice.

Dod Naboth had tested the grapes daily and deemed the east section ready for harvest. They had risen before dawn—her aunt and uncle, Gershon, Kadesh, and Jaedon. Miriam fed everyone a meal of unleavened bread, cheese, and dates. Food to strengthen them for the day's labor, without delaying their start. Naboth had promised they would finish the section early.

She and Gershon would be free to take Jaedon to the valley afterwards to practice archery, a special treat for the boy. Miriam encouraged his interest in the skill. She hoped he would not need to take up arms in battle, but with enemy nations surrounding them, that hope was unlikely. But even in peacetime, the ability to hunt for meat was valuable.

They each took a basket from the stack inside the gate. Dod Naboth pointed toward the eastern corner. "Start there, where the grapes get the morning sun."

Kadesh took the first row, Jaedon following closely while his uncle spun another tale about a scouting journey. "And did I tell you of the time I joined a caravan from Nabatea and had to pretend I was mute because I had not yet perfected my accent? They spoke at least three dialects ..."

After living in close quarters with Gershon's brother, Miriam saw where Jaedon had inherited his talkative ways. She smiled, noting how Kadesh's stories could slow the tide of the boy's tongue.

Her brothers, who for years had helped their uncle harvest his grapes in the weeks before their own vineyard ripened, would not come this harvest. Not that their labor was needed in Jezreel, with Kadesh and Miriam now part of the family work force, but she had looked forward to hearing from her brothers all her family's news. She had written asking Imma to accompany them. She still longed for motherly advice, even though she had been married a year. But instead of bringing her mother, Dov, riding guard for the king and queen's out-of-season visit to Jezreel, had brought her a letter.

Caleb wrote he was building a house for his marriage to Chloe next winter. Avigail, with one child just starting to wobble around, expected another any day. Once again, Seth would not leave his wife.

Turning her back on the others, Miriam lay a hand against her flat belly. According to Aaron the gatekeeper, the old ewe he housed in his courtyard produced a lamb each spring, without fail. And truly, spring had come, and a spotted lamb now frisked around with its mother. But earlier this month, her body assured her once again she was not with child. What was wrong with her? Was she too old to bear a child of her own? What did her husband think of her barrenness?

She derided herself. Such dire thoughts! If her mother were here, surely she would say it was far too early to think of barrenness. As if Jaedon and Gershon did not keep Miriam busy enough. She dropped clusters of grapes into her basket. But ... it had been a year since Miriam was wed, and still she mothered only another woman's son.

If she were only with child, might not that bring her and Gershon closer together?

Well, despite foolish doubts, time stretched in front of her. She was a healthy woman. She looked at her work-muscled arm, stretched to reach a purple cluster. *Very healthy. Yahweh, if it is not too much trouble, I would like a brother for Jaedon by this time next year.* Was that too presumptuous? She amended her prayer. *Only if it will not interfere with Your other plans.*

Miriam heard voices up near the city gate. She squinted into the sun and saw Dov walking down the ramp. He had spent the night at the palace after bringing Caleb's letter. He had told them he would be leaving in the morning for Samaria. Why was he not on horseback, prepared for the ride home? Aaron and another man followed him. When they reached the path leading to the vineyard, they turned. The last man was short and stoutly built, much like the gatekeeper, and gripped a cloth-wrapped parcel on one shoulder.

"Shalom, Dov, Aaron," called Kadesh from behind her. "On your way back to Samaria?"

"The plan has changed," Dov said, pausing to open the gate and allow the others to enter. "The king wants me to inspect the garrison here first, then carry a report back to the army captain at the capitol."

Aaron shifted his weight, drawing Miriam's attention. "I've been invited, but my leg won't tolerate riding a horse that far." He inclined his head toward the stocky man carrying the bundle. "But my son, Zuar, will ride with Dov."

Miriam felt her eyebrows lift. Aaron had never spoken of a son, not even a wife, though he had taken several meals with her family. She would expect to hear such topics discussed among the men over supper. Or at least when they sampled Naboth's wine. She glanced at Dov. His lips twitched, but he did not appear surprised.

Aaron grinned in a self-deprecating way. "After I came back wounded from war—about twenty years ago—" Again he turned his gaze upon his son. "—my wife went home to her father in Shechem. I couldn't blame her."

Aaron had a wife, and she had left him! How sad. After all the times he had supped at her table, how could she not have known? And yet, how much did she know about the other guests Dod Naboth brought home?

"I was nearly crippled. She doubted I could put food on the table," Aaron continued. "Until the king assigned me gatekeeper, she was right. I wrote informing her of my new, exalted position." He chuckled.

But Miriam saw that he had hoped his wife would return. Obviously, she had not. How strange that he was a lone man one instant, the father of a grown son the next. A giant of a son in breadth, if not in stature. At least Miriam's instant son had years of childhood ahead of him.

The young man said, "I don't know if Imma received that letter, but she never told Aaron … *my father* … I existed. She told me he had sent her away. That he no longer wanted her, and he would not want me."

"Neither was true." Aaron's face scrunched into a frown. "Sometimes disappointment can spread a heavy blanket over truth. After his mother died, Zuar showed up carrying an axe. Ready to take vengeance. I couldn't blame him."

Miriam blinked, trying to imagine this broad-bodied fighter showing up at the gate and introducing himself. Confronting Aaron, axe in hand. She felt an involuntary smile lift a corner of her mouth. Zuar. The *little son* Aaron never knew he had.

"You are good at not blaming, Father." He grinned at Miriam. "What do you suppose he said instead?"

"I ... I ..." Miriam stuttered as she searched for any reasonable response she could add to this strange conversation. Two men, one she never would have expected to speak a word to her about more than the weather, the other a complete stranger, were disclosing this intimate story of family troubles. Completely engrossed in their back-and-forth story, she had almost forgotten that her men, Gershon, Naboth, Kadesh, and Jaedon, worked behind her. She struggled against the impulse to turn and look behind, capture the expressions on their faces. But that would seem impolite. As if their news was an oddity.

Miriam threw a glance Dov's way, but he only shrugged.

"I could not guess," she said weakly.

"My father said, 'Ah. You brought your axe. Good idea!' Then he picked up a massive iron-tipped spear. Its shaft was so thick it must have matched Goliath's. I started to rethink vengeance, or at least confronting him so openly. As my father continued to babble, I decided to wait—go for the stealthy approach. 'Let me call the second gatekeeper,' he went on. 'He owes me for that time I worked his shift. I can show you the best hunting hereabouts. I have to say, I've never met a hunter who used an axe. What animal do you hunt with an axe?'"

"Babble?" Aaron raised both eyebrows, then resumed. "So then, my son said ... *my son* said," he repeated, as if liking the sound of the words. "'I use a bow for hunting. I was just *showing you* my axe.'"

"He said that?" Dov asked.

Miriam's shoulders trembled with suppressed laughter.

Chuckling, Aaron shrugged meaty shoulders.

Zuar went on with the story. "Then my father hefted his spear. 'Good,' he said. 'You get the deer. I'll go for the lions.'"

Laughter filled the vineyard.

Looking at Miriam, Zuar slid the bundle off his shoulder. "Now that my story is known, I suppose I will have to forgo stealth. But my father speaks fondly of you. So this is from my father and me. For the many times you have fed him."

"I thank you," Miriam said, smiling. "You must all come to supper tonight and help eat it. But ... is this venison or lion?"

The men guffawed.

She glanced at Dov. "You knew about these two?"

"Not until the battle of Aphek. Zuar fought with the foot soldiers. But when I saw him on the field, something about him seemed familiar." He paused, then said in a quieter voice. "He found Ben-Hadad."

Aaron growled. "He should have used his axe without—"

Dov stopped him with a hand on his shoulder and a significant glance toward Jaedon. But the whole city had heard of King Ahab pardoning Israel's long-time enemy and surely Jaedon had heard worse among his friends. All their fathers were angry too, but they kept their opinions at home. Miriam wasn't worried about Jaedon. Not yet. But she swept her gaze toward Gershon. He gave Jaedon a push towards her, pulled Dov and the other men aside, and they resumed their conversation. Gershon had the look he often got when the battle was discussed. Like a boy left out of the game the other boys played.

Except war was no game. And Miriam knew it meant much more than a game to Gershon. It was men's business, and he had not shouldered his share. Her husband felt ... emasculated.

Still, she was thankful Gershon missed the war. Glad their marriage had saved him from that, at least. Caleb had fought and she had glimpsed how it changed him. No more her lighthearted, prankster brother, he wore a more somber air. Though his battle scars had not been serious, Miriam feared the wounds left on his heart went deep. She hoped his marriage to Chloe could take place soon and healing would begin.

Jaedon shuffled toward her, scuffing up clouds of dust.

"Get your bow and quiver. We will walk down to the valley and practice while the men talk. They will not miss us." She motioned her intent to Gershon, and he nodded.

"Kadesh has told me all about being a spy," Jaedon said. "About listening at campfires and learning secrets. And when the land is at war—"

"Yes, well that would require that you talk less and listen more." She tweaked his nose, and he made a face. She would have to stop doing that. Soon.

They had left their bows and quivers near the vineyard gate. She slung hers over her shoulder, adjusting the quiver. She resisted the urge to reposition Jaedon's, so it wouldn't slap with each step he took. She had to stop constantly correcting him. She recognized the resentment she had felt at that age, when she thought she knew everything.

Once. Maybe twice, if he could be hurt. After that, she would let him learn on his own.

"I should not have said that. Actually, you get better at listening every day. If you really want to scout when you are grown, I think you would do well. But consider this. Your uncle has lived the life you admire. But now he happily works in the vineyard with his father and brother. He has had enough of spying and a scout's life. He even talks about expanding the family business with your father—buying more land in the valley with his share of—" She stopped herself from saying 'of the spoils,' not wanting Jaedon to glorify war in his mind.

And once, when she went late to the well, Miriam saw Kadesh talking with Davita. Gazing at him through lowered lashes, she had said something that caused him to throw back his head in laughter. Was he romantically interested in Davita? Miriam would like that. Her two best friends, one married to her brother, one to her brother-in-law.

Miriam stopped several paces from where they had stood to shoot the last time, wanting to increase their range. If Jaedon ever did need to face an enemy, she wanted him to have the advantage. And wild game never let one walk close. She lay a hand on his shoulder. "Do you remember where we hid the targets?"

Jaedon nodded and ran ahead to set them up. He had grown a bit in the past year. Though he was still very much a boy, sometimes she saw a glimpse of the man he would become—funny, confident, and bold. Would he like farming the grapes, or hold on to his boyish desire for a more exciting life, like Kadesh? A dangerous life. Miriam would not want that for him. But even a vintner could be conscripted—or volunteer for battle—as Caleb had done. As long as the surrounding nations wanted what Israel had—fertile land and access to the best trade routes—there would be conflict.

Jaedon came running back, hunching his shoulders and leaning into his pace as if he was falling with every step. His growth spurt had left him clumsy in his body. She could not help grinning. He was still her little boy.

"Do you think I am getting faster?" His mouth hung open a little and he puffed dramatically.

"I do. Now let's practice shooting faster. Here. Hold three arrows in your right hand instead of one." She showed him how to nock and shoot in rapid succession. The second and third arrows fell to the ground at his feet.

"Don't worry. I did that, too, when we were first taught." Miriam remembered Dov telling her the same thing when she had frowned at her own ineptness. "Pick them up and try again."

Several attempts later, he was able to shoot the second and third arrow, albeit slowly. But before long, he was shooting them at an even pace.

"Fine shooting! Shall we end now?"

"A few more. To let my fingers get used to what I am doing."

Feeling another smile coming on, Miriam pressed her lips together and nodded. "Good idea." She moved several paces away and practiced a similar technique while sweeping her aim from left to right.

Dov had explained she might use this when tracking moving game. "In the event your first shot doesn't take down the stag."

A horse whinnied. She would not have given it her attention, except it sounded as if it was above them, on the same terrace as the vineyard. Dov had not ridden his horse to the vineyard and was not leaving for Samaria until tomorrow. But perhaps the king had changed his orders again. Who else would ride a horse to the vineyard? She stepped back and craned her neck. The massive black stallion she had seen King Ahab ride during his previous visit to Jezreel clip-clopped along the path leading to the vineyard. She squinted. So that must be the king on its back, although he was dressed more simply than usual. A single guard accompanied him on foot. Not Dov.

She spotted Gershon in the vineyard, shading his eyes as he watched the king approach. Quickly he pivoted, speaking to someone. Naboth and Kadesh stood, apparently from stooping to pick low-hanging clusters. Dov, Aaron, and Zuar were no longer in the vineyard. They must have gone about their business sometime while Miriam and Jaedon were shooting.

Miriam felt a prickle of curiosity. The king must intend to speak with one or all of her men, as it was plain to see Dov was not there. What could Ahab want with any of them? She heard voices but could not make out their words. Greetings, certainly. She shoved her arrows back in her quiver. She looked at Jaedon. "I am tired. I doubt I can climb the hill as quickly as you. Do you mind if I start back?" It would take only a moment to get close enough to hear.

"Shall I stop shooting now and come with you? Do you need to lean on my arm?"

Her lips parted. *Sweet boy.* "No, I will stop and catch my breath if I tire. You finish getting your fingers used to what you are doing." She touched him. Why did it seem so important to do so, just now?

"Come along soon, though. Remember we have guests for supper. I would like your help tending the roast."

She walked quickly up the first part of the earth ramp, then slowed to tug her head covering forward so that it shadowed her face. She paused, listening. It seemed the king was praising the vineyard. Truly, their family kept it beautifully tended. The grapes they picked this morning were larger than last year's and the foliage lush with no trace of the red blotch that plagued some vintners.

She walked again, slower now. The king spoke again. She could make out some of it. "... vegetable garden. I will give you a better vineyard, or if you prefer, I will pay you a fair price."

The king asked to buy their vineyard? Surely not. The Lord forbad—Naboth would never—

Miriam quickened her steps, rushing up the last part of the ramp, stopping where the ground leveled, and the corner of the city gate jutted out. If she stepped behind it, those on the terraced hillside would not see her.

She heard Naboth say, "I cannot do that. The Lord forbids a man from selling land inherited from his fathers."

Miriam listened for the king's response. Silence stretched interminably, until finally he said, "Ah. You are negotiating. I assure you, I will give you a fair price. It is so convenient to my palace. It would make a fine vegetable garden."

So she had heard correctly. It made no sense. A vegetable garden! He would have to rip out the vines that produced the finest wine in Jezreel. Did the king realize his table wine came from this vineyard?

"I am sorry, my king. I cannot sell the vineyard. Not for any price."

She heard the horse moving about, the king grunting as he mounted, then rapid hoofbeats as the animal trotted in her direction. Glancing back, she saw Jaedon coming, then stepped through the city gate. She nodded to the second gatekeeper, relieved that it was not Aaron on duty, that this man did not know her by name, because the king was coming, and she knew he was angry. Though not quite sure why, she didn't want him to know she had overheard the conversation. She took several quick steps back from the gate. When the king passed her, he did not swerve his horse away, as if he would have been glad to knock her aside, though when he looked upon her face, his glare held no recognition.

Miriam asked Jaedon to tend the roasting meat in the courtyard and not leave it for any reason, lest it burn. She tried not to be obvious about checking on him, but guests were coming. The gazelle was fat and tender, but happily, her boy was doing a fine job. As they waited for the men to return from the vineyard, he turned the roast on its spit often, sometimes laying green grape leaves over the flames if they flared too high, embracing the sizzling meat with smoke. It smelled delicious. Indeed, Miriam pitied the neighbors who smelled it but were eating plain suppers tonight. She would have invited a few, had she not overheard the troubling conversation in the vineyard. She feared the mood tonight would be somber.

As soon as he returned, Dod Naboth took Yaffa to their room. Soon she heard the low murmur of his voice. Gershon had likewise drawn her aside. Before he said a word, Kadesh crossed the room, announced he was taking a walk, and disappeared through the door.

As Gershon told her what had happened, Miriam did not say she had overheard. She didn't want to add to the concern etched on her husband's face. Who would not be concerned to anger the king of all Israel?

"But what could Abba do?" Gershon asked, and she raised her hands in helpless agreement. Her father-in-law had given the only answer he could. He was a godly man. He must obey the law Yahweh had first given to Moses and handed down to all Israel. *The land must not be sold permanently, because the land is mine and you reside in my land as foreigners and strangers. Throughout the land that you hold as a possession, you must provide for the redemption of the land.*

Why would King Ahab have made such a request? Had no one taught him the Torah? From childhood, she and Gershon had heard the law repeated. Savta had made her recite phrases, allowing her a sweet date or bit of honeycomb if every word was correct.

"What would he want with it anyway? He owns a palace with marble and ivory fittings. It is surrounded by land, good land. I have never been inside, but it must have a beautiful view of the valley and the mountains beyond. Why must he have your vineyard?" Miriam saw her words had caused Gershon's brow to furrow deeper. She bit her lip. "I am sorry, my heart. Don't be concerned. He is a king. Tomorrow he will have forgotten. One humble vineyard will not hold his attention for long."

When Dov, Aaron, and Zuar arrived, neither Naboth nor Gershon brought up the disagreement with the king. Miriam checked the street for Kadesh, but he was nowhere in sight. What was taking him so long? Surely, he did not think it would take this long for Gershon to inform her about the king's request. Yet, when Kadesh walked out of the house, his expression had been purposeful, more than just a man allowing his brother to conduct a private conversation with his wife. Had Kadesh gone to speak with Davita?

Dov interrupted her thoughts, asking about the contents of the letter he had brought from Caleb. Miriam shared the news that Chloe's father had approved their betrothal.

Dov slapped his knee, grinning. "I suspected his interest, the day we taught archery to the women of the city. Sly fox! He said nothing to me about the matter. But then, the king has kept me busy since our return."

"I am so pleased he chose Chloe," Miriam replied. "She is a dear friend. I am only sorry that she will be leaving Jezreel. I will not see her at the well every day. And it is a two-day walk to Samaria."

Dov nodded, thoughtfully. "Perhaps there is an opportunity to make travel easier. The king acquired more chariots at Aphek. He housed some there, his stable in Samaria is already full from last year's victory. I will approach him about keeping a few in Jezreel for defense purposes. They could also be used now and then for transport between our two cities. To carry mail or supplies, for example. Or persons."

"I thank you." Miriam tried to summon a grateful expression. But she feared if the king had any inkling that the transport would benefit Naboth's family, Dov's idea would never come to pass. "Would you mind carrying a letter to my family when you go back?" She would write them about the incident. Abba or Savta would have advice to share.

She went to check the roast and found it was nearly done. "You have done such a fine job." She gave Jaedon a quick hug. "I will ask your savta for a tray and you can carry the roast inside."

Yaffa had already put bowls of sliced cheese, grapes, and bitter herbs with vinegar in the center of the rug they had spread. Miriam bent and said softly to Gershon, "Will you carry the pitcher of water and towel for washing?" Noticing the job had become difficult for Yaffa, Miriam had taken it over. But she wanted to help Jaedon outside before the roast was overdone. Gershon nodded and quickly rose to help.

She carried the tray and clean cloths outside. A few drops of juice sizzled. Eyeing the flare up, she decided to remove the roast herself. "Please hold the tray." Folding the cloths for padding, she lifted the roast from the spit and settled it on the tray. "Whew, heavy. Will you carry it inside for me?" Jaedon was growing up, but Miriam was not willing to risk him dragging a trailing cloth over the fire.

As she followed Jaedon inside, her mind whirled around her boy, Yaffa's growing weakness, the letter she would write, but most of all, the king's anger over Naboth's refusal to sell the vineyard. Would there be trouble? She had assured Gershon that Ahab would soon forget. But could she convince herself?

Chapter Twenty

But to the wicked person, God says:
What right have you to recite my laws or take my covenant
on your lips? You hate my instruction and cast my words
behind you. When you see a thief, you join with him; you
throw in your lot with adulterers. You use your mouth
for evil and harness your tongue to deceit.
~ Psalm 50:16-19

The palace at Jezreel, a few days later
Jezebel

WHEN OBADIAH, THE PALACE STEWARD CAME before her, hesitantly, eyes averted. Jezebel had to pull his name out of the past. He had not approached her since the drought, although she had seen him various places about the king's business. The steward was afraid of her, she remembered. Good.

"The king is ill," he said.

"Ill?" she asked. "How so?"

"He refuses to eat. I have tried choice meats, delicacies, music—"

"Music?"

"His illness seems a malady of the spirit, my queen. But music did not help. I hoped you might cheer him."

She frowned and waved him off, but she actually felt a little giddy. The king needed her.

This was the first time Ahab had summoned her in a great while. Well, *he* hadn't actually summoned her. But he must have sent the steward. She quickly donned her most beautiful garments, looped gold chains around her neck, and ordered her maid servants to brush and arrange her hair over her shoulders. Like molten fire, he used to say, running his hands through the strands.

She hurried to his quarters, though careful to keep her stride measured and regal.

But it was all to no purpose.

Jezebel narrowed her eyes as she viewed the dismal condition of her husband, king of Israel. There he lay, unmoving, face turned to the wall. His hair hung lank and unwashed and his tunic was wrinkled and twisted about his knees. She sniffed, the stale odor confirming her suspicion that he had not bathed recently.

Did the man intend to starve himself, make her a widow and their uncontrollable son king? She'd have none of it. She took a deep breath and purred. "Are you well, my love?" She placed her hand on his forehead. "You are feverish. I will send for scented cloths to cool your face."

"Leave me alone. I want nothing from you."

She flinched, but held her ground, remembering the moment he had nearly given her as spoils of war. As if she were just one more superfluous wife, along with his concubines and illegitimate children. Surely she, princess of Tyre, could regain her hold over him. He was a man, after all.

"Tell me what is distressing you, my lord. I cannot bear to see you this way." She sat beside him on the bed, running her fingers down the side of his neck.

Abruptly he rolled onto his back. "I planned to extend the palace garden down the hill onto the first terrace. That patch gets a good bit of sun. The cook said he could grow vegetables and herbs there all year."

Her husband wanted this land and could not get it himself. Perfect! She excelled at getting what she wanted. And once she had given him what he desired, the king would realize how much he needed her. "A delightful idea. What is the problem?"

He rallied a little, propped himself on one elbow. "The land belongs to Naboth the Jezreelite. I asked him to sell me the plot or let me give him a better vineyard, but he will not." He snorted. "Something about an ancient, obscure law. Not selling the land out of one's tribal unit."

"What! Are you not king of all Israel?" Quickly she softened her voice, hiding her exasperation lest he realize she rebuked him. "Please do not concern yourself further, my love. I can get you Naboth's vineyard."

She stood, looking down at him, then quickly bent and kissed him lingeringly. In many ways, he was a fool. He had let that prophet Elijah slip between his fingers, and he could not set aside his superstitious fear of the old god. And what king allowed a subject to tell him no?

Still, he had not given her to the Arameans—in the end. Instead he had gone to war to fight for her. He could not let her go, that was evident, whether he realized his ardor or not. If he did not love her, he at least esteemed her. She had brought to their marriage a valuable treaty with Tyre and a trade route to the sea. And if that were not enough, he needed her strength, for times such as this. When she set herself to a task, she could not be deterred.

After a final caress, Jezebel summoned servants to bring the king meat, bread, wine, and clean garments.

Next, she hurried to her quarters and composed letters to several of the elders and nobles of the city, those she knew were obligated to her husband for one reason or another. These she signed with the king's name.

Call the citizens together for a time of fasting before the Lord to ferret out any evil that would cause the nation trouble. Give Naboth, the vintner, a place of honor, for he sits to judge the people at the city gates. But seat two scoundrels near him who will accuse him of cursing Yahweh and the king. Then take him outside the city and stone him to death. Him and his sons. Thus we will purge the nation of evil.

She would slip into Ahab's bed later that night and see that she left with his seal to lend authenticity to the signatures. She kept plenty of silver hidden to pay scoundrels, thieves, and assassins. Ahab would have his garden, and Jezebel would have regained his esteem.

Chapter Twenty-One

Some time later there was an incident involving a vineyard belonging to Naboth the Jezreelite. The vineyard was in Jezreel, close to the palace of Ahab king of Samaria.
~ 1 Kings 21:1

Jezreel, a few days later
Miriam

MIRIAM ENJOYED THE PREDAWN QUIET WHILE the family slept. There were not many such moments when five adults and a lively boy shared one abode. Although she had moved to Gershon's home with him and Jaedon after the wedding, when Yaffa's growing weakness became more apparent, the three of them had returned to live with his parents. Not only did Yaffa tire easily, but stiffness in her limbs made it difficult to walk or grasp everyday objects. Miriam was glad to help the woman who had treated her like a daughter from the first.

There was sufficient room in the house for the five of them, but when Kadesh announced he had returned permanently, the quarters became uncomfortably cramped. But rather than live alone in Gershon's former house, Kadesh built a temporary structure on the roof. There had been discussion that perhaps he would purchase Gershon's house "someday," but now the family was deep into the grape harvest, and the proximity of Naboth's house to the vineyard made it convenient for the family—the entirety of the workforce—to live together.

Miriam stretched a hand over the hearth. Last night's embers still glowed. She added kindling, stirred up a flame, and placed several larger sticks over the growing fire.

Someday. If Kadesh decided to marry, and if it were Davita he wed ... Miriam smiled and bent into the task of grinding grain, letting herself dream. Davita already loved Miriam like a sister. Gershon's house would be perfect for a new couple, giving them the privacy so often in short supply. Time to grow acquainted with each other, time to talk over their pasts and their future together.

Miriam dragged the millstone back and forth. She and Gershon had not had that time, although Yaffa had offered to keep Jaedon for the first week. But a day later Miriam and Gershon brought him home, both agreeing they missed him. As for Miriam, the boy was always in her thoughts, but she also worried he was too energetic for Yaffa. But had it been a mistake, not setting apart time for her and Gershon?

She put the flour to one side. She and Gershon had a long future ahead. Plenty of time for them to grow closer. Every marriage was different. If theirs grew into a version of Naboth and Yaffa's, Miriam would be content. If he looked on her with a smile lighting his eyes. If he once said he loved her.

Time had passed, bringing changes no one could predict. She rinsed the lentils she had soaked overnight, added fresh water and seasonings, and set the pot in the hearth. It was pointless to chew over the past or worry about the future. Only days ago, she had been frightened by the king's conversation with Naboth, and nothing had come of it. Naboth explained Yahweh's commandment, and the king left. There was no trouble. Like she had told Gershon, the king had forgotten. One humble vineyard could not hold his attention for long.

Naboth took a deep breath when he walked into the front room. "Your bread smells wonderful. It is mornings like this I thank Yahweh that our fasts begin at sundown, not daybreak."

Miriam arched an eyebrow as she pulled flatbreads from the hearth.

Gershon, Kadesh, and Jaedon hurried in from outside. Gershon said, "What fast day are you speaking of, Abba?"

Miriam motioned for Jaedon to help her with the porridge. She quickly scooped lentils into wooden bowls, laying a flat bread atop each one.

Naboth inhaled again. "If there is one thing I can count on, it is your fresh bread every morning."

Yaffa gave his arm a light slap. "You used to say that

about my bread."

He chuckled. "I am a man of few words, so I must reuse them."

Miriam smiled, having heard this joke a few times. She glanced at Gershon, whose eyes fixed on his father, waiting. She knew Naboth had heard the question and would answer after he had chewed on it thoroughly, like a cow chews its cud.

Everyone sat on the cushions she had spread. Naboth blessed the bread and the porridge, and after he spooned up a few bites, he said, "The king proclaimed a fast."

Everyone but Jaedon stopped eating.

Gershon said, "A religious fast? He has never done that before. Do you think it strange?"

"No stranger than when he began worshipping in the Yahweh temple."

Kadesh said, "But he still worsh—"

Gershon cleared his throat loudly, jerking his head toward Jaedon. The boy's eyes flicked back and forth between father and uncle.

Miriam sighed. Another matter she had been meaning to talk over with Gershon. Since Elijah's triumph on Mount Carmel, Ba'al worshippers no longer held fertility rituals at the pagan temples, only in the high places. She was glad Jaedon would not see such sordid practices in his home town. But he was a curious boy and would ask questions. His father needed to explain that the Ba'als were what Yahweh spoke of when he said *Thou shalt have no other gods before me.*

Yaffa spoke hesitantly, as if her thoughts were not fully formed. "Perhaps the king's heart has been softened ... by the grace Yahweh has shown him." She paused a moment and then went on. "Ahab knows Yahweh's power. The miracles on Mount Carmel showed him. But he is a proud man. I think he was angry to be humbled in front of his nation and then the Arameans."

Miriam took Yaffa's hand. "Do you mean the siege?"

"Yes, dear. The Lord used a pagan nation to work on our king. He was ready to hand over his wives and children as tribute. And then that other prophet, saying Yahweh would give Israel the victory, so the king would know Yahweh is the God of Israel."

"Hmm." Miriam sat back, looking at the faces around the circle. The men appeared doubtful that Ahab had softened, but all gazed fondly at Yaffa. Who would not? She was a kind woman and often attributed the best motives to the worst people. But, perhaps in this case she was right.

In his letter, Caleb had written about the battle of Aphek. He was convinced Israel would not have won the battle without the rainy weather, the enemy's mass hysteria, and the crumbling wall—a convergence of events he attributed to Yahweh. But her brother had written nothing about Ahab's attitude toward Yahweh.

Likewise, when Dov spoke of the battle, he said the Israelites were grossly outnumbered, but Yahweh used both natural and supernatural means to give Israel a second victory. Dov saw the Lord's hand in the victory at Aphek, as did Caleb. But did the king?

If anyone had insight into Ahab's mindset after each battle, it was Dov. As a king's soldier, he was on the field each time. He overheard conversations and spoke to the king. Miriam knew Dov would never say anything disloyal. But if he had witnessed the king offer a sacrifice to Yahweh, make a speech, or utter a word of praise about the Lord's hand in battle, speaking of such actions would not be disloyal.

But Dov had said nothing specific about the king.

The rest of the morning's conversation concerned the ripeness of grapes, how many more bushels they expected to harvest, and how many new vines might fruit next year.

"I am sitting at the gate today." Naboth gave his wife a kiss on the cheek and grabbed the last flatbread. He winked at Miriam. "I must sustain my spirit so I can judge quarrels between brothers without despair."

"Remember to eat it before sundown," Yaffa said.

"Well before then, *Ishti*. The king called a town meeting and time of prayer midday."

A time of prayer with the elders and nobles of the city? The king had indeed had a change of heart.

When it was time to leave for the vineyard, Gershon pulled Miriam aside. "Kadesh and I can finish today's harvest without you and Jaedon. Why not go to the valley and practice your archery? Jaedon is becoming a good shot, and you enjoy it also. So go. But I need you both to help tread grapes when we return."

Miriam cleaned the bowls and cookpot while Jaedon put away the cushions and helped Yaffa sweep. How quickly the boy worked when an outing was promised.

"Would you like to come with us, Imma?" Miriam asked. "The sun is warm and there has been a breeze these last several days."

"Yes, come, Savta," Jaedon said. "Maybe we will see the eagles."

"No, dear. I plan to sit at the loom this morning and then rest a while. But I will have your supper ready when you return."

"You will not need to," Jaedon said. "The fast, remember? Abba says I am old enough."

"To fast?" Yaffa laughed and smoothed his hair. "Someday being "old enough" may not seem so desirable."

Miriam tucked cloth parcels of cheese and dates between the arrows in her quiver and filled waterskins. After situating Yaffa in front of her loom, they kissed her goodbye and strolled out the door. Passing the gate, Miriam grinned at Naboth, who listened attentively to a small crowd who had a grievance with a merchant. The sun gently warmed her face and the sound of Jaedon's chatter made her smile and required little more from her than an occasional "Truly?" or "Oh, my!"

How her mother would enjoy Jaedon. Imma had seen him as a toddler, when he was only her nephew's son. Now he was Miriam's boy. Even if he was not the child of her body, hadn't she fed him plump lentils, taught him from the Torah, and held a cool rag to his head during fevers? Those loving tasks made her his mother. She wanted to show him off to her family. Had it only been two years since she had lived in Samaria? Actually, somewhat less. Still, it seemed forever since she had felt Imma's arms around her.

But the possibility for a reunion was there. Dov had said he would ask the king to keep chariots in Jezreel. He said no more about it, but Miriam knew he had not forgotten. She thought of him bringing the pony for Jaedon to ride in the wedding procession. He was a man who provided more than he promised. There would be a chariot in Jezreel as soon as he could ask the king.

Gershon would not want to visit her family until after harvest. Another month, at most. Then at last she could have a long talk with Imma. She could ask her and Savta if any other woman had been barren in their family. How long it had taken before—

Jaedon tugged her sleeve. "This is where we stopped last time, Imma. Do you want to go farther?"

Surprised they had arrived so quickly, Miriam glanced up at the vineyard. She saw Kadesh and he waved at her. Gershon was bent over, not looking their way.

She waved back. "No, I told your father we would stay where he could see us. Will you get our targets?"

Jaedon nodded, reaching for the waterskins. "I hid them in that copse of trees. Want me to put the water there to keep cool?"

Miriam smiled, handing him the skins. "Good idea. Why not set up the targets just left of the trees? That is a little farther than we shot last time."

They took turns shooting and running after arrows until the sun was overhead and their arms ached. Then they ate their midday meal in the shade of the trees.

"This isn't breaking the fast, is it?" Jaedon's hand stopped on its way to his mouth.

"No," she assured him. "Not until sundown."

He leaned back against the tree, tossed a piece of cheese into his mouth, and looked up into the branches. "I don't see any birds."

"We have been making quite a bit of noise. If the birds are resting, they might pick trees a little farther away."

He picked up a date. "What if they are eating?"

"Like us?" She grinned. "Depends on the bird. They might be hunting seeds, berries, or insects in the grass or bushes. There is a spring nearby. They might be drinking or cooling themselves off. And some birds, like the eagles, as you know, eat meat."

She studied him, wondering if this might be the moment

to talk about hunting.

"You know," he said. "I am nearly a man."

She coughed. "You have not yet seen nine years."

"But you and Savta have been teaching me sections of Torah," he stated. "You said I am good at it."

"This is true. But you will not have to recite for at least three or four more years. Why do you bring this up?"

"I am good with the bow. You also said that."

She nodded.

"When are you going to teach me to shoot birds for food? If I am to be a man, I need to provide food for my family."

"Help. You would *help* to provide food. It will be many years before you must provide food for a family. You know you have a father and uncle. Not to mention your saba. Or those neighbors who want to trade meat for wine." She smiled. "But yes, hunting is a useful skill. This is something we will learn together. Even I have never hunted with a bow. You have seen my snares."

He twisted his mouth, spit out a date seed, then bit into another.

She frowned thoughtfully. "Perhaps we should talk to someone who bow hunts fowl. I am sure there are countless things we could learn from an experienced hunter. First, we must be very good shots. I do not like the idea of only wounding a bird and having it go off to suffer. And I don't think we should shoot birds in trees, if that is what you were thinking. For one thing, we might lose an arrow. Our shot might be deflected by branches or leaves, our aim spoiled. But most important, at least in my opinion, the tree is their home."

He nodded solemnly and a rush of warmth filled Miriam. He understood. The kindhearted boy!

After they finished eating, Miriam noticed a line of deeper green grass beyond the trees. She looked behind her, to the vineyard. Gershon shaded his eyes and looked their way, so she waved and pointed toward the spring he had told her about. He nodded and signaled his approval.

She called Jaedon and pointed. "See there? The spring your father mentioned."

He stared. "I don't see it."

"When you see deep green grass like that, especially when other grass is not so lush, a spring nourishes it. Let's look around. We might find bulbs or even ducks. If we do, we'll come back with snares another time."

They walked all around the spring, foraging bitter greens and wild onions for stews. "We have enough," she said. "Let's go home."

They were walking back through the trees when she first heard shouting, although at a distance, it sounded like animals being herded through the city. Recalcitrant camels, maybe, with angry drivers.

But when she stepped out from the trees, she saw them. A crowd of men in the vineyard. Shouting angrily. Dragging a man—Naboth! Shoving Gershon and Kadesh when they pushed into their midst to help him. Punching, grabbing, pinning the brothers' arms behind them.

Miriam ran toward the city, her bow and quiver bouncing. She clamped her arm over them, twisting to find Jaedon running close behind.

"Abba! They are hurting Abba!" His face was twisted, his eyes terrified.

She shot her attention back to the vineyard. The men continued beating Gershon and Kadesh, then shoved them toward Naboth, shouting the whole time. "*Sinner! Blasphemer!*" They were lifting rocks! Her men crossed their arms over their faces, protecting their heads. Jaedon screamed again and again. She could see the stones fly, some as big as melons, stagger Gershon, gut Naboth, and knock Kadesh to his knees. Rocks they were pulling from the vineyard wall. Gershon and Kadesh wrapped their arms around their father and turned their backs to the crowd. She ran a few more steps, feeling herself crumble, her legs dead weights.

"They are killing them!" Jaedon cried, his voice thin.

She wheeled, wrapped her arms around him. Shielding him from the sight with her body. Like Naboth's sons were doing for their father.

"Listen, little one. I will go help. But those men are wild animals. You must hide. Go back in those trees. Climb one and wait." She shook him by the shoulders. He must obey, must not follow her into danger. "Can you do what I say?"

"No. I am going with you. Abba! Saba!"

She grasped his arm and pulled him toward the grove. Finding a tree with some lower branches, she lifted him, steadying his foot on the lowest branch, shoving him toward a higher one, talking all the while. "I will go find them. If they are hurt, I will tend them before I come for you again. Your Savta and I will help them. Wait here until I come back. Promise me you'll do it. Promise me."

She shoved his bow up the tree. His quiver was secure on his shoulder. "If anything or anyone threatens you—" She gripped his leg. It trembled violently. "Hold your bow ready, arrow in your hand. Remember. Wait here for me. Still as a desert cat."

When Miriam reached the vineyard, no one was there. Stones lay everywhere. Trampled and torn vines. And the blood, everywhere blood. She heard the keening as she knelt among the stones. It was her voice, bewailing her husband, his father, his brother. What did it mean, the chaotic scene she had witnessed? All this blood, soaking into the ground. But where were they? Who had taken them?

She clamped a hand over her mouth, gulped down the sobs. Her husband. Jaedon's father.

Gershon.

She couldn't face telling ... she had to ... tell Yaffa. She wrapped her arms around her middle, trying to hold herself together against forces ripping her apart. Had they been killed? Murdered by that rabble! Why?

A flash of hope jolted her. Maybe they weren't dead. Maybe the mob had come to their senses and her men had somehow staggered home. Naboth had so many friends. Friends would have carried them home. But all the blood—

She stumbled out of the vineyard, making for the gate. She had to get to Yaffa, tell her what had happened. No! Can't tell her. It will kill her. Her husband dead. Both sons. All three men—dead.

Miriam's hands trembled, her head shook too, fighting what her senses told her. *This is not true. A nightmare.* No, believe it. Danger, danger is everywhere. You do not know what happened, why, or who those men were. Death may be waiting around a corner. Compose yourself. Look like a woman coming back from—from gathering greens.

Quickly, she reached into her quiver and yanked out a handful of greens. An arrow fell out, too, and she shoved it back inside. She lifted the neck of her tunic to dry her face, stood to her full height, and threw her shoulders back. *I am Miriam, the big woman no man wants.* She lifted her chin. When she walked through the gate, a hooded figure leaped out from behind one of the doors and yanked her back where he had come from.

"It's me, Zuar. I've been waiting for you," he whispered hoarsely, pulling off his cloak. "Officials are looking for you and the boy." He draped the cloak around her shoulders, drawing the hood over her head.

Zuar? Why was he here? Wasn't he to have ridden to Samaria with Dov?

"Let's go." He pulled her back toward the gate.

"But Yaffa." She trembled, fear pulling her down, at the same time she felt torn in two directions. She wanted to go to Yaffa, but where were the men?

"Wasn't she with you and the boy?"

"She was tired. She stayed home."

"You can't go to the house. Stay here." He shoved her into the narrow space between the open gate and the wall. "I will get her." He gently pushed her down, urging her to sit. "Make yourself small," he said. "And be quiet. The queen's henchmen are everywhere."

A donkey clip-clopped past, poked by a small boy with a stick. *Was her boy all right?* Had he obeyed her? Stayed in the tree?

Robed men passed by. Their sandaled feet shuffled briskly. "A grandson is still unaccounted for. An heir. The queen will not be happy."

Jezebel! Zuar had said the queen's henchmen.

"What about the wife?"

"The old woman? She has gone into hiding already. But a woman will not inherit. It does not matter if we find her."

"The queen said kill them all. No loose ends. She won't

like it."

Miriam shuddered, pressing deeper into the crevice. *Kill them all?* A woman will not inherit? What did this mean?

She spotted Zuar walking toward her. He passed without stopping, calling a greeting to someone out of Miriam's sight. He disappeared from her narrow range of vision, but a moment later, he slipped behind the open gate. "She was not at the house," he murmured.

"Some men were looking for her. I heard them. Will they hurt her?"

Zuar's mouth opened and closed. He looked behind him. "We'll find her. Keep that hood pulled forward. The queen's men mustn't see you—"

"But why? Why do they want me, Zuar? Why do they want Yaffa?" She squeezed further into the pocket of wall and gate.

"They say ... Naboth cursed Yahweh and the king."

"Cursed Yahweh! He is entirely devout. And why would that Ba'al worshipper care if Naboth cursed Yahweh?"

"It is a lie. Listen." He took both her hands and squeezed hard. "Something scared Yaffa. Does she have a friend?"

Her mother-in-law had many friends, but which of her friends were trustworthy? Where would she go? Why had none of the elders or nobles who knew Naboth spoken up on his behalf? Or Gershon's?

Why were all three men stoned? Even if Naboth had cursed God as they said, a son didn't die for this father's sins. She shook her head, as if she could rid herself of the cloud fettering her thoughts.

Zuar stepped back into the street, looked around, came back. "No searchers." He took her hand. "Come now. Where do we look?"

Miriam had two friends she trusted in Jezreel. One was gentle and one was bold.

"Davita. My best friend."

Miriam's gaze shot left and right as she crept from her hiding place. They walked the back alleys toward the house Davita shared with her father. It took them through a squalid neighborhood Miriam had never walked. Women lounged outside their doors in indolent postures, eyeing Zuar as he strode by. One even spoke to him as they passed.

"Come back another time, big man."

Zonah. Miriam saw his neck redden.

Miriam smelled the bread before they turned the corner and saw the line of customers. Zuar put an arm around her in a familiar way, bending his head down, she realized, to shield her face. "Is there a back door?" he whispered.

"That way." She swerved toward the back door, Zuar close on her heels. She knocked softly and Davita opened, as if she had been waiting. Her eyes were red-rimmed and teary. She took hold of Miriam and pulled her into the warm bakery.

"They're dead," she whispered. "I saw them drag the bodies to the refuse heap. At first, I didn't know it was them. But I went down. I saw them." Davita broke down.

So it was true. Miriam released her final thread of hope. "I can't find Yaffa. I thought she might—"

Davita wiped her eyes. "I got her out of the city. When I saw your father-in-law, Gershon ... Kadesh. You know, I thought he and I ... That doesn't matter now. I ran to Yaffa's house, took her to the valley, hid her in a thicket. I gave her a cloak, so she is warm. No one will find her. I will take you there."

"But Gershon—"

"He is dead. You cannot help him now. He would not want you to be taken. Miriam, I think they would kill you. Yaffa too. If Kadesh and I had—if those men thought we were betrothed—my life would be in danger, too. But as it is, I am only bereft." A sob escaped from her tightly pressed lips. She steadied, then whispered, "I loved him. We would have married. They took him from me, and they are not going to take you." Then at a sudden thought she grasped Miriam's arms. "The boy! They have been looking for him everywhere. Is he safe?"

"Jaedon is hiding in a tree outside the city. It is getting dark. He is so afraid." Miriam clasped her hands together. "So am I." Her voice grew small.

Zuar put an arm around each of them. "We are going. But not through the main gate. My father is watching the north gate tonight."

"I am coming, too," Davita said. "You will not find Yaffa

without me."

It was too much to think on. How could the vineyard matter so much to the king? He owned two palaces. And surely, he did not believe the lies about Naboth. No one could. And how did the queen become involved?

None of that mattered. Gershon was dead—her husband of only one year. Yaffa's husband, too. And Kadesh, with all Davita's hopes. Dead. All dead. Miriam looked at her friend's tear-stained face. Her own was dry. She was thankful for that. She had to think. How would they escape? How would they live? They were widows. Jaedon an orphan. Everything was lost—the vineyard, their home, their men, their safety. Could she make her way to Samaria without being found? Take refuge in her father's house? But ... her father was Naboth's brother. An heir. This might not be widely known. They lived in different cities and were beneath the king and queen's notice. But Miriam could not bring the danger to them.

She must become provider and protector for Yaffa and Jaedon. The three of them would have to live in the wilderness, hide in caves and wadis, always be on the run.

They would all die. She was not strong enough. Then, she must *become* strong enough. She must. Strong enough to overcome this tragedy. Shrewd enough to evade pursuit. She had to live and fight for Jaedon.

"You can't come, Davita," Miriam said. "Two women and a man leaving the city as night falls?"

"I told you," Zuar said. "My father is keeping the north gate."

But others might see them. "I could dress as a man," she said slowly. "I have often been called ... mannish."

"Mannish?" He laughed shortly. "That won't work. But, some sort of disguise—I have it. You can both dress as—I hesitate to say, but—*zonahs*." He cleared his throat as Davita gasped and continued quickly. "One man, two women, you can pretend to have drunk much wine, you will be veiled—it is perfect."

And it was. They walked through the gate unchallenged. When Miriam stumbled from grief and hung on his shoulder, it fit the tale they were weaving. If Davita's eyes were red, it was from strong drink, not mourning. Even her moaning, once choked by a sob, befit the image they portrayed. When they walked past Aaron, he gave Zuar a curt nod, but did not speak. Zuar whispered in her ear. "If my father is questioned, he can complain about his son's wild ways."

When they found Yaffa hiding in the thicket, Miriam gathered her into her arms, comforting her with the news Jaedon was safe. Leaving her in Davita's arms, Miriam ran ahead to the grove, calling softly, "Jaedon."

Only when she was under the tree did he whimper, "Imma."

"Can you climb down, my heart?"

He moved slowly, like an old man, stiff from cold and fear. She held up her arms, encouraging him. "Come, dear one." He stopped. When she heard him shudder, she quickly climbed up to meet him, chaffing his ankles, grasping his waist, kissing his cheek. She guided his hands and feet as they climbed down together.

When they reached the ground, they simultaneously reached for each other. But when she loosened her grip, he leaped up, wrapped his arms and legs around her, and clung.

When he showed no sign of letting go, she attempted to pry loose his fingers. Zuar moved in, gently grasping him by the shoulders. "Here, now, we must move on. You will get through this. Remember, you are almost a man."

Zuar led them farther from the city to a wadi. After they walked a while, he said, "Far enough. They will not find us here."

But when Miriam asked for a fire, he said it would point to their whereabouts, so they huddled together in the cold. Davita and Yaffa wrapped themselves in the same cloak, while Miriam held Jaedon.

She rubbed her cheek against his head, whispering, "Tomorrow, we will go to the eagles." That would put them far enough from the city. And there were many caves if they needed to hide.

He clutched her hand. "Do you promise?"

She arranged her cloak around him. "I promise." But she was not only promising the sight of eagles flying in the wide sky. She wanted to give him that joyful memory her family had experienced together. She remembered that moment, and so would he.

He was broken by grief. But he would heal. *Will he not, Yahweh?*

She shivered. There was another promise, a dark undertaking she held like an unspoken vow. She acknowledged it now. *Justice.* She would see to it. Her eyes felt dry, unfocused. The night was cold and she was tired— oh, so tired—but she would not sleep this night. She tried to pray, but could not. It was as if the words, like her soul, were weighted to earth. Thus tethered, they swirled around her, there in the dark. Words burning darkly in bitterness, flaming a path forward.

I don't know how. I don't know when. But there will be justice.

Chapter Twenty-Two

When my spirit grows faint within me,
it is you who watch over my way. In the path
where I walk people have hidden a snare for me.
~ Psalm 142:3

MIRIAM CLIMBED OUT OF THE RAVINE and took her bearings from
the cliff where the eagles had nested. The pale light of dawn
brushed the rock face. Now she understood how far they were
from the city. Not far enough.

Certainly, they must flee farther into the wilderness, but
neither Yaffa nor Jaedon were capable of a full day's walk.
Miriam recalled the peace that had filled her the morning
they watched the eagles soar. At that moment they were
happy—she, Jaedon, and Gershon.

The limestone cliff stood as memorial.

They could reach it today. Tonight, they would shelter
in one of the caves said to inhabit its face. One night for Yaffa
and Jaedon to gather their strength. They could not linger
this close to the city longer than that. They must flee as far
as possible, as quickly as possible.

She heard sounds of the others waking, so she
descended again into the wadi, sliding a little on the slope.
Her gaze met Jaedon's. Tears streaked his face, although
Yaffa held him close. Davita was pulling loaves of bread from
a pouch she must have packed as they left. *Bless her.*

And Zuar strode toward her, frowning. "You should not
have left without telling me. I understand the need for
privacy, but just—don't do it again."

She stared at him, trying to ignore a prick of irritation.
She owed him their lives. "You have shown us great
kindness," she said slowly. "I don't wish to cause you
concern."

He softened his tone. "We should leave quickly. East

into the hill country. Then south to Gilead. As far as possible from Jezreel or Samaria."

"A good plan." So why was she thinking of arguing against it? "But first, I have promised Jaedon we will go to the cliff." She would have overlooked this promise to keep Jaedon safe, but she knew the old woman and the boy were not yet ready for the trek Zuar described. She pointed. "It is not out of our way. Eagles have nested in a high cave there for a couple years. A second group of nestlings will fly soon. It would mean much to the boy to catch a glimpse of them, and as I have said, there are caves. Perhaps we would find one where we could rest a day or two. Until you and Davita go back."

"What are you talking about?" Zuar growled.

Davita jumped to her feet. "I am not going back."

"I have thought on this," Miriam said. "My friend, the whole city will miss you in your father's bakery. You bake, you take payment, you are there every day. How can you disappear without a word? For one day, perhaps two, your father can say you are sick. Then he will be questioned. It will come out we are friends, and he will be in danger. And you, Zuar, your father has told the whole city about your return. The queen will question the gatekeepers and his story will surface. What happened will be made known."

"Not the way we left the city. I am a degenerate son who runs with prostitutes—"

"Combined with Davita's disappearance, the stories will not hold up under scrutiny."

"Do you think I would leave three women and a child out here alone? Defenseless against the queen's men, or should they give up the search, against ruffians and assassins—not to mention lions and leopards that roam the land?"

Yaffa loudly cleared her throat. Jaedon was pressed closely against her.

Zuar paused. "Davita should go back," he said. "She would be missed."

"You must go with her." Glancing toward Jaedon, Miriam lowered her voice. "As you said, danger is everywhere."

He gave her a cold look. "I will take her back, but only if—"

"I am not a parcel, Zuar." Davita planted her hands on her hips. "Do not try to decide what I will or will not do. Miriam is my friend, and"—she threw a glance toward Yaffa and Jaedon and finished in a furious whisper–"she has lost everything. She is not losing me."

Miriam stepped over and wrapped both arms around her. "I love you my friend," she said in her ear. "But go back to your father. I cannot have his imprisonment or death on my conscience. Go back." She gave her one more squeeze and turned to Zuar. "Take her back—parcel or not—and we will watch for you toward evening, near the cliff face. Then we will be grateful if you will lead us somewhere farther, where we are no longer in danger." In her heart, Miriam wondered if there would ever be such a place.

Her leave-taking with Davita was emotional, yet restrained for Jaedon's sake. Zuar waited, standing apart. While Yaffa hugged Davita, Miriam approached him. "Take care when you go back to the city ... and thank you. I am glad we will not be on our own. Just yet."

He frowned, then said brusquely, "Wait for me near the cliffs. Do not forget. I will return well before dark." She nodded and turned aside, pretending she did not notice his eyes had grown moist.

Miriam held tight to Jaedon's right hand as she led him through the tall grass, Yaffa, his left. Miriam perceived her mother-in-law needed to feel his little hand to hold herself together.

It was also the only way to keep him moving. Once Yaffa had stopped to pluck berries from a bush crowding their path. But when Miriam let go of Jaedon's hand to help gather berries, he immediately curled onto the ground like a newborn babe.

Now she walked quickly, urging her companions along, while watching them for signs of fatigue. Her thoughts swirled questions that felt like accusations. What if she and Jaedon had not left to practice archery? If they had gone to the vineyard with the men, could she have prevented the stoning? Pleaded for mercy? Sent an arrow into each assailant until her quiver was empty? Or died with them?

How could she deal with this turmoil? She examined the little she knew. From the snatches of conversation she'd heard on the street and reports Zuar picked up, it seemed the queen was the force behind everything. But it seemed too senseless to believe—unless it related to the king's desire for their vineyard.

Then the pieces started to fit. Had the king and queen plotted to murder Naboth and any family members who could inherit or complain?

Miriam gauged their distance from the cliff. Another hour or two at this pace. She glanced at Yaffa. She was keeping up better than Miriam had hoped, though her bearing bore witness of the tragedy. She had lost her husband, not to the peaceful death he deserved, but to brutal stoning. Now the three of them were on the run, not sure why or exactly who pursued them. They could not discuss this as they walked, not with Jaedon listening. Not that she was sure he *was* listening. He had been so strange, so uncharacteristically silent, since the murders.

And no wonder. What young child could have lived through such a thing and remain unscathed?

For that matter, what adult? Miriam had never witnessed a stoning. There had never been one in Samaria, at least not in her lifetime.

But even if stoning were prevalent and Samaria filled with righteous followers of Yahweh, neither of which were true, Naboth accused of blaspheming the Lord? Never. Her uncle had been among Yahweh's most sincere followers.

Miriam trudged on through the grass, Jaedon's hand cold in hers. She sought a flicker in his eyes, some sign of awareness behind the staring gaze. She squeezed his hand. Nothing.

When would her family in Samaria know what had happened? How long would it take for news of Naboth's death to make its way to them? Dov had left in the morning, before the murders. Imma would not realize her daughter, newly married, was now a widow. Savta would have to be told her son and two grandsons had been stoned. Then it struck Miriam that her family would believe she, Jaedon, and Yaffa were also dead. The only persons who knew the truth— Davita, Zuar, and Aaron—would have to keep silent. In public, at least.

"Yaffa." She spoke quietly, keeping their presence as silent as possible. "Let's make for that line of trees." *Yahweh, please, let there be a stream.* Her feet ached, and they needed to fill their waterskins. She yearned for a running stream, where they could remove their sandals and wade in cool water. Would that revive Jaedon's spirit? Oh, how she longed to hear him speak, to pester her with questions as he used to. But for now, silence was a blessing, until she could be sure they were safe.

"Jaedon, look ahead." When he did not lift his face, she stooped down, touching her cheek to his. "See the trees? Those nearest us are greener than those in the distance. Remember what that means?" She waited for a reply that did not come. "There may be a stream or pond."

He gave a brief nod and her chest expanded with hope. She squeezed his hand and walked faster.

The pool at the foot of the mountain reflected blue sky and the fringe of trees. A breeze rustled the leaves and birds chittered in their branches. Miriam's spirit lifted. Yaffa smiled, swinging Jaedon's hand in the air as they approached. They drank deeply of sweet water and filled their waterskins. Yaffa recited the blessing of grain as they shared berries and the remaining loaf of bread Davita had left.

Afterward, Jaedon sat quietly, his feet in the water. Before long, however, he climbed out and fell asleep with his head in Yaffa's lap. Miriam wove a fish snare from reeds along the bank. She had seen more than one flash of silver under the gleaming surface. When she finished the snare, she waded into the shallows, placed it where a current flowed into its open mouth, and dropped bait toward the back of the trap—a few berries and a crust of bread.

Miriam waded up the shallow slope and dried her feet on the grassy bank. Glancing at Yaffa, she said, "Shall I take him? You need rest, too."

Yaffa gently smoothed his hair. "He feels good, right

here. Sweet boy." She hummed a tune she often sang when weaving. The tune drew Miriam's thoughts to the house where the loom leaned near the largest window. Yaffa would pause on a note with each pass of the shuttle, or circle around a musical phrase when she tangled a thread.

Yaffa had a left a nearly-finished tunic for Jaedon on the frame, woven in one piece. Who would wear it now?

Yaffa held the final note trembling between her lips. After a silent moment, she said, "I am grateful we are together, the three of us. That we were not separated."

She rested her hand upon her heart. "That I had the love of a kind man, for so many years. And that my son found you, my dear, after the loss of Jaedon's mother."

Yaffa spoke of gratitude after her husband and sons were murdered? Miriam's chest compressed, like a thread stretched almost beyond endurance.

Jaedon moaned in his sleep and the tightness expanded. She jumped to her feet, starting to pace, but turbulence in the pond caught her attention. She hurried to the bank and stepped in. A fat fish whirled in confusion. Miriam stiffened, recognizing the emotion the creature expressed—but here was supper. She had no room for pity, she must keep her family alive.

Yaffa leaned back on her elbows, watching. Jaedon had rolled onto the grass beside her. Using an arrow, Miriam strung the fish through its gills and placed it in a shady area of the pond. She baited the now empty trap with a few more berries and sat the other side of Jaedon. Resting her arms atop bent knees, she surveyed their surroundings. They were well hidden by the pond, backed against the mountain and shielded by trees. Sitting, she could just see over the top of tall grass. If she lay down, she'd be invisible among the grasses and reeds.

She could not see into the distance, but neither could anyone easily spot them here. This was a good place to wait for Zuar. At the foot of the cliff, as she had told him. Near water, which he would understand when he saw the line of green.

Little green bee eaters hopped along the pond's muddy edge, cheeping and snapping gnats out of the air. When two birds quarreled over a feathery moth, Jaedon stirred, but when the avian conversation resumed a steady beat of chip-chip-cheeerr, he sighed and went back under the spell of sun and sound.

Quietly she rose, threading her way through the trees to spy out the valley and what she could see of the road coming from the city. Peeking from behind an ancient oak, she could see the city wall. It was the north wall they had fled through, so she would not be able to see the vineyard on the south slope. Not that she wanted to.

No one pursued them. As far as she could see, they were safe. And then it settled on her shoulders, a gossamer scarf of gratitude.

"I am grateful we are together," she said softy, as though speaking to the trees. "That we are safe. That we have supper. That a kind and thoughtful man chose me to spend the rest of his life with. No matter how short it was." She choked, but went on. "That he trusted me with his son." She covered her face with her hands. They smelled like fish.

Oh, Yahweh, help me.

Jaedon sat up, stared around, and she saw his face start to twist in panic.

"I am here," she called softly. "Over by the trees."

He ran to her and she held him, humming Yaffa's weaving tune.

He leaned back and stared up at her face.

"Were you crying?" he asked. He had spoken three words.

She smiled. "Maybe a little, but I am finished now."

He took her hand and pulled her back to Yaffa, who was sitting and combing her hair with her fingers. Miriam showed him the fish. She should teach Jaedon to clean it. He needed to learn to take care of himself—and others—soon. But not today.

"Shall we look for the eagles? It is later in the day than last year. But we might spot them if we are quiet." She wished the words back, as soon as she spoke them. They faced danger, if an enemy came upon them. But she wanted her bright boy back to himself. "We don't need to be completely quiet. Eagles don't frighten as easily as little birds." She swept her arm toward the bee eaters swooping dizzily around a swarm of bugs, sending them chittering into the sky. "As long as we don't shout."

She noticed Yaffa attempt to hide a smile. Miriam supposed she was babbling, trying to make up for Jaedon's quiet.

"Yaffa, can you walk with us? I don't want to leave you alone."

"Of course." Her mother-in-law pushed herself up slowly, took a few tentative steps, and then hit an easier stride.

Miriam picked up the waterskins. Motioning toward Jaedon, she said, "Please check the trap. Never leave food for animals when you need it yourself."

Soundlessly he hurried to the pond and peered into the snare. He caught her eye, shook his head at the trap, but picked up the fish-laden arrow.

"Good thinking. That is our dinner. Now if we walk around the pond and toward the cliff in this direction, the sun is on our shoulders, not in our eyes. Don't walk close to the cliff, in case a cave animal rushes out. Keep your bow ready to shoot but pointed toward the ground. Watch for the eagles, be wary of wild animals, and keep an eye open for Zuar." And cruel people, she thought. How could she teach her boy to beware of the wicked?

They started in the direction she had laid out. As they walked, they entered an open area where the trees were not as lush nor the grass as green.

"There is a difference away from the water," Yaffa noticed. "But you see more sky."

Miriam nodded. And right then they heard a haunting eagle cry. They looked up. In a moment, a golden eagle launched from an outcropping and flew over their heads. Its wing feathers painted a shadow on the ground the length of a man. As the bird glided over, Miriam saw bands of white and brown under its tail.

It swerved away from them, circled back once, and dipped lower, as if beckoning for them to follow. It shrieked and they heard answering sharp chirps up ahead. A young one? Was there a nest on the outcropping from which the bird had flown?

Miriam looked for the mate, but it didn't show itself. The eagle looped back again, flying even lower. It swept across the field in front of them, right to left, and back again. Almost as if it searched for something. Prey, most likely. There could be marmots and hares in this grass.

Miriam heard the chirps again. Insistent. Just ahead.

The eagle circled higher. Miriam shook her head. It was beautiful. Immense. It gave another cry, long, mournful, and shrill. The sound echoed as the bird winged its way toward the sun. Miriam shaded her eyes, as the eagle flew directly into the glare, until its feathers seemed lit by fire.

Chapter Twenty-Three

*The Lord said to Gideon, "You have too many men. I cannot
deliver Midian into their hands, or Israel would boast
against me, 'My own strength has saved me.' Now
announce to the army, 'Anyone who trembles with
fear may turn back and leave Mount Gilead.'"*
~ Judges 7:2-3a

Gideon's Cave
Elijah

ELIJAH ADDED ANOTHER LOG TO THE small fire, then set his cook
pot amid the embers. In the hills surrounding the Jezreel
valley the nights were mild, and his solitary meal of grains
and wild greens needed only a small fire. It made for a snug
shelter in this cliff cave, said to be the location of Gideon's
threshing floor. Whether it was, or wasn't, Yahweh had not
seen fit to tell him. But Elijah sensed the Lord had *something*
to say.

It was not yet dusk and Elijah wasn't hungry yet. The
prophet picked up his harp and strummed softly, searching
for a melody that fit his mood. What was his mood, exactly?
Confused? Perturbed? He hoped not perturbed, for that
would indicate rebellion against The Almighty's will, and that
Elijah would not tolerate. At least not knowingly—which was
why he searched his heart.

Waiting. That was his mood. He rested the harp on his
knees. Nothing wrong with waiting. The Almighty had sent
him to this lonely cave, and he obeyed. Left Elisha and the
others at Bethel and Jericho and walked north alone. And
here he waited, in this abandoned cave on the shoulder of
Mount Gilboa.

That stand of oaks in the valley had hidden Gideon's
threshing floor from the Midianites and Amelekites. The
Harod spring meandered along the foot of the cliff. There God
had whittled down Gideon's army to only three hundred,
because they drank from their hands.

Elijah huffed softly. Wasn't that how Yahweh did things? Gideon's army of three hundred against a camp of thousands, thick as locusts. Shepherd boy against armor-clad giant. Elijah alone, against four hundred fifty prophets of Melqart. And Ahab's victories over the Arameans, kindnesses the wayward king did not deserve.

God had used Micaiah twice now to speak to Israel. Would The Lord use Elijah again? He would go if sent, but he was content to spend the rest of his days teaching the schools of the prophets or preaching to farmers in the countryside.

Running his fingers down the bent cypress he'd smoothed with stone and sand, Elijah tightened one of the gut strings. How had he left off playing music to the Lord? The hum of the lyre and words of the psalm helped Elijah hear the Voice.

> *Be still before the Lord*
> *and wait patiently for him;*
> *do not fret when people succeed in their ways,*
> *when they carry out their wicked schemes.*

Like a musical instrument, the Lord had tuned Elijah's thoughts to choose this Psalm. Wait patiently. Be still. These words were for him. Or for someone Yahweh was sending to him, a victim of great evil.

> *Refrain from anger and turn from wrath;*
> *do not fret—it leads only to evil.*
> *For those who are evil will be destroyed,*
> *but those who hope in the Lord will inherit the land.*

More slowly, Elijah repeated the song, his heart assenting to each phrase of his musical meditation. He would wait for the Lord to speak. Not like the time Elijah ran from Jezreel's walls, fleeing a queen's wrath. How had he, who served the Most High, feared that woman?

Soon. The Lord would speak soon.

When the last vibration of his harp hushed, an eagle's shrill cry penetrated the silence. *Ah!* Elijah was not alone. Laying his harp aside, he walked to the cliff ledge to scan sky and landscape.

A wind tossed the trees' topmost branches. The eagle circled above, focused on something on the ground. The grass flattened under the wind. The eagle shrieked again. This was no mating call, but a challenge to a predator threatening the nest. Why then, did the eagle dive for the ground?

Elijah craned his neck, but the tossing branches of the oaks blocked his view where the eagle had disappeared.

And then he heard another cry. A child.

Elijah. Go now.

Grabbing his staff and the pouch, the servant of the Most High obeyed.

Chapter Twenty-Four

*The Lord called to (Moses) from the mountain and said,
"This is what you are to ... tell the people of Israel:
You yourselves have seen what I did to Egypt, and
how I carried you on eagles' wings and brought you
to myself. Now if you obey me fully ... out of all
nations you will be my treasured possession.*
~ Exodus 19:3b-5

The limestone cliff
Miriam

MIRIAM STARED AT THE EAGLE CHICK, flopped sideways, and panting. So young. Pale down just sprouting a few brown feathers. She had meant to give Jaedon a memory of a better time.

"I'm so sorry, Jaedon. Its leg is broken. It can't live." She reached for the chick, turning her back so Jaedon wouldn't have to see when she—

"No!" He screamed, "Don't kill it. You can mend its leg." He turned his eyes on her, beseeching, the blank stare gone for the first time since the murders.

Keeping both hands fixed over the wings of the struggling bird, she knelt before her boy. He had spoken, but her words fled. The chick felt impossibly thin. The mother had stopped feeding it, knowing it could never fly and would die soon. Yet, its plight had awakened Jaedon.

"Please don't," he whispered. Her breath caught at the pain in his voice. She felt a tear streak her face. How could she hurt him again? Yet how could she care for a wounded bird, when she needed all her means to care for the three of them?

"Oh, my heart, even if I could splint its poor leg, it is a wild thing. It would not leave the dressing alone." A few dried shreds of flesh lay nearby, a witness that the eagle had tried to feed her chick. The chick's inability to balance on two feet must have made feeding it difficult, if not impossible.

"I will watch over it," Jaedon said.

A pang of remorse hit her. She'd put him in charge of the goat, which he had faithfully cared for. Who cared for it now?

A shadow fell between them. Yaffa mouthed, "Perhaps ..."

"It must eat meat. Where will we get meat?" Did she have to argue with both of them? Miriam lifted a hand to her throat, massaging the node of wretchedness. It would be hard enough to forage food for the three of them, let alone a crippled bird.

"We must trust the Lord." Jaedon thrust his chin out. "And we have the fish."

Miriam pressed her fist against her mouth, an urge to laugh warring with the threat of tears. The Lord had not done well by Jaedon thus far. His father, grandfather, and uncle killed, his vineyard stolen. Would he ever see his home again? Farm the grapes of his inheritance?

She turned her gaze upwards, hoping to see the parent eagle, but the sky was empty. If she did see it, what then? Lay the poor crippled thing back on the ground? She doubted the mother would care for the chick, now its injury was apparent and humans had handled it. Without flight or its mother's protection, the chick was at the mercy of predators. A quick end to its suffering. Miriam could accept that, but Jaedon could not. Indeed, she did not want him to cope with another death, not even one in the natural order of things.

She straightened, holding the chick level with her face. Steely black eyes glared into hers. Its downy feathers tickled her palm, and she drew a deep breath. *Phew, but the thing stank.* As if reminded, it shot a stream of foul-smelling scat out its vent. She would not have thought the scrawny thing had the wherewithal.

With a sigh, she turned to Jaedon. "Look at the length of his lower leg, from here to here." She touched the bends of its leg. "Find two sticks that long, and about as thick as your finger. Quickly, and don't go far."

Yaffa lifted the border of her tunic, reached toward her ankle, and pulled a wicked-looking dagger from a sheath.

Miriam raised her eyebrows. Her mother-in-law had

packed at least one useful item despite her chaotic departure.

Yaffa positioned its iron edge to cut a strip from her hem.

"Don't spoil your garment, dear woman." A big man, as gnarled and ancient-looking as the pines from which he emerged, walked toward them. He carried a shepherd's staff, crook on one end, club on the other. It suited as a weapon, but he leaned on it as he walked toward them. "I always keep strips of old cloth to bind up wounds or"—he gestured toward the chick as he kept walking"—set broken bones."

"Come no closer, old man," said Yaffa, stepping in front of Miriam and pointing the knife threateningly. "Who are you?"

"A shepherd, I suppose."

Miriam narrowed her eyes. A shepherd, *he supposes?*

"Where are your sheep?" She tensed her hands, reluctant to drop the bird if he was the harmless stranger he appeared, but ready to throw it in his face, disorient him if he made a wrong move.

He looked around as if a stray sheep or two hid in his shadow. "I heard a child cry." He shrugged. "My cave is just up there. Where is the boy?"

Miriam tensed. He heard a child cry. How did he know it was a boy? Had he had been watching them?

Jaedon came walking toward them slowly, his hands behind his back.

The man turned toward him unperturbed, as if he had spotted Jaedon before she did. "Did you find the grinding stone under the oaks?"

Grinding stone?

"You are *not going* to hurt my Imma!" With a deft movement, Jaedon swung what surely *was* an old grinding stone from behind his back. Running toward the stranger he lifted it over his head, ready to strike. But the shepherd's staff had a long sweep. With a quick move the man could knock Jaedon off his feet and get her and Yaffa on the back swing.

Surprisingly, the man dropped his staff, stepped back, and held his hand out, flat palmed. "Steady, lad." He glanced at Miriam. "Don't drop the nestling."

Jaedon slowed but kept the stone above his head. "I'll throw it if you move."

"I'm not going to hurt your imma. Or anyone."

"You're no shepherd," Miriam said. "Did she send you after us?"

The man looked at her with interest. "She?"

"The queen. Ouch!" The chick had clamped down on the skin between her thumb and forefinger.

He laughed at her question, it seemed, not the ungrateful chick. "No, the queen did not send me to find you." He stretched both hands toward heaven. "Yahweh, is there something you want to tell me?" He paused, as if listening, then asked, "Will that be enough?" He nodded toward the sky, then looked at each of them in turn.

"I am Elijah. If you need to hear more right now, in order to feel safe, ask your questions. But realize, our supper is cooking up there in the cave. There is enough for all. If we talk too long, it will burn."

How could she not have remembered him? He was older, yes, but that thick wild hair, the piercing eyes, the staff with which he had coaxed fire from heaven.

"I am sorry, sir. I remember you now. I was there on Mount Carmel."

"You were very young." He pulled strips of cloth from a pouch tied to a wide leather belt. He arched an eyebrow at Yaffa. "You were not so young."

Miriam's mother-in-law looked abashed at not having recognized him.

Jaedon piped up, "My savta told me about Mount Carmel. I was there, but too little to remember anything." He swung an arm toward the oak grove. "Wait for me. I dropped the sticks back there, when I picked up the grinding stone." He charged off for the trees.

When Jaedon returned, Elijah stroked the leg bone into place and positioned the splint. While Miriam continued to hold the chick and tried to fend off its angry nips, Jaedon and the old prophet wrapped the strips around the splinted leg.

He invited them all to the cave, but Miriam told him they

could not. Before she could explain about Zuar coming for them, the prophet said, "The man you are waiting for has been delayed. He will come tomorrow."

Elijah was very strange, but she believed him. He was a prophet of Yahweh, after all. So they climbed to the cave. Elijah went first, offering Yaffa his arm while he steadied them both with his staff. Jaedon followed close on the prophet's heels, glancing back often. Whether concerned for her or the eagle, Miriam did not know. She held the eaglet one-handed, close against her chest. Worn out from the struggle, it trembled with fright and pain and no longer tried to bite.

She understood how it felt. But Miriam knew her struggle had just begun.

Chapter Twenty-Five

*There was never a man like Ahab, who sold himself to do evil
in the eyes of the Lord, urged on by Jezebel his wife.*
~ 1 Kings 21:25a

Gideon's cave
Elijah

ELIJAH STIRRED THE POT, ENJOYING THE savory aroma of the fish
simmering with barley and wild greens. It made a tasty stew
for him and his guests, including the little eaglet. It snapped
the fish entrails from Jaedon's fingers and looked for more.
When the boy thought no one was looking, he fed it a few
more cooked slivers from his portion of the stew.

"That is sufficient," Elijah said. "If the chick is hungry,
it will be easier to manage and look to you for food. You can
feed it a mouse tomorrow."

While they sat around the fire, the little eagle flapped its
wings and chirped, its shrill cries reverberating around the
cave. Elijah cut and sewed on a small piece of sheepskin.
When he finished the tiny hood, he gently pulled it over the
eagle's head. The boy murmured to the little eagle and
stroked its feathers until it calmed.

"Good," Elijah said. "Remove the hood now, while it is
calm. It will learn not to fear it." Jaedon did so and the little
bird nibbled at the leather as it came off.

"One of the prophets in Bethel owns—or is owned by—
a hawk. Like you, he found it injured. Trained it to eat from
his hand, come when he whistles. He puts a hood on it when
it is time to sleep, or when he does not want it to hunt."

Jaedon asked to hear more about the prophet and his
hawk, but Elijah shook his head. "Not tonight," he said. The
Lord had not told him to say more.

Then Elijah rummaged around in the back of the cave.
He returned with a staff that had fallen in the fire and
partially burned before he took notice. Too short for him after
the mishap, it would be right for the boy and the eagle.

Elijah whittled the charred end flat, smoothed it with a handful of horsetail weed, and fixed a smaller branch across its top for a perch. Then he wrapped strips of sheepskin around the branch. He cut strips for ties such as he'd seen the hawk wear. Then he made a glove for Jaedon's left hand, with a long cuff extending to his elbow.

"Tomorrow, wear this on your hand and let the eagle sit there when you feed it. Train it to sit on the perch other times. That is where it will sleep tonight." Elijah helped him settle the eagle on the perch and tied one of the long strips to its leg, the other end to the perch.

"When you travel, it can ride on the perch, which is also a walking stick for you."

He had thought the boy would be too excited to sleep that night, but when Elijah added wood to the fire, he saw they all fought to keep their eyes opened. He knew something terrible had happened to them all today, something related to the song Yahweh had given him for meditation, but beyond that, he knew little more.

Elijah bedded them down in the back of the cave. He would bank the fire soon, but it would remain warm enough in that sheltered area.

Soon his guests were asleep. He prayed, thanking the Lord for the events of the day, smiling at the images of the young boy in the thrall of the eagle. Their budding relationship was something like Elijah's with his sheep—the sheep he had given to a friend, when the Lord sent Elijah to confront Ahab.

Sheep do not hunt, nor do they use claw or fang. They are entirely helpless. As the boy had protected the eagle chick, Elijah had protected his sheep. And then he had stood for the lost sheep of Israel, who were helplessly enslaved to false gods.

Eagles were protective of their young. Elijah wondered if this young eagle would bond to Jaedon, protect him as Daniel's sheepdog protected its flock. Elijah listened, but though the wind puffed at the entrance to the cave, Yahweh said nothing on the matter.

Elijah lay down in front of the fire and looked out on the stars and waited. He had been told to wait, but not—he yawned—how long to wait. His prayer had been interrupted by thinking about the boy, but Yahweh had sent these three—Jaedon, Miriam, and Yaffa. Four, if he counted the eagle. Elijah chuckled. He counted ravens among his friends, of course he would count the eagle. He began praying for them all, and as he prayed, he fell asleep.

Elijah sat upright and looked around. *Was that you, Lord?* A breeze cooled his face. His backside was cold, so he added a few logs to the banked fire.

Elijah, go down from here to meet Ahab, king of Israel. He is now in Naboth's vineyard in Jezreel, where he has gone to take possession of it. Say to him, 'This is what the Lord says: Have you not murdered a man and seized his property?' Then say to him, 'This is what the Lord says: In the place where dogs licked up Naboth's blood, dogs will lick up your blood—yes, yours!'"

Elijah bowed his head. He would go. But carrying such a message—would he return?

Wrapping his cloak around him, he picked up his walking stick, and started down the mountain. The women slept, but the boy sat up, rubbed his eyes, and ran after him to the cave entrance.

"Where are you going?" Jaedon asked. "Are you leaving us?"

Elijah walked back to the boy and put a hand on his shoulder. Elijah thought this task was related to the boy, but the Lord had sent Elijah with a word to Ahab, not to the boy.

"Fear not," he said. "The Lord will be with you." He took a step, and then turned back. "Watch for the mouse."

The palace at Jezreel, Jezebel

Jezebel ran to Ahab's chambers, her silk slippers slap-slapping on the marble. When they slipped a little on the polished floor, she giggled and then slowed to a more sedate, queenly gait.

Though awake and picking from a gold plate filled with

clotted cheese and almond-stuffed dates, the king lay on his chaise, propped on one elbow. He frowned at her. "What do you want?"

She had forgotten that he did not wake up well. She should have sent the steward earlier with wine. "Quick, get up," she said. "You know that vineyard you wanted, that Naboth the Jezreelite would not sell you? Well, he is dead now, so you can have it! Go down and take possession."

"What about heirs?" he asked.

"He has no heirs." She smiled. This was true. Naboth had heirs—once. But no longer. Every piece of her plan had been thought out. It all had worked beautifully.

The vineyard, Ahab

The gate to the vineyard stood open, broken on its hinges. Ahab bent to study it. The top hinge had been ripped violently from its fastenings. Strange.

Jezebel told him Naboth was dead but said nothing of the cause of his death. Ahab pushed it from his mind. The man was no friend of his. What did it matter now?

Ahab walked through the gate and down the first row of vines. Many were crushed, some ripped apart. He walked down another row, finding more crushed vines. A dark stain at the end. A third row revealed similar damage and more stains. He stared at the stains a moment. *Blood?*

Knowing Jezebel, an idea formed of what had happened here. He put it from his mind, focusing again on his plans. He had intended to rip out some, if not all, of the vines, to make room for the exotic vegetables the cook suggested he grow. He would hire a farmer to turn the soil and get rid of the bloodstains. Or whatever they were.

He paced off the vineyard, calculating in his mind how much more space he would have. He would rearrange the city wall so that he could walk from his bedroom into his beautiful garden, without walking outside the city.

He gazed across the valley of Jezreel, wondering if he could build up the level of the vineyard so that he could both keep the view and have a siege-proof enclosure. Then Ahab heard a voice behind him.

"Have you murdered a man and seized his property?"

Ahab turned slowly. It was the old prophet. Elijah. "So, you have found me, my enemy."

The vineyard, Elijah

Elijah stared at the man who had led Israel into idol worship. How could the king call Elijah his enemy—troubler of Israel? Was he oblivious to the wrong he had done in marrying the pagan princess, following her false god, and leading Israel into idolatry? Now she had committed murder on his behalf. And standing on this soil where the blood of Naboth cried out for justice, Elijah realized not only the murdered men had been wronged. Two widows and an orphan waited in Gideon's cave.

"Yes, I have found you, because you have sold yourself to do evil in the eyes of the Lord." Elijah said. And then he repeated the words of judgment.

"This is what the Lord says. 'I am going to bring disaster on you. I will consume your descendants and cut off from you every last male of your descendants in Israel, slave or free. I will make your house like that of Jeroboam, son of Nebat and that of Baasha son of Ahijah, because you have provoked me to anger and caused Israel to sin.'"

Elijah paused, expecting an angry retort or the flash of a sword, but the king stood silent. A flush slowly colored his face and he clenched his fist. But Elijah saw that it trembled. No wonder. The last time Elijah saw Ahab, lightning struck the ground near the king's feet.

Elijah continued, "And concerning Jezebel, the Lord says, 'Dogs will devour Jezebel by the wall of Jezreel. Dogs will eat those belonging to Ahab who die in the city, and the birds of the air will feed on those who die in the country.'"

His message delivered, Elijah started to turn. But the king grasped the neck of his own tunic in both hands and ripped it open to expose his chest. Then wailing in ritual remorse, he bent and picked up handfuls of dirt, which he sifted over his head and garment. Small clods of blood-soaked earth trickled through his fingers.

Elijah shook his head. Now the king repented. He had disobeyed the Lord countless times. Against the Lord's instructions, Ahab spared Ben-Hadad, who had attacked him twice.

Now the king stood before Elijah tossing dirt on his head. Next, he'd be going about in sackcloth and fasting.

Kings. They only repented when caught in the wrong. Snorting in disgust, Elijah left the vineyard and walked back to the cave and the three innocents.

Chapter Twenty-Six

*Like a roaring lion or a charging bear is a
wicked ruler over a helpless people.*
~ Proverbs 28:15

Samaria, a day later
Dov

"LET US GO FOR A WALK." Dov pulled the pouch of silver from its hiding place. "I want to see what exotic goods the caravan may have."

A caravan had arrived in Samaria. Dov and Maalik could wander the marketplace together. Not that he needed anything, but Caleb's grandmother had woven Maalik a new tunic—which he had sorely needed—and Dov had been given silver as part of his spoils of war. He liked the idea of sharing some with Maalik. After all, he had given Dov a home.

He placed several pieces on the table where Maalik sat. "Housekeeping money."

Maalik scowled. "You know I don't need that."

"I do. But I thought you might bring Caleb's grandmother a gift."

Maalik looked at the silver and grinned. "She would not take anything in return for the tunic. But a gift from a friend—how can she refuse?" He put away his writing implements, rolled a sheet of papyrus, and left to change his garment.

"What were you writing?" called Dov as Maalik disappeared in the back.

"An answer to the queen. She asked me to"—his voice became muffled as if he had drawn his tunic over his head, blocking the sound.

The queen contacted Maalik? "Asked you what?"

Maalik came back wearing the new tunic, its border a shade of blue Dov admired. "To work in the palace again."

"What? You told her no, did you not? You are too old for that." Dov rolled his eyes, wishing he had chosen other words, but working for the queen had nearly ruined Maalik's health, with constant intrigues and infighting among her servants. Dov's promotion to the army allowed Maalik to quit at the same time Dov left the temple guard. The man he thought of as father would not go back to the palace, not if Dov had any say.

Someone tapped on the door. Listening for Maalik's response, Dov walked to open it. Caleb stood outside, a letter in his hand. The letter Dov had delivered from Miriam.

"Did you know what was in this?" Caleb's tone sounded accusatory. His hair stood on end, as if he had just run his hands through it.

"In your letter? Of course not. Is something wrong?"

Caleb strode into the room. "Yes." He slapped the scroll against his palm. "She says in here that King Ahab asked Dod Naboth to give him the vineyard. Sell it to him."

Dov studied Caleb, who was obviously upset—angry, even. "Is something wrong with that?"

"Of course there is something wrong with that—sell the land of his fathers?"

Maalik held up his hand. "He doesn't understand, Caleb." He turned to Dov, "I did not teach you this from the law. It seemed pointless. The land is an inheritance. It cannot be sold. Yahweh forbids it."

The land is an inheritance. Dov thought about the burning house that plagued his nightmares. Land where his father's blood had spilled, leaving Dov to fight on the streets of Samaria for a crust of bread. An orphan, not an heir. He glanced at Maalik, seeing regret in the old man's eyes.

"Naboth told the king no?"

"He did. Miriam writes the king seemed angry. She is afraid." Caleb clenched the letter so tight the papyrus crackled. "Does she need to fear the king?"

Dov's forehead creased. Did she? Why would the king want the vineyard, such a small piece of land outside the city wall? But he did want it, or he would not have asked. And he had been told no.

Ahab was a proud man. A king. Dov recalled the scene at the side of the road when Micaiah the prophet gave the king an answer he did not want to hear.

You have set free a man the Lord determined should die.
Therefore it is your life for his life, your people for his people.

The king's face had suffused with red and he lashed his horses into a furious gallop.

There was great risk in telling a king no, especially when he was already angry. Micaiah's prophecy had enraged the king right before they returned to Jezreel.

"We will go to Jezreel and see she is safe."

"Then you do believe there is danger."

"I don't know," Dov said. "But we will make sure."

"I should go with you, Dov," Maalik said. "Not Caleb."

"What do you mean?" Dov and Caleb spoke over each other.

"Think." Maalik stretched out his hands. "If there is trouble between them about the vineyard, bringing another heir to the king's attention is not wise."

"Gershon is an heir," Caleb said. "And Miriam. She told me of this when I visited her in Jezreel."

"And your father is Naboth's brother," Maalik said. "Your entire family are potential heirs."

Dov shook his head, confused by all the family ties. Not surprising, since he had no living ancestors. "But Miriam? How can a woman inherit?"

"It is unusual, but Gershon wrote it into the *ketubah*," said Caleb. "To ensure she and the boy were taken care of, if Gershon should die during the war."

"But he didn't even go to war. He was not a soldier, and he took a wife. Besides, was it known that Miriam could inherit? Is not the marriage agreement private?"

Caleb ran his hand across his hair again, proving Dov's assumption true. "Right. Right. Perhaps I am overly vexed by the situation."

"If she were my sister, I would feel the same. Listen. We can deal with two situations at once. First, we can check on your sister's concern regarding Naboth. Second, when Miriam told me about your betrothal, she said she is happy Chloe will become a sister, but sad she will move to Samaria."

"What does that have to do with it?"

"Most of your family is here, and it is a long walk between our two cities. Miriam is lonely for family. Her imma was unable to attend her wedding and she misses her."

"And Imma longs to see her. But our sister-in-law's delicate health—"

Dov made a face and waved his hand impatiently. He wanted to avoid hearing details about women's bodily complaints. "Yes, yes, but the king's stables are filled with Aramean horses and chariots. I planned to bring several to Jezreel. It is an advantage to have chariots in strategic cities. Ahab will agree when I put it to him. We could expand their use by citizens, especially for trade. Farm produce, for example. Jezreel's farmers will help alleviate the food shortages in Samaria resulting from the siege. Communications between cities would also be swifter. As a runner, you see the value, yes?"

"You are saying Miriam could use the chariot to visit us?"

Dov paused, thinking how to rephrase this to ensure its support with the king as well as the populace. Ahab would not approve using his chariots and horses for family visits.

"If it is to the king's advantage, as I said. If a farmer brings produce between the cities, the horses would need to rest a night or two before returning. If the farmer has family to stay with, so much the better."

Caleb squinted, still puzzled at Dov's meaning. Dov sighed. "I will make sure the cities' interests are protected. Meanwhile, Miriam is eager to bring the boy here. Introduce your mother to a new grandchild. I could drive to Jezreel today, bring her and the boy back, and pack the chariot with fresh produce on our return trip to Samaria."

"So soon? You just arrived." Maalik said.

"You will drive only one chariot?" Caleb asked.

"This time. I will ask the king. If he agrees, I'll return with Miriam, grapes, and wine to sell in Samaria. It is best to not appear overly sure of his answer. He is, after all, a king. And a king dislikes appearing controlled—or even influenced—by a subordinate."

It remained only to decide when to leave. Dov announced he would go to the stable immediately, pick out a chariot, and be on his way. Caleb still looked tense. He probably didn't like the idea of being left behind when he was worried about his sister.

"Caleb, I will see the king and see what I can learn. But the whims of a king are like clouds on a windy day. As for Miriam, tell your mother to expect her tomorrow before evening."

Caleb bid them farewell.

They selected weapons for the journey and set them near the door. Dov helped put the house to rights. But when Maalik went to douse the hearth, Dov stopped him. "I see no reason for you to come. And it occurs to me Miriam would want to bring not only Jaedon, but her mother-in-law, or Caleb's betrothed."

"But, my son—"

"I agree with Caleb on one point. The king's actions were strange, especially if he understands Hebrew law. I did not want to raise Caleb's unease, but perhaps I will be needed a few days."

Maalik nodded. "In the past, I have seen the influence for good you have on the king. Which is why I am considering the queen's request." Dov stored this remark away for later discussion.

"Why did you not tell me of the law Caleb spoke of? Another man is farming my father's land."

Maalik met his gaze. "There seemed no point. You were a scrawny lad and I was no farmer. But mostly, when we became a family, I had no knowledge of the law."

Dov looked at the ground. "You know I am grateful. I would be dead if you had not taken me in. Even more, you, a Canaanite, instructed me in the ways of my ancestors. But you never told me. It occurs to me the land is still mine. I can take it back."

Maalik nodded slowly. "You are an honored warrior. If you ask the king, he will act. But, the man has sons. He has farmed there since—well, since you were a boy."

"Are you saying he has rights because he worked the land? He murdered my father."

"No. He bought the land, possibly from those who killed your father. A document was registered with the court scribe."

Dov closed his mouth. Inheritance was the only legal

manner in which to permanently acquire land, document or no. But the law was not always followed. Power, not law, often prevailed.

But there was another truth. Injustice, committed against a small boy long ago, must be rectified.

"I will think on this," Dov said. "But I have promised Caleb to see to Miriam's concern. Let us head for the stable."

All these years Dov had imagined the man who farmed the land had killed his father. If Dov asked, the king would take the land from him and give it to Dov. But the farmer was not the murderer. Something about that solution did not appeal to him.

Two voices argued inside Dov. The soldier would never have a family, thus did not need a farm. But the small boy longed for his family home.

Dov greeted the stablemaster. "I need a large and sturdy chariot to drive to Jezreel. On my return, I will carry passengers and supplies."

"Would a wagon better suit?"

Dov considered a moment. "No. I want to travel faster than a wagon would allow. A large chariot is sufficient."

"Do you have a preference as to which horses?"

"Only that they must be ready to travel now." Then, thinking that there was a chance Miriam could not come with him, he added. "I will bring my own horse, Uri, tied to the back."

The stablemaster called two assistants to bring out a chariot. They dragged out a large but plain vehicle made of wood and reinforced with iron. Dropping its center pole, they went back for the horses.

While the grooms harnessed the animals, Dov pulled Maalik aside. He had wanted to spend a quiet day with him. Two years in active conflict had left them little time together. "I am sorry our plans were interrupted. We will have our outing upon my return. I will not stay longer than necessary."

Maalik frowned. "The roads of Israel are not safe for a lone traveler. You need me and my weapon beside you."

Dov smiled. "Always, my friend. But if an armed soldier driving a chariot is not safe on a public thoroughfare, there is no hope for anyone. Ask the good Hadassah to say a prayer for me. I will see you tomorrow."

Maalik eyed Dov's bow and quiver. "At least take my shield and spear. You may have need of them. Or on the way back, Miriam may take my place. Hadassah says she is as capable as a man in many ways."

Dov grinned, as he always did when his friend began a sentence with 'Hadassah says.'

When Dov reached Jezreel late that afternoon, he drove straight up the ramp and through the city gates. He glanced across the terraces towards Naboth's vineyard but saw no one there. He shoved down the specter of concern that attempted to raise its head. The empty vineyard had nothing to do with Ahab's offer to buy the property. It was early for the family to stop working during harvest, but they probably started earlier than usual. No cause for worry. After Dov delivered the chariot to the stable and asked to see the king, he would go to their house. They would be eating an early supper and would invite him to join them, as they always did.

He drove directly to the stable, and when he didn't see Reuben, the stablemaster, he uncoupled the horses himself, not wanting to wait. A groom hurried out of a stall, looking at once harried and subdued.

Dov handed him the horses' leads. "You seem shorthanded. Where is Reuben?"

"Delayed. There's been trouble in the city." The groom's mouth flattened as he stroked the neck of the closest horse. "A stoning. I hope never again to witness such a thing."

Dov wanted to ask details—why and who—but the groom took the leads and tugged the horses to a rear stall. In a moment, Dov heard feed rattle into troughs. Dov led Uri into an empty stall and fed him. It was unfortunate Chloe's father wasn't here. Dov had planned to ask after the girl and have news to ease Caleb's mind when he returned. A sudden chill went through him. Could the stoning have impacted her father in some way? Certainly, a disagreement about horse care, even horse ownership, would not mean a death sentence!

As Dov emerged from the stall, he decided to go

immediately to Naboth's house and learn what had transpired in the city. But Obadiah, the king's palace steward, waited at the stable entrance.

"The king saw you on the road. He asked me to bring you to him immediately. Do not bother to make yourself presentable. And keep your wits about you, if you value your life. His mood is foul."

Dov forced himself not to gape at the steward's remarks.

Obadiah pivoted and strode back toward the temple, shaking his head and giving only terse responses as Dov tried to question him. Various townsfolk sent sidelong glances as they passed on the street. He didn't believe the steward knew nothing about the king's reason for summoning him. But Dov clearly saw Obadiah was terrified to be seen speaking to Dov, potentially about the stoning, or whatever else troubled the city.

What a time to approach the king. Dov mentally prepared a speech, emphasizing that housing more chariots in Jezreel was a military strategy and awaited Ahab's counsel.

To his surprise, Obadiah led him not to the throne room, but to the king's chamber on the upper floor. Obadiah spoke to two servants, who hovered near the entrance and motioned them inside. The king sat on his balcony, behind a curtain that would obscure him from public view, especially from the street. Even if someone walked atop the city wall or watched from a roof, it would be difficult to see the king sitting behind the balcony parapet. This was how the king had seen Dov approaching the city.

As they neared, Dov realized the king wore sackcloth and his predominantly black hair was dusted with ash. Strange. Dov bowed. "You summoned me, my king?"

"I saw you arrive. Is there trouble in Samaria?" Ahab's voice sounded restrained, in contrast to his normally firm, clipped manner of speaking.

"No trouble. It occurred to me the stables at Samaria are crowded with chariots and horses, while the Jezreel stable has several vacant stalls. I see advantages to splitting the military force between the two cities. I drove a chariot here planning to leave it and bring more if you approve."

The king nodded slowly. "Good idea. I approve." He gazed out the window, asking no further questions.

Obadiah had spoken of the king's foul mood, but Dov thought the steward meant anger, not wretchedness. Dov swallowed hard, gathering courage. "My king. You wear garments of mourning. Is the queen—" A terrible thought choked his words. Could something have happened to the queen or one of the king's sons? Not Ahaziah, the heir! Only a royal death would explain sackcloth and ashes.

"The queen is well." The king bowed his head over his open palms. "One of the city officials has died. You may go."

Naboth is a city official.

Dov quietly followed Obadiah out of the king's chambers, but when they reached the ground floor, he took hold of the steward, pulled him into a storeroom, and shut the door.

"Tell me now what happened," he demanded in a low voice. "Why is the king in sackcloth? Who was stoned yesterday?" When the steward hesitated, Dov impatiently stepped forward, asserting his authority.

"Naboth and his sons were stoned. I believe the queen was behind it—paid assassins to falsely accuse the vintner and incite the stoning. The king's seal was on a letter to one of the accusers, but the date it was written, I was in the king's presence. I know he did not attend to any official matters. In fact, he complained of not being able to convince Naboth to sell his property. But then the stoning. The next day, the king went to the vineyard to take possession—"

"Take possession! The land belonged to Naboth's family."

"Who are all dead."

An image flashed darkly in Dov's mind. Scorching flames scrambling across the roof of his burning home. Ruffians attacking his father in the field, too strong for the boy who fought back. Something closed Dov's mouth before he asked, 'What of Miriam? What of the boy?' If the queen—and the king—were willing to murder Naboth and his sons, nothing would stop them from killing Miriam and Jaedon. Dov wrenched his mind from that image and back to what Obadiah was saying.

"With Naboth convicted of blasphemy and treason, the land was claimed by the king. But there is more."

More? Would Obadiah speak now of what happened to Miriam and the boy?

"The prophet Elijah appeared. The first time he has been seen in Samaria since the end of the drought. He confronted King Ahab in Naboth's vineyard. He prophesied God's judgment—death to Ahab, Jezebel, and all of their heirs."

"Did the king tell you this? He said nothing to me."

"He did not. But guards were with the king. They saw and heard Elijah. Their story has been repeated throughout the town. Now the king fasts and wears sackcloth. That tells me the story is true. And that Ahab hopes Yahweh will relent."

Dov left the palace and stopped by the stable again. When the groom greeted him, Dov asked again about Chloe's father. He still had not arrived. Then Dov headed for Naboth's house. But when he reached the end of Naboth's street, palace guards were entering the home. He squinted, recognizing at least one of the queen's men, and backed around the corner, watching. When they came out empty-handed and turned for the palace, he headed the opposite direction for the city gate, even though he had not seen Aaron when he arrived. His friend still was not at the gate, nor was his son, Zuar. Where was everyone?

Dov asked the guard on duty for directions to Reuben's home. If the stablemaster knew nothing of Miriam's whereabouts, perhaps his daughter would.

Reuben's house, a white-washed structure, stood several streets from the stable. Dov reached over the courtyard wall and unlatched the gate. Heavy rugs were pegged over the windows. He knocked, but no one answered.

Looking around to see if anyone watched, he knocked again, speaking quietly through the crack between door and frame. "Chloe? It is Caleb's friend, Dov. I am concerned about Miriam and Jaedon." He waited, looked around once more, and added, "I am alone."

The door swung open and a hand pulled him inside.

With the windows covered, the door shut, and no lamp, it was nearly black inside. A deep, male voice said, "That you, Dov?" Not Reuben or Chloe but familiar.

"Haven't I said so?"

Someone fumbled in the corner of the room. A faint glow revealed coals on a hearth. Soon a lamp shone dimly, revealing the hulking figure of Zuar with that axe of his, standing beside Reuben, who lifted the lamp and held ... was that a chariot whip? Behind the two men, Davita and Chloe clung to each other.

"Why are you all hiding in the dark? What has happened?"

Reuben spoke first. "We sheltered here because my wife is too ill to move. The city has been in turmoil. Naboth was stoned, along with his sons, on the charge of blaspheming God and cursing the king. Obviously, the charges were false. But they were dead before their friends learned of it."

How could none of Naboth's friends have known that he was attacked? A mob would not have been silent. Houses were close in the city, Naboth's and his neighbors' were built along the wall. Their rooftops provided a clear view of the vineyards on the terraced hill.

Reuben continued. "Immediately after, soldiers went throughout the city searching for Naboth's wife, Miriam, and the boy. Some of their friends protested the search and were beaten or arrested. There was much confusion yesterday."

Davita spoke next. "Zuar was very brave. He disguised Miriam and me as zonahs and we walked through the north gate without incident."

The north gate. Disguises. "Wise choices," Dov said.

Zuar cleared his throat. "It helped that my father was guarding that gate."

"No one else recognized Miriam," Davita said, "that was important. No one can report seeing either of us leave the city."

"Davita was bold." Zuar said. "She hurried Yaffa out of the city before anyone thought to look for her. Then she came back looking for Miriam."

"But Zuar found her first when she came through the main gate. She thought her mother-in-law would have come to me, so they came together to my father's bakery."

"And he smuggled the two of you out." Dov hesitated. "What about Jaedon?"

"Miriam hid him in a tree and then came looking for Yaffa. That is how we both were in the city for Zuar to save."

Even in the dark, Dov detected trembling in Davita's voice. But the ordeal for Naboth's surviving family was not over. "Where are they now? Yaffa, Jaedon, and Miriam?"

Zuar thumped his axe on the floor. "Miriam demanded Davita return to her father, sure that if Miriam and Davita disappeared together, her father would be questioned. Perhaps imprisoned. She was probably right. No one will suspect Davita now. Once I had her safely home, I was to return for Miriam and the boy at end of day."

"Yesterday? But you did not return."

"No, there was too much upheaval yesterday. I believe they will have waited for me. They were deeply distressed by everything they had endured. Yaffa and the boy, especially, seemed unfit to travel far. I did not want to leave them, but Miriam insisted I see Davita home. Miriam planned to take them as far as the limestone cliff. She spoke of finding a cave there in which to shelter."

Dov walked to the rug-tacked window, pulling an edge slightly away and peering through. "The street seems quiet now. Not many are out of their houses. Perhaps, like you, they are staying out of sight of soldiers.

He swiveled to face them. "Listen, Zuar, I have a chariot. We could go together to the limestone cliff and see to Miriam's safety. Reuben, I think you and your family are safe in your house. You could probably go back to work even today, but perhaps Chloe would be afraid?"

"I am not afraid," Chloe said in her gentle voice, speaking for the first time. "But what of Davita? She needs to go to her father, be at his side at the bakery as usual. Even if the streets are quiet now, she should not walk alone."

"I will take her," Zuar said. "I promised Miriam."

"We were on our way," Davita said, "But we came across Chloe returning from the well when a riot broke out on the street."

"So it is decided. Zuar, you take Davita home. I'll get the

chariot and pick you up outside the gate. If you bring your bow, we appear to be hunting. North or south gate?"

"North."

Dov set off for the stable. Reuben's decision to wait until tomorrow to return to work was understandable. Despite her protest, Chloe was frightened and with cause. Naboth's murder had devastated his friends and unsettled the city.

According to Obadiah, the queen was behind a plot to frame and murder Naboth. The queen's involvement didn't surprise Dov, but had the king known before her plan was set in action?

Dov couldn't be sure. Two things he did know. The king had wanted the vineyard, and now he owned it.

Chapter Twenty-Seven

*Some time later the brook dried up because there had been
no rain in the land. Then the word of the Lord came to
[Elijah]: Go at once to Zarephath of Sidon and stay there. I
have commanded a widow in that place to supply you with
food. So he went to Zarephath. When he came to the town
gate, a widow was there gathering sticks. He called to her
and asked, "Would you bring me a little water in a jar so I
may have a drink?" As she was going to get it, he called,
"And bring me, please, a piece of bread."*
~ 1 Kings 17:7-11

*Gideon's Cave
Elijah*

ELIJAH WALKED SLOWLY ACROSS THE JEZREEL valley, stooping to
gather seeds, rising and bending again to snap greens as he
went. Not only for food, but wanting to delay the encounter.
Years ago, in much the same way, he sat a while at the well
of Zarephath, resting from his journey. Delaying. Then
Yahweh sent the woman *to him*, gathering broken sticks for
fuel. Who would want to tell a poor widow, preparing her last
meal, to give him the first baked morsel? But Elijah obeyed,
there was never any question of that. He knew his request
would deepen her sorrow, but her obedience would
ultimately save her life.

Yahweh was like that. Asking his followers to obey,
despite their questions. Sometimes He answered those
questions. Sometimes not. And sometimes He answered
questions not asked.

The vision had come upon Elijah suddenly. No staring
into a fire this time, no music or meditation. Just the
sunshine warming his mantle and the grass rustling as he
walked through, speaking with the Lord. *Thank you for not
allowing the king to run me through with a sword when I told
him his future.* Had there been a sword? Ahab had not worn
one as he strolled about Naboth's vineyard, as unconcerned

about the innocent blood he trod upon as a lion over its kill. But the king's guards had been armed, and Elijah's head still rested on his shoulders.

Thank you for that, Yahweh. But if you did require my life, you will notice I did not promise the boy I would return.

And then the vision opened before him, as if the Lord himself had sliced the landscape and inserted the whole of the city of Jezreel into the valley. Elijah heard the sound of cart wheels on the pavement, an oil merchant shouting his daily bargain, a woman singing softly to a child. He heard the sound of a thousand footfalls as the townsfolk walked to and fro, going about their business. A horse snorted, a dog barked, and an old man's broom swept sand from the cobblestones.

Then a hush fell, like fog settling over the city, and the king walked haltingly among his people. He wore the sackcloth Elijah had spoken of in irony, and ashes continually sifted from his head, leaving a trail like fish traces in a pond. Ahab moved through the marketplace meekly, his gaze cast down. He did not speak, nor did anyone address him. Through the stillness, Elijah heard the Lord whisper.

Have you noticed how Ahab has humbled himself before me? Because he has humbled himself, I will not bring this disaster in his day, but I will bring it on his house in the days of his son.

The vision rolled shut from the edges like a scroll. Elijah closed his eyes. He wiggled his toes in his sandals, felt the firm ground beneath his feet. Next, he drank from his waterskin, reality trickling through his veins along with the water.

He listened, nodded, and walked to the edge of an abandoned field where he gathered handfuls of lentils. Next, he walked to the pond where Miriam's trap held another fish.

Now he must return to the cave, tell them of Ahab's judgment, and the rest. Like the widow of Zarephath, Miriam would have words with him. Further, she would have a choice to make.

As Elijah climbed to the cave, he heard the sounds of pursuit and attack. *Scuttle. Wood striking stone. Chirrup. A shrill shriek.*

The mouse.

Elijah sighed. He had hoped it would be finished before he returned. He trudged up the last incline and stepped through the entrance. As the mouse scurried towards him he saw the boy running after it, wielding the staff Elijah had given him. *Whack.*

This time, the boy did not miss.

The eaglet seemed to have no understanding of how to eat the mouse, so Miriam cut strips for Jaedon to dangle in front of its beak. "I will not do this again," she warned, and Jaedon nodded. Yaffa ducked her chin and smiled as she mended a torn section of Elijah's cloak.

Jaedon had chased the mouse and killed it himself. Miriam's stomach gave a little lurch as she relived the moment, glad there was no reason to protect Jaedon from that unpleasantness in the future.

"From now on, you will have the displeasure of finding and cutting up food for the eaglet. *Your* eaglet," Miriam said. Did her boy wear the ghost of a smile? It was as if caring for the bird lifted Jaedon from his mire.

She watched them together, thinking of Gershon. Did he see? The eaglet rocked back shakily as Jaedon fed it, talons curled in pleasure, sometimes excitedly flapping downy wings where tips of pinion feathers peeked out. The splinted leg caused the bird to list to one side, but otherwise seemed not to trouble it. Boy and eagle gazed into each other's eyes as the chick fed, Jaedon's lips pressed together in rapt concentration.

Thank you, she breathed. Some contrary part of her argued this was not much, considering what her boy had lost. But this morning, the eagle's shrill chirps as it fed seemed a promise of healing.

Hadn't she also glimpsed the unexplainable? Her longing, yesterday, to find water. A prayer, actually. *Yahweh, please let there be a stream.* And then, there it was. A stream that deepened into a pool that fed as well as refreshed them. *Did I thank you properly for that, Lord?*

The chick stared at her with round black eyes. Beyond

the eaglet, the prophet's gaze fixed on hers. Could he see into her mind?

She turned her back on them both. She had requested, the Lord had given. Everything came from Yahweh. Even the stones.

After the eaglet fed, the strange lids on its round eyes shuttered a few times and closed. Jaedon had built a little nest in a corner with branches and grass. Yaffa studied the structure and praised his artistry. Visibly encouraged, when Elijah pulled a fish out of a pouch, Jaedon volunteered to prepare it for the stew that would be their next meal.

Elijah built up the campfire, glancing at Miriam a few times in a way that seemed almost furtive. Well, it did not take a prophetess to realize he was a very old unmarried man, not used to sharing a cave with two women and a child. The eaglet, she thought with a smile, would be least worrisome to the prophet who had been fed by ravens.

"I have something to tell you," he began. "All of you." He poured water into the cook pot, adding lentils from the same pouch that had held the fish. "You know little of prophets and may find me strange. Often, I myself—" He broke off and loudly cleared his throat. "One cannot always make sense of life. But in everything, I find it best to ask the Lord, listen, then obey. The one who asks will receive an answer, and the One who speaks will not be ignored."

Jaedon scooted forward. "The Lord told you to leave early this morning and you did. He did not speak to me." Jaedon looked at Miriam, a faint crease between his eyes. "Did He speak to you, Imma?" Miriam tucked her lips, hiding a smile. Her boy was back.

"Perhaps. I am not sure." Seeing he meant to question her further, she held up her hand, tipping her head toward Elijah.

The prophet gave her another look. She thought she rightly interpreted this one as relief. "The Lord had a message of judgment for King Ahab. Regarding a matter of which you are concerned." He paused—looked at Jaedon—then he stared out the cave entrance. She could swear he was listening. He could only be speaking of the murders in the vineyard. Did he not know how to go on?

"The king has done great evil, and he has been judged."

Miriam tensed. Judged? Was he dead? Did this mean they could go home?

Elijah stirred the pot beside him, then stood to place it on the fire. "The Lord is a just God. He knows the thoughts and intents of all hearts. I am only a man. Yahweh speaks to me on some matters, but not all."

He paused. "I know what you lost that day." He was looking at Miriam at that moment, but quickly his gaze went to Yaffa, and finally to Jaedon, whose attention he held the longest.

Elijah's gaze returned to her. "Justice is demanded. And yet ..."

And yet?

"Yahweh is also a merciful God."

Merciful? Did the prophet speak of their escape from Jezreel? Yes, Jaedon and Yaffa lived. And the mercy shown to them since, but why—

"The king has repented. He has humbled himself, going about in sackcloth and ashes."

Repented? The king? What did this mean? Sackcloth and ashes did not bring back her husband. And what about the queen? She had hounded them out of Jezreel. Surely the prophet did not mean they were to ignore or forgive?

Miriam leapt to her feet, took hold of his arm, and pulled him outside the cave entrance. She put enough distance between them and the others to keep their conversation private.

"You said he had been judged"—her throat was so tight, it came out as a croak. She choked and continued—"that he committed a great evil. Which he did. My husband—Jaedon's father—his grandfather and uncle—all dead. Killed on our land. You said Yahweh is just. The king will die, will he not?"

"He will die and all his family. Every one. Just not yet."

Not yet? That wicked king needed to be dead now! Miriam hated the look on Elijah's face, the compassion she saw there, which left no room for argument. Oh yes, she could argue, but it was decided. Done. How did one argue with the Almighty?

She tried, though. *Yahweh, give us justice. Serve him as*

he has done. Let us return home. Hot tears salted her eyes, but she blinked them back. Why cry now? She cut off the thoughts that crowded forward. Angry thoughts at the unfairness of it all.

"We cannot go back, can we? Does the king's repentance include returning the land to my son?"

Elijah listened. "Yahweh does not speak of that now." He put a hand out in appeal. "Since He first spoke to me, I have learned He gives me what I need to know at that particular moment. What I need for the next step. One step. Never the whole journey."

Miriam saw it again. The prophet grew very still. His eyes became unfocused. He tipped his head—listening.

"Has the Lord spoken to you—just now—of another matter?"

"Two matters. He says, 'It is mine to avenge, I will repay. In due time their foot will slip. Their day of disaster is near and their doom rushes upon them.'"

Miriam felt everything in her close against the words, like a boarded-up house. "And what else?"

"Someone is looking for you."

She stared at him, then whirled to return to the cave. Should she gather up Yaffa and Jaedon and run? Or pick up her bow and fight?

Miriam picked up her bow.

Chapter Twenty-Eight

Look at the birds of the air; they do not sow or reap or store away in barns, and yet your heavenly Father feeds them. Are you not much more valuable than they?
~ Matthew 6:26

Near Gideon's cave
Dov

"SURE IS SLOW GOING THROUGH HERE." Attempting to steer the chariot along the foot of the cliff, Dov clenched his jaw as they came across another outcropping. After circumventing the rocks, he again swung close to the cliff, craning his neck to find the ledge Zuar described.

"There it is," Zuar said. "The eagle's nest. Miriam said they would meet us somewhere in this area."

Dov looked up and spotted the evidence of an abandoned nest. "Look at the size of those branches. Amazing they can fly, carrying that weight."

He stepped out of the chariot, securing the reins to a sturdy tree growing out of the cliff. The chariot hadn't saved them time so far. They would have navigated this woodsy area better on horseback. Still, once they found Miriam and the others, travel by chariot would remove them from danger faster.

Dov and Zuar searched the area on foot for any sign of the three. It didn't take long. Not far from the ledge, Zuar found an area of trampled-down grass. "Appears they rested here."

Dov found a single set of footprints which seemed to come into the scene from the cliff area. "This looks like someone else came upon them."

Zuar knelt to study the trampled area. "No sign of a scuffle. Just a place they all sat. They may have taken a meal here and then moved on. The single set of prints could indicate one of them walked along the cliff, perhaps found this spot and called the others. They came from this direction." Zuar indicated the path where footprints departed from the clearing. "See the underlying prints showing they came into the clearing before?"

Dov nodded. "But they left. You were sure they would wait for you." He searched for other signs, like snapped branches. What was this? He bent to get a closer look at small, dry strips. Fragments of a dead animal.

"Still am." Zuar pointed. "See those trees?"

Dov studied a thicket of bright green leaves a fair distance away. The topmost branches stirred in a breeze. Less vibrant foliage provided a long backdrop. He nodded. "They'd head for water." He would see her soon. Relieve his mind.

The thirsty horses quickened their pace as they drove toward the stand of trees. It became apparent, as they neared their destination, that Dov couldn't drive the large chariot between these closely-spaced trees.

They uncoupled the horses and left the chariot. The thirsty animals tugged them towards the water. The horse Dov led walked into the stream, grazed its muzzle over the surface, and noisily sucked water through its lips.

"Miriam?" Dov called, quietly at first, then realizing how far they had driven without seeing another soul, with more force. "Miriam! Jaedon!"

When he stopped to catch his breath, Zuar cupped hands to his mouth and shouted.

Then Miriam came walking through the trees, Jaedon beside her. Each carried their bow and quiver. She looked thinner and there were dark shadows under her eyes. Had she eaten since she'd fled the city? Had the boy?

"Miriam, you are safe!" Zuar splashed out of the stream, pulling his reluctant horse behind, muzzle dripping.

"Dov, you are here?" She looked grief stricken and surprised. Of course, she had expected only Zuar. But there was something else in her expression. Anger? At him? Why would she be angry?

Jaedon broke and ran toward Dov. He braced himself for the impact, but the boy did not splash into the stream and hug him, as Dov supposed he might, as he had in the past. Instead, the boy clamped his arms to his side, looking even slighter, frailer than before. "Did you know? The king killed my abba."

"I only just learned, then I came to find you. Find you both." He turned his gaze on Miriam, seeking signs of physical injury, although he knew the worst injuries to child and woman would be invisible.

"And my savta. She is here, too."

"Is she well?" Dov cringed at the stupidity of his question. How could any of them be well?

"She is resting in the cave, caring for our eagle."

"Eagle?" Dov felt his eyebrows lift, then he glanced again at Miriam. A dripping Zuar had an arm wrapped around her shoulder.

"We found an eaglet," Miriam said. "And a prophet." Her mouth lifted slightly in a smile. Had he been wrong about her anger?

He heard a rustle of leaves. Elijah! His stride was not as long or steady as Dov remembered, but it had been several years since he had last seen the prophet in Jezreel. Right before Queen Jezebel threatened to kill him.

Zuar smiled at Miriam. "I worried unnecessarily, with a man of God to guard you."

Dov pulled the chariot horse toward the bank and closer to Miriam. Every time he prepared to speak, Zuar spoke first, saying what Dov had meant to say. He fumbled for suitable topics. Should he ask how they had come across the eagle? It seemed trivial in view of the danger they were in. No. Miriam would want to know what had happened in Jezreel since they fled.

"The city is troubled by Naboth's murder. There are those who would seek justice"—Dov caught sight of her face and broke off. She looked furious. At him? For speaking thus in the boy's presence? Or because Dov worked for the king? He glanced at Elijah, who looked wary and at Jaedon, who looked only sad.

"There is much confusion about what is to be done," he continued haltingly. "Behind closed doors, some speak for Naboth's innocence. The palace steward found evidence the queen paid scoundrels to accuse him. Hired thugs are searching for Naboth's heirs. They watch your house. There is no question you three are in danger should your whereabouts be discovered." Dov glanced at Zuar for agreement.

"True," Zuar said. "So, as I promised, I will take you to a safe place."

Dov wrung the end of the lead rope, and water streamed onto the ground. What was this? Exactly what had Zuar promised?

"Where might that be?" Miriam asked.

Zuar shrugged. "Somewhere farther south. Or east of the Jordan. Maybe near Shechem."

"What do you know of those areas?"

"My mother and I lived in Shechem, so I have friends there. I am not as familiar with the other areas, but they are remote and should be safe."

Dov stared at him. Two widows and a boy in a city filled with strangers?

He could not let Miriam go alone into uncertainty, with responsibility for an aging mother-in-law and a child not even her own. He had known her first as a young girl, who had grown to an appealing woman—before he learned she was betrothed. He wished Caleb had come with him after all. Her brother would not approve of Zuar's haphazard plan.

Dov was here in Caleb's place, so he must be the one to protect Miriam, the boy, and his grandmother. Find a safe place for them. He stopped there, coming up against an obstacle. The impropriety of an unmarried man traveling with the beautiful young widow. Were the boy and mother-in-law sufficient to protect Miriam's reputation?

"I have another idea." Dov searched her eyes, hoping to find approval. "Marry me. I have a fair amount of silver from the war. I will quit the army, buy us a small house somewhere, and take care of the three of you." Even as he said the words, he saw the confusion in her face.

"Somewhere? And you would marry me? Why would you do that?" Miriam asked.

"You can choose the city, if you like. This is similar to what Zuar proposed, but a woman alone is not safe. I want to help you. What the king has done is wrong. I've been loyal to him my whole adult life. I thought him a strong military leader, capable of protecting our country, but now, he allows this. Even if the queen was the instigator, I have lost all respect for him."

But was that an answer? Yes, Dov had lost respect for the king, but that had nothing to do with his desire to wed Miriam. He wanted to protect her and the boy. And Yaffa, of course. Right the wrong done to them. Truth was, he felt responsible. If he had stayed in Jezreel one day longer, wouldn't he have learned of the queen's plot? Could he have changed the tragic course of events? He felt weighed down with guilt, but marrying Miriam felt right.

Then Elijah said, "I have one more option, Miriam. At this time, no city is safe for you. You can come south with me to the hill country of Ephraim. The school of the prophets where I will take you is in a hidden settlement. You will be safe with us, for I am returning to teach them, until Yahweh sends me elsewhere. You will not be a woman alone. Some of the prophets are married, so you and Yaffa will have other women to befriend. Your snares and bow will be useful in the community. And the prophet who hunts with a hawk, will teach Jaedon to train the eagle."

Elijah's voice was sonorous, his proposal compelling. Listening, Dov himself wanted to join the school of the prophets.

Jaedon sidled next to Miriam and took her hand. "Wherever you go, Imma, take me with you. Please don't leave me behind."

She fell to her knees, putting both hands on his shoulders. "Do not think I will ever leave you, my boy. You are mine. And you are very precious to me."

Dov turned aside, moved by her declaration. When nightmares of the streets had plagued him as a young boy, Maalik had made similar promises to Dov.

Were there any such words that could convince Miriam that she would be safe with Dov? That he would protect her and the boy with his life?

She turned now, to face him, and he saw what her answer would be.

"Dov, what a kind gift you have offered. To burden yourself with two widows and a boy and forever forfeit your chosen profession. I will not ask it of you. Elijah has offered a solution that seems right for us. We will go with him. But may I ask a favor?"

Disappointment crushed his chest. "Of course." He would give her anything in his power.

"Watch over my family in Samaria. My father is Naboth's brother. He will not dare to claim the stolen land, but if the queen hears of the relationship, they will be in danger. If you continue to work with the king, you will be in a position to hear if there is a threat."

Dov ran his hand along the horse's neck, needing to feel the solid warmth. Miriam was right. He would return to the army. But he would never be the same young recruit who had first joined Ahab's forces, blinded by duty. Dov's eyes had opened to what the king was. The king *and* the queen. He would watch, and so much as he was able, he would prevent such evil from happening again.

Then she turned to Zuar. "I thank you also, my friend. You and your axe were fearsome protection indeed. When you return to Jezreel, will you watch over my friend Davita? Although it is not widely known, she and my brother-in-law Kadesh had talked of marriage. Because they did not become betrothed, there should be no danger to her, other than the fact that she—and you—helped me escape Jezreel. Should that ever become known, who can say? Just keep watch over her, please. And another friend in Jezreel, Chloe, who is my brother Caleb's betrothed."

Zuar shuffled his feet. "With pleasure."

Dov forced a smile. So Zuar would protect her friends in Jezreel, and Dov would protect family members in Samaria. It seemed for the best.

Elijah cleared his throat. "Come with us to the cave. Assure yourselves that Yaffa is well and allow her to hear news of the city from your lips. Stay the night, if you wish."

Dov thanked him and hobbled the horses so the animals could graze. Zuar retrieved the provisions from the chariot. Elijah led the way, Miriam and Jaedon side-by-side behind him, and Dov followed.

They walked silently through a grassy clearing approaching the cliff edge. Miriam paused and bent to touch

Jaedon's shoulder. As she did, Dov spotted long brown ears protruding above the grass. The boy pulled two arrows, letting fly one after another. Miriam clapped her hands, praising him for his fine shots. Tossing a grin over his shoulder, Jaedon ran ahead and grabbed up a hare.

Dov was taken aback. Even if he made no rebuke, the prophet would not let them eat an unclean animal.

Miriam glanced at him, reading his shocked expression. "Our supper is lentils and greens. But the eagle is not under the Law."

When they reached the cave, Jaedon introduced the eagle. Although huddled in a nest built of bushy branches and rags, it chirped loudly when it saw him. Dov noticed its splinted leg, evidently the reason they had captured the young bird. "He is hungry," Jaedon said, starting to cut strips of meat from one of the hares. The eagle snapped up the strips greedily as the boy offered them.

"He?" asked Dov.

"Well, I am not sure. Miriam says he—or she—must be older before we can know. But he seems like a boy to me. I have named him Hevel."

Dov smiled at the name's meaning. Jaedon's imagination saw his lame chick floating on the wind one day, like a breath or vapor. Well, the eaglet certainly had the appetite of a growing boy. When it devoured the strips Jaedon had cut, Dov offered to cut more.

Miriam flashed him a look of relief. She appeared tired and went to sit quietly beside Yaffa. Meanwhile, Zuar showed Elijah the provisions he had packed in Jezreel, which included two large loaves of bread from the baker, Davita's father.

After Hevel ate its fill, Jaedon demonstrated how it allowed him to put a small hood over its head. "When he is not meant to hunt, he mustn't spot game." Jaedon put it on and off several times, finally leaving it on and putting the chick in the nest. "He will sleep a while and wake me when he wants to eat again. Elijah made me a perch he can ride on when he is older." Jaedon showed Dov a staff with a cross-bar at the top for a perch. "He is too young now, his legs too weak to grip long enough, especially the injured one. But he will learn. I will teach him."

Dov gripped the boy's shoulder. He was young and had come through a harrowing time, yet showed this sense of responsibility. He would be a help for Miriam and Yaffa. It was good he would be in the company of Elijah and other prophets, not only for protection, but to learn how a man should act.

Once again, Dov told himself Miriam had made the right decision. The old prophet was wise, and he heard the voice of Yahweh. Dov's offer to marry her, as strongly as he had felt it, was ill conceived. He was an officer in Ahab's army and had trained recruits from throughout the land. Anywhere they went, he might be recognized, then she would be found.

Elijah came to hunker beside them. "Will you return to the city tomorrow?"

"I thought to offer you a ride to the hill country. Zuar could walk back to Jezreel. Or wait for me here."

Elijah smiled. "Best you two go hunting as you originally planned. Bring back meat to share with the townsfolk. It will establish a reason you took the chariot out of the city. No, driving us south would leave a clear track for anyone to follow. We must walk, but we will take it slow. For my old legs." But then he glanced significantly at Yaffa, who was dozing.

"It is a pity, though," Elijah said. "I would like to take such a trip in a chariot."

Chapter Twenty-Nine

For I know the plans I have for you,"
declares the Lord, "plans to prosper you and not
to harm you, plans to give you hope and a future.
~ Jeremiah 29:11

Journey to the hills of Ephraim
Miriam

THE DAY DAWNED CLEAR OVERHEAD, BUT a storm raged inside Miriam. Last night's supper of lentils and greens disagreed violently. She hurried out of the cave behind some boulders, and there she emptied her stomach.

Her emotions were in disarray and had made her ill. Calming herself would set her to rights. She held her hand over her middle and took several slow breaths until the wave of nausea settled. Then she slowly walked back to the cave.

Yaffa gave her a level look when she returned. "Are you well?"

"Yes. Just upset at everything—as are you." Miriam was thankful everyone else, including Jaedon and Elijah, were below making ready the chariot. It was difficult enough to face Yaffa's gaze.

Now a crease deepened between her brows. "I thought you might wish you accepted Dov's offer."

Miriam stared at her mother-in-law. "How can you say that? I am a widow of only a few days. I loved my husband." She turned aside, pressing her hand to her hollow middle. If she had not yet grown to fully love Gershon, she had been on her way. Was not that true of most marriages? Love would have bloomed, in time. But their time had been cut short.

The horror of his murder stalked her dreams and cast a pall over her days. Dov worked for King Ahab, who had either conspired with or had been duped by his queen. How could she ever marry a king's soldier knowing he had a part, however small, in her husband's death?

Yaffa folded her hands in her lap, drawing Miriam's

attention. When had they grown so gnarled and wrinkled with age?

"I lost my husband, too, and both sons. Yet, in this evil time, you need a protector. And your children will need a father."

Miriam took in her mother-in-law's knowing expression. "Children? I am only upset because—"

"No, my daughter. I have seen you go pale at the sight of blood."

It was all she could do not to clap her hand over her mouth at the mention of blood. "I am not pregnant. I cannot be. We tried so long—"

"And now you are. It is a blessing. Listen. Dov is a good man. Jaedon admires him. Go down and stop him. Tell him you changed your mind."

"I cannot. Besides, if I am pregnant—"

"He is a good man, my dear. He already said he would care for you and Jaedon. What is one more child?"

Now Miriam clasped her hand over her mouth and ran outside. She retched several times behind the boulders. Then she sat on a flat stone, resting her head in her hands. She stayed there until the sickness passed. She heard Jaedon calling and shakily got to her feet. The chariot was ready. Zuar stepped inside and gathered up the reins.

Elijah stood beside the horses, stroking one. Jaedon sat atop the horse, waving at her. Dov had a hand on his leg to steady him. He was a good man. A kind man.

"Are you coming down?" Jaedon called.

"No, my heart. I will say goodbye from here. Dov, Zuar, thank you. And safe journey." She felt tears form. Why were there tears?

"And you," Dov said, then quickly turned away.

Shortly after Dov and Zuar departed for Jezreel, Miriam, Jaedon, and Yaffa left with the prophet. As they headed south, there were times Miriam nearly forgot they fled from danger. Mornings seemed only a pleasant walk along a high path where she gazed upon layers and layers of hills. Elijah strolled ahead leading the way, and they followed until he stopped. Miriam found it peaceful walking atop the ancient limestone ridge, steep slopes falling away on both sides, under a wide expanse of blue sky. In every direction she looked, more hills crowded upon each other.

Jaedon carried the eaglet. Sometimes it rode on his gloved hands, sometimes on the staff-perch Elijah had made. When it tired, Yaffa seemed to reach the end of her strength as well, and even if there were hours of daylight, they would stop and rest, sprawling over the steep grassy hills.

Though she would not say so, the traveling also drained Miriam's reserves, and she appreciated the frequent stops. Thankfully the sickness she had experienced in the mornings subsided. Grief and her sole responsibility for Yaffa and Jaedon weighed heavy and must have made her sick. It was a mercy she was not pregnant.

She was reminded of their need for concealment a few days later, when they bypassed the first town they came upon. "Too close to Jezreel," Elijah said. So they dropped down the hill on the other side until they were out of sight of the cluster of homes built on the side of the slope. There they made camp.

As he had the other nights, Jaedon lay close to Miriam, making a nest for Hevel between them. Though she never fed the eagle, it seemed to accept her as a second parent. Wearing its hood, it rested quietly between them, with only an occasional chirp or rustle. Yaffa lay on Jaedon's other side. The prophet bedded down the other side of the small campfire. In this way, they stayed warm. But though she was tired, Miriam sifted the silence for menace—a rattle of stones, the snort of a horse, the soft tread of a jackal. Would the prophet be alert to danger in the night? Did the young eagle, especially hooded, retain its instinct of self-preservation? She prayed, *Protect us, Yahweh. I am a woman, alone. Well, not alone perhaps. But I am without a man. Well, there is this prophet with us. Your prophet.*

Had Gershon ever felt alone, incapable of protecting her and Jaedon? Had he worried about caring for his aging parents? If he had such fears, he had not confided in her, nor prayed aloud about them. He prayed only the ritual prayers of their people.

She drew a deep breath of the night air, inhaling the sour smell of her own helplessness. How could she ever make this right?

I heard Gershon's prayers. And I hear yours. Sleep now.

The next morning, Miriam awoke refreshed. They resumed walking the main road along the ridge until they approached Tirzah, which they also skirted. "Too many people, too many tongues, and too close to Samaria." Elijah said. "We will stop with an old friend."

He again led them down the slope to a mostly dry wadi that swerved southeast from Tirzah. They walked in the gravel stream bed, Miriam stopping from time to time to gather reeds for snares. They would need fresh food soon.

She held an armload of mottled reeds when she heard footfalls running toward them. Her heart lurched. Not a horse. A wild animal? She dropped the reeds, snatched the bow from her shoulder, and nocked an arrow. She aimed toward the approaching animal, but Elijah yelled, "Hold!"

A black dog rounded the dry stream bed, tongue lolling. Elijah knelt on one knee, and the dog greeted him with excited yips and sweeping wags of a white-tipped tail. A bearded, dark-haired shepherd rounded the corner, the dog's owner, by the way it dashed back and forth between him and Elijah. A small herd of sheep followed, starting to wander up the hill when they saw the dog and shepherd otherwise occupied.

Elijah leaned on his staff to rise. "This is my friend Daniel," he called to Miriam.

Miriam glanced back at Jaedon, walking slowly toward her with Yaffa and the eaglet. Might the dog jump on Yaffa or go after the eagle?

Elijah, unconcerned, gave the dog a final scratch behind its ear. "Are you camping nearby?"

"I do better than that." Daniel gestured with a sinewy arm toward a mud-brick house crouching on the side of the hill. A stone wall extended from one side. "My boys and I built this last year. The wall was already standing, put up by some other shepherd who must have moved his flock along the same routes I take. The house is comfortable if I bring my wife or children along. But I am alone this trip and welcome company."

As she neared Elijah and his friend, Miriam stayed in front of Jaedon and Yaffa in case she needed to divert the dog. Then Daniel turned his attention her way, raised his eyebrows when he spotted the eagle, and spoke to his dog. "Hey, old fellow." He pointed at the sheep wandering the side of the hill. "Go watch." Intrigued, Miriam watched the dog run in a low-slung gait to circle the sheep. It found a satisfactory lookout point and lay down, its attention fixed on the herd. When a sheep wandered beyond the dog's self-determined fence line, it jumped up and headed off the stray.

With his dog taking charge of the sheep, Daniel was free to admire Hevel, listening closely to Jaedon's description of how they found it injured and splinted its leg. Daniel reached to run a finger along the break, and in a flash, the bird stretched its neck, clamped down on his finger, and twisted. The shepherd yanked his hand free, laughing, and cradling it with his other hand. "My fault," he said when Jaedon apologized for the bleeding wound. "I know better than to touch a wild thing."

Miriam watched as Jaedon stroked the bird's ruffled feathers and talked quietly to it. Then he turned it so Daniel could see the splinted leg. "He puts weight on it now. Grows stronger each day. I will teach him to hunt when he is old enough."

She felt her face relax at how easily Jaedon spoke to the shepherd. Finding the eaglet had been good for her boy. The responsibility had given him something other than his grief to focus on.

"How will you do that?" Daniel knelt to get a closer look at the eagle, who turned a suspicious glare on him.

She liked how Daniel talked to Jaedon as an adult and showed interest in the eagle.

"I am not exactly sure. But I have changed the way I feed him. I used to dangle the food above his beak. Now I toss the meat in the air and he catches it. Like I once saw grown eagles take a dove."

Jaedon perked up under Daniel's continuing questions,

chattering about his ideas for training the eagle, what he thought it liked and disliked, and how he looked forward to meeting a certain prophet Elijah said had raised a hawk to hunt.

"Although we must carefully introduce him to the hawk. They are enemies in the wild, but they must get along if we are to live together." Miriam smiled at such wisdom, but her thoughts flew next to the enemies who had made her and Yaffa widows and Jaedon an orphan. Even if she felt sure the king and queen were behind it, who were the faceless murderers? How could her little family ever feel safe if shadowy figures might follow wherever they went?

They stayed with Daniel a week. He moved his sheep each day so as not to overgraze the land, he explained. They followed, stopping when he did, one day beside a bubbling spring with willows growing at one end.

It was there Daniel cut a fresh shoot, whittled a flute for Jaedon, and taught him to play a simple tune. "The prophets will teach you more, I expect. They are musical fellows." He then tweeted a more complicated set of sounds, and birds bickering in the bushes answered him back, their quarrel forgotten.

Enjoying the music and Jaedon's soft laughter, Miriam leaned against a willow trunk, motioning for Yaffa to lie beside her. She gently combed her mother-in-law's hair with her fingers, bringing forth hums of pleasure.

"The sickness has not troubled you again, daughter?" Yaffa murmured.

"No, Imma. I am fine." In the background she heard Elijah and Daniel talking together, with Jaedon lacing his opinions between. They spoke of sheep, herbs that flavored mutton, and the best springs from here to Bethel. The shalom of the moment embraced Miriam. The sun warmed her, and her eyelids slid down.

Gershon climbed the hill towards her, the sun bathing his face as he made his way through the sheep. He lowered himself beside her, leaning back against the willow. "It is pleasant here," he said. "I am glad you left Jezreel, Ishti." He stroked her hair and she breathed in the sweet scent of ripe grapes. "My graceful, long-necked heron."

When Miriam woke, she looked around, blinking to disperse fragments of sleep. Yaffa snored softly beside her. She spotted Jaedon tossing meat at the eagle, which it jumped to catch. Was that safe for its leg? But it seemed to land squarely each time, flapping its growing wings.

Elijah and Daniel conversed at the far edge of the herd. Where was Gershon?

And then she remembered. A cavern opened inside, and she felt herself sliding into its depths. It was the first time she had dreamed of Gershon, and waking was like losing him again.

She drew a deep breath, hugging herself. Daniel had said they would have mutton stew for supper. She walked slowly around the spring searching for herbs, something ordinary to fill the empty place, pleased to spot small heart-shaped leaves of mint winding along the spring edge.

He had called her Ishti.

Chapter Thirty

*I am in the midst of lions; I am forced to dwell among
ravenous beasts—men whose teeth are spears and
arrows, whose tongues are sharp swords.*
~ Psalm 57:4

Jezreel Valley
Dov

DOV HAD BEGUN TO WONDER IF he and Zuar must go back empty handed, but two days after they left Miriam, they finally killed a deer near Jezreel. When they loaded the carcass into the chariot the horses stamped uneasily.

"What do you suppose that is about?" Zuar asked. "These are battle-trained horses, are they not? They should be used to the smell of blood."

Dov shrugged, stepping over the big buck to take the reins. "Human blood. Maybe game smells different. This thing is huge, though. It nearly fills the chariot. Maybe we should butcher it here after all." He disliked that possibility, however. He planned to use the antlers and hide, and many in town would gladly help for a share of the meat.

"No, you were right. No more time to waste. We will be taunted already for our lack of hunting prowess. Gone four days and only one buck to show. Yet, such an animal! We're lucky it ran across our path. Almost as if it were looking for us."

Dov spoke gently to the skittish horses, then turned them away from the forested hills. They'd make it to Jezreel for the midday meal, he estimated, if the horses settled down. When he loosened the reins, however, the horses sprang forward, eager to gallop. But the uneven ground was riddled with the tunnels of burrowing animals, so he took up the slack in the reins. The horses bent their necks to his pressure but persisted in their reckless pace.

"Behind us!" Zuar yelled.

Dov twisted around. A female lion bounded after them,

only strides from the chariot's open rear. Thrusting the reins at Zuar, Dov slid his bow from his shoulder, nocked an arrow, and shot. It hit the lion in the shoulder. She snarled her rage but kept coming. He sent two more arrows. One missed, one bit into her neck.

With a mighty leap, the lion sprang into the chariot, landing on the carcass. As she crouched to latch onto the deer, Dov grabbed his sword, bracing against the side of the chariot. If the lioness would just take it and back off, it could have the stag. But Zuar lunged toward her, axe raised. Neighing shrilly, the horses swerved, throwing him and the lion together. It let go of the stag and crunched on Zuar's arm. Swearing, he struggled to wrench free. Dov shouted, "Let him go!" as he stabbed the lion, but his blade glanced off bone. Blood flowed from the animal, but intent on its prey, the lion seemed not to feel its wounds. Dov aimed for its throat, but it sat back on its haunches, yanking Zuar between them. Before Dov could regroup, Zuar, the lion, and the carcass fell from the chariot, tumbling man over deer over lion.

Dov grabbed the reins and tried to turn the horses back. They stopped but fought him when he whipped them toward the lion. He jumped out of the chariot, waving his arms and shouting as he ran.

Cradling his savaged arm against his chest, Zuar grasped his fallen axe. He struggled to his feet. The lion shook her head, stunned by the fall. Then she fixed yellow eyes on Zuar, who slowly backed away. She staggered, then crouched.

Still running, Dov shoved the sword into his belt. He wasn't going to reach them in time to use his sword. He grasped the bow and clutched a handful of arrows. Aiming as he ran, he sent them one after another toward the lion.

When the first arrow hit her side, she hissed and snapped at it. The second hit her flank. She roared and wheeled around. The third hit her in the shoulder, near the first he shot, then Dov was upon her. He dropped the bow, snatched the sword from his belt, and as the lion faced him, stabbed her full in the throat.

She tried to roar, but her damaged throat only gurgled.

Zuar staggered forward and swung his axe, but she had already crumpled. Dov didn't blame Zuar for the extra blows. The lioness had seemed indestructible.

And crazed.

Jumping in a moving chariot to take a kill? With two humans? He studied the animal, looking for signs of disease. He had seen a dog with a frothing mouth once that attacked its own master, but he saw no evidence of that. But its ribs showed, and the coat was rough and lackluster. He kicked its side and when there was no response, Dov knelt and pried its jaws open with his knife. The gums looked grayish and the tongue ulcerated. He got to his feet, thinking over the moments before the attack. The horses had been skittish when they loaded the buck. Had the lioness been stalking the buck before they shot it?

"She was starving. After our deer, I expect." Zuar said, holding his arm tightly.

"Let me see your arm." Dov stepped close. A ragged wound, filthy from the lion's saliva and the rolling fall from the chariot. He unwrapped his belt and tied it around the cut. "We must get you to a healer." The belt seeped blood, so he tightened it more. "Feel all right, my friend?"

"A cup of wine would suit. But I'll settle for water."

"It's in the chariot." Dov turned to run for their vehicle, but he only saw its dust in the distance. The panicked horses would enter Jezreel without passengers, unless someone stopped them.

During the attack, uncanny strength and speed had infused him. Now it drained away. Dov glanced down. The front of his tunic was shredded, and bloody claw marks crossed his chest, arms, and legs where the lioness had swiped him. How had he not felt any of this during the attack?

"Looks like we're walking. Here, sling your good arm over my shoulder."

Zuar slapped his hand away. "Save your breath. Carry my axe, if you insist."

They walked until the sun stood directly overhead, Zuar growing visibly weaker with each step. "Need rest," he gasped hoarsely, then he fainted. Dov grabbed him in an embrace before he hit the ground. Then he grasped his friend's undamaged arm and hitched the limp body across his shoulders.

"Stubborn, unreasonable lout. You weigh as much as a bull," he muttered, clamping his friend's leg and arm as he took a hesitant step. Then he followed Zuar's advice. Saved his breath to put one foot in front of the other.

I should have asked for help before this, Yahweh. Please give me strength to carry my friend to the city. Don't let him die.

A breeze cooled Dov's face, and he quickened his steps. One foot after another. He trudged along until his shoulders felt like they would slide off with their load. He hitched Zuar forward a bit, twisting to see his face. Dov saw only the back of his head, but he heard rasping breaths. At least he still lived.

Dov looked toward the city. He could almost make out the gate. He estimated he might make it before dusk. Step, step, step. What kind of fool loses a chariot? He examined each moment. He'd had to jump from the chariot to help Zuar fight the lion. From the time the lion leaped in the chariot, Dov had reacted. He could have done nothing different. But before, when the horses were acting nervous, he should have known. Known a lion was near? How could he possibly?

With every step he trained his ear to any further threats. Lions were pack animals. Another might be near. But there was also danger from two-legged predators. Those who had murdered Naboth and his sons were now hunting his women and grandson. Anyone known to help them would also face death.

Where was Miriam now? Far from Jezreel, he hoped. Hidden in the uncharted hill country from Jezebel's assassins. He staggered, then regained his footing. She had an old woman and a boy depending on her. So much responsibility on such a young woman. Yet she had the prophet with her. An old man.

He stepped into a dip and his knees buckled. He quit worrying about Miriam and the prophet and fixed his attention on the ground in front of his feet.

Thirst tormented him. Why hadn't he tied the waterskin

on his shoulder? Because the bow had been there—and now Zuar, heavier with every step.

His bow. Where was it? Had he lost it when he hoisted Zuar on his shoulder? No, before that. He'd dropped it to pull his sword for the killing blow. Had he not picked it up again?

Well, there were more Aramean bows in the city arsenal. If he made it back. If another lion did not accost them on the way.

Zuar's weight pressing on his neck, Dov wrenched his head up to measure the distance to the city once more. At the foot of the ramp leading to the gate, dust churned in a furious cloud. He sighed with relief. By all appearances, it was Aaron who drove the chariot at full speed, behind what appeared to be a fresh team of horses. Aaron, faithful old Aaron, must have been searching the valley from his guard post.

Dov grinned, carefully slid Zuar to the ground, and waved both arms over his head.

Jezebel leaned over her balcony wall in the palace of Jezreel, looking over the courtyard below. There he was. Wearing sackcloth, Ahab looked like an impoverished farmer whose ox had died. He descended the palace steps in his daily pilgrimage to the temple of the Israelite god.

Where had her plan gone wrong? Her husband had been so pleased, when she first got him the vineyard. Then that terrible man Elijah confronted him, spoiling everything. She ground her teeth. Would the old seer never cease to plague her?

Looking up, the king caught sight of her and scowled. Jezebel backed away from the window, her breath coming quick and shallow. Suddenly she picked up a glass bowl and threw it across the room. Green glass shards scattered everywhere. She felt a pang—she had brought that bowl from Tyre. Her father had given it to her. Another hateful man who had betrayed her.

A servant girl came running. What was her name? Well, it mattered not.

"Clumsy of me. Clean it up."

The girl bowed deeply. "Yes, my queen."

Jezebel turned away as the girl did her job. There was another matter Jezebel needed to clean up. She couldn't trust just anyone with the delicate request. Who could she rely upon?

The girl swept the debris onto a bronze dust pan and began backing from the room.

"After you dispose of the mess, summon the steward for me."

"To the throne room?"

"No. I will speak with him here." Jezebel rolled her eyes. Why should she walk down a flight of steps and across the palace to meet with a steward? These people were so narrow minded.

The girl quickly lowered her head and backed from the room.

Shortly, Obadiah stopped at her open door. "You summoned me, my queen?"

She tilted her head. "Yes. I would like to speak to an army officer I spoke to several years ago. I don't recall his name. He was captain of the king's guard."

Obadiah hesitated. "Would you like to speak to him here?"

She sighed. "No. In the lesser throne room. But I will wait here until you announce his arrival." It had been five or six years since she last spoke to the young officer. She remembered him as virile and decisive. Importantly, he had admired her, as most men did. Yes, he was the man for the job.

Jezebel had felt no qualms in meeting the young captain in her quarters at that time. But that was when the king, if not *completely* enamored of her, was firmly under her thrall. Now, she could not forget that Ahab had nearly given her as war booty, so she must be more circumspect. It was one thing to raise the servants' eyebrows by speaking alone with the king's trusted steward, another to meet privately with a handsome officer.

Because they all talked. From palace servants to city officials, none could be trusted. Wagging tongues. That was why she needed a military man now. The captain could be trusted to take care of this matter.

Obadiah hurried to the army barracks. The meeting room was empty except for one soldier warming himself beside a dying fire.

"Where can I find the captain of the king's guard?" he asked.

"Most of the officers are in the valley training new recruits and volunteers. The captain should be there."

"Will you carry a message? The queen wishes to speak with him immediately. He should ask for me at the palace. Obadiah, the king's steward."

The soldier agreed and promptly jogged toward the city gate. The captain should arrive within the hour. Obadiah returned to see that the room was set to rights.

Since the lesser throne room had not been used in months, Obadiah called several house servants to sweep, dust, and polish. It was imperative the queen find nothing with which to be displeased. When the palace doorkeeper announced a soldier had arrived, the last two servant girls left with brooms and polishing cloths. Just in time.

Obadiah smoothed his robes and walked sedately to the entrance. But he was disturbed to see the soldier he had just sent to find the captain.

The soldier bowed, his face flushed. "I am sorry, sir, I gave you bad information. I did not know the captain was injured in a hunting accident. He is still unconscious. But I left a message with his adoptive father, and the captain will come as soon as he recovers."

Obadiah nodded. "Where does he live? In the event the queen wants to send another message."

"He lives with Maalik," the soldier said. "The old eunuch that brought the queen from Tyre."

The next day, Dov woke to find Maalik sitting beside his

sleeping mat, staring at him with concern.

"I thought you would never wake."

Dov raised himself on one arm, noticing both were now wrapped in clean cloths. He inhaled the sharp aroma of balsam ointment, remembering how Maalik had salved the many cuts and scrapes he had sustained. A bitter tea made of balsam needles and bark had eased his pain before he drifted into a deep sleep.

He sat up, vaguely thinking something was wrong. The window was in the wrong place. "Where am I?"

"We are in Jezreel, a few doors from Zuar and Aaron. The queen sent a chariot to bring me from Samaria and rented this house. I thought it was kind of her to make it easier for me to care for you."

Dov doubted that, but Maalik held a somewhat fond regard for the queen, remembering her as the sad Tyrian princess he had accompanied to Israel.

"We always stayed with Naboth or at Gershon's. Both houses are empty now, but I couldn't bring myself to stay there." Maalik glanced away.

The thought made Dov shudder. "How is Zuar? The lion gave him the worse time of it."

Maalik shook his head. "The healer saw to him first, before coming here. His arm is in bad shape. A wild animal bite sometimes become tainted. The healer gave particular attention to cleaning and packing the wound with garlic, as for you. You have many deep claw marks."

Taint? The healer feared infection. Dov remembered the animal's grayed gums and emaciated condition. "I prefer balsam. But if garlic will heal Zuar's wound—"

"He instructed Aaron to change the dressing daily. Asked me to help if Aaron's work schedule makes it difficult. But—"

"I am well enough. I can help." Dov sat up, sending a rush of pain to his head. "I will go see them today."

Maalik looked down. "I have told Queen Jezebel I will return after you are sufficiently healed. Not because I want to return to the palace. But because I learned, from the time I escorted her to Israel as a young bride through the years I served as her temple guard, one does not tell the queen, no."

Dov massaged his throbbing temples. "I fear you are right. The things I learned about the deaths of Naboth and his sons make me want to send you into hiding." He told Maalik everything Miriam and Elijah had shared at the cave.

"Do I need to tell you I would not leave you?" Maalik got up to stir a pot simmering on the hearth.

"I know you would not want to leave your house and friends. But it seems clear the queen was behind this dark business. She is a dangerous woman."

"And Elijah found the king walking in Naboth's vineyard, prepared to take possession." Maalik ladled steaming liquid into a cup. "It does not seem the king is without fault. He did not don garments of mourning until the prophet condemned him." He knelt beside Dov and handed him the cup.

Dov inhaled. "Mint."

"And feverfew. Davita suggested it."

"Davita?"

"She brought the concoction and two loaves of bread after visiting Zuar's bedside. Said the tea would ease pain without making you sleep." Maalik's eyes glinted with humor. "The girl seems quite concerned for your friend."

Dov shuddered. "I am concerned, too. That lioness leapt into the chariot, grabbed him by the arm, and dragged him out. He lost much blood. But you said the healer—"

"Also is concerned, my boy, lest the wound become putrid. But Zuar is in Yahweh's hands. And Davita's, it seems. Although I am sure he will appreciate a visit from you, his friend. But not until you are better."

Dov sipped the brew, the freshness of mint and sweetness of honey taming feverfew's bitter taste. He swallowed the rest, longing for respite from the searing pains throughout his body. He slowly lowered himself back to the mat.

"The king. How can I continue to serve him now that I know—"

"That he is a king? That he takes what he wants from whomever?"

"I thought he wanted the best for Israel." Dov no longer believed that. The king had unjustly killed—or allowed the killing of—a loyal subject.

"Did you now? Perhaps before we befriended Caleb's family and learned the ways of Yahweh. When you were younger, I suppose I tried to shield you from the darkest truths of the pagan temples. But you knew the king visited the temple prostitutes."

Dov nodded. "But he is a king. And a man."

"Once you were tempted by one of the priestesses, I think."

Dov felt his face heat. He did not like to discuss such things with the man he thought of as father. Yet, who else? He had never spoken of his feelings for Mara, all those years ago. Even now, he would not name her.

"She was a strong woman. And she wanted to leave that life. I admired her. The way she fought to protect her sons. But I knew she was not for me. Nor I, for her."

Maalik smiled. "I have tried to teach you the ways of your father's people. It seems I have done well enough. Or perhaps I have made you too reticent. What of the brave Davita? Bold, yet devout. And unattached. Would you have me speak to her father on your behalf?"

Dov's hand flapped the air. "No. She is a fine woman. Otherwise, she would not be Miriam's friend. Enough. We were speaking of my continued career with the king."

"Oh, is that what we spoke of? Well, I think you should continue to work for the king for the same reason I will again work for the queen."

"Because one does not say no to the king or the queen?"

Maalik raised his eyebrows. "You are a friend of Miriam, are you not? And she is in great danger."

Dov nodded slowly. "I think I understand. We will be in positions to learn of any increased threat if the king or queen learns of her whereabouts."

Maalik quirked an eyebrow. "Do you know where she is?"

"I do not. I can swear to that in all honesty. But I know how to find her."

For the second time that week, Obadiah walked into the

lesser throne room. He greeted the soldier who awaited him, recognizing him before he gave his name, despite the cuts and bruises on his face and nearly all exposed skin on his arms and legs.

"I am Dov, captain of the king's guard. I have been summoned by the queen." He stepped forward and bowed, wincing, if Obadiah was not mistaken. He caught a whiff of the balsam and thyme used to anoint wounds.

He remembered this soldier. He had been one of the young officers who led the rout of the Arameans, but even before that, he remembered Dov during the time of Elijah. Dov had been a friend of young Aban, a former acolyte of Melqart who helped the prophet Elijah.

"We have met." Obadiah inclined his head. "You have been injured." It was not a question.

Dov nodded, shifting his weight awkwardly, but offering nothing. A discreet man, Obadiah reflected.

"The queen will not come until I announce your arrival. Do you know why you have been summoned?"

"I do not."

"Nor do I. I will go to her now." And if not prevented, Obadiah would stay and listen.

Dov nodded again.

Jezebel had changed to her purple gown, painted her eyelids with kohl, and donned her crown. She must appear not only beautiful but powerful. The soldier's gaze told her she had succeeded. But what was this? He was not the man she sought.

She studied him curiously. She had heard two soldiers had been mauled by a lion. This man's fresh wounds and bruises told a tale. But who was he?

He bowed low. "I am Dov, captain of the guard." He clenched his hand and thumped his heart in salute. Then he winced.

She studied him. "I asked for the captain of the guard— but you are not the man I sought. Five or six years ago I spoke to a young officer ..." Her voice trailed off. "You are not him."

Dov waited a respectful amount of time as if expecting more, but she remained silent. Often silence produced the desired result.

"I was promoted after the siege and subsequent rout of Aram," he finally offered. "Commander Ocran was formerly captain. Perhaps he is the man you seek."

Seeing admiration in the younger man's eyes, Jezebel briefly considered giving him the task. But no, she would find the man who had already proved himself discreet.

"Is this Commander—Ocran—in Jezreel?" She would remember his name.

"Yes, my queen."

"Then send him to me."

Deciding to wait rather than return to her quarters, Jezebel sat on the throne and ordered refreshment. A servant brought bread, olive oil with herbs, and wine from the king's new vineyard. After the old seer scolded him, her husband had lost interest in his plan for a vegetable garden. But when she learned the best wine in the country came from that vineyard, she hired someone to tend the vines and kept the wine for only his use. She took a sip. Lovely.

Finally, the right captain—now a commander—arrived. Commander Ocran. He introduced himself and bowed.

A narrow window cast light on his face. He was a little older, a little stouter, but he was the man she remembered. And yes, she saw respect and regard in his gaze. He would carry out her orders without misstep.

"I have another task for you. It must be handled discreetly."

He nodded. "Yes, my queen."

"I will give you four names. Two are city officials. Two are unsavory individuals. I want all four arrested and imprisoned. Discreetly."

He waited, expressionless.

She gave the names of the two officials she had ordered to accuse Naboth. Then she named the witnesses who had sworn to the vintner's guilt.

"Yes, my queen."

He performed the salute, less crisply than the younger officer had, but what did a salute matter? Perhaps she ... sometimes ... moved a little less crisply than she used to. Yet she was every bit as resolute. A trait the king often lacked. But she had been a princess in Tyre, where subjects immediately obeyed when their king commanded, or they died. And that was why he needed her.

The afternoon sun glared as it sank toward the temple of Astarte, a dull place these last years. Another offense she laid at the feet of that troublemaker, Elijah. Ahab should have killed him when he had the chance.

But what mattered now was silencing those gossips. Ocran was the man to get the job done. And once they were in prison, she would have their tongues cut out.

No. At least two of them could write. Taking their tongues would not be enough.

Chapter Thirty-One

*Keep this Book of the Law always on your lips; meditate on it
day and night, so that you may be careful to do everything
written in it. Then you will be prosperous and successful.
Have I not commanded you? Be strong and courageous. Do
not be afraid; do not be discouraged, for the Lord your God
will be with you wherever you go.*
~ Joshua 1:8-9

In the hills of Ephraim
Miriam

MIRIAM AWAKENED BEFORE DAWN WITH AN urgent desire to scrub
every corner of Daniel's house. She could no longer ignore
the spider that busily spun webs overnight. If Daniel's wife
accompanied him on his next pass through the countryside,
the woman should find the house as clean as she left it.

Carrying two jugs, Miriam hurried to the shady spring
where cool water burbled over a tumble of rocks. She filled
the jugs and twisted a broom of willow twigs to banish the
spider. Then she headed toward the sound of sheep bleating,
where she should find the men. As the sun cleared the
distant hills, light fell on her path.

She smelled smoke before she came upon the herd.
Daniel knelt in a clearing, feeding sticks into a small
campfire. "I will make the meal this morning, in thanks for
all your cooking." He glanced significantly at the water and
broom. "Although it appears that resting is not in your
plans."

Miriam tried to smile but felt her chin waver. The jugs
grew heavy. Why had she filled them so full? "I'm impatient
to begin my tasks, so your kindness is welcome. When will
the bread be ready?"

He indicated a cloth-covered lump on a wooden slab.
"The dough is waiting and the coals nearly ready."

Eying the flames, Miriam reckoned she easily could
clean and return with Yaffa before Daniel finished.

"Where are Elijah and Jaedon?" Her son had begged to camp with the men, and she had agreed. After all, Jaedon could be in no safer company than the prophet's.

"At the house by now. Jaedon wanted to feed his eagle away from the dog. I sent it to watch the sheep, but raw meat was too great a temptation. My dog kept circling back."

Miriam stopped herself from nodding and spilling the water balanced on her head. "When he finishes with the eagle, we will return for your delicious meal."

She started back to the house, trying to walk faster, but the jug on her hip felt uncomfortable. Why did she feel so awkward? She had been managing two jugs of water for years.

She recalled when Caleb had gone with her to the well in Jezreel, dropped his water jug, and drenched himself. When they returned to the well for more water, the moment sparked his courtship of Chloe. Now they were betrothed.

Suddenly, she teared up. When would she see her brother again? Her imma and abba? Could she go to Caleb's wedding? Would she ever meet Seth's children?

Miriam blinked several times, awkwardly trying to wipe her eyes as she approached the house. She heard voices inside.

"And the dog ran over and tried to grab the strips right out of his beak, so Hevel snapped at his nose." Jaedon giggled. "Daniel said I should come back here."

Miriam stopped in the doorway.

Yaffa sat by the hearth, smiling at Jaedon. Elijah stood just inside. But when he caught sight of Miriam, he hurried to take the jug of water. She quickly set the other on the floor and pressed the palms of her hands against her eyes.

"What is wrong?" Yaffa asked.

"Nothing." Miriam put the broom to action in the corners. "Sweat in my eyes."

The house went silent a moment, and then Yaffa said, "Elijah said Daniel is preparing the morning meal."

"It will take him a while for the fire to burn down. Jaedon, please take Hevel outside while I clean. Elijah, will you make Yaffa comfortable in the shade? I won't be long."

Jaedon hesitated, his mouth slightly parted, then did as

she asked. Elijah moved toward Yaffa, offering his hand to help her rise. She took it, but she gave him a gentle push toward the door. "I will help Miriam with the cleaning. We will join you soon."

Miriam heard the two talking as they walked back the way she had come.

"Do you think the eagle would let me hold it?" they heard Elijah ask.

"No," Jaedon said. "He only likes me."

"Hmm."

She looked at Yaffa and grinned.

Yaffa smiled back, but said firmly, "Tell me what this is all about, my girl."

"The house needs cleaning, and I want to get after it. The eagle—"

"Jaedon has cleaned up after the bird," Yaffa said. "You have seen to that. As have I, for that matter."

"But we are guests. I think I should give the house a good cleaning. I want Daniel's wife to find it without spot."

"Then, let us start." Yaffa dampened a rag and scrubbed a low stool, the door frame, the window ledge, and the corner Miriam had just swept. "Shall we do the walls?"

Miriam frowned. "Yes, I planned to wash the walls. But I don't want you doing such heavy work."

Yaffa put her hands on her hips. "The house is made of mud. A good sweeping is all it needs."

Miriam tossed her hands in the air. "I am unsure. I suppose I am ... unsettled."

"This frenzy to scrub and clean. Your tears. You are certainly unsettled, because you are with child. I remember when last you bled. You have stopped being sick in the mornings and brim with energy to ready your nest. Make no mistake. Your child—my grandchild—will come late this winter."

Miriam sat on the just-cleaned stool and covered her face with her hands. "It cannot be! Am I to have a child that Gershon will never see? Raise him alone without a father?"

Yaffa patted her shoulder. "There, there, daughter. It is not so bad. You have me and Jaedon is becoming a dependable boy."

"Oh! I am on your stool." Taking hold of her hands, Miriam pulled her mother-in-law onto the seat. Then she knelt and lay her head on Yaffa's lap. "We are running from enemies."

"But the Lord is with us. And his prophet."

"The child will be another heir. His life will be in danger."

"My daughter." Yaffa stroked her hair. "You must trust the Lord. Your grandmother must have taught you these words of the Lord, as given to Israel's leader Joshua. She taught them to Gershon and to me, for my parents were not devout."

Miriam closed her eyes and listened to Yaffa recite, recognizing the sing-song cadence in which Savta spoke when reciting the Torah.

"Have I not commanded you? Be strong and courageous. Do not be afraid; do not be discouraged, for the Lord your God will be with you wherever you go."

Yaffa had a faraway look, as if folding the promise away for a future time of comfort. "Daughter, I, too, have been broken. I asked the Lord, 'Why were you not with our men in that vineyard?'"

"And did He answer?"

Yaffa hesitated. "I am not a prophetess, but yes. A quiet whisper, as if on the wind. He said, 'What makes you think I was not there?'"

Miriam turned her face into the folds of cloth, clenching her fists. She was angry with Yahweh and weary of hiding it. Naboth and his sons had kept the law far better than King Ahab. They had never broken the first and greatest commandment, *Thou shalt love the Lord thy God with all thine heart and thy neighbor as thyself.* How many laws had Ahab broken? He had worshipped the Ba'als. He had coveted Naboth's vineyard and lied and murdered to steal it. Yet he lived, and her husband was dead.

The father of her child. If there had not been a great passion between her and Gershon—yet—a flame had been kindled. It would have grown, but his life had been snuffed out.

After a moment, she raised her head, feeling hot tears spring fresh. "Why did He not save them?"

Yaffa's voice quavered. "Death comes for us all, my dear. The Lord has commanded us to obey, be strong, and be courageous. He will be with us."

Cupping Miriam's face, Yaffa smiled, though her eyes glistened with unshed tears. "The house is set to rights. Now let us wash our faces and taste Daniel's bread. I have learned that the best meals are those made by another."

They washed their faces with spring water, checked each other for traces of tears, and set off for the campsite where Miriam had left Daniel. They smelled bread and smoke as they drew close to the site. Jaedon strode among the sheep, the eaglet riding on his shoulder and the dog bounding by his side.

Elijah and Daniel sat by the fire. Logs had burned to embers, and small loaves of bread roasted on stones, wafting sweetness and smoke. Two wooden bowls sat on a log beside Elijah, one filled with olive oil, the other with salt. Elijah indicated Yaffa should sit on the log.

Miriam sat cross-legged beside Daniel on a patch of grass. "Do you trade for the salt?"

"No need. Each year, I go to Jerusalem for Passover and to the Dead Sea on the way back."

She nodded. Savta had spoken of the beautiful temple in Jerusalem, where she had grown up. She told of moving north with her husband Nathaniel, wondering if she would ever see Jerusalem again. But her grandmother always expressed the desire for the family to keep the Passover in Jerusalem one day. Now that journey could never come to pass.

"Jaedon has eaten his fill of bread." Daniel grasped a loaf between folds of a cloth, tossed it in the air a few times to cool, and dropped it into Yaffa's lap. Quickly, he snatched another loaf and dropped it in Miriam's lap.

Yaffa dipped her bread into the oil beside her, then into the salt. She took a bite. "Mmm. Did you add honey? It is sweet."

"No, I have none. But I roast half the grain before grinding. I like the flavor it gives the bread." He ducked his head as if embarrassed.

Miriam smiled and bit into the crusty loaf, nodding her

approval. As she ate, she turned her attention to Jaedon and the eagle. The bird nibbled at the long hair brushing his shoulder. When the dog drew close, the eagle flipped its wings and made an irritated sound, like a bird curse that made her want to laugh.

Elijah walked over to dip bread into the oil. "Yahweh has told me we must leave today."

Yaffa nodded, but Miriam repeated, "Today?" She closed her fingers around handfuls of grass, as if tethering herself to the spot. Why was she reluctant to move on?

"As soon as you have eaten."

"I will pack bread for your journey," Daniel said.

"Where will we go next?" They were truly leaving everyone behind. No one would know where she had gone.

Elijah smiled. "Wherever Yahweh tells me."

Chapter Thirty-Two

*Fix these words of mine in your hearts and minds. Teach
them to your children, talking about them when you sit at
home and when you walk along the road, when you lie down
and when you get up. Write them on the doorframes of your
houses and on your gates, so that your days and the days of
your children may be many in the land.*
~ Deuteronomy 11:19

The hill country of Ephraim
Miriam

WHEN THEY DEPARTED THAT MORNING, JAEDON cried, whether
for leaving Daniel or the dog Miriam did not know, but she
felt her own eyes moisten. Yet another loss.

She refused to sink into self-pity. A blue sky welcomed
them to the ridge they had walked before. Miriam was
grateful for the fleecy white clouds that laced the sky,
sometimes drifting over the sun and offering respite. She
recalled the words Daniel had taught them, which he called
'a shepherd's prayer'. *Then we your people, the sheep of your
pasture, will praise you forever. From generation to generation
we will proclaim your praise.*

Jaedon strode ahead, the eagle on his shoulder wearing
its hood. Yaffa walked beside her, limping a little. "What are
you thinking of, daughter?"

Miriam smiled, glad she had turned her mind from
complaint to praise. "I was thinking of the words Daniel
taught us. Thankful for this"—she swept her arm in an
upward arc—"and the fragrant breeze. Do you smell the
wildflowers?" Noticing the hitch in her mother-in-law's stride,
Miriam felt a twinge of concern. "Lean on me, Mother. We will
stop soon for our midday meal." After staying several days
with Daniel, she had hoped Yaffa had gained strength for the
journey. But though they had only walked half a day at an
easy pace, her mother-in-law was already tiring.

Yaffa laughed. "We only just broke our fast."

Jaedon turned, causing the eagle to lift its wings to maintain balance. "No, the sun has moved this much." Spreading his hands, he indicated a wide expanse of time. The eagle swiveled its head as if considering Jaedon's words, then bit into a fold of his tunic.

Elijah, coming up behind, said, "We are approaching Shechem. Turn off here. I know families who farm in the area. We will take a meal with one of them."

Miriam spotted a footpath ahead, angling down from the main path. In the distance she saw many small dwellings built halfway down the slope, mudbrick houses like Daniel's. Below the settlements, she saw long, cultivated terraces along the lowest parts of the slope. The earthen floor of the wadi, where it was not covered with crops, grasses, or wildflowers, was red-brown and fertile.

Before she left the ridge, Miriam looked back. She could see a good long way behind them. But no one was coming.

As they began their descent, Yaffa clung tightly to Miriam's arm. Elijah stepped forward and took her other arm. "Do you enjoy almonds, my friend?"

"Indeed, I do." Yaffa smiled, though her lips were compressed and her face had gone pale.

"Then we will stop with Imlah, Micaiah's father. He tends the most fruitful almond trees in the hills of Ephraim. I daresay we shall eat our fill and depart with a sackful."

Miriam breathed a sigh of relief when they reached the grassy floor. Yaffa walked easier on the lush carpet as they passed a stand of fig trees and approached row upon row of almonds, growing on terraced levels up the side of the slope. Elijah led them past the last trees in the orchard, then the mountain opened into another wadi branching off the one they'd walked. A wiry, gray-haired man spread seed on freshly tilled ground. A knock-kneed donkey happily grazed the field's borders where long blades of grass clung to overturned dirt clods. Its plow and harness lay discarded, off to the side.

Elijah patted Yaffa's hand, let go, and walked toward the farmer. "Ho, Imlah, what are you planting?"

"Elijah! Glad to see you, old friend." He clasped Elijah in an embrace. "I thought you were with the prophets at

Bethel."

"And so I was. But Yahweh sent me north to Jezreel."

Imlah stepped back, studying the prophet, perhaps waiting, as Miriam was, for further detail on his mission to Jezreel. When it did not come, the farmer cut his gaze to Miriam, Yaffa, and Jaedon. Miriam was not surprised when his attention stayed a while on Jaedon and the eagle.

Elijah reached an arm as if to encompass them. "Miriam, Yaffa, and Jaedon are friends I met near Jezreel. Jaedon found this injured eagle where it had fallen from its cliff nest."

Imlah bowed from the waist, then turned again to Elijah. "My wife will not forgive me if I don't bring you and your friends for a meal."

"I was hoping you would say that. Does Noa still keep hives?"

"She does. Always welcome in trading. Are you hinting for honeyed almonds?"

"I am sure the boy would appreciate a taste." Miriam saw Jaedon perk up, but he did not add his response to the conversation. She felt warmed by his reserved behavior. It was not the despondent silence she had observed after the murders, instead, a boy gaining wisdom.

Imlah gave Elijah a playful shove. "You old deceiver. You cannot leave them alone."

"True." The prophet grinned, then shifted his attention to the donkey. "Have you finished your plowing?"

Imlah nodded. "I am out of seed wheat. Are you heading for Bethel?"

"Is that Adi, Micaiah's donkey? Never seen another stand so contentedly by the plow."

"I always drop a little grain nearby."

Elijah whistled admiringly as he walked toward the donkey. Jaedon followed on his heels.

The farmer tipped his head, smiling. "One must look for simple solutions when Yahweh does not whisper in his ear."

Miriam hid a smile. How many questions had Imlah asked and Elijah side-stepped? Ha! He asked another question when he was asked his plans. She had begun to realize he either waited to hear from Yahweh, or the message was for him alone.

"Don't be sure Yahweh does not whisper in your ear. Where else would you receive wisdom?" Elijah picked up one of the ropes lying atop the harness. "Do the village children still ride this old girl?" He approached the donkey, stroked her rounded forehead, and fastened the rope to its halter.

"Every opportunity they get."

Elijah led the donkey toward Miriam and Yaffa. It stopped and faced them, gazing in their faces with deep liquid eyes. The animal was so small Elijah barely needed to lift Yaffa for her to sit on its back. It seemed to tiptoe on tiny hooves when it walked, effortlessly carrying Yaffa's weight, its back swaying not at all. "Such a sweet little thing," Yaffa said, pleasure warming her voice. "Truly a jewel." She ran her hand down its neck and Adi stretched her neck in satisfaction, launching into a cheerful bray that made everyone laugh. Elijah led them deeper into the wadi, presumably toward Imlah's house.

Miriam peered along the ravine at the few houses built halfway up the slope. More terraces below held lush grapevines. At the far end it appeared there was yet another curve to the wadi. This area would be easy to protect if necessary. An army could not drive chariots through nor armored troops easily navigate these wadis, where the residents knew every twisted path, stand of trees, and layer of hills. And for what? She counted four or five closely packed houses at the end of this wadi, and even the larger grouping she had seen from the ridge was a cluster of fewer than twenty homes.

A woman stood at the door of the first house, wiping her hands on a towel tied around her middle. Though she was not a tall woman, the door frame was inches above her head. Only one small window allowed light into the house. Another protective measure, wise, but Miriam would not like to cook in such a dark house. A picture of her Jezreel house unfolded, with its large windows and courtyard that had made the house so pleasant.

But even as the memory faded, Imlah lifted a hand and called to his wife. She smiled hugely and hurried down to meet them.

"Shalom! Oh, how pleasant to have guests. I am Noa."

Imlah introduced them as Elijah's friends from Jezreel and, surprisingly, he remembered all their names.

Noa glanced up the hill, where smoke curled above the roofline. "Oh, dear. I must check on supper. Keep me company? My oven is behind the house."

Miriam glanced at the slope, then at Yaffa, so comfortable on the donkey. Before she asked, Elijah handed her the lead rope.

As the women and donkey walked uphill, Jaedon glanced between Elijah and the donkey, clearly torn. "Shall I help Elijah and Imlah?"

"Yes, that is good." Miriam smiled at his polite question. The boy grew more heedful every day. She still saw sadness in his eyes when reminded of that day, but following Elijah and being responsible for the eagle did him good.

Miriam led the donkey up the slope to the source of the smoke, a tannur oven behind the house. "Noa, sudden guests can be an imposition, I fear. But we brought food to share."

"I am pleased to meet another woman, more so, one from a city." Noa's eyes creased with her smile. "But you must keep your food for the journey. When you travel with Elijah, you will be moving on with little notice, or be left behind. There will be no shortage of food. The neighbors will all want to hear him teach, as he did the last time. You must stay the night."

Miriam breathed a sigh of relief. A roof and walls for the night. She helped Yaffa off the donkey, keeping her steady as she slid the short distance to the ground. If Noa longed for news outside of the hill country, Miriam hoped Elijah would be the one to share it. She was not prepared to speak of the vineyard and their flight.

Noa fed kindling and dried sheep dung into the tannur oven. "You can turn Adi loose, she will stay close. Hang her halter on the lean-to. She will graze all afternoon and go into the shelter at dusk."

After releasing the donkey, Miriam returned to study the oven with interest. Jezreel offered tannurs for public use, but Yaffa had preferred cooking on a grate or griddle in their own hearth. Although these houses huddled close together, several tannurs were uphill of the homes so the heat and smoke rose. Noa slapped rounds of wet dough on the upper walls, then peeled off crisp-crusted flatbread. A clay pot of lentil stew simmered directly on the coals.

Miriam found there were many things to speak of without talking of their great sadness. She told Noa of the Jezreel marketplace and the kinds of goods to be found. It surprised them both that the gossips at Jezreel's well sounded like Noa's neighbors. When Noa expressed amazement to hear Miriam trapped birds for food, Miriam offered to show her how to make snares.

Imlah's wife had rightly predicted her neighbors' welcome. They carried baskets and pots, walking single file along the sides of the slopes so as not to disturb the crops.

The people of the village had recognized Elijah's distinctive clothing from afar. They brought bowls of grapes, quartered pomegranates, and soft goat cheese. Noa's almonds, which she roasted and drizzled with honey, were passed in wooden trenches. While they ate, several families invited them to stay in their homes. Yaffa and Miriam would stay with Imlah and Noa. A sheepherder, who was handfeeding a suckling lamb, originally claimed Elijah and Jaedon, but when he realized the eagle went with Jaedon, it was quickly decided a bachelor farmer with no animals was a better choice.

After supper, the community gathered around several campfires. Elijah stood below them on the slope so all could see and hear.

"You have heard of the miracles Yahweh worked on Mount Carmel. The false prophets prayed and danced, even cut themselves, calling for their gods to send fire upon the sacrifice. But when I asked Yahweh to send fire, it fell upon His sacrifice, consuming not only the bullock and the kindling, but the stone altar and the barrels of water poured over everything. We serve a powerful God, who keeps His promises.

"Later, my servant Aban and I prayed all night for Yahweh to send rain. Seven times I sent him to the cliff's edge to search the sky. Finally, he saw a cloud in the distance, the size of a man's hand. I sent him to tell King Ahab. 'Hitch up

your chariot and go to Jezreel before the rain stops you.' And
as the sky grew black with clouds, the wind rose, and a heavy
rain came on, the king drove off to Jezreel. But the power of
the Lord came upon me, and I ran ahead of Ahab all the way
to Jezreel."

Elijah chuckled at the sound of murmurs. "You don't
believe? Yes, this old man who stands before you. Never
doubt the power of God."

Most of the northern kingdom had been at Mount
Carmel that day, Miriam among them. Everyone wanted to
see if the strange prophet could end the drought as he
claimed. Her family had traveled from Samaria and met with
her uncle Naboth and his family.

Miriam remembered the false prophets, their loud cries
to their gods and their dancing, though her parents had
covered her eyes when the pagan priests began cutting
themselves. Even as a child, her heart had stirred when
Elijah confronted her people. *How long will you waver
between two positions—Yahweh or the Ba'als?*

Then Elijah prayed 'Let it be known today that you are
God in Israel, that I am your servant and have done these
things at your command. Answer me, Oh Lord, so that these
people will know that you are God, and that you are turning
their hearts back again.'

Though she was a small girl, Miriam had felt her heart
turn, like a pin in a lock. She had known, for the first time
in her life, that Yahweh was her God, by choice, not because
He was the God of her parents.

And then fire had flashed from heaven like a thousand
thunderbolts.

Elijah paced around the fire. "I have reminded you of an
event that revealed the power of the Lord. But Yahweh is also
merciful."

As Elijah spoke, Miriam saw similarities between the
prophet's life and hers. Jezebel threatened to kill Elijah. She
sought to kill Miriam, Jaedon, and Yaffa. Elijah fled from the
queen, ending up in a cave on Mount Horeb. Miriam fled with
her family and hid in a cave with Elijah.

Elijah had despaired. Miriam fought despair each day.

"He told me about you," Elijah said to the people. "He

said, 'There will be seven thousand who will not kiss the Ba'als. Prophets and believers.' He told me to find Elisha, who will follow after me. To teach others about Him, as I do tonight. You who believe are numbered among His seven thousand."

The response was the hush of fifty or sixty people holding their breath. And the flutter of a young eagle ruffling its feathers against the night.

Once again on a mountain, Miriam felt a turning. A turning away from despair, walking into the seven thousand who would stand behind Yahweh. Waiting for Him to … *what?* Move? Work? Speak?

Miriam had seen when Elijah physically turned his ear and listened.

Listen. Should she listen for the Lord to speak … to her?

"The Lord had more to say to me that day, words for me alone. But I tell you this. Yahweh is all powerful. He expects His commands to be obeyed. But He is also compassionate. In my weariness and discouragement, the Lord was gentle with me."

Elijah folded his arms, rocking a little as he seemed to wait, listen, as Miriam had seen him do before. The wadi was quiet except for the sounds of fires crackling and the occasional night bird, answered by the imperious chirp of the eaglet.

Elijah turned his gaze on those seated around the hillside. The gaze of a teacher. A man of God.

"Hear, oh Israel, the Lord is our God, the Lord is one, and you shall love the Lord your God with all your heart, all your soul, and all your might."

Miriam felt something open, at the prophet's words, like petals of a flower unfurling. She wanted to know more about what he had seen and heard on Mount Horeb.

"He said this to your ancestors, those led by Moses, 'Fix these words of mine in your hearts and minds. Teach them to your children, talking about them when you sit at home and when you walk along the road, when you lie down and when you get up. Write them on the doorframes of your houses and on your gates, so that your days and the days of your children may be many in the land.'"

Miriam had never worshipped another god, nor even thought of it. Her grandmother's teaching made sure of that. And Imma ... Miriam pictured her mother. When stirring lentils she would say, 'God is good to send sun and rain to grow crops,' and when weaving, 'I am thankful the Lord gave skill to your father's hands to build this loom.' And Abba, after working hard in the vineyard all day, would read to them from a scroll by lamplight, 'Blessed is the man who does not walk in the way of the wicked...'

It was her job now to teach Jaedon. Her's and Yaffa's. To do all Elijah had bidden, as her parents and grandmother had done, almost without Miriam's notice. The enormity of the task flooded over her, leaving her gasping for breath. She put a hand to her chest, then feeling something lower, put a hand over her belly.

She felt another turning, or opening, or blossoming.

Chapter Thirty-Three

*Even my close friend, someone I trusted, one
who shared my bread, has turned against me.*
~ Psalm 41:9

Jezreel
Dov

DOV HAD NOT STOOD SO LONG since the lion attack, but more
than that, the queen's summons had unnerved him. When
he realized she actually wanted Ocran, indicating she had
dealt with him in the past, Dov determined to look into the
matter.

Awkwardly shrugging out of the military uniform, Dov
noticed the wound on his arm had seeped through the
bandage again. The wound was still red and swollen, but
worse, the hand was stiff and near useless. He one-handedly
changed the bandage, wanting the job done before Maalik
returned from the palace.

Dov had just finished sliding his tunic over his head
when Maalik walked in. "Home earlier today?" Dov measured
the light slanting through the window.

"I made sure to limp when the queen was having her
hair arranged." Maalik winked. The queen, relieved to have
her trusted servant oversee new, untrained slaves, allowed
Maalik certain latitudes in deference to his age.

"Good. There is something I want to talk to you about
before Davita arrives."

Maalik settled onto a cushion. "What troubles you?"

"Did you know the queen summoned me to the palace
this afternoon?"

Maalik drew his brows together. "No. What was it
about?"

"I am not sure. She quickly remarked I was not the man
she expected. She wanted the captain of the king's guard.
But the captain she sought was a young man during the time
of the drought."

"Your commander—Ocran. I saw him there as I left."
Maalik blinked, shifting his gaze to the door.

"What is it?"

"I was thinking back to the time Elijah barged into the temple of Melqart. He interrupted fertility rites and proclaimed a three-year drought. Jezebel was furious at the insult to her god, the god of rain. Remember?"

"Of course."

"What you did not know was, she summoned the captain of the king's guard. Sent him and his men on a quest. Said bring Elijah's head in a basket."

"Ocran."

"Yes."

A knock sounded and a musical, "Shalom!"

Dov settled back onto his cushion. "We will speak of this again."

That night as they ate their supper of bread and stew, Davita had good news. "I have changed Zuar's dressings every day, watching for putrefaction. The wound edges did turn red, but when the healer stopped by, he was pleased with their appearance. I am so relieved. At times I feared for our friend's life. He suffered high fevers and delirium until last night, when he finally sweated them both away."

"How kind you are to spend so much time nursing him," Dov said, noting the weariness etched on her face. "But you should not stop here again. I was not wounded as badly. The lioness preferred the taste of Zuar." He felt his mouth twist in a wry grin.

Davita giggled, putting a hand over her mouth. "The lioness had good taste."

Had her cheeks grown pink? She was a kind and beautiful woman. Zuar could do worse. But maybe he was wrong. Too soon after losing Kadesh. Dov glanced at Maalik and saw a glint in his eye.

Clearing his throat, Dov said, "Thanks be to Yahweh that he is healing. May the Lord bless your kindness. When Zuar is ready, I will visit."

Leaning her cheek against her palm, she said, "Unless he worsens, he should be ready for visitors in two or three days."

On the third day after Davita's visit, Dov felt much recovered. Although stiffness remained in his arm, most of the wounds had closed and his bruises faded to yellow. He donned the tunic Maalik had bought in the marketplace, his old one shredded in the attack. The new garment was soft and comfortable and inexpensively made of undyed wool. He approved of its black border around the neck and hem, woven from wool of black sheep.

Maalik emerged from the back room wearing the tunic Hadassah had woven for him.

Teasing, Dov preened for his stepfather. "We are too fine for the likes of Zuar. I need a second garment for humble purposes."

Maalik laughed. "You are right that we are finely dressed, but we cannot afford two new tunics."

"Nor do we need them. The queen gave you garments for serving at the palace and the king provides garments for war." Dov had tunics he'd worn during the last two battles. Each had been damaged, but between the two, he was able to make a patched garment that suited for weapons practice. No, he didn't need another garment, but he regretted losing his other tunic to the lion. It had been practical, comfortable, and in good condition. Sometimes a man wanted a garment like that when he was among friends.

A firm hand pounded their door. Who was calling so early? Dov lifted the latch.

Commander Ocran stood outside. Why was he here? They stared at each other a moment.

"Come in, Commander." Dov moved aside to allow him entry. As long as Ocran was here, Dov intended to ask questions.

The commander removed his leather helmet, holding it in a hesitant manner. Cross-hatches appeared on his forehead. "Would it be possible to speak to you alone?" He glanced at Maalik. "Here, indoors, if you would not mind."

Maalik cleared his throat. "I was just going to the baker's. I will be back shortly." He picked up his cloak, fumbled in the clay jar for a piece of silver, and left. Dov admired Maalik's quick thinking, wondering if he'd mention to Davita's father Zuar's fine attributes, or only purchase bread.

Running his hand around the helmet's rim, Ocran began. "My apologies. It is hard to know who to trust with what I have to say. And best we not talk in public, where we could be overheard."

Who to trust? Dov folded his hands. "Maalik is trustworthy. But we are alone now. Speak your mind."

"There have been four executions this week. Secret executions. According to gossip, two public officials disappeared quietly. Rumors are they moved to Jerusalem, having embezzled money from the queen. The others, witnesses against Naboth, were scoundrels passing through the city.

"None of this is true. The individuals were hired by Queen Jezebel, with different roles in the murder of Naboth and his sons. All four are dead." Ocran looked intently at Dov. "You may have heard of this, although the queen paid well to ensure the executions were handled covertly."

Dov forced his response through tight lips. "I was not aware. But if these individuals were responsible for the murders, their executions were just."

"There is more. I know you were friends with Naboth's family."

A crawling sensation went up Dov's back, like the charged moment on Mount Carmel before fire shot from heaven. "Many were friends with the vintner. His wines were unequaled. And now you say his killing was unjust."

"His remaining heirs are in danger."

"Are they not all dead?" Dov suspected Ocran was the queen's executioner, and was giving nothing to him, despite their long friendship.

Ocran narrowed his eyes. "Not Naboth's wife, an old woman called Yaffa. His grandson, Jaedon, a boy of eight or nine years. Nor Gershon's wife, Miriam. Kadesh, apparently, was unmarried. The queen has sent a man to kill them all."

"How do you know this?" Dov studied his commander. This was a perfect soldier. A man he had looked up to, who had mentored him for years, since the time he first joined the king's army. They had talked over campfires cold nights before battle.

"Because I am the man."

They stared at each other with mutual distrust. Ocran had admitted to four murders, possibly planned three more.

"Why are you here, Ocran? What do you want from me?"

"First ... I want you to believe I would not do such a wicked thing. Would not murder those women, nor an innocent child."

Dov did not want to believe it. He remembered Ocran's face falling into hard lines as he spoke of the instructions he gave his wife, to first kill herself and then the babe, should the city fall to the vile Arameans. He remembered his fists, clenching and unclenching, as he told Dov to do the same for Maalik. The man deeply loved his wife and child. But countless wars had hardened him.

"Did you execute the four?"

"Yes. But as you said, it was justified and swift. Not what the queen had ordered." Ocran shuddered, a strange reaction from a hardened soldier.

Dov rubbed the back of his neck. "What is your other request?"

"I want you to tell me where they are. Yaffa, the boy, and Miriam. So I may go and warn them."

Dov laughed harshly. "What would I know of that?"

"Consider this." Ocran lifted a hand in appeal. "If the queen believes they are dead, she will cease searching. But if she believes I am unsuccessful, she will send another. And another."

"It does not matter. I don't know where they are."

Slowly putting the helmet back on his head, Ocran searched Dov's face. "I believe you," he said. "You never were a good liar."

Nor were you, Dov thought. *But it seems you have learned.*

Ocran's gaze was steady. "Think about what I said. If the queen thinks I am unsuccessful, she will find someone else. She will probably have me put to death by the new assassin, and he may be a better tracker. Now that no new wars are imminent, scouts have no work. Not all can return to the family vineyard as did Kadesh.

"But don't think too long. They are in danger. I know you cared for the family. I even noticed ... your tenderness ... toward the woman."

A jolt went through Dov which he struggled to hide. "Well, you know the story of my parents. I often thought of Yaffa as a mother."

"I did not speak of Yaffa. And I am sure you know how to find them." Ocran strode to the door. "I will not be back. If you decide to help me, send Maalik with a message."

After the commander left, Dov paced around the small house, but he could not walk off the storm inside him. He grabbed his bow and quiver and strode to the gate, down the ramp, and to the practice area in the valley. There he sent arrow after arrow toward a stump until he emptied his quiver. At least half missed the stump. He stalked over to retrieve them, then repeated the process over and over again. He did this until his muscles trembled and sweat drenched his body.

Chapter Thirty-Four

*Lord, how many are my foes! How
many rise up against me!*
~ Psalm 3:1

STANDING OUTSIDE THE HOUSE IN THE settlement, Miriam pulled
her cloak around the mound of her belly. Though the air was
still, a light snowfall covered the hills, lit by morning's pure
yellow sun. She went back inside for the squares of sheep
hide Elijah had given them, grunting as she bent to tie them
over her sandals, fur side in. She was glad for their warmth,
but it was cold, even in the house. She would go to the spring
later.

She crept past Yaffa sleeping soundly near the hearth.
Quietly stirring up the banked coals, Miriam added kindling
and sticks. Though they had been here several months, she
still had not gotten used to snow. It was beautiful, but she
sent up a prayer this was the last of it.

The nights had grown cool before they finally reached
Gilgal, the little settlement of prophets north of Bethel. Here
Elijah explained they would remain.

"The Lord sent me to teach at both camps for a time. It
is but a short distance between them, so I will travel back
and forth as the Lord instructs. But you will live here, where
there are married prophets. They will watch out for you
during the days I am away, and their women will be good
company, especially as your time grows near." Blushing, the
prophet had averted his gaze from Miriam's growing belly,
with the embarrassment of an old man who had never
married.

She felt enormous, but Yaffa and the women in the
settlement assured her she was a perfect size. Jemima, one
of the first to greet them, had given Miriam a larger tunic,
replacing the one that constricted her every move. It was

thicker as well, woven from wool. And other women had kindly shared warm clothing with Yaffa and Jaedon.

The day after they reached the settlement, a slight, wiry prophet arrived holding an armload of long, smooth branches. "I am Javan. My wife says you need a loom." He hurried to the corner and built the loom with swift motions and faster mallet raps. Then he handed Miriam a pouch filled with several skeins of wool yarn. "Jemima said this should get you started. Visit her, when you are settled. We live in the house at the end of the row." Then he had swooped out with the air of a man who wasted neither time nor words.

Giving a last stir to the coals, Miriam crossed to the loom and fingered the half-finished blanket suspended from the warp strings. After Javan had left, Yaffa began weaving with Jemima's yarn. She promised the blanket would be complete in time for the babe, who would arrive within a month. Just then, a series of kicks announced the child was awake. Miriam put her hand over it, filled with a deep inward purring.

She hoped for a girl, an easy child to stay home and keep her company while Jaedon roamed the hills with his eagle and the prophets. Hearing movement across the room, Miriam turned her attention to where Yaffa slept near the hearth.

Rolling to her side, Yaffa raised on one elbow. "Are you ready to go to the spring? Wait, and I'll go with you." A strand of gray escaped from the braid in which her long hair was twisted each night.

"It has snowed overnight. I'll start our meal and go to the spring later when it warms."

"I will help you, Imma." Jaedon came from the small room he shared with the eaglet. She heard the muted chirrups that the bird made when resting in the crate she had built. Yaffa had woven a rug to cover the crate at night, which seemed to calm the eaglet and help keep it warm.

"Thank you, my heart. But feed your bird first so he will be quiet while we eat." She busied herself grinding grain. Jaedon returned to his room, and Yaffa pulled back the smoke flap. Miriam shivered at the rush of cold air through the opening, very grateful they now sheltered in a house, no longer on the open trail.

Finally, Miriam sat back from grinding the grain. Instead of mixing the flour on her knees, she hove herself up and carried the flour to a waist-high worktable Jaedon had begun and the prophet Elisha helped him finish. He and Elijah would be here soon to take the morning meal with them.

Her mind wandered to the strange set of circumstances that had brought them all together—two prophets and three exiles.

Miriam, Yaffa, and Jaedon had settled into a vacant house in the Gilgal settlement. Elijah, who dwelt with the prophet Binyamin, had accompanied her to the spring to carry an extra jug. She could not go there without stopping to gaze across the landscape, and it seemed Elijah felt the same. They stood laughing at a flock of quacking ducks making their way south. Then Miriam spotted a man climbing the final ascent to their village. She started at the appearance of a stranger, but Elijah laid a gentle hand on her shoulder.

Then the stranger waved at them with his walking stick, grinning. Someone Elijah knew? The man was older than she, maybe thirty years younger than Elijah, with dark, thinning hair. His garments were plain homespun, like Elijah's, but belted with cloth instead of leather.

"Elisha! I've been expecting you." The prophet patted her shoulder and hurried down the path.

Though she had heard of the man anointed to take Elijah's place, she had not met him. She wondered if there was any rivalry. That thought was soon dispelled by their camaraderie. After that day, Elisha was nearly always with Elijah. Miriam had grown to respect and care for the younger prophet.

The memory dispelled like flour settling. Standing at the table, Miriam kneaded the dough a final time and patted it into cakes. It was nearly time for the men to join them.

Jaedon came around the half-wall that marked the alcove he shared with the eagle. "I fed the eagle as you said." He washed his hands in the water set aside for that purpose. "Can I help now?"

"Will you bake the bread?" Miriam handed him the plank holding the rounds of dough.

Humming his agreement, Jaedon hurried over to the hearth. He gently laid the pieces on shards of broken pottery placed over the coals. Glancing over his shoulder, he said, "Elisha can help train the eagle to hunt. He worked with that prophet who owned a hawk."

Sunlight through the door dimmed suddenly as the two prophets stooped and entered. "That's right," Elisha said. "After we eat, we will build a lure."

"I am familiar with lures," Jaedon interjected. "My imma uses grubs and bits of meat to capture birds." His voice sounded respectful, Miriam noticed, not the brash little boy that used to cause her to cluck in disapproval. She smiled, wiped her hands on the cloth tied over her middle, and served up bowls of grain porridge.

Though the air was still cool, some of the snow had melted. Yaffa stayed at the house to continue weaving the baby's blanket. Miriam, Jaedon, and the two prophets walked to the valley nestled between the hills.

Jaedon carried the eagle, now the size of a small hen, on his gloved fist. Glossy brown feathers had replaced the white baby fluff and the eagle's head glinted with golden plumage. Jaedon had fashioned leather bands around its ankles and leather strands secured its legs to Jaedon's wrist. Boy and eagle had practiced until the bird was comfortable traveling this way. Miriam's eyes settled on Jaedon, a strong boy approaching his tenth year, attending to everything Elisha did and said with a serious expression on his ruddy face.

While Elijah also watched the pair, Elisha unwrapped a bit of rabbit carcass, a furred pelt with bits of bloody flesh still attached. This he wrapped around a stick the size of his forearm. Then he took two long coils of thin cord from a pouch and tied one to the lure. "Fasten one of these long cords to Hevel so he cannot fly off before he has learned to hunt." Elisha helped Jaedon find a tailfeather with a strong enough quill to which he could fasten the cord.

"Let him play with the lure for a little while—get used to its look and smell. I will stand at the far end of this field. When you are ready, settle him again on your fist or let him stand on the ground, but take him off the lure. Signal when you are ready.

"I will pull it down the field in short jerks to catch his interest. We want him to chase it. Once he seizes the lure and spreads his wings over like a mantle, you must run and push him away from the lure—the kill. He will not like that, but this is how you teach him you are the master. You will not take the kill completely away, but block him from eating on his own, and then direct him to bits of meat. Put some in the pouch I gave you before you start."

Miriam winced. It sounded complicated. Jaedon had been responsible for the eagle, feeding it, cleaning up after it. The bird bonded to him, as if he were a parent. But sometimes the eagle had a mind of its own. She had heard it scold Jaedon in loud chirps when he didn't feed it fast enough, squawk, even bite when it was thwarted.

Elisha walked away carrying the end of the cord. Jaedon coaxed the eagle to stand near the lure. It cocked its head, stared at the fur-covered stick, and bent to give it a curious peck. Jaedon rewarded it with a bit of meat from his pouch. Then he pressed his gloved fist against the back of the eagle's legs until it stepped onto the glove. He gave it another bit of meat and signaled Elisha.

Elijah chuckled softly. Miriam watched the younger prophet jerk the cord, and the lure gave a sudden leap. The eagle whipped its head around. Staring intently at the bait, the eagle sprang toward it, but Elisha quickly gave his line another jerk. Then he started hauling it in, hand over fist. The eagle hopped a few more times, wings spread, in pursuit of the fleeing lure, and then flapped its wings and flew, keeping low to the ground as it chased the bait, chirping excitedly all the while.

The eagle landed atop the lure, clutching the fur with talons and beak. Jaedon ran after the bird and, when he reached it, shoved it off the lure. The eagle screeched and jumped back on the lure. Jaedon shoved it off again. The eagle tried to strike Jaedon with its feet, but Jaedon calmly shoved it back with his gloved arm. Miriam was glad for both the glove and the long sleeves on Jaedon's tunic.

"Get in close, feed it a piece of meat," Elisha said. "But hold it near the lure." Finally, the eagle seemed to understand Jaedon was not going to steal its prey but was directing it how to behave. Like a parent bird might do.

"Enough for one day," Elisha said. "Feed him this way now, using the lure, making him work for the bits of meat. You could even do this by yourself, drive a post into the ground across the field, loop the cord around it, and pull from here. Soon you will have him hunting."

Jaedon took the eagle back to its crate. Then he followed Elijah and Elisha to meet with the other prophets. Miriam often accompanied the other women to listen to the teaching, prophesying, and music. But today she decided to take her bow and find another rabbit for Jaedon's eagle.

When she returned to the house, her mother-in-law sat at the loom on the tall stool. Javan had returned with the seat after he met Yaffa and observed her difficulty in standing for long periods. "Jaedon went with the prophets," Miriam said. "Do you want to join them? I will take you."

Yaffa worked the shuttle through the hanging warp strings. "No, daughter, I would rather weave in this bright sunlight." She glanced at the bow and quiver slung over Miriam's shoulder. "One of the prophets brought lamb for supper."

"Jaedon needs another rabbit for the eagle. But he and Elisha began teaching it to hunt for itself."

"Good. That eagle needs to finally earn its keep and hunt for you."

Miriam chuckled. "Another prophet uses his hawk to hunt doves and pigeons. Still, the eagle has been good for our boy."

Yaffa nodded, smiling. "Try not to be late. The prophet who brought the lamb is unmarried."

Miriam rolled her eyes and pointed at her enormous stomach, which should be enough to deter any man.

Since she had not yet gone to the spring, she decided to go there first. She might find a rabbit, and if not, she could leave her jar, return to the valley to hunt, and draw water on her way home. She still wore her cloak. The weather changed in the hills too suddenly to be caught without it.

Taking the high route to the spring, Miriam saw a stranger climb over a nearby hill, reminding her of the day she had met Elisha. The man started down the hill and toward their settlement with the doggedness of a man with an appointment. Two or three hills behind him, she saw another figure trailing the first. Slowly, she removed the bow from her shoulder.

Two men coming from the north, not traveling together. Could one or both be looking for Jaedon? For the three of them?

She stepped back from the edge. The first man had his eyes fixed on the terrain and might not have seen her. The second, however, seemed to be constantly searching the hills around him. Should she run and find Elijah? Yes. She turned.

And there he was. As if the prophet had also felt the danger.

"Two men coming from the north. I am afraid they seek Jaedon."

Elijah peered intently over the edge, although he seemed to be looking down the valley, rather than at either man. He took her hand. "The first is a friend. The other, we will see."

Miriam searched the valley, trying to see what had caught the prophet's eye there. She caught a flash of movement in the shadows. An animal? She turned her gaze back to the north. Elijah said he was a friend. She wanted to believe him. But the stranger came along the ridge road, walking fast, his stride long-legged and strong. Traveling alone, yet without fear. No attempt to hide, though he looked back often as if he sensed his pursuer. Aware and in control. Like ... a soldier.

Dov.

How had she not known him? The wide shoulders of an archer, the graceful strength of a swordsman. Something emerged from the shadows of memories held within her. Dov standing in the dale beneath the cave as he prepared to leave, his hand on the chariot horse. Looking up at her.

Then the babe kicked her sharply. Miriam rested her other hand there to soothe the child. *I will care for you. I will.*

Miriam and Elijah waited together as Dov turned off the ridge. Elijah cupped a hand to his mouth and called just loud enough to be heard. "Ready your bow. Bring us the first rabbit you see."

Looking a little confused, Dov nonetheless pulled his bow, nocked an arrow, and went still. Miriam watched, wondering what went through his mind as he scrutinized the winter-dried scrub. Exasperation or expectation? She had felt her share of both, but he had spent less time in the company of the prophet. When a rabbit darted across Dov's path, destined to become the eagle's next few meals, Miriam sensed a ripple of completion.

The second traveler reached the turnoff and followed in Dov's footsteps. There was something of his bearing that echoed Dov's. Another soldier. Two northern soldiers far south of King Ahab's military centers of Samaria and Jezreel. What could it mean? Again, her mind leapt to threat toward her remaining family.

But not from Dov, certainly. He was Caleb's friend. On that basis, he had even offered to wed her. He was not a danger.

But he could not miss this fellow following him. If they were friends, why did they not travel together? If they were adversaries, why had Dov not lost him somewhere in the hills, instead of striding in plain sight along the ridge?

Stones rattled down the path as Dov climbed the final ascent. Miriam felt an urge to step into his arms, welcome him as a brother.

Where had that come from? It was only that the last time she had seen him she was devastated by grief and fear, then she had journeyed south into an unfamiliar landscape—an unknown world. Then he came, a breath of the familiar. A reminder of her brothers, her imma, abba, and savta. She missed them so much.

As Dov walked by the spring, he stepped into a marshy spot and staggered, nearly falling to his knees. With a grin, he righted himself and kicked water and mud from his sandal. He walked over to Elijah and gave him the rabbit. Dov stared hard at Miriam, before taking three slow steps to stand in front of her. His arms folded around her, and he rested his chin on her head. He twisted to adjust for her belly. He smelled like sweat, chaff, and berries.

"Hello, Miriam," he said.

Dov couldn't fathom what induced him to embrace her. Was it her laugh, when he stupidly stepped in mud? But surprise at his action was surpassed when he felt the hard mound of pregnancy between them. She hiccoughed. Or ... was that a kick? He held her overlong, trying to pull his wits together, wipe any foolish expression from his face. What should he say?

He took a half step back. "Hello, Miriam."

The prophet was a little behind her, still holding the rabbit, smiling. Dov sucked in his lips, glad he had not made such a fool of himself as to kiss her.

"I am so glad to see you both." He looked across to the ridge turnoff. Empty. Ocran had already begun the descent to the valley. Soon he would be on them.

"And I need to talk to you." He looked behind him. "Now."

Elijah motioned to an outcropping of rocks. Dov took Miriam's hand and helped her sit on a large flat rock. Elijah sat beside her. Dov stayed on his feet, facing the path he had just climbed. Then he quickly told them everything Ocran had revealed about the murders of Naboth and his sons, Ocran's part in bringing justice to the conspirators, and the queen's order to kill the remaining heirs. "Ocran, my commander, swore he meant you no harm. That he wanted to warn you. I refused to tell him how to find you, but I wanted to warn you of the danger. He followed me. At first, I wasn't sure it was him. I pretended not to know he followed."

"And now?" Elijah asked.

Slowly, Dov pulled his sword from the scabbard, hitching the bow to be ready. "I have known him a long while. I always believed him a good man. But his confession that he carried out four executions and he has been ordered to kill any living possible heirs—"

"You are no longer sure of him?" Elijah's gaze strayed to the path.

"The fact that he followed me—I cannot chance Miriam's life—or that of Yaffa or Jaedon. Murders to steal a farmer's land. It is inconceivable."

"Yet you still work for the king."

"Yes. I am not sure why, but I feel I cannot let him out of my sight."

Chapter Thirty-Five

*He lies in wait near the villages; from ambush
he murders the innocent. His eyes watch in secret
for his victims; like a lion in cover he lies in wait. He
lies in wait to catch the helpless; he catches the
helpless and drags them off in his net.*
Psalm 10:8-9

Gilgal
Dov

THE SUN BEGAN TO SINK BETWEEN the hills. Patches of snow
crusted as the day waned, but Ocran did not show himself.
Dov paced the knoll, sighing as he scrutinized the shadowed
valley or peered across the layered hills. Elijah waited with
him, sitting on a rock, seeming lost in thought. He had sent
Miriam to prepare dinner. Dov was glad, but not because he
was hungry. He wanted her safely away when they
confronted Ocran.

Dov had wanted to trust the man who had brought him
through the ranks. Who had sworn, 'I want you to believe I
would not do such a wicked thing.' But as Dov had walked
south, he sensed a presence tailing him and smelled the
smoke of unseen campfires. And then, at the end of his
journey, he had lost sight of his former mentor.

There had been plenty of time for Ocran to climb the
ascent, to present himself openly to Dov and Elijah. The
commander should realize they would not let him near
Miriam and Naboth's heirs until they heard his reason for
coming south—until they were sure he meant them no harm.

Dov had turned for the knoll again when Elijah rose to
his feet. "Come, it grows late. Miriam will have supper ready."

Guilt stung Dov for bringing this trouble upon them. He
did not deserve to warm himself by a hearth, nor eat a hot
supper. "I will stay here and guard the path. I have dried
meat in my pack."

Elijah leaned on his staff. "It will snow again tonight. No

one need sleep outside. Besides, although this is the main access, many paths approach the settlement—several points along the valley and from at least three wadis."

Dov opened his mouth to argue, but Elijah struck his staff against the ground. It hit earth with a muffled thump. "You stand within a community of prophets. Listen."

He listened but heard only the sighing of the wind, as if the wind wearied of his stupidity. A prophet had said it would snow, and no one need sleep outside. Supper was ready. He should listen.

He nodded, accepting the advice of both wind and prophet. "I am hungry, and I have not eaten hot food for days." His stomach rumbled loudly to confirm.

The prophet smiled. "You will enjoy Miriam's stew. The prophets see that she always has meat to add. But she adds a spice that renders her stew irresistible. She won't tell anyone her secret."

Dov quirked an eyebrow. "Did you remind her she lives in a community of prophets?"

Elijah chuckled.

They smelled the enticing aroma long before they reached the mudbrick house. Dusk had settled. The window and door were dim rectangles of light from the hearth fire and oil lamp. Elijah ducked when he walked through the door. Dov removed the bow from his shoulder and bent, but once inside, the ceiling height allowed him to stand upright.

"Shalom, Dov," said Yaffa. She turned her gaze to Elijah. "Elisha is not coming?"

"He stays with Binyamin and his wife tonight."

"Ah." Yaffa indicated a mat near the hearth where Miriam stirred a pot of bubbling stew.

Jaedon moved to give Dov the closest spot. "Did you bring horses?"

After storing his weapons near the door, Dov sat beside Jaedon. "Not this time. I walked."

"So did we," said the boy. "All except Yaffa. She rode Adi part way."

"Adi?"

"A donkey," Yaffa said.

Dov glanced at the older woman, thinking of the

distance and terrain. A donkey would have been a godsend.

"Yes." Elijah closed a pair of wooden shutters over the window. "We borrowed her from Imlah, Micaiah's father."

Micaiah. Dov had not seen the prophet since he foretold the victories at Aphek and a year before that at Samaria. "Is Micaiah well?"

"Ah yes, he is well. I had forgotten you met him. He is teaching at Jericho just now." Elijah slid a bolt over the shutters, then closed and bolted the wooden door.

As she handed them small bowls of stew, Miriam looked curiously at the prophet as if it was not his custom to bar the window and door.

Perhaps they could eat in peace. Even though there were several ways to access the settlement, with the window and door secured, at least Ocran would not surprise the household. Dov meant to stay alert all night.

Jaedon slipped a finger in his stew and tasted it, glancing guiltily at Yaffa when she cleared her throat.

Still standing by the window, Elijah prayed. "Oh Lord, God of Israel, there is no God like you in heaven above or earth below. Bless, we pray, this food you have given us. May you watch over us, night and day, your people you have promised to lead and care for. May you always hear our prayers. Yes, hear us from heaven, and when you hear, forgive."

Dov heard a little pop and when he opened his eyes, a coal had flared on the hearth. Thoughtful, he watched it burn down until the flames flickered evenly again.

Miriam handed him a loaf. He broke a piece for himself, passing the loaf to the others. He dipped a corner of his bread into the stew, bit, and closed his eyes in pleasure as the savory flavors filled his mouth.

"I hope Maalik is well." Miriam seated herself across from him.

"Yes," he said. "And your family. Of course, they were terribly upset over the murders, and not knowing what had become of you, feared for your lives. They were relieved when I said you were safe with the prophets."

Miriam leaned forward, her mouth parted softly. "Is my mother well? And Savta? And what of Avigail's children?"

She had seen neither child, he realized, and deserved a full report. "Well. Let me start with your niece and nephew. The little girl, pretty and quick, has barely seen two summers. She follows her brother everywhere possible and cries if he runs off without her. They call her Miri ... for you, Miriam."

He hesitated, fearing this might be hard. "The elder, a boy, is more than a year older. He is smart, kind to his imma and baby sister, and chatters like a magpie. They named him Kadesh." At the name of her brother-in-law, tears sprang to her eyes.

He talked on, wondering how he found so many words. "Your mother continues to grow herbs in her courtyard. Unlike you, she shares the herbs with her neighbors. Even tells them what they are called."

Her lips quirked as if she suppressed a smile. "A woman must have her secrets. Especially in a village of fewer than fifty residents."

Dov grinned. "I imagine secrets are hard to keep when more than half your neighbors are prophets."

Her gaze shifted to Elijah then back to him, "Difficult for anyone who is near them, friend or foe. You were about to tell me how Savta fares?"

"Your grandmother is well. She and Maalik continue their friendship. Their daily walks." He paused, thinking of their strange attachment.

Miriam trailed a morsel of bread through her stew. "Maalik is a kind man. Savta was so lonely after our Saba died. She loved us, her grandchildren and children, but when Maalik took her outside and described everything he saw as they walked, it was if he opened her eyes again."

Dov blinked at the sudden sting in his eyes. "He opened my eyes, too."

"How is that?"

"Did you not know he took me in, an orphan living on the streets? My mother died in childbirth, and my father was murdered when I had seen only six years. Maalik was a father to me. Though a Canaanite, he sought to teach me the ways of my people. That is why he absorbed your grandmother's stories like bread and wine."

"No, I—no."

Everyone knew Maalik had raised him, but Miriam had not heard the story of his parents' deaths. Of course, he would not have shared such a thing with the young girl she had been at the time he and Caleb became friends. Why had he done so now? He saw her eyes fill with sympathy. She twisted the front of her tunic, tightening it as the babe rolled within her, causing the fabric to ripple with movement. Dov could not tear his gaze away from the intimate sight only a father should see—that Gershon would never see.

Disconcerted, he looked up and caught her watching him. She unclenched her fingers, letting the cloth fall loose. Averting her eyes, she said, "Jaedon, please put more wood on the fire."

"Is there more to cook, child?" Yaffa asked.

"Noooo. I thought I might enjoy a warm herbal drink. Anyone else?"

After counting the murmurs of agreement, Miriam shifted around, bracing an arm to shove herself up.

"Let me," said Dov. She who had always been graceful and strong, had become ungainly. She also appeared tired, with shadows under her eyes. He pointed at a filled water pot. "Is that for drinking or washing?"

"Drinking," she said. "But—"

"Sit yourself. Just point. Which cook pot?"

Elijah's eyes flitted back and forth between them as he slowly wiped a crust of bread around his stew bowl.

Miriam pointed. Rolling his sleeves, Dov filled the cookpot and set it amid the coals. Then he asked, "Is your recipe for herbal draughts a secret?"

Before she could answer, Jaedon jumped up. "It is, and I know it!" He hurried to a covered box, dipped out various ingredients into the lid, and carried it to the heating water. He shook the herbs into the water, gave it a quick stir, and returned to the others. The prophet smiled.

They sat for a long while, asking questions and hearing news about family and friends in Samaria and Jezreel. As Jaedon passed cups of the hot herbal brew, Yaffa said, "Those are fresh scars, and Israel is not at war. What happened?"

Dov chuckled ruefully. "Zuar and I went hunting before we returned to Jezreel. A lioness attacked us."

Miriam gasped, drawing back. "That is not funny!"

"Perhaps not, but for a soldier to be bested by a cat, even a big one—no, you are right. It was not funny then, and not for several days afterwards. Zuar, especially, had a difficult time. Had your friend Davita not nursed him back to health, he might not have lived. His arm was badly mauled and became infected."

Miriam gaped at the crisscrossed scars on his forearms, her brows drawing together. "And you?"

"The lioness got in one good swipe across my chest, and as you see, cuts and scrapes on my arms and legs. Some I suffered when the lioness pulled Zuar from the chariot. Perhaps the chariot had not quite stopped when I jumped out to help."

Jaedon pressed for more details while Yaffa and Miriam listened in horror. Elijah finally cleared his throat and brought the questions back to Miriam's family.

Dov paused to sip from his cup. "Though the betrothal was arranged between your father and Chloe's, your brother is enamored of his future wife. They will wed soon, since he does not need to build a house. There is enough room in your father's house because—" he broke off, realizing there was enough room because Miriam's room was vacant.

Enough room in your father's house. Why did he not understand this detail would remind her of all she had lost? Dov felt clumsy, off balance, telling her news of home, ignorant of how to soften words that might come as a blow. A woman should be telling her all this.

Her smile was tinged with sadness. "I suppose I will not see the wedding of my brother and one of my dearest friends."

Dov had no answer, for it was most certainly so. She might never see them again. His mind cast about for solutions. On what pretext could he bring family down here? Could he smuggle her into the city? No, it was madness to think such things. While Jezebel was queen of Israel, these three were not safe anywhere in the land. By bringing warning, he himself had endangered them. Resolve hardened inside. He would see that Ocran did not harm them, even if he must kill his former commander.

His thoughts in turmoil and wanting to tame the excitement of the lion attack story so young Jaedon would not be sleepless, Dov spoke again about Davita's kindness. Not only nursing Zuar so faithfully, but bringing strengthening broths and herbal draughts to Dov, to ease pain and stave off infection. Miriam's eyes grew thoughtful as he described Davita's daily visits to Zuar. Would she resent Davita's attentions to Zuar, knowing her friend had begun to care for Kadesh before his murder?

Jaedon's eyelids began to droop during lulls in the conversation. Finally, Elijah put a hand on his shoulder. "Elisha bade me remind you, he will work with you and the eagle at dawn. Rest now. You will see Dov in the morning." Jaedon obediently trudged to the alcove he shared with Hevel.

"Will the boy be warm enough so far from the hearth?" Dov asked. "Am I taking his place?"

"He is content in the alcove. Though Jaedon cleans the cage often, the eagle smells." Miriam scrunched her nose. "With no door, enough heat reaches the area for a hardy boy, and the bird has more shelter than in the wild."

Dov looked around the room, wondering where he would lie down. With Ocran prowling outside, he would not sleep.

Miriam said, "When Elijah or Elisha stay the night, we move the loom to the center of this room for privacy." Noticing his expression, she blushed. "We hang a blanket over the top."

The loom was no taller than Yaffa. Blanket or no, he could easily see over and around it. Yet, it was a divider. An honorable man would not look.

Elijah went to the loom and took hold of a side pole. "Help me position it now. Then we will have a look around the settlement while the women make their preparations."

At last. All Dov's instincts sprang to readiness. Ocran could no longer be counted a friend, not when he was out there in the dark, skulking like a spy or assassin.

The sky was overcast, filled with the morrow's snow, save for a patch surrounding the moon. As they strode past house after house, replicas of the one in which Miriam prepared her pallet, bolted doors were outlined with slivers of light.

"Where shall we search next?" Dov asked after they had circled the cluster of houses.

"We need not search." Elijah pointed toward the moon, which shed light on a cliff that jutted into the darkness. "He is there." A drift of smoke rose up to meet the light.

"Follow me and step lightly," Elijah said. "A narrow path leads down to the wadi. Stay close to the cliff wall."

They soon found the banked campfire with Ocran sleeping nearby. When they were within a stone's toss, Elijah signaled Dov to halt.

"We waited too long," Elijah said. Ocran jolted awake. "I didn't want you to sleep outside." A small flame flickered above the coals inside the round of stones.

Ocran grabbed for his sword, but the campfire flared suddenly into the sky, sending him scrambling back, crablike and empty-handed.

"Why are you here, Ocran?" The firelight lit Elijah's face and threw a huge shadow of cloak and staff.

"I ... I am seeking the heirs of Naboth, the vintner." Ocran's sword hand clenched and unclenched.

"That is true. Why do you seek them?"

"I want to warn them."

"Only partly true. You plan to kill them on the queen's orders, though you know that is unjust." The fire flared higher with a roar as if fueled by wind.

Ocran scrambled to his feet, the firelight revealing his fear. "Tell him, Dov. That I planned to warn them. That I said I would not hurt them."

"You said that."

"Ocran, let us not waste time," said Elijah. "I know your intention. But the Lord has placed a wall around Miriam, Yaffa, and especially Jaedon. You will not touch them."

Dov felt the ground move. No, it was only in his head. Beside him, Ocran staggered to maintain his balance. Not imagination, then. Earthquake? The Lord Himself protected the three. If that was true, Dov need not concern himself for their welfare. So why did terror grip him?

Ocran threw himself upon the ground at Elijah's feet.

"Man of God, take my life. I deserve to die. Yes, I planned to kill these innocent people at the queen's behest. When Dov would not tell me where to find them, I told her they had disappeared. Then she seized my wife, whom I treasure, and our only child. Said she had confidence I would carry out her orders. Otherwise, she would slay my family in place of Naboth's if I did not return with proof of their deaths by the new moon."

Ocran lifted his head, his face twisted with remorse. "I am a sinful man. Put me to death, but please ask the Lord your God to extend his wall of protection around my wife, my child, as He has around the family of Naboth."

Elijah raised his staff. "The Lord my God? Why should He protect your family? Who is your God, Commander Ocran?"

As if it were meant for Dov, the question pierced like a spear. He would protect Miriam and Jaedon at any cost, though she was not his wife, nor the boy his child. Dov began to understand Ocran's terrible choice.

Extending his hand in supplication, Ocran said, "I command nothing. The Lord God holds all power. He can turn even the minds of kings to his will."

"So you believe?"

Ocran lifted his face to the scrutiny of the flames. "How can I not? The fire burns with no fuel. The Lord sent it to attest that you are his servant. But I hid murderous intent in my heart. I am not worthy of forgiveness."

Elijah reached his hand into the flame, palm down. Without flinching, he slowly moved his hand, pushing the flare back into the circle of stones. Once more, crumbling coals glowed among tiny flickering flames. Contained. Tamed.

Then the prophet prayed, words Dov remembered spoken over their supper. "Oh Lord, God of Israel, there is no God like you in heaven above or earth below. May you watch over us, night and day, your people you have promised to lead and care for. May you always hear our prayers. Yes, hear us from heaven, and when you hear, forgive."

Elijah took Ocran's hand and pulled him to his feet. "You spoke correctly, saying you do not deserve to be forgiven. You stand at a crossroads."

"What should I do?" Ocran's anguished voice tore at Dov's heart. Who could see what they had witnessed and not be moved?

"You must pray." Elijah leaned in. "And you have a decision–but I have this message for you. Words Yahweh put on the heart of a man such as yourself, long before you were born. 'If I had cherished sin in my heart, the Lord would not have listened; but God has surely listened and heard my voice in prayer. Praise be to God, who has not rejected my prayer or withheld his love from me.'"

The next morning, Dov woke to the sound of sheep bleating and hooves thudding outside the open window. A cock hopped to the ledge, crowed loudly, then flapped away at the threatening *shrrreee* from Jaedon's eagle in the alcove. A wise decision on the part of the rooster. Jaedon's magnificent eagle had tripled in size since Dov had seen it at the cave. The boy had told Dov they were nearly certain the eagle was female, rather than male as Jaedon had first supposed. Dov smiled, remembering the boy's closing comment. *But Elijah does not know. He says, he does not need to know.*

Rubbing his eyes, Dov rolled and cast a quick glance around. He heard the women murmuring from the other side of the blanket-draped loom. Not seeing Elijah, Dov straightened his clothing, grasped his cloak, and shoved to his feet.

Miriam spoke from the direction of the hearth. "Elijah went to bring your friend to eat with us. He slept at Binyamin's house."

"I met Binyamin before. Isn't he one of the prophets Obadiah hid in your cave?"

There was a pause before she answered. "You remember."

Dov hesitated, recalling the dark, damp cave where this girl had led him. The sound of men crying. Deep, choking sobs. A sound heard often, nights after battle. "He was sad that night."

"They all were. But no longer." She pulled the blanket

from the loom, folded it, and tucked it into a wooden chest. Her dark hair was twisted into a braid that reached below her waist. He looked away.

Yaffa turned from stirring a pot. "Binyamin married Eden, a sweet girl, daughter of an olive farmer."

At the wedding talk, Miriam's cheeks turned pink. "Will you help me move the loom near the window?"

Dov wanted an excuse to come closer. A sudden thought stopped him. "But should you—won't the child—I will move it alone." He lurched forward, grabbing the wooden frame without giving her a chance to argue.

Her eyes flickered, following him, as he strode toward the window, carrying the loom. Miriam only said, "I thank you," and turned away, hurrying toward the hearth, where she took the spoon from her mother-in-law.

Due to her prominent belly, she stood well back from the fire and bent awkwardly to stir. The braid fell over her shoulder, baring the tender nape of her neck. He longed to run his hand along its curve.

Suddenly, Dov went still, remembering Ocran's words. *Then Jezebel seized my wife, our only child. Said she had confidence I would carry out her orders. Otherwise, she would slay my family in place of Naboth's if I did not return with proof of their deaths by the new moon.*

An idea began to form.

He cleared his throat. "How long before the food is ready? I must step outside."

"Take your time, young man," Yaffa said. "The others are not here yet."

As he bent to walk out the door, Dov pretended to have nothing more on his mind than a need to relieve himself at the refuse heap. As he wandered among the houses, he kept a sharp eye for Ocran or Elijah.

A prophet walked down a path toward him. "You are Elijah's friend from the north? He's with your other friend"— he pointed up the path. "Turn right, when you reach the top. Or just—well, you decide." Then he walked on.

At the summit Dov looked over the edge, then turned right. Immediately he saw Elijah, followed by Ocran and Elisha. In the ravine below, he spotted bloody animal skins, piles of ash, and rotting dung. The refuse heap.

After quickly taking care of his needs, Dov rejoined them. "Ocran, what you said last night ... about the queen ordering you to kill Miriam and the others."

"You know I will not—"

"I know. But she *will* demand proof." Beyond Ocran, Elijah and Elisha watched. They appeared interested but not ready to offer opinions. Or prophecies.

Ocran blanched, a strange look on the face of the formidable commander. "Their heads."

"My thought as well."

They stared at each other, the silence blooming.

"Apart from being sinful, that would be an arduous task," Elijah said. "One that would require time and privacy."

Ocran turned. "She demanded your head—in a basket—when she sent me for you during the great drought."

"I know. But my death was not in Yahweh's plan. Nor are the deaths of Miriam, Yaffa, and Jaedon."

A wind stirred the trees edging the refuse, filling Dov's nostrils with a rank odor. Less rank than the stench of Jezreel's dump. His insides roiled again, as they had that day he pulled Naboth, Gershon, and Kadesh from beneath the rocks and refuse and prepared them for burial. He'd done so alone and in secret, because showing respect to those who "cursed God and the king" was also a crime.

"There is little privacy in a community this small, especially one holding so many prophets. If Ocran had killed Miriam and the others, and if his terrible deed was not heard or immediately discovered, he would have no time to continue on to ..." Dov could not bring himself to name the grisly action. No need to speak what would need to be done and how long it would take, when a terrible picture was full-front in each of their minds. "But he could take their blood-splattered clothing back to the queen as proof."

"She would never accept that. My wife and son are as good as dead," Ocran bemoaned. "Every person in this settlement wears a similar woven tunic of undyed wool."

"Every person except Yaffa, Miriam, and Jaedon," Dov said. "Have you not noticed the blue threads woven into each of their garments? The color has meaning to their family. The formula of herbs and flowers used in the dye has been passed from mother to daughter."

"Another secret recipe," Elijah said. "Like the lentil stew."

"What do you mean, secret?" Elisha asked. "Can't you see?"

"I have no need to know," Elijah snapped. "The cook lives in my home."

Ocran nodded understanding. "So if we took the blue-threaded garments, splattered them with blood—"

"And buried them—briefly—in the refuse, so they smelled of decay like a body—"

"The queen will recoil from the stench, cover her nose with her hand, and shout for me to immediately remove the garments from her presence! That might do it!" Ocran slapped his thighs.

Elisha looked at his mentor, then at Ocran. "That *will* do it."

Slowly, Dov let his fists uncurl.

As they headed to the house, the others pulled a little ahead. Elijah walked beside Dov, his shepherd's crook thudding the dirt path. "I have a word for you."

A word for you. Not for Israel, not for the king. When a prophet said that, it didn't mean random advice or town gossip. Dov wanted to back away from the prophet, get out of reach of those feelers, or whatever they were, that pulled thoughts from a man's mind. Then he remembered Ahab's dismissal of Micaiah's prophecy. *He never prophesies anything good about me.*

"Yes, Elijah. I'm listening."

Elijah nodded in approval. "You must go with Ocran. Possibly he needs you, although I'm not sure of that. But you must keep your vow to the king."

Dov turned his face away, his breaths shallow. What about Miriam? He'd thought this time, that things were different between them. That she, the boy, and the coming child needed him. She carried these responsibilities alone, while the king had an army. He turned back to look at Elijah, who appeared to expect a response. He trudged on.

They waited until after eating to explain their plan to the

others. Miriam looked horrified as Ocran explained his original intent in coming to Gilgal. When she glanced at Jaedon, even making a move to push him outside, Dov realized her desire was to protect the boy from the dark tale, but she couldn't shield the lad. He would soon be a man and must understand the world's dangers.

As the very-pregnant Miriam struggled to rise, Yaffa laid a restraining hand on her arm. "Will you return the clothing to us? Even if the blood remains, I want it. The blue yarn was a gift from my Naboth."

"I will do my best," Ocran agreed. "I am sorry there is no other way."

Jaedon had remained uncharacteristically quiet. "It is time for Hevel to hunt. We will get you the blood." He went to the alcove, returning with the hooded raptor.

Elijah and Elisha stood and, surprisingly, so did Yaffa. She always stayed close to Miriam, as if fearing she might give birth if left alone.

"I need fresh air, and I love to watch the eagle fly." Yaffa started for the door. She cast her gaze on Elijah, then as if a second thought, on Jaedon. "You do not mind, do you?"

"Not at all." Elijah took her arm and they followed behind Jaedon and the eagle. Elisha hesitated and half-turned as if to stay, a propriety, Dov realized. He and Miriam would be left alone in the house.

Without looking back, Elijah reached his free arm to grasp the other prophet, and Elisha followed the others.

Again, Miriam performed that lurching roll to her feet, and Dov extended his hand. She took it, her hand strong and cool in his own. He pulled, and they stood face-to-face, her eyes black and lustrous as obsidian. She turned away, reaching for an iron pot steaming in the coals.

He stepped in front of her. "Can I help?"

She looked at him, then quickly glanced away. What was that expression? Confused? Irritated?

"If you would carry the water to that table. Pour half the water in the basin."

He did so, then motioned to the pitcher sitting alongside. "Shall I pour in some of this to cool the water?"

She nodded. Then, making a shooing motion, she

hurried over with a stack of bowls. As she bent to reach into a small jar behind the basin, her braid again fell over her shoulder. Dov quickly stepped back, clasping his hands behind him.

She pulled her hand from the jar, a green-gray substance clinging to her fingertips. Swishing her hands through the water caused bubbles to crowd the edge of the basin. *Borith.* "I suppose ... that is, will you be returning with Commander Ocran?"

At the same moment, he said, "That smells nice."

Gazing coolly over her shoulder, she lowered several bowls into the foamy water. "The borith? Ash made of elm, vegetable scraps, and herbs I found last summer."

"You are so competent. You comb through the countryside, not only finding game, but foraging for edible and useful plants. Since you were a girl."

That had not been what he meant to say. She needed someone to care for her. She needed him.

"You have the boy and his aging grandmother to care for." He laughed. "Evidently a somewhat smelly eagle and at least two prophets who enjoy your cooking and seek to steal your secrets."

She laughed too, as she motioned toward a drying cloth. "And fending off marriage proposals. It seems every prophet, whether he previously sought a wife or not, sees the benefit of a cook at his hearth."

Dov froze, forgetting what she had told him to do. She gingerly dipped a bowl into the iron pot, steam still rising above its rim. When she lifted it out, letting the hot water drizzle off, she stared at him pointedly. "The drying cloth?"

He snatched the cloth and reached for the bowl. "But the coming child. You will need a man. Did you not want to accept an offer?" Dov felt pressure crease his forehead. One of many offers. Of course, every man in the settlement would want her.

Miriam frowned. "I have Yaffa. She will help me with the child, when the time comes. While one of the musicians might be handy to soothe the child with his lyre, many a prophet bumbles about with his mind elsewhere."

"But food. And protection." Dov faltered, because even

as he asked questions, answers came to him. She had fed a houseful during this visit. Yahweh had dramatically protected them from Jezebel's plot and turned Ocran onto a new path. And whether she married a prophet or not, this whole community looked out for her and her household. She didn't need him.

"I don't need to marry a man for protection," she was saying.

Dov brought his attention back to her voice, which had been a pleasant murmuring backdrop to his thoughts and now became actual words.

"I was married to a man, recall, and had a father-in-law, also a man, and a shrewd brother-in-law, an honored spy for Israel. They are all dead."

Now his gaze was fixed on her moving lips, the fascinating way they pursed for the word *shrewd* and came together as she breathed *man*.

"These men could not even protect themselves. I mean no disrespect to my beloved, but you see my reluctance to marry for protection."

He was nearly undone when the tip of her tongue appeared between her teeth. She was staring at him now. What had she just said? *... my reluctance to marry for protection.*

Well, that did it for him. He had nothing to offer her, save his protection. He had no land, and if he left the king's service while he was still under his vow, he would have no wealth. All he could offer was his ... admiration. His long admiration. His memory played back images of the wiry girl, hands on hips. *These are my birds. I caught them.* The young woman, striding down the hill, bow in hand. Now this young widow, beautiful, on the brink of motherhood. She was ... lovely and brave. He ... he loved her. She was ... *turning away.*

Elijah had been right to tell him to return with Ocran. Of course, he was right. He was the prophet of the Lord.

"You never did answer my question," she said.

Question? What question? "I am sorry. What—"

"Are you returning with Commander Ocran?" She sighed, looking pointedly at the stack of rinsed bowls and the drying cloth limp in his hand. He quickly went to work. He could do that much for her.

He became a callow youth in her presence. Worthless. She had turned him down once and would have today. Certainly, he would *not* have asked her again, even if Elijah had not explained his duty. Would he?

Dov dried the final bowl, then carried the stack to the shelf. "Yes, I am returning." He stood there a moment, his back to her. "I would like to stay. I love—" He clenched his fists. "The peace. The presence of the Lord's spirit, moving among the prophets. Sometimes it almost feels as if—"

She made a sound behind him, and he turned. Her eyes shone as if tears clung by sheer strength of her will.

"As if God's Spirit brushes your shoulder?" she whispered.

She was so lovely. He took a step toward her. Were her lips trembling?

"We have the blood for you." Eagle on his shoulder, Jaedon stood at the door, holding a dripping badger. The eagle, its eyes covered with a hood, made a sound very like grumbling.

"Do not bring that thing inside. Go around back, where you usually feed Hevel."

"Take her, then," Jaedon said. "This was her first kill of the day and she has not yet eaten. She is not happy with me." The boy carefully transferred the bird to Miriam's shoulder as she murmured endearments. It trilled something back and fluffed its feathers.

"Elijah said I should bloody the garments while the kill is fresh. Where are they?"

"A moment." Miriam walked carefully to the chest where she had stored the blanket. She dug through its contents and, depositing the eagle on a corner perch, returned with a small stack. "A tunic you have outgrown and one I wore before—" She twisted her mouth and glanced wryly at her stomach.

Glancing at Dov, Jaedon took the tunics. "Elijah said you are to help me with this so it looks authentic." Then he shook out the tunics, each with borders and tassels of light blue. "Where is Savta's?"

Miriam hesitated. "She made a shawl entirely of blue. And the tunic she is wearing is bordered like these." She shook her head. "She must decide. I would not choose for her."

Dov remembered Yaffa's request. The blue shawl must be quite meaningful. And yet how could the old woman give up her only tunic? "We will try to salvage the garments and return them to you. But I fear blood will stain them irredeemably."

As if coming to a decision, Miriam whirled and hurried back to the wooden chest. The garment she carried was entirely blue. "Take this. Do ... what you must to this garment. Do it first."

She handed the rolled-up garment to Jaedon. He shook it out. "Imma, are you sure?"

Dov felt as if turned to stone. It was Miriam's. Her blue wedding tunic.

"Yes, my heart. Your grandmother would be heartsick to give up her shawl—a last gift from your saba." She laid her hand on her belly. "Your sister—"

"Brother," said Jaedon.

"There, you see? A brother would have no need of this wedding tunic. And should the little one be a sister, well, there is plenty of time for me to weave the garment. And who knows if she will like blue?"

Dov followed Jaedon behind the house. As they splattered Miriam's blue tunic with the badger's blood, Dov prayed a blessing on her and those under her roof. He prayed for their safety during the perilous times they all faced. And he prayed that, after his duty to King Ahab was discharged, he might see her again on this earth.

Chapter Thirty-Six

*Jehoshaphat son of Asa became king of Judah in the fourth
year of Ahab king of Israel. Jehoshaphat was thirty-five
years old when he became king, and he reigned in
Jerusalem twenty-five years. He did what was right in the
eyes of the Lord. The high places, however, were not
removed, and the people continued to offer sacrifices and
burn incense there. Jehoshaphat was also at
peace with the king of Israel.*
~ 1 Kings 22:41-42a, 43-44

Samaria, about two and a half years later
Dov

ONCE MORE, DOV GAZED AT THOUSANDS of tents beneath the
city, recalling the Aramean siege. How shocking, for Israel
and Aram, when Israel had beaten and disgraced their
enemy. At Aphek, Aram was beaten again, but their king was
pardoned. Although the Arameans later joined Israel, Egypt,
and others to subdue the Assyrian threat, Dov remained
wary of another attack from their long-time foe.

But these tents housed allies not enemies.

King Ahab had requested help from King Jehoshaphat
to retake a city of refuge—one of the cities Ben-Hadad had
promised to return in exchange for his life. He had not kept
that promise. Now the army of Judah stood ready to help
Israel.

Commander Ocran turned to Dov, his ceremonial
helmet and breastplate gleaming in the sun. "It is time."

Dov saluted and ran down the brick steps that hugged
the wall. After Dov and Ocran returned to Samaria from the
settlement at Gilgal, their former trust had been renewed.
However, their paths had then parted. King Ahab ordered
Ocran to fight with him in the war against Assyria while Dov
was stationed in Samaria to stave off attacks from Moab or
the Philistines. Ahab's forces returned victorious from the
battle of Qarqar, and Ocran taught new military tactics in the

barracks.

Israel's army was stronger than it had ever been.

As Dov headed for the gates, he cast a glance around the city streets, cleared for the occasion. Curious townsfolk huddled inside open doors and poked their heads through windows. They'd been warned to keep the streets clear, until the second shofar blew.

"Open the gates," Dov told the gatekeeper, who sent assistants scurrying to drag the iron gates apart.

As if on cue, the palace doors also opened. City officials in fine robes carried two thrones toward the open gates.

Ivory engravings on the thrones caught the morning light and the shofar sounded its two-pitch call. King Ahab descended the palace steps in full purple regalia. Beside him, King Jehoshaphat wore a long-sleeved tunic of bleached linen, its sash embroidered in purple thread. Kingly, but simple.

The kings walked together through the gates, taking their places at the top of the ramp leading from the valley floor. When they paused in front of the thrones, soldiers cheered from the valley before them and from the city behind. Near the base of the dirt ramp, a large group of prophets bowed. Hundreds of them. Dov noticed they wore linen tunics similar to King Jehoshaphat's but with plainer sashes. Still, it was finery such as Dov had never seen on the prophets of Yahweh. None of these had been with Elijah at Gilgal. Perhaps wealthy patrons backed them.

The shofar sounded again, thrumming with pomp. As the final note faded, the kings sat, and a hum of voices marked the townsfolk heading for the square near the gate. A few notable citizens were allowed through the gates and proceeded to a reserved area at the base of the ramp, where they would enjoy the best view. Dov had arranged for Maalik and Hadassah to stand there, so he watched for them until the flow of citizens stopped. Where were they?

King Ahab raised his scepter, and the chatter quieted. "I thank my brother king from Judah for standing with Israel. Though Ben-Hadad agreed to return the cities his father took, he will not return Ramoth Gilead. I asked King Jehoshaphat, 'Will you go with me to retake Ramoth Gilead?'

and he said—"

"I am as you are, my people as your people, my horses as your horses." The king of Judah smiled congenially. "But first, let us seek the counsel of the Lord."

Dov spotted Caleb moving through the crowd. When he stood beside Dov, Caleb said in a low voice, "The king of the south follows Yahweh. This is good."

Dov nodded. Perhaps King Jehoshaphat would influence Ahab for the better and Miriam could bring Jaedon and Yaffa back home. Miriam's child had seen two summers. A girl, as Miriam had believed? His thoughts of a lively child warmed him like a summer breeze, but like a breeze, they turned. The minds of the king and queen were fickle, changing with any prevailing wind. Though Naboth's vineyard had not become Ahab's vegetable garden, grapes from its vines produced wine for only the king's table. Miriam could never return. The risk, should the king feel threatened, was too great. And Ocran, if his deception were revealed, would be executed.

King Ahab motioned toward the four hundred. "As you see, I have assembled the prophets." He called, "Shall I go to war to retake Ramoth Gilead, or shall I refrain?"

One of the prophets stepped forward. "Go, for the Lord will give victory to the king."

There was a smattering of conversation, hands over mouths, bent heads. Dov glanced at Caleb.

Caleb spoke from the side of his mouth. "Those are not prophets of Yahweh. I recognize priests of the Ba'als who went into hiding after Mount Carmel."

Hadn't they all been killed at the Kidron brook? Dov almost asked, but he didn't want to be overheard.

King Jehoshaphat turned to Ahab. Though he did not shout, his voice carried to where Dov and Caleb stood among the archers. "Is there no longer a prophet of the Lord in Israel?" There was another ripple of comments.

King Ahab rubbed his nose. "There is still one man through whom we can inquire of the Lord, but I despise him. He never prophesies anything good about me."

Dov's jaw clenched. How could Ahab speak of despising a prophet? Yahweh had handed the king two battle victories.

It seemed he no longer remembered the fear that had compelled him to dress in sackcloth and dust his head with ashes.

King Jehoshaphat turned to look at Ahab. "That is not the way a king should talk. Let's hear what the prophet has to say."

Ahab caught Dov's eye and beckoned. As he strode toward the king, Dov watched the crowd of prophets, sickened by what he saw. Their leader brandished a set of iron horns like those previously used worshipping Melqart in his incarnation of the bull. "This is what the Lord says, 'With these you will gore the Arameans until they are destroyed.'"

More prophets at the foot of Samaria's hill spoke over each other saying much the same. "Attack Ramoth Gilead and be victorious, for the Lord will give it into the king's hand."

Masking all expression, Dov saluted his king. The prophets felt wrong. They promised the king what he wanted to hear.

"Bring Micaiah son of Imlah." After giving the order, Ahab frowned, propped an elbow on the ivory armrest and, in a bored manner, motioned for an attendant to fan him and Jehoshaphat.

Dov nodded and walked back toward the archers. Two years ago, Elijah had said Micaiah was teaching in Jericho. If he was now in Samaria, Dov had no thought where to find him. Then his lips twitched into a smile. On each occasion they met, the prophet had found him. Dov bent and spoke into Caleb's ear. "The king wants Micaiah."

"Come with me," Caleb said. They started walking, heading, it seemed, for the home shared by Caleb's extended family. "I came to tell you Maalik decided against bringing my grandmother to the place reserved for honored guests. Worried about the crush of a crowd and too many strangers. The family has gathered on our roof." He quickened his pace.

Curious, Dov hurried after his friend. Was the prophet there with them? Or did one of the family know his whereabouts? Soon they were climbing the outside stairs to the rooftop. Three stories high and adjacent to the city wall, the roof afforded an excellent view.

Lemuel and Dorcas came to greet them. Caleb's brother Seth held his squirming young son and his wife Avigail their young daughter. They waved without rising. Maalik spoke to Caleb's grandmother, who turned her ear toward him. "Hello, Hadassah," he called, "And everyone else." But the prophet was not among those gathered on the rooftop.

And neither, though she should be, was Miriam. If she were here, she would be standing near Avigail, the girl cousins shyly taking measure of one another. Jaedon would tell Lemuel stories about the eagle, because the bird's feats truly were amazing. And Yaffa? Would she be arm-in-arm with Hadassah, unable to let go of her ancient mother-in-law? Or would she be weeping, telling Lemuel stories from his brother's last days?

"You heard?" Caleb asked.

"Most of it," said Hadassah, "Except what the king told Dov."

"He told me to bring the prophet Micaiah. Anyone know where he is?"

"The Lord knows," Hadassah said.

Dov blinked when Maalik started to pray. "Yahweh, we want to hear your words and our city needs them even more. Bring your prophet so he can speak. We have not always listened to your prophets, Lord, but we are listening now. Forgive our people for the wrong we have done. Help us do right. We look to you, O God, our rock and our deliverer."

Lemuel also prayed, followed by Hadassah. To Dov, the blind grandmother's words seemed to hum with pent up power. They circled him like cords of flax, pulling him back toward the meeting at the city gate. Opening his eyes, he nudged Caleb. "Let's go."

Dov hesitated at the top of the stairs, then resolutely started down. Perhaps he should have waited a while longer, his hope for an answer to prayer kept afloat by the raft of believers.

As he descended, he heard Caleb's footsteps behind him, heard voices in the streets and alleys below, even heard the false prophets chanting outside the city. Spewing false hope. He stopped for a moment and turned his head, as Hadassah had done. He closed his eyes and listened.

He heard footsteps. Of course he did, he was in an alley that joined others, in a city that housed thousands. But he heard *one set* of footsteps among many. He heard Caleb gasp. And he smelled sheep.

"Hello, Dov."

Recognizing the voice, Dov opened his eyes. They had prayed for the prophet to appear, and here he stood. "Micaiah. We asked Yahweh to send you. King Ahab asks to see you."

The prophet smiled wryly. "Let us go, then."

As the three walked together, Dov said quietly, "Listen. He wants to know if he should go to war against Aram. There are many prophets with him, already prophesying victory."

"Many prophets, eh?"

"I thought you should know."

Micaiah shrugged. "I can only tell the king what the Lord tells me."

They walked the rest of the way in silence, but every step felt charged with meaning. Even the crowd quieted, recognizing the prophet and parting to let them through.

King Ahab studied Micaiah with an expression of distaste. Dov had heard and smelled the prophet with closed eyes and looked only at his face as they walked back. Now he noticed the state of his clothing—worn sandals, patched tunic, and a ragged sheepskin for a mantle.

The king curled his lip. "Micaiah, shall we go to war against Ramoth Gilead, or shall I refrain?" It was clear Ahab did not want to ask Micaiah to prophesy.

Fear for the prophet chilled Dov. *Agree with the king. Live to prophesy again.* Yet even as the cowardly thought took shape, Dov realized he would never do such a thing, nor would Micaiah.

"Attack and be victorious," the prophet replied in a sarcastic tone, bowing deeply. "The Lord will give the king victory."

King Ahab struck the armrest of his throne. "How many times must I make you swear to speak nothing but the truth in the name of the Lord?"

Micaiah nodded. "Very well. I saw all Israel scattered on the hills like sheep without a shepherd, and the Lord said,

'These people have no master. Let each one go to his home.'"

King Ahab turned to the king of Judah. "See? Didn't I tell you that he never prophesies anything good about me, but only bad? My valiant army will be scattered?"

Jehoshaphat's eyebrows drew together, forming a crease between them. He opened his mouth to speak, but Micaiah spoke first.

"Therefore hear the word of the Lord. I saw the Lord sitting on His throne ..." He paused, staring pointedly at the two kings sitting on ivory thrones. "On *His throne of light* with all the host of heaven standing around him. And the Lord said, 'Who will convince Ahab to attack Ramoth Gilead and go to his death there?'"

As he listened to the prophet's vision, Dov imagined angelic beings standing in awe of the radiant throne of the Most High.

"One suggested this, and another that. Finally, a spirit came forward, stood before the Lord and said, 'I will entice him.'

"'By what means?' the Lord asked.

"'I will go out and be a lying spirit in the mouths of all his prophets,' he said.

"'You will succeed,' said the Lord. 'Go and do it.'

"So now," Micaiah said, "the Lord has put lies in the mouths of all these prophets of yours. You know they are not the Lord's prophets. Yahweh has decreed disaster for you."

Dov let out the breath he'd been holding. Now Ahab would see the false prophets for who they were. Micaiah's prophecy was as clear as a mountain spring.

Exclamations, loud questions, and angry voices filled the air. King Ahab turned to Jehoshaphat, raising his hands in exasperation. "You see?"

Then the leader of the false prophets stalked forward and slapped Micaiah in the face, sending him stumbling backward. "Which way did the spirit of the Lord go when he left me to speak to you?" he asked sarcastically.

A red mark, the shape of a hand, colored Micaiah's face. "You will find out on the day you run to hide in an inner room."

"Enough!" shouted King Ahab. "Take Micaiah and send

him to Amon the ruler of the city and to my son Joash. Put this fellow in prison and give him nothing but bread and water until I return safely."

Sick at heart, Dov watched the soldier take hold of the prophet of the Lord. In order to speak the Lord's truth, Micaiah had risked his life. Would he die in prison? Not if Dov could help it.

As they dragged him away, Micaiah declared, "If you ever return, the Lord has not spoken through me. Mark my words."

Chapter Thirty-Seven

So the king of Israel and Jehoshaphat king of Judah went up to Ramoth Gilead. The king of Israel said to Jehoshaphat, "I will enter the battle in disguise, but you wear your royal robes." So the king of Israel disguised himself and went into battle. Now the king of Aram had ordered his chariot commanders, "Do not fight with anyone, small or great, except the king of Israel."
~ 2 Chronicles 18:28-30

The road Ramoth Gilead, shortly thereafter
Dov

AS DOV'S TROOPS MARCHED UPWARD TOWARD Ramoth Gilead, he understood why Ahab had been determined to take back Israel's former city of refuge. Not only was the city stationed on a major road through Gilead, the afternoon sun revealed rich land. Along the narrow Jabbock river, terraced farmland bore lush crops of olives, grains, and vines. They passed thick forests smelling of balm, like the expensive ointment Davita had applied to his wounds after the lion attack.

Yes, this was fertile land, but a more compelling cause burned in Dov's chest, perhaps goading Ahab as well. Ramoth Gilead belonged to Israel. The land been given them by God. It was a Levite city, a place set apart for manslayers to receive refuge and a fair trial. Surpassing all that, Ben-Hadad had promised to return the cities his father had taken in exchange for his life. These were the reasons Israel and Judah marched to take by force what was theirs by right.

Yet, the same prophet who had correctly foretold two victorious battles had seen a vision of King Ahab's death during this battle. Dov would have never made the decision Ahab had. He had seen the prophets' predictions come true so many times.

But so had the king. He had seen fire and rain fall on Mount Carmel at Elijah's behest and led his armies to two victories prophesied against overwhelming odds. Yet Ahab ignored this dire prophecy. The only way to explain it was the second part of Micaiah's prophecy. The lying spirit.

A scout galloped his horse toward Dov, flinging up bits of black earth. "Basecamp ahead, Captain. The kings have already pitched their tents."

Dov observed where Ocran led his troops and signaled he would take his men to the left, so the two platoons would secure the kings' position. Scouts and guards would keep watch all night. Ahab had ordered the attack for the hour before dawn.

After his own tent was pitched, Dov set out to walk the camp's perimeter. He stopped to offer encouragement to young soldiers who faced their first battle. He reminded them of their assignments during the attack, each set well behind the front line and flanked by seasoned fighters. He breathed in the aroma of lentil stew enriched with the meat of the stag they had taken today. When he passed the food wagon, he instructed the cook, "Ensure the men eat lightly tonight. A heavy meal will make them sluggish tomorrow."

Soon he came upon Ocran. "Walk with me?" They set off together, walking past soldiers carrying firewood, tending to horses, or checking weapons and armor.

Although in plain sight of both armies, the two had a measure of privacy as they walked. Keeping his voice low, Dov said, "One usually does not know what to expect in a battle. But I fear we're on the wrong side of things. I cannot understand why the king did not avoid this battle."

Ocran frowned at the path before his feet. "If you'd been at the battle of Qarqar, you might understand. It was an enormous victory over the Assyrians. Many kings allied with us gave Ahab credit for tipping the battle with Israel's army. We fielded more chariots than any country. Ahab was cheered in every city as we marched home. After such a victory, he must think himself invincible."

Ocran paused. "There is something else. I heard the king say he would enter tomorrow's battle in disguise, but he told King Jehoshaphat to wear his royal robes.'"

"What? The king of Judah did not consent, did he?"

"He did. He is an agreeable fellow and seemed to realize no special threat to himself."

"But you told me that all the commanders at Qarqar were impressed with Ahab's military skills. And Ben-Hadad was among them."

"Yes, he was on our side in that battle. Now we face him."

They both fell silent.

As they walked, they approached a group of men kneeling on the ground tossing stones. What were they betting on? The hungry days of his early childhood never far from memory, Dov could not understand a man risking his wages on outcomes beyond his control. As they passed the group, he heard a man call out a prediction for tomorrow's battle—that Israelite chariots would surpass the Arameans in number.

If he were a betting man, Dov would place his silver on two facts. Ben-Hadad knew Ahab's military strengths and would put a high price on his head. And Micaiah had prophesied the king's death.

Dov resumed speaking. "Disguised, eh? So Ahab thinks he can outmaneuver God." It was as if the king gambled that Yahweh's goodness to him would continue whether Ahab obeyed or not. After all, he'd been given three consecutive victories.

"I am torn," Ocran said. "Like you, I have taken an oath to serve and protect the king. Yet, if the Lord has destined the king's death, should I fight against God?"

Dov nodded slowly, his tumbled thoughts of the past few days falling into place. "Elijah sent us back, though I longed to stay. So we must be here for a reason. There is a line we must walk. We must perform our duty to the king. We were also told to lead the sheep of Israel. Be shepherds to our people."

Ocran huffed in exasperation. "We know the prophecy, yet there is still much we do not know."

"We know enough. Like any battle, we fight the enemy, back our fellow soldiers, and protect our king."

"But if Yahweh has foretold his death, should we ...?" Ocran's voice trailed off with an inflection at the end. As if he could not bring himself to voice the murderous thought.

Dov, too, had considered it. Ahab was not the same king

he had been during the siege of Israel, nor the battle at Aphek. Or perhaps it was Dov who had changed. He had always seen the right and wrong of things, in that, he'd not changed. But lately he saw something beneath the surface, a battle being waged by a different army.

The army of the Lord. In which the battle was always about right and wrong, with a finer edge to it, like that of a sharp sword.

Dov said slowly, "The king made a choice to ignore the prophet of God. Each of us have choices—to go into this battle or not." He paused and lowered his voice. "To try and fulfill the prophecy by our own hand. The benefits of each decision can be argued. But the choice is simpler when we remember the ways of Yahweh. He tells us to keep our oaths and to faithfully serve our king—as long as we can do so without disobeying Yahweh's law. You made such a choice—rightly so—when you chose not to carry out the queen's command."

Ocran nodded. "Even before Elijah showed me my error ..." His lips twisted in a scowl. "I could not stomach the idea of putting the sword to innocent women and a child. Or betraying our friendship by using you to find them. But more than my own aversion, I thought back to the stories my mother told me. Of King David, after he had been anointed king by the prophet Samuel, but Saul was still on the throne trying to hunt him down. To kill him."

Dov nodded. Maalik had shared stories Hadassah told him about King David. Once, David and his friends hid in a dark cave and Saul entered to relieve himself. David crept close and cut off a corner of the king's robe. After Saul left, David followed and confronted the king. Showing him the cloth, David pointed out he could have easily killed Saul then, if he planned to.

"I remember that story," Dov said. "From evil people come evil deeds."

"Yes," Ocran agreed. "David quoted that old proverb as the reason for his promise to never harm Saul. I had nearly forgotten that story. But after that night when I met Elijah, and my dying campfire roared up to meet the stars, I remembered the proverb. I remembered the evil I had considered toward three innocents, and my heart cracked as if Yahweh had reached inside and squeezed it with His mighty fist."

Their walk had taken them to an area where the horses were tied among trees, to provide sturdy tethers and obscure their presence. Dov quickly spotted Uriel tied apart from the others to the branch of an ancient oak. The stallion didn't like other horses crowding him when he ate. Dov walked over, took hold of the feedbag, and peered inside. Uriel snorted a protest and turned his head aside, just as Dov released it, chuckling. "I'm glad they feed you well, old fellow. You will earn your rations tomorrow."

Ocran came alongside. "He is a fine animal. You have done well with your mounted archers."

Dov ran his hand along Uriel's neck. "It takes a horse sensitive enough to respond to leg and voice commands yet steady enough to comply in the thick of battle. I received Uriel as payment for the siege. He was already battle-seasoned and when I began to shoot from him, he took to it easily."

"Wish I'd taken to shooting from horseback. I'll be in a chariot with Ahab, or one of the two flanking him." Ocran removed his leather helmet, running his thumb along the chin strap. "I'm the experienced officer, but I struggle with indecision. When they come for him, do I fight, when Ahab's death is foretold? I can't run away. That would be against everything I think right."

"You have said it. Do what you think right. This is always what a follower of Yahweh must do."

"Then we will die together."

Dov replied slowly. "Do not underestimate the power of the Lord. Think of what you experienced in Gilgal. Could you have imagined any of that experience? Yahweh said Ahab would die tomorrow, but He did not say how."

Dov checked Uriel's tether and then walked through the cluster of horses inspecting ropes and feedbags and searching for any sign of illness or injury. When he was satisfied all was well, they continued their circuit. Each stopped to speak with those reporting directly under them. The troops were ready to fight on the morrow.

In the hours before dawn, the camp readied for battle in silence and stealth. Dov's scouts had chosen a hill with a gradual slope for the king's lookout. Riding through thick darkness, Dov led the way on Uriel ahead of Ahab's chariot. Scouts on either side eyed dark shapes that could hide an enemy, sometimes shoving a spear into thickets, startling sleeping birds that exploded into the night sky. Finally, Dov stopped at the crest of the designated hill, where the king would be able to look down on the battle.

Dov prickled all over as if the darkness were a hair coat. He wanted to be anywhere but here, but more than anything, he wanted to be with Miriam. To help her plant another vineyard, give her and the boy another inheritance, however small. Keep her safe. Then he reminded himself. She was there with God's prophets. He was here with a proud, half-mad king.

This was a bad business. If only the king had killed Ben-Hadad as Yahweh had ordered, if only he had believed Micaiah, they would not be here.

The king's chariot rumbled up beside him. Ahab's shape was staunchly erect. He was always ready for battle, as if he had been born to that purpose.

"Dov, I will go down with the army as the battle begins. To encourage the troops—get this battle over quickly."

"Yes, my king." Soon the light of dawn would touch the battlefield. Was this how the king would die? In the confusion of the first surge?

Dov steadied Uriel as another chariot rolled close. He recognized the form of Ocran with his bow, the driver in front, and a spearman on the right.

Movement caught Dov's attention, on the adjacent hill where the king of Judah was to muster his troops, but he could only make out black contours against a starry sky. Footsteps rustled the grass and wheels creaked behind him. Another chariot pulled alongside Ahab. He was flanked now by the best fighters in the army. *Protect these soldiers, Yahweh. Do not punish the innocent for their king's disobedience.*

He looked behind. Large black shapes revealed more chariots. Spears sliced the darkness. Dov turned, peering intently through the murk where the armies would converge. Dawn approached. He held up his hand, signaling the troops behind to wait. He searched the distance for the city of Ramoth Gilead. Would he see any lights? Probably not. If Ben-Hadad's men infiltrated the city, watchmen would not be allowed to carry torches. The wall would obscure lamplight from homes. Except—yes, there on what must be a rooftop in the farthest corner, a light glowed dimly. A signal from a loyal Levite? The chariot horses stamped impatiently, and Uriel tossed his head. Dov pushed his weight down heavily, signaling his horse to stand. A shrill whinny sounded in the distance, and yellow light crested the eastern hills.

Bearing Aramean standards, chariots, lancers, and foot soldiers flooded the valley.

"Follow me, oh Israel!" Ahab raised an arm skyward, barely recognizable in his undyed tunic and simple scale armor and helmet. His driver slapped the reins, and the horses galloped down the hill. They flew no royal standards. Dov raced just behind the king. Ocran's chariot drew abreast of Ahab's, Ocran holding his drawn bow as they charged the enemy.

Dov sent one arrow flying high toward the Arameans, watching it arch over the Israelite frontline, then whipping his attention back to nock a second arrow. Soon he lost count of the number of arrows he sent into the mass of Arameans, for his eyes could not track their end amid all the movement.

"Help! Help the king of Judah!"

Dov swung Uriel toward the shouts. Spotting ten or more Arameans converging on King Jehoshaphat's chariot, Dov urged Uriel into a flat-out run. Wind stung his eyes as he pulled his bowstring and fired. His arrow sank deep into a lancer's shoulder. The warrior fell, spewing curses. His comrades glanced around uncertainly.

One shouted to the others. "This is not King Ahab. Retreat. Find the king of Israel." The Aramean fighters turned aside, casting their gazes over the conflict, apparently searching for the other royal chariot.

Dov urged Uriel on, drawing alongside the king of

Judah. "Are you all right?" Ahab's plan had worked to his benefit but not to Jehoshaphat's. Although at least one Aramean recognized Ahab from three previous confrontations, when they saw a leader wearing kingly garb, they attacked. If Jehoshaphat had not cried out, he would be dead now.

The king of Judah lifted a hand signifying assent. "My swordsman is wounded," he called. As the driver moved behind a line of Judah's slingers, Dov saw the wounded man sitting on the chariot floor, holding a blood-soaked cloth to his forehead. A lancer leapt in beside him, and the chariot wheeled back into the fighting.

Dov offered a prayer for his fellow soldier, then cast about for King Ahab. Dov spotted him at once, still flanked by guarding chariots. Pressing close together, they plowed through the Aramean ranks, easily turning aside swordsmen and cavalry fighters with their three-pronged attack.

Dov turned to aid a band of slingers who had advanced too far into the enemy's ranks. He sent arrows to deter their assailants while they retreated behind a hedge of Israelite shields. As they had been trained, now that the first line of attack had met the enemy, they would make their way into the forest, advance with the trees as cover, and assail the enemy with flying stones along their flank.

As he trotted back toward the fray, a foot soldier offered up a fistful of arrows as Dov rode by. Nodding in gratitude, he kept one out and replenished his quiver with the others.

He nocked the arrow but gave the fletching a second look. Eagle feathers were hard to come by, but Jaedon had given him several from Hevel during his visit to Gilgal. This was Dov's own arrow. The arrowhead and shaft were bloodstained, though he always cleaned them before battle. So one of the arrows he'd arched over the front line had hit someone and drawn blood. Perhaps killed him.

Somberly, he guided Uri into the forest, parallel to the battle, searching for an enemy to engage. An armored Aramean parried swords with an Israelite Dov recognized from his training sessions. The Israelite was weakening, falling back as his foe lunged forward in quick succession. Dov nocked, drew, and let fly his arrow. At the same time the

Aramean swung for the Israelite's head, Dov's arrow pierced him under one eye. Blood spurted as the enemy slumped.

Cantering back into the battle, Dov drew and fired several times in succession. Before he ran completely out of arrows, another soldier provided him with retrieved arrows. He caught sight of Ben-Hadad, galloped toward his chariot, and shot. Shot again. The shield bearer deflected both shots. Dov slowed to avoid a tangle of hooves, heaving haunches, and splintered wood as two chariots collided. The Israelite driver crawled out, followed by an archer. They hurried to unhitch their struggling horses. The Arameans lay still.

Seeing they could manage without his help, Dov swerved around the pileup to pursue Ben-Hadad. He continued to shoot, but the shield bearer skillfully blocked his arrows. Then the chariot turned and bounded straight for him. He continued shooting until they were almost on top of him, then he aimed his last arrow for Ben-Hadad's center.

Screaming and clutching his middle, the shield-bearer fell. The chariot swerved towards Dov and the man fell from the chariot onto the battlefield. Ben-Hadad shouted for the driver to stop the horses, not to see to his armor bearer, but to aim his own arrow at Dov.

The first arrow pierced the right side of his leather armor, cracking a rib. He gripped the arrow to pull it out, but agonizing pain stopped him. He must break the shaft so he could continue fighting until he could get to a healer. Drawing a ragged breath, he grasped the shaft close to the leather armor and closed his other hand farther up the shaft.

But just as he snapped the shaft, Uriel swerved violently. Dov looked up, ready to calm his horse, thinking that in his pain he must have signaled Uri to leap sideways. But a sword slashed down. An Aramean had ridden close enough to engage. Throwing his weight sideways, Dov avoided a death blow. But the sword caught his bow arm instead, slicing the flesh to the bone. Blood gushed from the wound.

With fierce determination, Dov clung to consciousness. How had he let this happen? Purposefully, he pushed breath in and out. The swordsman's horse side-stepped as he tried to kick it into position, and Dov painfully suppressed a laugh.

The enemy's horse was a mare, and Uri had issued a frightening squeal. Challenge or invitation, the mare wanted no dealings with a stallion. Pain shot up and down the side of his body. He hunched over, pressing his forearm under the extruding arrow shaft and gripping his slashed arm to slake the flow of blood.

As the Aramean beat his mare with the flat of his sword, Dov turned to escape into the forest. Dodging branches, he glanced back. The Aramean was dangerously close.

But behind him, outside the forest, a chariot slid to a stop and Ocran jumped out. Grasping a spear, he darted between the trees after the Aramean. Dov's pursuer must have heard crashing through the underbrush, because he turned and swung for Ocran, who vaulted behind an oak. The sword sliced deep into the trunk and stuck.

Ocran leapt forward and thrust his lance into the soldier's side. Clutching at his wound, the horseman slumped to the ground.

Gasping, Dov curled around his wounds, fighting off the faintness that threatened to topple him.

"Let me see." Ocran examined the protruding arrow. "We'll leave that for now." He ripped cloth from his tunic and tied it high on Dov's bow arm to slow the bleeding. "Let's get you to the chariot. If I lead your horse, can you stay in the saddle?"

Somehow, Dov did not lose consciousness. Ocran loaded him into his chariot and drove it to the hill where they'd begun the battle. He settled him under a tree. "Must get back to it, old friend. I'll send a healer when I can."

The sun crossed its high point, the battle continued, and Ocran did not return. The fighting was fierce, but as Dov faded in and out of consciousness, sounds were muted, cries of death, and shouts of valor too distant to matter. Clashes of swords and flights of arrows grew dim. The thudding in his ears, the scent of his blood, were more real than the fight for Ramoth Gilead, a city he had never entered. Heaviness draped over him, feeling as though his body were sinking into the ground. Disjointed resolutions wove through his mind before the darkness took him. Never again would he fight for an evil king. He would fight for a mudbrick hovel. He would fight for Miriam and her children.

Dov woke to the sound of chariot wheels and shouting. His mouth tasting of blood and dirt, he turned his head and spat. Ocran knelt beside him, holding a waterskin. "Drink now. The king has been wounded."

The water tasted like heaven. "You brought his chariot?"

"Yes. His driver is propping him up. He is gravely wounded and doesn't want his army demoralized." Ocran coughed hoarsely. "A soldier to the end. A leader."

The prophecy. Dov struggled to lift his head. "Is he dying?"

"He will not live the night."

Dov squinted, trying to make out Ocran's face. "You? Were you wounded? His guards?"

"We are well. And no one got near the king. An enemy shot a random arrow. Somehow it lodged between a chink in his armor."

The ways of Yahweh.

Refusing more water, Dov lay back, panting against the burning pain radiating from the arrow. Overhead, the sky looked gray. "Are there fires?" he asked.

"No. The sun is setting." Ocran turned as another soldier approached.

"The king is dead, Commander."

"It is over then. Relay this order to our troops. 'Everyone return to his town. Quickly, before the enemy realizes Ahab is dead.'"

He heard the order going through the soldiers on the hill, fading as it spread to the valley. With Ahab dead, was Miriam now safe? Would she be able to bring her little clan back to Jezreel?

No. Jezebel still lived. Dov drew a short breath, let it out slowly. It was getting harder to breathe, as if that arrow blocked passage, harder still to move, as if all his strength had leaked out the wound. Would he die on this hill? Would he never see Miriam again?

Ocran leaned over him again. "Drink this wine. I've found a healer to remove the arrow."

When Ocran put a skin of wine to his lips, Dov took several swallows. He'd once seen an arrow removed from a man's cheek, close to his eye. Remembering the blood and greenish tint of exposed flesh as the arrow was pulled, he poured the wine down his throat.

Pain woke Dov once more as they loaded him into the chariot.

"We must carry the king's body to Samaria," Ocran said.

Startled, Dov rolled his head sideways and saw the body of Ahab beside him, still in the plain tunic and armor he had worn to save him from death. His face was covered with a cloth.

"The healer said he's done all he can for you. Maalik can best care for you as you convalesce, but we need to get you there soon."

"Uriel?" As he spoke the horse's name, Dov heard him whicker.

"I tied him to the chariot. You are shivering. I'll get you a cloak."

Ocran came back shortly with an unfamiliar blood-stained cloak. It was warm, and for that he was grateful. *Yahweh, bless the owner of this cloak. Accept him into your presence.*

Ocran climbed into the chariot, stepping between Ahab's body and Dov. He bent. "I'll aim for the smooth spots in the road."

Dov grimaced, knowing those were few.

"Ready? More wine?"

The chariot rocked forward and back as the horses anticipated departure.

Dov understood their eagerness. "No. Just take me home."

Chapter Thirty-Eight

*So the king died and was brought to Samaria, and they
buried him there. They washed the chariot at a pool in
Samaria (where the prostitutes bathed), and the dogs licked
up his blood, as the word of the Lord had declared.*
~ 1 Kings 22:37-38

Samaria
Dov

DOV WOKE TO AN EAGLE CRY. At least, he thought that was what
woke him. Sunlight poured through an open window,
blinding him. Had he slept through the night? He threw his
arm over his eyes and was seized by pain. Bandages covered
his bow arm from wrist to shoulder.

Maalik busily tied up the window covering, his shape
blocking some of the glare. "Sit up. Time to eat."

Dov groaned. His head felt like a boulder and his whole
body throbbed with pain. "Not hungry."

"Davita brought oat and lentil gruel, though you didn't
have the courtesy to wake when she was here. You will eat it
or wear it. I am done playing nursemaid. After you eat,
bandages come off. If your wounds have continued to
improve, we might leave them off."

Davita?

Eyes closed, Dov hesitantly reached for his forehead. It
felt cool and, despite throbbing pain, the grogginess began to
lift. "How long have I slept?"

"Through the king's burial, all the speeches about his
building projects, the ivory palaces, the pagan temples"—
there was the sound of Maalik spitting. Dov's eyes popped
open and Maalik continued—"all the commendations. No one
spoke of the dogs licking his blood where they washed his
chariot, at the pool where the prostitutes bathe."

Dov knew a little about royal burials, having heard of
the ceremonies for Ahab's father. Although King Omri was
buried the day after his death, feasting and speeches lasted

a week. "I have slept for a week? Where am I?"

Maalik brought a basin filled with warm water. He dipped a cloth in, wrung it out, and handed it to Dov. "Wash your face and hands." Then in a gentler tone, he said, "You are here in our own house, of course. You've slept ten days or more, through the coronation of Ahab's son, Ahaziah. In my exhaustion, the days have run together, and I am not sure. Your wounds were grievous, so the healer mixed ground poppy seeds with your broth."

"Ten days!" Dov attempted to shove himself up, then wheezed as pain shot through his arm and side.

Maalik brought the gruel in a small wooden bowl, exchanging it for the wet cloth. "You must move carefully for a while. Can you manage this yourself, or shall I get a spoon and feed you like an infant?"

Dov grinned ruefully. "Is that what you have done?" He reached for the bowl and nearly dropped it. Despite the fact there was no visible injury to his left hand, it was painful to move it. And it seemed he had no strength. Had the lacerations impacted sinews? He took firm hold with his other hand, merely resting the limp one against the bowl.

"Like an infant," Maalik confirmed. "The healer stopped the poppy milk two days ago, but you continued to sleep. I admit, I was glad to see you move this morning."

"But why is Davita in Samaria?" Surely she would not have come for the funeral, nor even the coronation.

"You needed her." Maalik's voice caught. "I thought I might lose you."

Sniffing the gruel, Dov thought he detected cinnamon. Awkwardly, he tilted the bowl to his lips. Honey.

Maalik came back with another bowl and sat on the edge of Dov's sleeping mat. Taking a sip, he nodded in approval. "I will miss Davita's cooking once you are better." His voice grew serious. "She has been here every day, sometimes accompanied by Zuar, bringing food for us both, helping me change your bandages, carrying water. Such a help. Some days, Caleb brought Hadassah to encourage me. He insisted we walk around the city while he sat with you. We have staunch friends, my boy. Hadassah would say—no, I say—Yahweh has blessed us."

"Zuar is here, too? Has all Jezreel come?" Dov asked.

Maalik's eyes creased, and he said slowly. "Nearly. Davita's father accompanied her for propriety, and Aaron came with Zuar. The men rented a vacant house, and Davita sleeps on a pallet in Hadassah's room."

Dov looked away, embarrassed by the trouble he had caused. He must regain his strength quickly. He tried flexing his fingers, noticing only slight movement. He slid his good hand to the bandages circling his middle. Pain radiated from the arrow wound.

His body was in a terrible state. It seemed he would lose the use of his bow arm, ending his career as a soldier. But wasn't that what he wanted?

"Now don't give me that look, my boy. The fact that you live at all is a blessing. You lost nearly as much blood from your shredded arm as did our dead king. Not to mention taking an arrow to the side. The healer said if not for the leather armor and your rib, it would have gutted your bowels. Still, both wounds became infected. That alone might have killed you."

Maalik was right. Dov thought he would die as he lay wounded beside the dead king. Now all he needed to do was heal. If he lost the use of a hand, even an arm, he had another arm, his right one at that. He could retire from the military with honor, and he would do so. He felt strangely grateful, knowing his injury meant he would not serve another king from the house of Ahab.

"I am grateful, Maalik. Especially to you. Thank you for caring for me. That I am alive is a miracle, is it not?"

Maalik looked away. "Well," he said hoarsely, "Enough talk of infirmity. Finish your gruel. As soon as Zuar and Davita arrive, you will get up and walk. The sooner you recover, the sooner I stop waiting on you like a servant."

"You mentioned them visiting together often. Their friendship continues?"

"So it seems. Perhaps we will celebrate a wedding."

Caleb and Chloe were expecting their first child. Now Zuar and Davita, an unlikely couple, seemed on the brink of an understanding. Could Dov hope that if he regained his strength and asked Miriam again to marry him, that this time she would say yes?

Suddenly, he recalled the uncomfortable conversation he'd overheard between Miriam and her father before her marriage to Gershon. Because of the siege, Gershon had been unable to obtain her father's permission, and they had become betrothed without his approval. Her father was insulted and reproached Miriam, embarrassing her.

Hadn't Dov made the same mistake, asking her to marry him when she was first widowed? He would not do so again. As soon as he could present himself whole, a man who could care for Miriam, he would offer Lemuel a *mohar* for his daughter.

A week later, bored with circling the street where he lived, Dov crossed town to the house Zuar and his father had rented.

He rapped on the wooden door. "Come with me to the marketplace. I want to purchase a new bow."

Zuar cocked an eyebrow. "Have you forgotten you are now retired, *Ex*-Captain Dov?"

"Come with me to the marketplace, if you please." He bowed slightly, aware of the still-tender area the arrow had pierced.

"You have a fine bow. Why do you need another?"

Dov tipped his head toward his injured arm, hanging stiffly at his side. "I can no longer string mine, let alone shoot. I'd like to try a lighter weapon." The sword wounds, pieced together like a garment, were beginning to heal. But though he massaged the arm daily with rendered animal fat, the stiffness had not improved.

Scratching his head, Zuar said, "If you like. But why purchase a bow? Surely you can choose one from the king's arsenal. After all, you were wounded in his father's service."

"Perhaps I could. But I've been released from my duties and paid my wages. I have means. And I want no favors from King Ahaziah. I doubt he knows my name."

Zuar grimaced. "Perhaps it's best to avoid his notice. I know he's a young man, but he has a love of banquets lasting long into the night, and he's not so good in the morning."

Dov frowned. With potential future conflict with Aram and Assyria, Israel needed a wise leader. Ahaziah was young and his sudden rise to power seemed to have gone to his head. Still, he had Ocran to advise him, as well as other senior officers. The young king should settle into his responsibilities in time.

"Bring your axe. After I find a bow, I want to go to the valley and practice."

Zuar looked dubious but fastened the weapon to his leather belt.

They walked through the narrow streets to the gate market. A donkey seller praised the attributes of several animals, one a pretty white jenny, unusually tall and long-legged. Like Miriam.

Attempting to flex his stiff hand, Dov turned to examine pottery displayed by a merchant from Zarephath. Beautiful glazes. Blue-greens, warm golds the color of ripe wheat, clear reds. He pushed away the memory of blood pooling on the ground. He had seen too many battles. He summoned instead the memory of calanit blooms in the meadow near Jezreel. But he could not make himself respond to the reds.

He ran the fingers of his good hand around the rim of a beautiful pitcher, the blue-green color he had first admired. The color of a clear mountain spring. The artist had etched a wavy line around the top, more like a winding stream than the stylized ocean waves typical of Phoenician pottery. "How much for this?"

The merchant named his price and Dov nodded. "Have it wrapped for travel and delivered to the home of Maalik." He gave directions, then selected several more pieces, including one of the calanit red. Though he did not like it, he knew someone who would.

As they walked on toward the weapon maker's booth, Zuar said, "He overcharged you. You should have bargained with him. I am sure he was insulted."

Dov barked a laugh, then pressed his arm against his ribs. "I thought the price fair, especially to have the item delivered."

"Your home is no far distance. But are you planning a journey south, by chance?"

Dov scoffed, glancing significantly at the hand pressed against his side. "I am not fit to travel."

"Hmm." Then Zuar lifted his head, sniffing. "I smell roast pork." He veered toward the outskirts of the market, where the food vendors sold roast meat, baked items, and produce.

Dov followed, thankful for the distracting aroma. The roasting meat did smell good, but he, like Maalik, had given up pork when Caleb's family, especially Hadassah, had explained to them the Hebrew dietary laws. Out of respect for the family and Yahweh, they attempted to learn the sometimes-confusing rules. Giving up pork was the hardest.

Evidently Zuar had no such compunction. While he was waiting in line, Dov walked over to a woman cooking what smelled like lamb. "Can you tell me, did this meat come from the temple?" Since King Ahab's death, the prophets of Ba'al had grown emboldened by Jezebel. No longer worshipping only in the high places, they returned to the Temple of Ba'al Melqart in the city and resumed the sacrifices and fertility rites.

The woman scowled. "I should say not. This lamb is from our own herd."

Dov thanked her and ordered several pieces. While he waited, she cooked over a wood fire and wrapped the roast meat in grape leaves. He motioned for her to hand him the final piece in a loosely folded leaf. He bit into the savory lamb, juices dripping through his fingers.

Zuar came to stand beside him, empty handed. "Line's too long. What is that you are eating?"

Motioning for him to take the pile of wrapped pieces the woman had prepared, Dov said, "Roast lamb. I got enough for us both."

Zuar took a bite. "Mmm. Better purchase a few more for our midday meal."

The woman smiled and sliced several more pieces. "If you have more shopping, sirs, I will have these ready for you when you return."

They made their way back toward the weapon seller. Dov selected a plain bow with a gentle curve, several bowstrings, and smaller arrows to fit the bow. If he was in

Gilgal, he could borrow the one he had given Miriam, seized after the siege of Samaria. But if he had stayed in Gilgal, he would not have been wounded in the last battle, nor need such a bow to regain the use of his arm. Worthless thoughts. One could not change the past, and Elijah's teaching had convinced Dov that keeping his vow to the king was part of Yahweh's plan. Were even his wounds part of Yahweh's plan?

That thought was entirely too complex to dwell upon. Dov motioned to his selections and asked the vendor for the price. This time Dov bargained, albeit half-heartedly, and gained a boar skin quiver suited to the smaller arrows, at only a slightly inflated price.

Zuar came to stand beside him, a bulging cloth bag slung across one shoulder. He indicated a vegetable vendor. "You owe that merchant for this sack and several squash. We can fit our meat in here also."

Dov nodded, grinning. Zuar knew easy prey when he spotted it. "Developed an appetite for squash, have you?"

"Not exactly. But let us gather our purchases and head for the valley. It is nearly midday."

Dov paid for the extra meat and the items Zuar had selected. The sun warmed his shoulders as they descended the earthen ramp to the valley. Did Zuar walk more slowly than usual? If so, Dov was grateful for the consideration. His rib pained him, walking downhill.

When they reached the valley, Zuar pointed at a stump used for target practice. "I'll move that a bit closer. I can't throw that far." He trotted off.

Dov watched. How long before he could move that swiftly again? He doubted he'd ever be able to move a stump with only his two arms. He pulled the unstrung bow from the quiver, searching with his fingers for one of the strings he'd stuffed in the bottom. He tried bending the bow with his hands. It was small enough, he should be able to, but he could not. The left arm was not only weak, but without the ability to grip, his hand was nearly useless.

Then he tried a variation of the technique he used for his large bow, stepping through the bow with his left leg and using his right foot to secure it, left hand to bend it. With the shorter bow, although the angle was at first strange, the

349 | DANA MCNEELY | 349

bow's tension was manageable. After a few mishaps, he succeeded. He lifted his head and grinned.

Zuar stood a little apart and shot his fist into the air. "Well done!"

Next Dov tried nocking an arrow. He fumbled even more with the new arrows. Because he couldn't completely close the fingers on his hand, the small arrows slipped through his grasp, landing on the ground by his feet or flipping into the air a few steps away. He shrugged. "A success and a failure. On to the next thing."

"I am prepared." Zuar reached for the market pack, pulling out several squash and a ball of undyed yarn. He handed Dov the largest squash.

Dov barely needed to close his fingers to hold it, so he handled it easily, passing it back and forth between his left and right hands as Zuar instructed.

"Toss me yours and catch this." Dov tossed his squash but fumbled the one thrown to him. He'd had more skill as a boy. Heat suffused his face, and he felt an urge to throw the squash to the ground and stomp it. The thought of such a petty response made him shake his head. Instead he tried tossing the squash back and forth between his own hands, slowly at first, then attempting more speed, until Zuar again said, "Well done."

Next Zuar pressed the yarn ball into Dov's hand. "Squeeze this. Imagine it the neck of the man who carved up your arm."

Dov squeezed, as usual, his fingers barely moved.

"What about—" Zuar cupped his two hands around Dov's stiff fingers and squeezed. "Does it hurt?"

"Actually, no. As if I am wearing a thick glove over my fist."

"Yet your fingers bend, which is encouraging." Zuar stared at his own hand as he opened and closed his fingers. The two worked together, talking the whole time of different methods to gain flexibility—picking up rocks, grooming Uriel with brushes and cloths, preparing a garden for planting. It made sense that performing normal activities would improve his movement and strength. Except for the last.

"A garden? Where did you get such an idea?" Dov asked.

Did Zuar blush? "Well, Davita is staying with Caleb's family, you know. His mother, Dorcas, and Davita want an herb garden, and I offered to dig the soil in their courtyard."

Dov started to laugh, but stopped himself at the expression on his friend's face. "It is a good idea. And so are the others—your squash and yarn, my smaller bow. I will work to relearn everything I do with this hand, which thankfully, is not everything. And if it does not improve, I will find ways to do what I must despite it."

"So, you will help me with the garden?"

He did laugh now, thinking of Caleb, Seth, and Lemuel. A family of farmers. What would they think when two more men showed up with shovels? "I will."

Determined, he moved through the drills again. It was true. As an archer, not being able to hold his bow steady with his left arm seemed devastating, but in fact, it was only inconvenient. He was right-handed after all. He could learn other ways to shoot his bow, or he could use other weapons. Become more skilled with the sword or sling.

When his arm trembled and he dripped sweat, Dov called a halt. "Maalik will scold if I am late for supper." His muscles were already spasming. He knew pain would ensue. He considered it progress.

Chapter Thirty-Nine

Let no foreigner who is bound to the Lord say,
"The Lord will surely exclude me from his people."
And let no eunuch complain, "I am only a dry tree."
For this is what the Lord says: "To the eunuchs who keep my
Sabbaths, who choose what pleases me and hold fast to my
covenant—to them I will give within my temple and its walls
a memorial and a name better than sons and daughters; I
will give them an everlasting name that will endure forever."
~ Isaiah 56:3-5

Samaria
Dov

DOV HAD SLEPT TOO LATE. DIGGING that garden with Zuar yesterday had sapped him of strength like a maple in winter. As sunlight poured through the window facing the street, Dov drank honeyed water and shoved flatbread into his mouth. Dropping more into the sack which already held several stones, a sling, and a package of goat cheese, he called, "Are you sure you don't want to come with me?"

"You know Hadassah and I walk the city each morning." Maalik emerged from the back room wearing the tunic Hadassah had woven and smelling of mint leaves and myrrh. Dov suppressed a grin.

"Why don't you both walk to the valley with me? It looks to be a fine day."

"She doesn't like unexpected change."

"Are you so sure of that?"

Someone rapped on the door. Dov frowned. He wasn't expecting anyone and Maalik would call for Hadassah. No matter who it was, he would send them on their way. No one would interrupt his training.

Caleb stood with his arm around his grandmother. "Savta told me you have been practicing archery—among other things—in the valley each day. I thought we might join you."

Dov slid his hand to his side, glancing at Maalik. Yesterday, Dov managed the shovel by laying the handle against his left palm, performing most of the gripping and shoving with his right. But if Lemuel realized how crippled he was—

"You are kind to include us. It's been an age since I've been to the valley." Hadassah directed a smile towards Dov, her hands folded around a cloth-wrapped bundle. "I brought date bread and an invitation to supper. To both of you." She lowered her eyelashes so that they fell like petals against her lined cheek. Miriam's long lashes softened her face in such a way.

"Of course," he answered. "I will be happy to have an audience." It was a lie, but he would strive to make it true. Caleb was his best friend, though circumstances had kept them apart lately. His wife claimed most of his time, and rightly so. Yesterday, he had been with his father and brother at the vineyard. But there was an awkwardness between them Dov couldn't quite put his finger on.

"I heard you are practicing with the sling," Caleb said. "I am an expert slinger, in the event you need advice."

"Who does not need advice?" Dov forced heartiness into his voice. "Yet I have only seen you with your bow."

"As boys, Seth and I chased foxes from the vineyard with our slings."

There it was, the awkwardness. Caleb's mention of his family's vineyard, but nothing of Miriam, nor of his dead cousins and their father's vineyard. *Does he blame me for not preventing that terrible injustice?*

Dov composed himself. "I see. Well, I will take this date loaf with us for our midday meal. Wait while I wrap a package of goat cheese."

"Not necessary." Caleb lifted the bag he'd been holding at his side. "Chloe packed a meal, and there is plenty to share. Cheese and grapes, for certain, and who knows what other surprises."

Dov slid the bow over his shoulder and grasped his spear. "Your wife enjoys surprises?" He raised an eyebrow at Maalik, who growled under his breath.

"Very much." Caleb winked. "With twin sons, how could

she not?"

A wave of emptiness rolled over Dov. Hunger. He felt only hunger. "They are well?"

"Like two puppies, constantly crawling into trouble. Chloe invited Davita to visit this morning. They're going to the marketplace with Imma. Surely three women can manage two troublesome little boys."

The twins had not yet seen a year, and Caleb called them troublesome. How would it be when they walked? Yet Caleb, who had first returned from war angry then despondent, now wore laughter wherever he went. Fatherhood suited him.

Maalik walked outside and took Hadassah's arm. Dov glanced around the room once more. He had his weapons and the sack of food. He closed the door.

"I brought you a broken-in sling to try," Caleb said. "Zuar told me you bought one in the market." He shook his head.

Dov strode ahead, Caleb close to his side. Maalik and Hadassah fell in behind.

"This is not the route we usually take," Dov heard Maalik explain. "We are walking toward the southern gate. I see Aaron is manning the entrance today. Just there."

Dov glanced behind and saw Maalik gently turn Hadassah's chin. She lifted her hand toward the gatehouse. "Hello, Aaron. A beautiful day, is it not?"

"It certainly is. Out for a stroll?"

"We are going to the valley to watch Dov and Caleb practice."

"For a while," Maalik said. "And then to pick flowers."

When they reached the valley, Maalik seated Hadassah on a flat rock and sat beside her in the grass, murmuring.

Caleb pulled two slings and a parcel of stones from the sack Dov had thought contained only food. He fished around for his sling, then tipped stones into his upturned, claw-like hand.

Caleb's gaze rested briefly on the hand, then he extended a smooth, water-stained sling. He ran his fingers along it. "Try this instead. Old leather is softer, indented from the stones. You may find it works better."

Dov enjoyed using a sling—the force of the circular swing in his right hand, his easy ability to drop just one side of it with his good right hand. But he had not perfected his aim. The stones flew too high or kicked up bits of earth. He examined Caleb's sling, slid the loop over his finger, and pressed the pouch around a stone. Counting one-two-three, he let go the string, and the rock hit the ground. Disgusted, he made a clucking sound with his tongue.

"I see what you are doing. Lift your elbow a bit higher. Look at your target."

Dov nodded, embarrassed to have to be told such a basic fact. "As for any other weapon."

Caleb grinned. "Yet a sling is completely different from a spear or a bow. Try again."

He did, with better success. Several more attempts rewarded Dov with consistent thwacks against the post. He shot until he had flung all his gathered ammunition, then strode to the post to retrieve the stones. Recent rains had uncovered a few larger ones, and he picked them up also.

"Those are far too large." Caleb laughed.

"Not for my purpose." After offering the sling back to Caleb and being told to keep it, Dov stowed it away. Then he showed Caleb the exercises he practiced several times each week. "The fingers in this hand remain stiff, but my arm is back to full strength. I intend to keep exercising with larger and larger rocks."

He ignored the accusing voice inside. You are half the man you were. What woman would trust you to protect her?

When the sun was halfway to the horizon, they headed for the city. Dov's feet dragged. Trying to appear strong, he had pushed himself too far. He wished he hadn't agreed to Hadassah's supper invitation.

She and Maalik walked ahead, chatting happily.

"It seems they don't feel their years," Caleb said.

"Just what I was thinking." Dov smiled. "I am glad they are friends. Hadassah has taught Maalik so much about the ways of Yahweh. And he passes it on to me."

"She is the matriarch of our family. Has always been our

teacher. Did you know her father was a scribe to King Asa of Judah?"

"I heard some of her story. When she lost her inheritance, she moved to Israel with Nathaniel, her husband. But why? I know she missed the temple."

"She disputed an inheritance provision that would have required her to marry her cousin, a man she did not respect. Instead, she married a poor soldier for love." Caleb cast a glance at Dov. Was he drawing some sort of parallel between Dov and Hadassah's soldier? No. He said a poor soldier. Dov had fought in several successful battles. He had sufficient means to support a wife, but he was a cripple.

"Miriam loved that story when she was a girl." Caleb grinned. "So did I, though I would not admit it. Such impractical stories are for girls. And yet, I chose my bride."

"You did? I thought your father—"

"Oh, he went to her father with the bride price, but I told Abba to get her for me. And Dov, I knew Chloe was agreeable. Miriam had told me."

They walked a while in silence. Dov cast several glances toward Caleb to see if he had more to say. He was not sure if he wanted his friend to go on, or speak of something else. He liked that he was talking freely. It seemed as if the discomfort between them was ending, but Dov wasn't sure the direction they were going was—

"You know, Dov, I always thought that you and my sister—you know."

"What do you mean? She was betrothed."

"Of course, but before we knew that. And then … after what happened."

Caleb had been forthright. Should Dov?

"Did she tell you I offered to wed her, and she refused?"

Caleb appeared stunned. "When was this?"

"When Zuar and I searched for her after the murders. When we found her with the prophet."

Caleb sighed, lifting his hands as if that explained everything. "Well, of course. That was only days after. She and the others had suffered a terrible ordeal. She could not think rationally."

"I spoke to her again shortly before the battle at Aphek."

"Where you were wounded. You asked her to marry you then? She agreed and reneged upon learning you were wounded? I can't believe that of her! I will speak to her. She—"

"No, Caleb. I did not exactly ask her to marry me. I spoke to her of marriage ... in general terms. She said she did not need a man to protect her."

"Well of course she would say that, that is Miriam all over. From the time she was a girl, she insisted she could fight her own fights. Seth and I had to *secretly* beat the young bullies who tormented her about her height." He sighed. "I realize now, they admired her, the stupid dolts. I mostly blame myself—but Seth must take his share of blame—that there were few offers for her hand in Samaria. That is why my father sent her to Jezreel. But I always thought you would be right for her. As a girl, when you helped Aban and his family, she thought you were—" Caleb choked and looked off toward the city, his cheeks reddening like a maiden's. It seemed he would not go on.

Dov could not stand it. "What!"

"She thought you were heroic." Caleb rolled his eyes.

Dov took a deep breath. "I will speak to your father."

"Tonight?"

"If you think I should." Dov's heart pounded, but the thuds were strangely calming.

Caleb let out a long, slow breath. "At last."

"Are you ready?" Maalik came from his room, resplendent in the tunic Hadassah had woven.

Dov awkwardly tied a sash around his middle, glad he did not need to fasten on armor. He would never do so again. "Do I bring the *mohar*?" He fidgeted with his sash again, hoping the answer was yes. His hurried trip back to the market had produced the desired results.

Maalik laughed. "I admit, I am not sure. Perhaps not the *living* portion, since we have been invited to supper." He tied the small pouch onto Dov's belt containing the *ketubah* scroll and the silver pieces.

He beamed at his step-father, wondering why he had

never called him *Abba*. Maalik looked as proud, and as sure of the success of their undertaking, as any father of the son of his loins. Dov embraced him, holding the old man hard against his chest before they both stepped back and grinned at the floor.

Maalik picked up the two cloth-wrapped packages, then they walked together to Caleb's house. *Lemuel's* house. Energy whipped though Dov's body like lightning strikes before a storm. He prepared himself to surmount any obstacle.

As they approached, the savory aroma of lamb wafted from the house. Dov tensed and Maalik rested a hand on his shoulder. "Steady, boy."

Dov scoffed. Nearing forty, and he was still *boy* to Maalik. And suddenly Dov's age as well as his weak left arm seemed impediments. Yet, he was not *that* much older, was he? She had been nearing twelve when he was a young guard. He pushed the thought away, mentally bolting a shutter against any worrisome thought. Caleb had given his approval as elder brother. Age brought wisdom, did it not?

Maalik knocked on the door. Immediately it flung open. Lemuel stood in the doorway, frowning. "Hello." He paused, then added, "Come in."

"Shalom upon your house," Dov responded politely, waiting for Lemuel to step aside. After an awkward moment, his wife Dorcas came and took his arm. "Come in, come in." She guided them into the room. "How good to see you again, Maalik. I am happy you are better, Dov."

Hadassah sat near the hearth. Caleb, dropping a cushion beside her, said, "This is your place, Maalik. Dov, sit here between father and me."

Maalik and Dov obediently went their separate ways. Dorcas bustled behind Hadassah and looked expectantly in Lemuel's direction. He stood where Dorcas had left him. "Will you pray for us, husband?"

"Yes, *Ishti*."

After the prayer, the room seemed to mellow. Dov had felt the almost audible sigh of relief as Lemuel ended with "so be it, Yahweh." In that moment, their hearts were as one. Perhaps the watered wine Lemuel handed around also helped ease the tension that threaded around Dov. He did not think it was only he who felt it, an observation confirmed when Lemuel poured himself a measure of the rosy liquid, tipped it down his throat, and refilled his cup before coming to sit beside Dov.

Dorcas began dishing up bowls of stew, which Caleb distributed. Maalik and Hadassah murmured quietly, Maalik doing much of the talking, sometimes gesturing with his hands, not for Hadassah's benefit, Dov had come to realize, but to put form to the word pictures he painted for the blind woman.

The conversation turned to Miriam's letters, as it had on previous occasions. Like Maalik, Dov had painted word pictures about Jaedon, Yaffa, and the eagle, expanding upon the spare lines she had written in the letter he carried to them from Gilgal. But to his surprise, Lemuel unrolled a new parchment inked on both sides and began to read.

"From your daughter Miriam, to my beloved abba and imma. I hope you are well. I am writing to tell you of the birth of my first child, a daughter I have named Gershoni, in memory of her father. I have not written before, as there was no one to carry this missive, but Elijah is sending a prophet to minister to the people of Beth-shan, and he agreed to put it in your hands.

"Gershoni is now two, an active strong-willed child who toddles after her brother everywhere. Jaedon allows it good-heartedly, mostly, I believe, because he misses his eagle. Hevel finally took a mate and left us, although we have seen the pair of them fly overhead a time or two. We believe they have nested nearby, and we listen hopefully for chicks when we forage in the hills or hunt, as we must now do for ourselves, since our eagle has abandoned us, ungrateful creature.

"Yaffa is well, and as you can imagine, thrilled to have a granddaughter on her knee—when the little one deigns to perch momentarily. And I wish you, dear parents, could somehow find your way to us. Daily, I ask Yahweh for this gift. I know the dangers continue, so you must come discreetly. It is not a long journey, two or three days. Even Savta, I daresay, could manage on a donkey, as did Yaffa.

Even with King Ahab dead, I cannot return to the north, as long as Jezebel lives. We are safe here, in the company of the prophets, nestled in our dear hills. Come to see us and hold your new granddaughter.

"Give my love to Seth and Avigail, Caleb and Chloe, and Davita. And if you see—"

Lemuel rolled and tied the parchment. "Some final personal remarks follow. But I thought you would be interested to hear how they fare." He lifted his bowl of stew, blew across its surface, and set it down again.

Dov could not bear the thought of eating. Best get this over with. He fumbled for the pouch tied on his sash and retrieved the *ketubah.* "Lemuel, I would speak to you privately."

Miriam's father glanced at his wife, whose eyes had widened, and then around the room. "Speak to us all, Dov. I am not sure my wife or mother would allow us out that door."

Dov glanced around the room, finding every set of eyes trained on his. There had been a reason, probably more than one, Lemuel had read the letter aloud. That surprising letter, the first news since he had left Gilgal with Ocran. A baby girl—no, a child, already two. There was no time to think on any of this. "I have prepared a *ketubah* with Maalik's help."

Lemuel reached for the document and Dov laid it in his palm.

"I want to marry your daughter—be father to her children."

"Hmm." Lemuel ran his finger down the *ketubah,* nodding his head at intervals as he read. "In recognition of the loss to your family of her service, I offer you a *mohar* of a mated pair of goats, another of sheep, and twenty pieces of silver. For her *mattan,* a white jenny and twenty pieces of silver." He looked up. "Generous recompense for a daughter who has given no service to her family in over three years. A widow, with *two* children now, who is an enemy of the queen mother. I take it, you love my daughter?"

Dov leaned in. No question about the extent of his injury? Where they would live? How he would provide for her? "With all my heart." Miriam, he vowed, would never need to ask that question.

Lemuel glanced at Dorcas. "The *mohar* is generous."

She nodded, smiling.

Over by the hearth, Hadassah moved about, seeming about to rise. "I am not satisfied with the arrangement. You have just told me my only great-granddaughter has been born—is two years old already. And marriage is discussed for my only granddaughter. From how many of her weddings must I be absent?"

Maalik laid a hand on her arm. "No more, Hadassah. Dov has a plan."

Lemuel looked interested. "Go on."

"The white donkey is gentle enough for Hadassah, led by Maalik or Caleb. And my horse Uriel is well-behaved. I will lead him and Dorcas can ride."

"But where will we stay?" Miriam's mother asked.

"That will not be a problem. Elijah has friends all along the way. The prophets will be glad to take you in when we reach the settlement. Sometimes a house is empty, when the owner is traveling. The prophets go throughout the countryside, telling how Yahweh is working."

Lemuel raised Miriam's letter. "This prophet's house is empty now."

"We must make preparations." Dorcas clapped her hands together and stood, as if ready to begin. "How long before we must leave, Dov?"

He was suddenly afraid to say. "I planned to leave as soon as I had Lemuel's blessing. Tomorrow."

Lemuel shrugged, but the women gasped. "Food for the trip. A wedding garment."

Dov tapped his chin. "What if she says no?"

"She will not say no." Hadassah scoffed.

"Imma Hadassah," Dorcas said, "Are you so sure? She has always been a willful child."

"As to the wedding garment, though I would gladly wed her in patched garments, I think that would trouble her. Shall I—would it be wrong to—purchase a fine tunic?"

Dorcas looked at Hadassah. "Even if you were to wait a week, we could not get it done in time."

Hadassah sighed. "This is true."

"So, yes. It is a kind thought, Dov."

"Then you must accompany me to the marketplace. It must seem you are buying the garment for one of you."

Hadassah laughed. "Miriam is much taller than either of us. We will bring Davita."

Dov sighed. If they brought Davita, Zuar would come. And Caleb. How could all the talk be contained with such a large party looking for a wedding tunic—when most women wove their own garments? No one must know he was traveling south to take a wife—he was just traveling south. He must think up a plausible story for the gossips to spread. Sneaking out of the city with such a procession would be impossible. "I am concerned about Miriam's safety. All the talk our departure would produce."

"You are right. What if someone became suspicious and guessed Miriam and the others are alive? We should shop in another city where we are unknown," Hadassah said.

Dorcas nodded. "Yes, let us go tomorrow as you planned. We can say—we are going to Jerusalem for Passover. Let us not concern ourselves with the tunic. Who knows, we may come across a caravan."

"But Passover is a month away," Lemuel said.

"We do not want to walk among crowds," Hadassah said definitely. "After all, I am an old blind woman." Maalik laughed and stroked her hair.

Dov smiled at the women, continuing to chatter about plans, what they would take, what was ready, what was not. He wondered if they really meant to proceed on to Jerusalem. It mattered not, he would take them anywhere they desired. The family was on his side in this matter. An indefatigable army. Miriam had no chance. When there was a break in the conversation, he said, "When I purchased the jenny, I also found something for each of you. Nothing impressive," he added quickly.

Maalik handed Hadassah one of the wrapped packages, then carried the other to Dorcas. He hurried back to help Hadassah unwrap hers. When she felt the softness of the woven blanket, she made a cooing sound of approval. "So soft," she murmured.

"The trader said they are made of the softest wool of a type of animal raised in the eastern mountains. Not quite a sheep nor a goat. The trader's wife said you will ride in comfort."

Dorcas ran her fingers over her blanket, admiring the colorful stripes. "Thank you, Dov," she said. "You are a thoughtful boy. We will be ready to leave at dawn."

Dov smiled. *A thoughtful boy.* At least Miriam's mother did not think him too old to marry her daughter.

He almost stood to leave, now that the reason for their visit was resolved. But then he looked down at his now-cold stew, remembered his manners, and ate the supper the women had prepared, remembering to compliment them lavishly. But he barely tasted it as he mentally packed the animals for travel, wondered if they would need a wooden cart to carry tents, or perhaps another donkey for a pack animal.

Finally they all stood, said their goodbyes, and walked along the row of houses, lamps glowing from windows leading them home. All the words spoken crowded Dov's mind. But there was one thing left unsaid. "Without your help, with the *ketubah*—with everything—I would have been lost." He put his hand on Maalik's shoulder. "Thank you ... Abba."

Chapter Forty

May your fountain be blessed,
and may you rejoice in the wife of your youth.
A loving doe, a graceful deer—may her breasts satisfy you
always, may you ever be intoxicated with her love.
~ Proverbs 5:18-19

Gilgal Settlement
Miriam

MIRIAM AWOKE BEFORE DAWN TO THE sound of the iron cook pot clanking onto the hearth. She bolted upright. What was Yaffa doing lifting that heavy pot? Beside her, Gershoni whimpered at the noise. Miriam shushed as she got to her feet.

But Elijah, not Yaffa, turned to stare at them sheepishly, the iron lid held in his hand. "I am sorry to have woken you. I was looking for your stew recipe. There is a wedding today."

She swiped her hair back from her shoulders as she settled the little girl on her hip. "Elijah, I have no recipes. I just cook. And I am out of the spice you all love, so we will need to prepare something else."

"You have none? But one of our number is marrying today. How disappointing. Can you get more?"

"I could but I—"

He put his hand over his heart, huffing, as if he had climbed a steep hill. "Oh! That is reassuring. All right, you go find the spice—take Jaedon to help—and I will take Gershoni and Yaffa and meet you later at Eden and Binyamin's house."

"No, I—"

Yaffa, fully dressed, emerged from the alcove that used to house the eagle. Jaedon followed, carrying a basket, a waterskin, and their two bows. "I hear we are in search of your lentil stew spice. I thought we might find game at the same time."

Miriam studied their faces, carefully devoid of expression as if they all were privy to a joke of which she knew nothing. "Why am I the only one who has not heard of the wedding?"

Yaffa and Jaedon shrugged. Gershoni mimicked by hunching one shoulder and gurgling.

Elijah said calmly, "I believe I mentioned it first thing this morning. Now hurry, so you can get the stew started. It must cook several hours, if I remember correctly." He reached for the little one who happily leaned into his arms and patted his white beard.

Miriam sighed. "How many guests will there be?" Why ask? It would be all the prophets and their families, and whatever nearby farmers and vintners could leave their chores for the afternoon celebration. She amended, "How many will bring food?"

"Nearly everyone," Yaffa said. "But your stew is a favorite. It is your fault, child, for hoarding the secret."

Yaffa and Elijah hurried out of the house. Miriam regarded their retreat, then asked Jaedon, "What do you know of this?"

"I think they said a wedding." He reached in the basket and handed her some flatbread left from the night before. "Come. We can eat while we walk." He took one himself. "Mmm, I am starving." Crumbs fell from his lips. "The sooner we find that spice, the faster we can get to Eden and Benyamin's house. She keeps chickens."

And Jaedon was fond of eggs. Miriam was too, for that matter. When they got to Eden's house, her friend would tell all.

Miriam led the way to the stream in the wadi, circumventing the refuse heap. The smell always reminded her of the day their garments were splashed with badger's blood and kneaded like dough into rotting garbage. The ruse had worked as they hoped. Ocran sent word with the prophet Micaiah when he was released from prison. At the stench, Jezebel turned her face away, handed Ocran a pouch of silver, and dismissed him. With Ocran's message, Micaiah also brought the garments which her mother had washed. How many times had she helped Imma scrub the family's garments in the stream below the city? Her mother would have labored to remove the blood, yet the stains remained.

Miriam wished Ocran had burned them. She considered doing so herself, but in the end, folded the three garments into the bottom of a trunk, though nothing would induce her to wear her ruined tunic. It would be like wearing a death shroud.

Such terrible images! As she walked through knee-high grass, she turned her face to the sun, searching for a pleasant thought. A breeze lifted her hair. Almost ... like Imma, brushing Miriam's hair by firelight. How good that had felt, how peaceful a moment.

She had not seen her mother since before the siege of Israel. More than five years.

Could she ever return to Samaria? Not while Jezebel lived and schemed. Sadness filmed Miriam's eyes.

Jaedon came running from the stream. His legs pounded the dirt, healthy as a young calf. He and Gershoni were safe here with the prophets. And Yaffa was still with them, though Miriam had feared she would die of sadness after losing Naboth. Her little family had thrived. They were what mattered.

Between panting breaths, Jaedon said, "The patch has spread since we last gathered wild cumin."

"Then fill the basket. We will share the cumin with everyone and tell them about this place."

"Tell them?"

"Yes. Such things should not be kept secret." She had enjoyed wearing a mantle of mystery in the small settlement where everyone knew what went on each day, and even when prophecy was not involved, heard their neighbors speak around their hearth at night. It was the earth's gift, for everyone to enjoy. Why keep the recipe a secret? But no more.

She heard someone's donkey braying and a woman's laughter. The high-pitched eee-aaah went on as if announcing something of importance. There were only a few donkeys in the settlement, and she knew them all. All had a more guttural bray. Wedding guests must be arriving, or the wedding party itself, from a nearby settlement. She tipped her ear toward the ridge road. Yes, voices were coming from that direction. Curious, she craned her neck. Trees dotted the slope and hid the travelers from view. *And her from them.* Probably best. Anyone could be on that road.

"Imma, is this enough?" The basket was filled with the fragrant wild herb.

"Plenty. Thank you, my heart."

Jaedon ducked his head, took her hand, and turned. "We should go. Eden will have those eggs boiled and hot."

She looked at him quizzically. "What about hunting?" Hunting always came first.

"I said we might come across game. Let us walk silently on our way back. But we should not make them wait for us."

A lot of conversation came through Eden's window. A pretty white donkey was tied in front, a long-legged jenny who turned her head and greeted Miriam and Jaedon with another of her high-pitched brays.

Eden popped her head through the open window and waved. "Hurry Miriam, everything is ready!" She pulled her head back inside and the room went quiet.

Miriam quickened her steps, but Jaedon ran past, opening the door and slipping inside ahead. She frowned. He always held the door for her. Just because he was excited about those eggs, that was no reason to forget his manners.

The door stood slightly ajar, so Miriam shoved it open.

And stopped breathing.

First she saw Imma, tears streaming down her dear face. Then Hadassah, clinging to her arm. Maalik stood behind them, his hand resting on Savta's shoulder. There was Abba, hurrying toward her. Caleb holding a child crooked in his arm, Chloe leaning against him, holding another by the hand. Twins!

Miriam pressed a hand against her mouth, holding a sob at bay. "How is this?" she choked out.

"What kind of greeting is that," said her father, crushing her to him.

Dov came from around a corner. Davita and Zuar behind him. She could make no sense of anything.

But Dov! Here. He seemed taller, somehow. And there were new lines on his forehead. She could not take her eyes off him.

"I am conducting them to Jerusalem for Passover."

Stranger still.

"Passover? But that is a month away. Who of you have gone to Jerusalem for any feast day ... in my lifetime?"

"Change is coming, Miriam. Israel and Judah are allies. King Jeshoshaphat's son is married to a daughter of Ahab and Jezebel. Travel to Jerusalem is no longer forbidden."

She shook her head. "But Passover is still a month away. Why have you come—"

"So early?" He took her hand in his calloused fingers. "To ask you again to marry me. Not because you need protection, because you do not. Yahweh and all living in these hills protect you. But because I need you—and I want to be here for you. I want to be father to your children. These two, and others we may have.

"I love you, Miriam."

She began trembling and he talked faster.

"I have spoken to your father. He holds the *ketubah* and agrees it is fair—"

"Generous," Lemuel said.

Dov shot him a smile, but then his expression turned serious again. "But you must agree. I would never try to force you into acting against your will." He squeezed her hand and gazed earnestly into her eyes.

Those eyes, with creases of concern at their corners. She wanted to smooth them away.

Was this a dream? She had awakened to Elijah's words. *There is a wedding today.* She had told Dov no twice and regretted her answer each time. She would not make the mistake again. But while there were witnesses ...

"You will never force me into acting against my will?"

"Never—after this."

Then he pulled her to him and his lips descended on hers. He smelled of road dust, sweat, and wild mint. He kissed her soundly, which she knew was unseemly in the midst of all these people, but it was not against her will.

The music began after the kiss.

Accompanied by gentle lyre notes, Miriam floated around the room, holding onto Dov's arm as she greeted each person. After all her prayers that they might be restored to her, her family had come. They passed Gershoni among them, chucking her under her chin. Not only her family, but her dear friends Chloe, toting two babies of their own, and Davita, arm-in-arm with Zuar.

Had they formed an attachment? She tugged Dov toward the pair.

"Miriam," Davita began, "I was so sure you would accept Dov. I longed to be at your wedding, and so I asked my father ... and Zuar," she squeezed his arm, "and they agreed we would travel with the others." She shared news of Jezreel, which often involved Zuar having experienced it with her. From that and the glances that passed between the two, Miriam saw her friend would not remain single much longer.

The guests had brought so much food, the house could not contain it. Jaedon and Benyamin carried a table outside for food, drink, bowls, and cups. Dov offered her bits of food, some of which she took, but talking to those she had thought lost to her was most important.

Eden swept toward them and stopped to grasp Miriam's arm. "You do not mind if I steal your betrothed for a moment, do you?" she asked Dov. Then, turning to Miriam, she said, "Several months ago, Elijah proposed an idea for your wedding gift. Come see."

Several months? How many others had known of her wedding before her? Perhaps even before Dov knew he would ask again?

Motioning for Imma and Yaffa to follow, Eden led Miriam to a small room, the same location as the alcove in their home. The women crowded close as Eden pulled aside an embroidered tapestry.

Savta, still holding to Yaffa's arm, lifted her nose and sniffed. "What do you see, Yaffa?"

"A pretty room. The first thing I see is a wool rug in shades of brown and cream from speckled sheep. Sleeping mats and blankets are rolled behind a low table holding a clay oil lamp. And a wooden chair stands in the corner, made by Benyamin himself. It gleams with beeswax. Touch it, my mother."

But while Yaffa led her mother-in-law to the chair,

Miriam's gaze fixed on the blue garment draped across its back. Could it be?

Eden hugged Miriam excitedly as Yaffa continued, "Feel that? Can you guess what it is?"

"A woven garment." Savta held it up, gave it a shake, and slid her fingers along one edge. "A fine garment with long sleeves. Blue." She gave it another shake. "And of a length for our girl."

Eden hugged Miriam. "For your wedding! Yaffa helped me weave it here. But how did you know it was blue, Hadassah?"

Savta smiled, her black eyes glinting with a lifetime of smiles. "The dye. It smells like Asp of Jerusalem."

Miriam held the tunic against her, feeling it brush her ankles. "How did you find the time to dye the wool, weave this incredible garment—and keep it secret from me?" Even as she asked the question, she remembered the times Yaffa had gone to visit neighbors, without saying exactly who. Or the times Elijah expressed a desire for roast partridge, if only Miriam could trap some.

"Elijah said we must, and so we did. Here now, put this on. The day has come."

She would marry today? She reached for her mother, and they embraced. Yes, why not? Everyone she loved was here. Who knew when they might be together again?

Giggling like girls, Imma and Yaffa helped pull off the tunic Miriam had donned that morning, until she stood in only her sleeveless linen shift. She dipped a cloth in a basin of scented water and washed. Then Eden slipped the blue tunic over her head. It drifted down like first snow.

A tap sounded on the wall, and Davita stuck her head in. "Chloe and I have something for the bride. May we come in?"

"Of course!" Miriam smoothed the tunic over her hips. "Look what Eden and Yaffa made."

Chloe clasped her hands in admiration. "A beautiful shade of blue. If Dov had not told us about the ploy to deceive the queen—that wicked woman—I might think it the same gown."

Davita stood with her hands behind her back. "It must

be strange, surrounded by prophets." She brought her hands forward. In one she held a wreath of flowers—blue, white, and yellow. In her other hand, she held a sheer white veil with an embroidered edge.

"The wreath is lovely, Davita. Did you make it just now? And Chloe, I remember your beautiful veil. How did you know to bring it?"

Davita giggled. "When we arrived, Elijah told me to pick flowers for a bridal wreath to match a blue dress. And to hurry, because you would be back soon."

"This veil called to me from the bazaar, and a good thing I heard," Chloe said. "Before we left, Dov told us your wedding tunic was ruined. On our way, he tried to buy a suitable garment from a caravan. But they had nothing but Egyptian harem garments." Even Yaffa and Hadassah laughed at that.

They fussed over Miriam, adjusting her tunic, fastening a wide embroidered sash around her hips, and smoothing cream of red ochre on her lips.

Once again, someone tapped on the door post. This time no one poked their head inside, but Caleb asked, "Are you nearly ready? The men have taken Dov to wash in the stream. Elijah says he will be back soon."

In a flurry, the women put the veil over her head and face, fastening it with the wreath. Eden touched Miriam's neck, wrists, and arms with drops of almond oil infused with lilies.

Then they heard a horn—it was not a shofar, but the musician sought to mimic the distinctive two-pitch tone— and shouts were heard. "The bridegroom comes! He is coming!"

Miriam's heart pounded in a way she had never felt before. A flutter of desire dragged her toward him, while something like fear bid her run away. But this was Dov. She had known him—watched him—since childhood.

"Caleb," called Eden, "Please carry this chair to the center of the front room." The women pulled Miriam with them, seated her on the chair, and readjusted her tunic and veil. Laughing, she jumped up and hugged her brother, then sat back down. Outside, the voices grew louder, the donkey began braying again, and it sounded like a troop of goats came up the hill after the men.

Dov walked through the door, the afternoon sun shining around him as if its rays pulsed from his body. He wore a different tunic, white as new snow, and Davita ran to drop a wreath on his head, white flowers and bay leaves.

Dov kneeled in front of her. "I have long waited for you, my love. I pray our life together will be longer still. I bring gifts." He leaned forward and whispered.

She sat back and laughed. "The white donkey? She is beautiful."

"She reminded me of you." The room erupted in laughter. "I mean—her beauty—her long legs—"

"Stop!" She held her curled fist to her mouth, shaking with mirth.

Giving himself a shake, he continued. "For the *mohar*, I gave your father sheep and goats."

"And I give them to you, Daughter," Lemuel said.

There were murmurs of approval throughout the room.

"I bring you this silver, that you may have sustenance should death take me first." Dov laid a small pouch on her lap.

He opened the pouch and pulled out a gold ring. A round stone, deep blue with light-colored veins running through it, was set in overlapping scallops of silver and gold. "I give you this ring, to remind you of our joy on this day."

Then others walked over to place gifts in her lap and around her chair. A beautiful rug, shaken out for all to admire, then quickly rolled again and leaned into a corner. Carved wooden spoons. A pair of chickens in a crate, one of Miriam's own, which made her smile. Maalik guided Savta over, and she laid a pair of gold earrings into Miriam's lap. "I have saved these for you, my heart. My father gave them to me when I married." It felt like the blessings of heaven descended around her, drenching her with longed-for rain. Her family. These friends. To have them with her on the very day she thought all were lost to her.

She spotted Jaedon holding Gershoni, her fist in her mouth. Miriam beckoned them to her. Jaedon leaned against her.

Dov said, "May I?" He held out his arms and the baby

went to him, shyly burying her face in his shoulder.

He handed her back to Jaedon, squeezed his shoulder, and whispered something in his ear, as Elijah came over. Placing her hands in Dov's, Elijah began praying. The words whirled inside her as she listened.

"Blessed are You, Adonai, our God, Ruler of the universe ... who created delight, glad song, and love ... let there soon be heard the voice of the loving couple, the sound of their jubilance from their canopies and of the youths from their song-filled feasts. Blessed are You, who causes the couple to rejoice, one with the other ..."

Several prophets had picked up their lyres and were strumming in melodious currents, the music itself a prayer. Elijah spoke blessings and Miriam felt carried along like a dove caught in a gale. Coils of dizziness wound tight, as if she would faint from the beauty of the moment. Shards of light sliced her wedding veil and Miriam saw years ahead, unfurling like scrolls, Dov and her grown old, their children and grandchildren clustered around them, safe in these hills.

And then she heard a scream. "She's fainted." She felt Dov's arms around her, gently lowering her to the ground, whispering, "You are safe, Beloved," and calling her *Ishti*.

He asked for water, stroked her hair, and soon held a cup to her lips. Honeyed water. Miriam raised her hand to her forehead, gazed at her wedding ring, and vaguely wondered what had become of her veil.

Elijah knelt beside her, leaning on his staff and grunting a little as he descended. "The weakness from the vision will pass soon," he quietly told her. "Afterward, sit in the chair a while." Then he used his staff and allowed Caleb to help him stand.

"Let me see my daughter." Imma pushed Elijah and Caleb away, but Dov continued to hold her. Imma felt Miriam's forehead. "No fever." She cupped her cheek. "But you are flushed. It is warm with all these people. Take her outside, Dov. No, first give her something to eat—dates and almonds or cheese, if you have them."

Dov picked her up and carried her to the chair. He brought her a selection of dates, grapes, almonds, cheese, and roasted grain. Imma watched her closely, but after eating some of the food, Miriam was ready to walk outside for a breath of mountain air. Holding her arm, Dov accompanied her. The prophets plucked their lyre strings in a lively tune that reminded Miriam of gusts of wind tossing the tree tops. Music that must be danced to.

The guests agreed, because as soon as Dov and Miriam faced each other and began slowly moving their feet, others joined in dancing, twining their arms to the breezy rhythm. Jaedon danced by, Gershoni in his arms. Holding a red flower in her chubby fist, she bounced it on his head. The music and dancing continued, fueled by feasting on all the many dishes brought by the guests and watered wine. When the stars began to come out, it was time for the wedding procession to the groom's house.

But Dov had no house. Miriam supposed they would spend their first night in one of the homes belonging to an absent prophet, away ministering wherever Yahweh had sent him.

She sat in the chair where she had first seen her wedding tunic. Imma, Savta, and Yaffa kissed her. Jaedon bent over, threw his arms around her neck, and said, "I love you, Imma. We will all be happy."

Then he ran off, returning quickly with two lit torches, one he gave to Dov. Other men came forward with torches they lit from Dov's and Jaedon's. Then several of them lifted the chair to their shoulders, with her clinging to it, and the men started up one hill and down another. Davita and Chloe led the women with tambourines and singing. They trudged through deep grass and along the stream, following Dov's lead, far from the settlement. Finally, they came to a tent pitched under the oldest oak in the forest.

"It is beautiful here," Imma said. Tears glistened in her eyes. "I love you, darling girl."

Jaedon took her mother's hand and said, "Follow me, Savta," and headed back to the settlement. Others followed, calling their good-byes, a few of the men teasing Dov, but thankfully they followed the others. Miriam was alone with her thoughts, with Dov, and the stars.

He lit a fire with kindling and wood already laid within in a ring of stones. Ducking into the tent, he returned with cups, a skin of wine, and a cloth-wrapped ball of goat cheese. "Hold these," he instructed, and went back into the tent for a blanket which he spread in front of the fire.

After they were settled under the lacy canopy of the oak, he asked, "What did you see?"

She sipped her wine. "It began with the music and Elijah's voice. Another voice too, like the whisper of God. His voice and the wind, became one, a force that drew me in. A whirlwind. And I saw our future."

Stars twinkled where they shone through the branches. Miriam felt tears come to her eyes. He gazed at her with concern, reaching his finger to gather a tear, its calloused tip rough on her cheek. "You saw our future ... and it brings tears?"

She nodded, feeling her face crumple with the effort of holding them back. "Only because it is so beautiful."

He chuckled, pulling her close. His arms were very warm. "I could have told you that."

Chapter Forty-One

Now Ahaziah had fallen through the lattice
of his upper room in Samaria and injured himself.
So he sent messengers, saying to them,
"Go and consult Baal-Zebub, the god of Ekron,
to see if I will recover from this injury."
~ 2 Kings 1:2

A year later
Elijah

"ELIJAH, AWAKE."
There was no mistaking the voice. He lived alone in the small house he'd once shared with Miriam, Yaffa, and Jaedon, but he now he had company. The angel of the Lord.

Light filled the room, though dawn had not pinked the sky. "Yes, my lord?"

"Arise and go north. You will meet messengers from Ahaziah, king of Samaria. Say to them, 'Is it because there is no God in Israel that you go to consult Baal-Zebub, the god of Ekron?'" The light flickered, like an oil lamp in a breeze.

The god of Ekron! Once before Ekron had sparred with Yahweh and been humiliated with painful tumors.

The angel continued, "Tell the king, 'You will not leave the bed you are lying upon. You will certainly die.'" After the Presence left, the light slowly faded.

Elijah got up and donned his tunic. Not the soft one Yaffa had woven, but the hairy one he wore to confront King Ahab at Samaria, Carmel, and Naboth's vineyard. Elijah strapped on his leather belt, packed some food, and slung a waterskin over his shoulder. Finally, he picked up his staff. He would need it for such a journey.

As he left the mudbrick house, he gazed down the hill to the vineyard. He spotted the curve of Dov's back bent over the vines, the quick step of Jaedon. Well, if the Lord wanted them to know where he had gone, He would tell them.

By midday, Elijah leaned heavily on his staff, his legs blocks of wood. Planning to stop for refreshment, he came upon the troop of six soldiers wearing leather armor and helmets. He stepped to the middle of the road. "Ho there, soldiers of Ahaziah. Is it because there is no God in Israel that you go to consult Baal-Zebub, god of Ekron?"

"Out of the way, old man. We are soldiers of the king."

Another soldier spoke. "Sir, I've seen this man at Carmel. He prayed down fire from the sky."

The first man swaggered a bit, but he tilted his head as the men behind him stepped back.

"Best you go back and tell the king what I said." Elijah turned his back on them and sought shade. He spotted a small forested hill in the distance. Green grass to the right promised water. He would wait there.

One of them hollered, "Who should we tell the king spoke to us?"

Elijah shook his head and kept walking, the heat of the sun on his back.

When the soldiers returned to the palace with their message, the royal physician took them to the king's chambers. He lay rigid, his face contorted in pain. "What kind of man told you this?"

Their leader said, "He wore a hairy tunic, a wide leather belt, and carried a shepherd's staff."

Ahaziah groaned. "Elijah, the Tishbite. My father called him 'the troubler of Israel.' As if I didn't have enough problems—Moab refuses to pay their tribute, I cannot rise from my bed to punish them, and Elijah stops me from seeking a healer. Go to your captain. Tell him I said take a company of fifty soldiers, if six men can't handle one old seer." He grimaced. "But bring me that prophet."

From atop his hill, Elijah saw the soldiers marching toward

him. Idly, he counted them. Thirty, forty-five, fifty, and the captain. Leather armor, as before, for the soldiers. But this time, a captain led them, decked in bronze battle armor and helmet.

On the other side of the road, a flock of sheep crested a hill. Probably headed for the lush grass at the base of this hill or the spring he'd found yesterday flowing into a pool.

But when the shepherd saw the soldiers, he whistled to his dog, turned the sheep, and left the way he had come. A wise move.

When the troop reached Elijah's hill, they massed closely, their captain at the fore.

"Man of God," he shouted.

Yes, Elijah was God's prophet in Israel.

"The king summons you. Come with us!"

It seemed the captain had no respect for Elijah's position. As it happened, Elijah had little respect for the Captain's rank or his bronze armor.

"You have said I am a man of God, yet you have spoken to me without respect, as if I am not. Let us put this to the test. If I am a man of God, may fire come down from heaven and consume you and your fifty men."

With a loud crash of thunder, a lightning bolt encased the soldiers in fire, shook the earth, and sent a boulder rolling down the road. The fire burned, clean and white, until it licked up everything, just as it had at Carmel. Even the bronze armor. *Thank you Yahweh for causing the captain to stop at the base of the hill.*

Elijah glimpsed the shepherd raising his head above a boulder.

Elijah rubbed his ears. He had forgotten how deafening was the Lord's thunder. The fires burned low. Soon there would be nothing but scorched earth. Not even an odor, for which he once again thanked the Lord.

Then Elijah went to reassure the shepherd and visit. Perhaps they would eat supper together.

The next day the soldiers came even earlier, arriving shortly before midday. Fifty again. Elijah hoped they would be more respectful when they arrived. Not for his benefit, but for the Lord's. And theirs.

While he was waiting, Elijah wondered what King Ahaziah thought when his captain and troop did not return. Only the shepherd had seen what happened, and after sharing supper with Elijah he watered his sheep and disappeared into the hills. Did Ahaziah think they had deserted?

"Lord?" Elijah listened, but Yahweh had nothing to say about the king. Elijah understood His displeasure. After Yahweh had proved himself so many times—the drought, the fire and rain at Carmel, Ahab's odds-against battles—despite all, Ahaziah turned to a false god instead of the One.

This time, Elijah held up his hand, signaling them to halt farther back. He wanted them to see the scorched ground, which glistened with a black shiny substance, similar to the sand around the pottery ovens of Zarephath. Perhaps the sight would give the Captain reason to reflect.

"Man of God! Get down from that hill and come with us. The king of Israel commands you to appear before him."

Elijah sighed. "If I am a man of God," he said, "May fire come down from heaven and consume you and your fifty soldiers." He put his hands over his ears.

It was as before. The fire burned faster, consuming everything in a boom and a flash. Perhaps the Lord had stoked His lightning, since the troop had stopped farther away. He glanced up. "Thank you, Lord. Please tell me, are more coming tomorrow?" He nodded. "Then I will wait."

He peered into his sack of provisions. A crust of bread, a day old when he left, now hard as stone. He glanced up again. "Is there another shepherd in the area?"

He waited for another answer, but when there was none, decided to stretch his legs. Descending the hill with his food pouch and waterskin, he walked to the pool. It bubbled merrily, as if an orb of fire hadn't just consumed fifty-one men. He hiked up his tunic and waded in, wiggling his toes in the mud. Something bit him.

With a yelp, he grabbed for the creature, coming up with a large scaled fish. He threw it on the bank, broke off a stiff reed, and climbed out again. After killing the fish, he built a ring of stones, lay the kindling, and piled on a few larger sticks.

"Thank you for the fish." He threaded it on the reed. "I should have thought to bring my fire starter."

The heavens rumbled. Elijah looked up and smiled. A lone spark drifted down on the kindling.

On the third day, the soldiers came later. So late that Elijah wondered if they learned what had happened to the others. Had one of yesterday's bunch hung back, run away before the burning, and alerted the king? No, Elijah had watched the whole thing, sickening as it was. Why would men fight God?

Halfway to dusk, they came. Fifty soldiers and their captain. All as before. Elijah held up his hand to stop them. It had worked well yesterday, so he would use the same plan. Should Elijah send one man away, one from the last row? If not, the king might deplete his whole army, fifty-one soldiers at a time.

But the Captain was walking forward, despite Elijah's signal for him to halt, he was—falling on his knees! Holding up his hands in supplication. Elijah squinted, but the man was too far away to see clearly, and his bronze helmet shadowed his face.

"Man of God," he began. The same words as the others, but a respectful tone. "Please have respect for my life and the lives of these fifty men, your servants." He looked around at the scorched earth. "I see that fire has fallen from heaven and consumed the first two captains and their men. Please spare our lives. Please come and speak to our king."

Elijah squinted again, recognizing the voice. Ocran.

Elijah heard a whoosh of wings behind him. The angel of the Lord said, "Since he speaks to you with respect, go with him. Do not be afraid to give the king the message I told you before. Because he sought the help of a false god, Yahweh will leave him to his own devices. He will never rise from his bed again."

Elijah nodded, knowing better than to look back. "May it be as you have said."

Chapter Forty-Two

The waters saw you, God, the waters saw you and writhed; the very depths were convulsed. The clouds poured down water, the heavens resounded with thunder; your arrows flashed back and forth. Your thunder was heard in the whirlwind, your lightning lit up the world.
~ Psalm 77:16-18a

Gilgal Settlement
Miriam

MIRIAM DESCENDED THE ZIG-ZAG PATH TO the vineyard, holding Gershoni's hand. The settlement at Gilgal had buzzed for days with a new prophecy. A storm was coming. One that had everyone watching the sky and Dov and Miriam concerned for the vines.

There he was, her love, bending over the row of vines, fastening branches to supports. Jaedon was beside him. They looked like father and son, their turbans wound into identical circles to shade their faces. As one, they directed worried gazes toward the sky, then turned their attention to her.

"Abba!" Gershoni shouted. "Jay-ton!"

The girl's cries woke the baby, but the good-natured child only crinkled his face in a gap-toothed grin. Miriam adjusted the scarf under his chubby legs so he could sit upright astride her hip and wag his little arms.

"Ba!" he yelled in her ear. She cringed at the pain of it while laughing.

When they reached the vineyard, she spread the scarf under a vine-covered trellis, similar to the one in her father's vineyard in Samaria. She laid the baby on his back, handing him the cloth doll he loved to chew.

"Any more word from the prophets?" Dov asked. They had built their house opposite the hill where Miriam, Yaffa, and Jaedon first lived. In the years after Ahab's death, more prophets joined the settlement near Gilgal and additional homes were built. Miriam enjoyed the nearness of neighbors. She lay her palm against her slightly rounded belly. Especially now, with yet another child growing inside.

"The same. A storm is coming."

Dov looked up at the sky, then at his vines. He had turned to farming with alacrity. "It is a privilege to nurture," he had told her. Rather than kill, she had interpreted, though he never voiced such a thing. He avoided speaking of battles or his interactions with King Ahab, the only king Dov had served.

But when Ocran came to Gilgal with Elijah, after the death of King Ahaziah, the two men had talked long into the night around a smoldering campfire. Supposedly sleeping inside the walls of their half-built, roofless house, Miriam overheard some of their conversation.

"It was hard to serve such a king. Drinking, carousing, finally killing himself in a foolish fashion. Sending one hundred soldiers to their death."

"Until you."

"I could never understand why the young king lived the way he did. To be sure, his mother taught him to worship the Ba'als. Yet, during his father's reign, he saw the power of Yahweh. When on his deathbed, he sought an answer from Baal-Zebub. Ultimately, he heard from the Lord. But he never sought Him."

"Therein is your answer." Miriam heard a crunch as if Dov tossed a branch into the fire. The crackle of flames grew louder. "Ahaziah wanted no answer from Yahweh. All his life, he wanted to go his own way. He looked for gods to tell him what he wanted to hear. Instead he found judgment."

"He had no son to succeed him. Now his brother Jehoram is king. More of the same, I am afraid." There was a long silence, broken only by pops and rumbles as the fire burned. "It is beautiful here. The stars burn like a thousand oil lamps in the heavens. I wish ..."

Miriam gazed at the stars. Ocran's description was apt. She sighed at the loveliness of the sky, wishing they need not cover it with a roof.

Ocran never said what he wished. After a long while, Dov said, "Bring your wife and son, Ocran. Then never return."

"Never return? Wouldn't that be breaking my vow?"

Dov sighed. "Perhaps. But much can happen in a year." There was another pause. Without a woman to grease the conversation, there were often long pauses.

"You sound almost like a prophet."

Dov chuckled quietly, probably trying not to wake her. Miriam smiled in the dark.

"There is something about living among prophets. The Torah readings. The music."

Would he speak of the things she had seen? She had never told him not to. But their late-night conversations seemed like secret treasures, for only them.

"You have spent time with Elijah," Dov continued. "Did he ever speak to you about the years of the drought?"

"Some. After I came to him with the company of soldiers, he told me about the fire on Mount Carmel. How it burned up the sacrifice, the altar stones, the ring of water, even the dirt beneath. Turned everything to black glass, like the ground where we stood. I tell you, Dov, fire from heaven is not like this campfire."

She could almost see her husband nodding. "I was at Carmel. It changed me."

"I was fighting the Arameans. I wish I had been on the mountain with you. My life might have been different."

"And yet, here you are. Maybe Elijah will tell you more sometime about the earlier years. When Yahweh first sent him to confront Ahab, sent him to hide at the brook Cherith, and then to Zarephath. Each time, Elijah said, he spoke to Yahweh about a deep concern and asked Him what to do. Each time, Yahweh told him what to do next. But only one thing. Elijah did it, and then Yahweh told him the next thing. One thing at a time."

"So, I should tell the Lord I no longer want to serve a wicked king. Then what?"

"Wait."

"Will Yahweh whisper to me?"

Dov chuckled. "He might. But it is more likely that in a quiet moment, a persistent idea will come to you. A deep desire or what seems a wise thought. Or a friend will give advice that seems right."

"Like bring your wife and son to Gilgal?"

They both laughed loudly, followed by shushes. Miriam put her hand over her mouth.

Finally Ocran spoke. "I am a soldier."

Miriam again stifled a chuckle. *As if he is talking to a merchant.*

"You are the one who said, 'I wish.' Ask your wife what she thinks. Miriam will welcome her."

Her husband knew her. She loved having Hadassah and Yaffa close, and Dov enjoyed having Maalik only steps away. Sometimes the old man worked in the vineyard, but mostly he stayed close to Hadassah.

"Hadassah and Maalik built the house up the hill. There is room for another."

"They married?"

Miriam heard the surprise in Ocran's voice.

"They wanted to spend whatever time is left to them together," Dov said. She liked how her husband said little about other people's affairs, but what he said was affirming.

She remembered smiling and must have drifted off to sleep, because the next morning she woke with the sun on her face—when sleeping in a half-built house, better sun than rain on your face. But that night she had learned a little about how Dov's life as a soldier must have been. It helped her understand his silences.

Now he moved among the vines, preparing for the coming storm. She studied the sky. It did have a strange look, surprisingly bright rather than dark.

Her attention was captured by a disturbance on the opposite hill. Elijah came out of their old house tying his cloak over his shoulders. Elisha followed on his heels. Another journey. In the years since King Ahaziah's death, the two traveled to speak against false gods, teach the ways of Yahweh, and establish schools of the prophets.

"Elisha, stay here, please," Elijah said. "The Lord has sent me on to Jericho. I do not know when I will be back. No need for you to travel so far."

"I am going. There is no way I will leave you."

Elijah shrugged and set off at a fast clip, his staff

striking the ground.

That was strange. Miriam had never known Elijah to request his successor stay behind. They always travelled together.

Along the line of houses, other prophets emerged. Micaiah had returned from north of Samaria. He stood in a group near Benyamin's house. They eyed the two leaving, seeming to discuss whether or not they would follow. They did.

More prophets came from houses, some with their wives and children. First Eden, shouting for Benyamin to wait. He waved her back inside, but she ran after him anyway. Then another woman followed her prophet husband. Several women, after their husbands had left, went back into their houses and remained there with their children. Another couple with a young family took the children to her parents' home, then joined the crowd trailing after Elijah and Elisha.

"Something important is happening," Miriam said. "I don't understand it, but I want to go. Let's take the little ones and Yaffa to stay with Maalik and Hadassah."

"But what about the storm? You are with child."

She took his hand. "You will keep me safe, my love. Hurry."

By the time the children were settled, the prophets were far off. "We will never catch them on foot," Dov said. The sky had darkened, but was strangely fractured by light, like a cracked vessel. "If you still insist on going, we will ride."

Dov saddled Uri and the white donkey. She had a comfortable, ground-covering gait, not as swift as the stallion, but adequate. When they reached Bethel, where Elijah and Elisha had founded a school of the prophets, people were streaming out of the city.

Miriam slid down from the donkey, handed the reins to Dov, and nodded at the prophets of Bethel. "They expected him."

It illustrated a peculiarity she and Dov had mused over. If the Lord sent a vision, many in the community experienced it. Miriam often caught a glimpse. Perhaps it was not so odd. If rain fell in a city, more than one person got wet.

Dov led their animals to a water trough. A townsman

handed Elijah a waterskin. He upended it, taking a long drink. Meanwhile the school of prophets had crowded around Elisha. "Do you know that the Lord is going to take your master from you today?"

"Yes, I know," said Elisha, "but I don't want to talk about it."

Elijah was going to die? Miriam reached for Dov, and he closed his arms around her, whether he understood the reason for her pain or only understood she needed comfort.

Elijah walked over to Elisha. Was he walking more stiffly than usual? Had she ignored signs of illness? No, he seemed perfectly well. "Stay here, Elisha. The Lord is sending me on to Jericho."

Elisha shook his head. "As surely as the Lord lives and as you live, I will not leave you."

Why was the old prophet still trying to convince Elisha to stay behind? They were never apart, these last years.

The two walked on, side by side.

When they reached Jericho, it was almost as if Elijah tested his friend. The prophets of Jericho also came out to greet the travelers, and upon recognizing Elisha, said, "Do you know the Lord is taking your master today?"

Elisha snapped at them. "I know! Keep quiet about it."

Miriam didn't want to hear about it either. Why this procession across the country? If the Lord was going to take Elijah, why did half the country need to witness his death? He had served the Lord well. He deserved a quiet and dignified passing. To die during his sleep.

Accepting a cup of goat milk from a young prophet, Elijah looked across the crowd at Miriam. He mouthed, "You should go home."

She shook her head.

Then he said to Elisha, "Stay here. The Lord is sending me on to the Jordan."

"It does not matter where He sends you," Elisha said. "I will not leave you."

When they reached the Jordan river, Dov and Miriam stayed with the crowd of prophets, who stood a little way off, almost as if they expected Yahweh to send fire and lightning again. They could be right, because Miriam felt a prickling over her skin.

Dov dismounted and helped Miriam off her donkey. "Let me hold them," he said. "If something unexpected happens, it is best our feet stand on firm ground."

A stiff wind picked up from the north, tossing the clouds overhead. Elijah took his cloak, rolled it tightly, and struck the water. Mounds of water divided to the left and right, and they crossed the Jordan on dry ground.

Miriam gasped, and Dov clutched her to him.

Elijah called to Elisha, his voice carrying over the wind. "Tell me, what can I do for you before I am taken?"

Elisha bowed his head, an expression of humility. Then he lifted his chin, his expression resolute, as if bracing himself for the years ahead. "If I am to be your successor, let me inherit a double portion of your spirit, lest the task be too much for me."

Elijah smiled. "Now that is difficult, being it must come from the Lord, not from me. Yet, if you see me go, it will be yours. Otherwise, it will not."

The wind grew stronger and the crowd of prophets banded close together.

Elijah and Elisha went on farther, talking, their arms moving about to words their watchers could no longer hear. Wind whipped everyone's hair and garments.

Despite the wind's rising volume, Miriam heard an eagle cry. And there it was—the eagle floated on the wind like a breath, skimming over the crowd, dipping down over Miriam's head, then circling back toward Elijah.

"It is Hevel, is it not?" Dov asked.

She nodded mutely.

In the sky overhead, the clouds parted, morphing into translucent silhouettes of horses. Manes and tails seemed to stream in the wind. One tossed its head, the other pawed the ground, and the clouds swirled into backdrops for living, fiery horses. A flaming chariot appeared behind the horses, tendrils of fiery harness miraculously attaching chariot to horses, and the apparition swept down to earth, landing between Elisha and Elijah.

As if the wind would whip her away, Dov clutched Miriam against him as Elijah stepped into the chariot. The flaming horses whinnied shrilly and, accompanied by thunderous hoofbeats, galloped up into the sky.

The wind became a whirlwind, sweeping the prophet, the horses, and the chariot into its maelstrom.

The eagle shrilled once more, circling the whirlwind at a distance as the horses carried Elijah farther into the sky, until they disappeared into the highest heavens. His cloak fell from the chariot, twisting and tossed by the wind as it fell to earth at Elisha's feet.

Dov spoke into her ear. "He once said, 'I have always wanted to journey in a chariot." Miriam clutched his hand, feeling tears spring to her eyes.

Elisha tore the neck of his tunic. "My father! My father! You were the chariots and the horsemen of Israel."

It was true. Elijah had been Israel's warrior protector. And now he was gone.

Yet Elisha had asked for a double portion of Elijah's spirit. And he held the prophet's cloak in his hand.

Grasping Elijah's cloak in one hand, Elisha strode back to the river. "Are you there, God of Elijah?" He struck the Jordan. And the waters parted.

Author's Note

Biblical fiction readers often ask what is true and what is fiction in the novels they choose. Believing that the Bible is the Word of God, I begin by adhering to the biblical account where it is clearly stated and layer in history, settings, and customs. Then I add characters who desperately want something.

I invite you to check the scripture and tell me how I've done. Whirlwind continues the story of Elijah beginning in 1 Kings 20 and continuing into 2 Kings 2. When I began cross-referencing, I found a surprising fact in 2 King 9:26 that forced me to go back and rework all I had written up to this point. To avoid spoilers, I'm not going to say more, but after you've read Whirlwind and these scripture passages, contact me via my website (https://danamcneely.com) if you haven't guessed why I was thrown for a loop.

I've never served in the military so I researched the battle scenes with maps, photos, and a fantastic resource, Battles of the Bible by Chaim Herzog and Mordechai Gichon. The book neatly laid out probable battle plans. The section titled AHAB IN THE GOLAN HEIGHTS, which set the city of Aphek near En Gev, near the shores of the Sea of Galilee, was especially helpful. If you're a military history buff, you may find this book interesting.

When I name characters who either do not appear or aren't named in the biblical account, I try to find a name that is meaningful for the character's part in the story and doesn't sound too much like another character's name. You might find it interesting to look up some of the meanings of names. A couple that might not be easy to find would be the eagle, Hevel, which means breath or vapor and Dov's warhorse, Uriel, which means light, or flame.

Hevel enters and leaves the story like a breath or vapor. The book of Ecclesiastes uses the word *hevel* as a metaphor for the brevity of life. Uriel is an archangel, mentioned in the Apocryphal Book of Enoch, who warns Noah of the coming flood. I thought it was appropriate for the horse to be given the name of a flaming angel bringing news of judgment.

Rain and Whirlwind, books one and two in the Whispers on the Wind series, are stories of men and women who interacted with the prophet Elijah during his time on earth. Look for two more books in this series to relate stories about his successor, the prophet Elisha, and other characters from Whirlwind.

I hope you enjoyed Whirlwind. If you did, I would love to see your review on Amazon, Goodreads, BookBub, and any other sites you frequent. Reviews are extremely important to writers. Without them, their stories become lost in the universe of available books.

Let's stay in touch. Sign up for my free newsletter where I share book news and bits of my personal life. When you subscribe, I'll also send you a free ebook, The Eyes of the Lord. This novella tells the origin story of a beloved character from Rain.

All my contact information, including social media info, can be found at this one link: linktr.ee/dana_mcneely. I look forward to hearing from you!

Made in the USA
Monee, IL
20 May 2023

33849120R00236